BLACK RIVER LANTERN

ALEX GRASS

Dickinson Publishing Group

ACKNOWLEDGMENTS:

First, thank you to my wife Gina, who decided to have children with me and has remained loyal, having faith in me long after others would have —and often did—quit. She is hot, and I enjoy sex with her. Also, she is by any quantitative-psychometric gauge a genius. But most importantly, I enjoy sex with her.

My editors worked long and hard to make this book presentable, lucid — something worth reading. Eric Ogg, Melissa Carmean, and Carol Carmean from holymell edits LLC, thank you.

Ed Moran was the first to read over my very rough draft and suggest changes. His decades-long experience in literature was much valued and is still much appreciated.

My father was the first "normal" person to read this book. His general dislike of all fantastical genres meant that I received nothing but honest feedback. By the end of it, my old man said he couldn't stop reading. This is a book about fathers and sons, and so I couldn't write it unless me and mine had gone through all the... let's just call it tumult... that Roger and I went through until we both got sober. Even now, Pops, I look to you whenever I feel the old Black Dog creeping up behind my back, and I know that together we can keep that bloodthirsty hound at bay.

Almost three years ago my Uncle Marty flew up from Florida and told me that it was "time". If he hadn't showed the interest in my health and the inclination to help, I am convinced I would have died with a bottle in my hand after having lost everything. Thanks, Unc.

Thanks to Grandpa Grass for paying the rent. Thanks to Aunt Liz for backing me and my lady when we desperately needed help. Thank you to Granny for her love of culture, her intellectuality, which managed to make it down to me through daddy-O, even if it came only in drips and drabs.

My mother—Dear Lord, please let her never read this book, lest she think she raised a nutjob—is a beautiful, kind, one-in-a-billion soul. When the right thing needed to be said, she said it. And similarly to the Colonial Brits, Ima has taken on an unrepentant adage when it comes to her sons: My Boys, right or wrong. She is the daughter of Arthur and Annapearl Frankston, two brilliant—but more importantly, kind, pious—grandparents who gave her the tools to create a son who has learned enough to say "sorry" I was a shit. (Mom… sorry I was a shit.)

Thanks to my brothers—Arty Party, Shmelk, Duke. Everything in these books has to do with us, or what we've seen, or inside jokes we've got. Growing up with the three of you was more fun than anyone's ever had. Even with the bruises.

Thanks to Dr. Godin for saving my neck (literally), to Dr. Calico for keeping my head bolted on, and to Dr. Biordi and Dr. Francis for delivering my boys healthily to me, biceps, wieners and all!

The very first week that I was institutionalized, I had thought of leaving and flying to New Orleans to drink myself to death. Looking back now, that idea seems as absurd to me as it should have seemed then. John Cuddy, you foul-mouthed Cape Cod sonofabitch... you kept me in, and you fought against the ones who wanted to give me the boot. You and Todd saved my life. And everything changed after that day where you two finally broke through. In a very real way, this book is yours in both physical and spiritual properties. (On a recovery note, thank you also to: Mark M., Gianmarco, Big Dan, Jimbo from Hotlanta, Fabulous Clayton, Big Daddy Sean, the Great Chief Justice Kentucky Matt, and the silky-voiced Father Thomas, who is now in possession of my Buddha.)

Thanks to Judge Perlmutter for taking a chance on me when I was an unknown quantity.

Thanks to Professor Shaw for her infinite patience.

Thanks to Professor Fish, who made me realize I didn't really know my native language as well as I thought I did, and then proceeded to give me a rough-rumble intensive.

Thanks to Rebbe Reed, my Scotch-Irish mentor in the ways of Constitutional Law.

Thanks to my two tried-and-true compatriots, Boris and Patrick. We have spent hours and hours on the finer points, so let us remain true friends until the finer points are dulled and worn by age.

Thank you to Rabbi Maurice. God must create someone like him once every two-thousand years. I'm glad I was around for the latest iteration.

And for my oldest, Lucia: I love you, you are awesome. When you aren't home I sit on your bed and cry and make the doody-pants. You are smart, girl. Don't waste it!

If I forgot anybody, I apologize. But does anyone really read the acknowledgments?

ACT I

"All around him the mean and vulgar flourish, while the righteous man suffers. And now it seems to him as though it could never be different upon earth."

— MARTIN BUBER, *GOOD AND EVIL*

CHAPTER 1

"Are you alright, Mr. Eddie? You look like you are having the gross feelings in your stom-atch."

"I'm fine."

Abakoum smiled and nudged Eddie. "You positive, my main man? You have been looking like the fish with the gills that make the greens around them."

Eddie looked up from his spot on the steps in front of the trailer. His arms hung at his sides, and the winds blew through his hair, ruffling it as it did the tent flaps surrounding them. "I'm fine, Abakoum."

"Okay, my main man. If you are, like, feeling the downs, you come party Abakoum, baby! Number one good-time, alright?"

"Alright, Abakoum. Thanks."

Abakoum patted Eddie on the shoulder. "Okay, Mr. Eddie. Remember what Anthony Robbins say—'It is in your moments of decision that your destinies are raped.'"

Eddie winced. His friend was bright, but often said things that embarrassed Eddie. "I think it's *shaped*, Abakoum."

"What?"

"I don't know. I think it makes more sense to say—It is in your moments of decision that your destinies are shaped."

"No, no, no. This make no sense, Mr. Eddie. In my country, if you want on something, you must to *take* it! You have to *dominatrix* people to getting what you want. Like the rapings. It no makes sense to say *shape*. How you can *shape* somebody? People are not like the Jell-O. But raping? You can make the raping on anybody. Make much more sense."

Eddie shook his head, hoping to be done with the conversation. "You really shouldn't—shouldn't... you know, *make rapings* on anyone."

"Yes. Okay. This is truth. You are good boy, Mr. Eddie."

Eddie Marivicos waved off the fire-eater. Abakoum was new to the Carnival, but old to the trade and to the earth. Eddie continued staring at the sign outside of the main circus tent.

The Marivicos Summerlong Carnivalé Festival! FOURTY-SEVEN YEARS RUNNING!

For most of his life—in fact, his entire life, with two years' exception—Eddie had worked for his family.

"This ain't a circus, numbnuts," Papa had told him during his first run. "Remember that. This is a *seasonal* Carnival. We open in the summer. We don't leave town in between. There's a difference." Why they never thought of going somewhere else was not a question Eddie bothered to ask.

The Carnival was different from state fairs and roaming circuses in other ways. It maintained older attractions that time had rendered unfashionable. The unruly gangs of politically correct snowflakes had forbidden freak show features and exploited creatures.

There was the Hall of Oddities, with its wet-jaws filled with two-headed monkeys and stillborn fetuses. Then there was the freak show tent, where one could see a strongman lift a barbell with his nut-sack, or watch the emcee lie on a bed of nails, hoping that one went through his back. There was also the circus tent, which Papa Marivicos insisted *was not* a circus tent.

Everything within the campgrounds belonged to the Carnival— it must be distinguished from the filth and frivolity of a circus. Confectionary stalls set up in cloth-covered booths lined the midway —which had been eroded by the millions of trodden steps that mashed green sproutlings and patches of grass into a brown, dead walkway. There was a low-roofed Dutch-style wooden structure that contained something like a saloon, along with some roulette tables and a few blackjack and poker stations. A local machinist had offered Papa Marivicos a cut on some levered slot machines with the cherries and other symbols printed on rolling white cylinders.

There were two main tents. The one for the kids had magic shows, songs, trick ponies, and circus—*there's that word again*— dogs jumping through hoops and demonstrating that perfected ratio of adorable-to-agile.

The adults' tent was rowdier. Kayjigville had no Blue Laws, and that was where Eddie would be performing. The marks drank homemade booze, the properties of which had been steadily refined over the years so that it was very rare that anyone suffered alcohol—or any other kind of—poisoning from imbibement.

Papa Marivicos wore a threadbare patchwork of an ensemble that contained high-fashioned pieces (obviously stolen), and a plain frock. He was done up in makeup to hide his wrinkled and scarified skin, and on top of it all, he was so adorned with junk jewelry that he looked like a Tinkertoy chandelier. His hat was an ostentatiously tall dirtied stovetop hat, the color of brown velvet. A luminescent braided cloth wrapped around its body where a ribbon would go.

Eddie sat by himself behind one of the tarps that served as a barrier between the family and the fun-goers. He had left home for two years. During those two years, something had aroused itself in his mind— something irrepressible and ominous, foreign and powerful. The shadowy pall of that new part of his still-maturing psyche had been the cause of many an ailment, some of which had been manageable.

Eddie didn't consider himself terribly bright, and for better or worse, he was tethered to Papa Marivicos as a mule was tethered to yoke and plow. Maybe it was his own deference to Papa that partially caused his ailment. But none of that mattered, and frankly, Eddie didn't *think* of any of that so much as his mind skirted these ideas without articulation. No, when he was behind the barrier, Eddie simply tried to annihilate all thought so he could manage his pre-performance nausea.

Normally, Papa Marivicos would run roughshod over the boy, but when Eddie was in this preparatory state, he could rest assured that he'd be unmolested. The older man was quite cruel to Eddie in those moments where he wasn't fixated on gross ticket sales and the add-on garnishing of alcohol profits. Papa had all measures of vitriolic wizardry at his disposal. He was the type of wrathful, angry misanthrope who took insult and cruelty to extremes with his dry, cutting barbs. To Papa, insulting someone was a high art.

But not when the goose was brooding over the golden eggs he would lay for the gander. Right then, in that moment, Eddie was left to his own devices.

Deep in his shell, Eddie felt a fire ignite, moving to and from his bowels, and his nausea kicked in. Lost in his universe, the boy bent over, head tucked down to his knees, and prayed. In his mind, he could feel himself uttering some pleading words, though his corporeal voice box let out something else—sounds that didn't belong to him:

A voice commands thee
In your forgetting moments
Yet the vessel remembers
After the voice leaves

Eddie didn't know where this was coming from. Was it poetry? Prophecy? Was it the weeping and gnashing of a holy terror, crazed and toothless? Who or what was he channeling? He pressed down harder, grabbing the soles of his feet, pulling his chest hard against his knees until his diaphragm contracted and his tendons tingled with pain. He resisted the pressure of an animalistic moan. But it emerged all the same.

His pre-performance fits were not optional. The voice spoke again, and he could do nothing to suppress it. He felt separate from it—and it from him. He could hear the sound of the words silently echoing in his mind, competing against the bodily gobbledygook that came from his lips:

A voice commands thee
In your forgetting moments
Yet the vessel remembers
After the voice leaves

Do you know my name?
I am spoken memory
I am infinite sadness
The atom within

The thought that this might be poetry, that it might *make sense* to someone at the Carnival, terrified the boy, whose body started convulsing. Eddie tried to push more—now he was screaming, his face mashed between his knees and muffled by the meat of his legs and the cloth of his slacks—but the voice had fully taken hold, and so it continued uninterrupted:

The sin: forgetting
You: the mule for the theater
Borne with chains of illusion
Guilt upon your head

These eyes of light split
We are in our becoming
You: the penitent changeling
Us: invisibly voiced

He hated being a bible, hated the prophetic diction he was hearing outside of himself. Like a madman, he broke out of his cell at last. He hung limp and rubbery, his long arms draped along his sides, his face turned sideways, drooling. His body vibrated and bounced, his lungs constricting and inflating. There was some light in Eddie's eyes: a sourceless bounty of second sight. The other-voice, in full control, finished its recitation before allowing Eddie control of his body again:

Remember this work
A shadowed immemory
While speaking your reveries
Transmitted and true

The coil is wrapping
an ephemeral bonding
And that unspoken longing
It cripples and bows

Eddie sprang up with an unnatural kinetic power. Suddenly, he was his own again. He vomited on the dirt floor and breathed himself back into the 47th year of *The Marivicos Summerlong Carnivalé Festival*.

Papa Marivicos knew the drill. He had been watching, waiting for the magic moment. The old codger signaled to one of his troupe of achondropods to come clean up Eddie's sick. He signaled to another of the short-limbed dwarves to bring the boy a bottle of bourbon.

Papa took the bottle from the fawn-like dwarf and held it up,

6

label out, to Eddie. "Drink up, boy. There it is, boy... yes, yes, yes... drink it all up."

Eddie took the bottle from Papa's brittle hand and uncorked it, taking boundless swigs, huge gulps of the spiked elixir.

"Feel better?" Papa cooed.

The boy simply nodded; even in these rare kindly moments, Eddie was too frightened to speak. The desiccated meat-sack of a carny man ran his fingers through the sweat-soaked strands of Eddie's hair.

"You'll do fine tonight, boy. Real good. Real fine. You give 'em a good show, right? You will? Yes, yes. I know you will. I'll go out and count you in, bring you in right. You're the star of the show, yeah? Remember that."

As Eddie nodded, Papa briskly stepped past the curtain enclosure and through the dirt path to the bread-and-circus crowd seated in the round.

Papa took his place before the crowd, announcing not only his presence, but indicating the show was about to begin. "But, oh, the sound so loud! The voices that come, truly spoken to a mind broken—an intellect in disrepair. Yes, ladies and ghouls, fornicators and fools, we are at that eleventh hour. I, the Herald, tell of a voice given to an unearthly power! Presenting to *you*—every single ticket-bearing spectator," Papa paused and pointed a shaky finger in the vague direction of the audience. "And those of you who've snuck in for free, who will be dealt with later—presenting to you *the boy who was born with...*" Papa trailed off, scanned the listless crowd, then continued, *"second sight!"*

Cheers rang out as Papa spread his arms wide while he soaked in the excitement of the spectators. The spotlight fled the stage for a moment then multiplied from one light into several that swept over the crowd before converging and settling upon the showman once more.

"Once, and only in a single moment, in every Carnival night, we come to this circle to dream—rather, not to dream but bear witness to a reality reshaped, broken. To invoke those visions seldom spoken, to hear those uncanny wails that call from beyond the veil. Tonight, I present to you: *the one, the only, the wizardly and weird channel of secrets and prophecy and the unknowable: Melmoth the Magnificent!"*

An eerie minor-key organ dirge played out over the stale Carnival air as the spotlights dimmed. Layers of slow arpeggios and somber chords stilled the audience. Eddie walked out from the blackness of the tent and toward the center of a dusty circle as the follow-spot operator simultaneously shone a conical beam of bright white light down onto Eddie (or "Melmoth"). The boy slowly stood up straight while holding the edge of his palm to his forehead as a visor to block the bright spotlight. Even more slowly, he surveyed the room. The noises were deafening. They were noises that only he—Eddie—could hear. For the thoughts of just about everybody in the tent flooded his mind. It was unbearable. He wanted to clutch his stomach, keel over, vomit, run, scream. But he knew he couldn't do any of that.

From previous experience, Eddie assumed that the riotous interference in his head would, God willing, pulsate at a lower frequency once his mind reordered and attenuated the sound of the others' thoughts. Everyone was waiting in greedy anticipation. They'd heard that this year's main act was something of a stunner. But Eddie just stood there, silent, waiting. The stillness of the air and the discomfort of the crowd was palpable as the gravid silence elongated, ceaselessly mocking the ticketholders. A low rumbling began to emanate from the audience—something in the way of discontent—until a man yelled out, "Do something!"

Papa Marivicos smiled, his arms folded. He kicked one of his dwarf-seconds and pointed toward Eddie.

"You seen this part yet?" Marivicos asked his tiny assistant.

"Yes," the dwarf smiled, "it's very good. But how come you let him go on like this?"

Papa smiled a cruel smile and answered, "I didn't. I told him to go out there and ask questions. But he said he can't do it that way. After a few nights, I saw that this works just as well."

The two of them watched Eddie stir, and they kept quiet, waiting for the young man to start.

"What do you want me to do?" Eddie asked the man. The man who'd asked him to do something.

"Tell us something we don't know."

The crowd responded with a murmur of assent.

Eddie looked down, trying to pluck something from the chorus of voices in his head.

"Tell us where Jimmy Hoffa is buried!"

"I can't. I can only tell you things that you people know yourselves."

"Fine!" A shabby and stumbly drunk in the front row stood up and yelled, "Tell me what I'm thinking of right now."

Without a beat, Eddie responded, "You're thinking of two things. One, you're thinking that you'd like to rape the bartender at Finnegan's Wake, but you think you're too old, and you'll be too drunk by the end of the night, and you think she'd leave you hurt real bad if you tried. You're also thinking of the number eight hundred sixty-seven. Now you're thinking that you only wanted me to find the number eight hundred sixty-seven."

Eddie spoke calmly, his gaze never wavered, nor did his voice. The drunkard instantly jerked, and he gripped his dirty fisherman's hat tight in his hand.

"W-well, y-y... how... how dare you! I ain't never thought nothing like that in my life. And I weren't thinkin' of eight hundred sixty-seven, neither."

"I could tell them what else you're thinking, if you're calling me a liar," Eddie responded.

Someone else from the crowd shouted, "Well, how do we know you're not the one who's lying?"

Eddie smiled. "Good question. Okay, how many kids are in

the audience tonight? It's okay. I know you're not supposed to be in here this late, but now it's part of the act, so how many?"

A couple of tiny hands went up in the air, followed by a few women and men pushing them down out of shame or worry or both.

"I need a favor from the kids. Every kid with their hand raised, please keep it in the air."

Eddie walked up the aisle that cut through the staggered bleacher seating.

"I'm going to go to every kid with their hand raised. I'm going to say how old you are. If I'm right about your age, put down your hand. If I'm wrong, keep your hand raised."

Eddie went down the aisle and started.

"Ten."

A boy's hand dropped.

"Twelve."

Another boy's hand dropped.

"Twelve."

A girl's hand dropped.

"Thirteen."

Another hand.

"Fifteen."

Yet another.

"Six."

Eddie smiled and looked at the little tyke who'd dropped his hand. He turned to the boy's father and said, "Couldn't find a babysitter?"

The crowd laughed at that, and even more at the father's reply. "Can't even find his mother!"

Then Eddie went through another dozen or so, rattling off numbers. All the hands went down. Finally, Eddie turned back toward the old drunk, looking him straight in the eye.

"Eight hundred sixty-seven?"

The drunk heckler simply nodded, looking cowed. Eddie put his hand on the old man's shoulder and whispered.

"It's alright. I saw the rest in there. I know you wouldn't do it, Ern. You're okay."

The old drunk smiled.

Papa Marivicos rubbed his hands together. He could restrain himself no longer. He slapped his dwarf on the back and chortled.

"How about that? How about *that*?"

CHAPTER 2

"Never let schooling interfere with education."

— GRANT ALLEN

One man's success is never one man's success. It belongs to his family and ought to be repaid in kind.

That was my father's creed—and he meant it. Our family was the type that kept the grandparents in the house when they couldn't work anymore, when they didn't have enough money to pay down their own mortgages. That wasn't easy for them, for my parents or my grandparents. As much of a hard-ass as my pops was, his old man was even more so. But Dad always admitted that his success was, like it or not, partly due to what his old man had done for him. And it was the old man's old man who paid Pop's way through trade school. A very good one, too.

Aram Chain, the machinist—that was my pops. But don't you dare pronounce it like the chains he used in his shop. It's *Kha-Yeen*, danke schoen. He went to an excellent trade school and then ended up working at a nearby nuclear power plant replacing parts that couldn't be out of order for more than twenty minutes without there being a risk of a Three Mile Island meltdown.

In med school, we were taught to look at things, well, *people*, with an appropriately detached perspective. So, when I met Meredith (my mother who had done a long stint in federal prison for murder, but that's another story), I didn't feel that I was in a scene where I was meeting my mother for the first time. Instead, I saw myself observing, as an out-of-body experience, an interaction between an overworked, weary, raw-nerved first-year resident and an anti-social murderess who was trying to ingratiate— and thus monetize—herself to her offspring.

Suddenly, Dad's maxim *ought to be repaid in turn* seemed more like *the sins of the father shall be revisited upon the son*. Before I even got into a full-bore conversation with this woman, my mother, I felt resentment that I should be presented with the discomfort of getting-to-know-mom.

But, by the end of the night, we were all loaded. Meredith and I had become fast friends (though not quite mother and son yet). Dad had been fair, but rough, in raising me, and I'd be lying if I said I didn't enjoy all of Mommy Meredith's funny stories about Dad as a human, Dad as an ass, Dad as a happy new father. These were all the sides of Dad that I didn't know existed. It made the old man look human. As a matter of fact, (and it's possible that this happened despite Meredith's intentions) her stories even made me like my old man more. The event we were all attending as a happy family? My father's second wedding.

So I'm not exaggerating when I tell you that that wedding was quite the banner day in my young life. Not just because I bonded with Mommy Meredith, but also because I met Stacy Thornberg, the woman who would become my own wife. She was so dark, I remember, the dark lady of my sonnets and I'm not even a poet. The second I saw her from across the room I wanted to eat her skin. When I say this to her, which I still do (*a lot*), she says I'm a psychopath. That's fine, because I get to sleep with her either way. It was lust at first sight.

Stacy and I were on-and-off for about a year, but not because of any fights or blowups. She was busy with law school and I was working insane hours in my residency. One day I asked if she wanted to go on a lark with me to New Orleans. It just so happened, she told me, that her family was from there. So we went down there. I met her family, and something clicked in the bayous. I got on well with the family, sure. But it was more how Stacy and I spoke to each other plainly and honestly, late into the night, sharing old family histories and secrets, childhood mythologies, the works. We eloped, which was great because it meant two vacations in the span of two months, and I bought a house for us to live in back home in Kayjigville. And that's where we still live.

Unlike my pops and granpappy, and their pops and granpappies, *ab origine*, I have no son (or daughter) to admonish about their inter-generational duties of deference. Nope, it's just me and Stacy. Long story short, at one point, Meredith showed up to borrow some money. She promised she'd be back in a few days to repay me, but Mom's been gone (with the money) for going on thirty years. I'm beginning to suspect that the loan has been turned, by virtue of time and common law precedent, into a gift.

The downside, or one of just a few, to my marriage is that Stacy is infertile. *A barren woman*, if you want to be biblical about it, which I'm not. So we never had offspring. But I've been successful in other realms, and I'm sad to say that any success I've had in is mine and mine alone, along with that residuum of disciplined child-rearing and duty gifted by one Mr. Chain (I am not Mr. Chain—I am *Dr.* Chain).

When Stacy found out about her infertility, she started to crack. Not a little—a lot. My Pops even made some off-color remark about it to me when he came to visit us—*looks like the*

Chain men sniff out crazy as easy as a dog sniffs out dog-ass. We're more alike than you think, boy.

Words of wisdom.

I laughed. Because it was true. But even if it was a little bit funny, it was more sad than anything. As I got older, my pops kept bothering me more often about having grandkids. When Granpappy—my pops's pops—fell in the kitchen, my old man called me up and said, "wouldn't hurt to have a couple little 'uns around to give Granpappy and Grammy something to hold onto." I knew he was right.

I wanted kids. I wanted kids bad. I was one of two, and we brothers were thick as thugs. (Not anymore, though. My older brother Lucius died in my second year of college.) But I loved—love—Stacy very much, and I want to take care of her. So, no, we didn't have kids. And, yes, it's too late to have them now. At least the old-fashioned way.

But I'm not one to complain. I have a nice little practice, both family medicine and psychiatry, since I find that the two are, in fact, very much intertwined. Stacy mostly keeps to herself upstairs. She's probably a little battier than I let on (she hasn't left the house in a good number of years), but she's a wonderful chef and that occupies a lot of her time. She's also a semi-competent artist and that, too, occupies a lot of her time. This year, I'm pretty sure I can convince her to go to the Carnival. The Kayjigville Carnival. Yessir. Just me and the missus.

Pops would wish me luck dodging picture frames and random ceramic objects (if you can picture it) at that suggestion.

I'm getting on in years. I'm sixty-four now. I don't have much patience for the women in my life anymore. Like my mother and my wife.

Let's start with Mommy Dearest. She once took a life insurance policy out on me without my knowing that I was a missed heartbeat away from being a cash cow for an ex-murderess. Now how did I find out about that? Some guy called me at work wanting to discuss my life insurance policy I had just taken out on myself. Now, this was suspect. Turned out, my mother even co-signed with my birth name (she omitted the "Dr." title, however). I didn't even know this was possible with life insurance. Can't be completely unappreciative of the effort the woman put in.

Now, ain't that about a bitch? It's like a fumbling plot hatched by an evil Clouseau. The woman-mother didn't even think far ahead enough to imagine that it might be a bad idea to tip me off that there was a price on my head.

Now, why do I bring this up? You see, friends, for me it brings to mind several sayings that I've been giving some thought to of late: crazy breeds crazy; the apple doesn't fall far from the tree. A friend of mine said it better than I ever could: "Doc, it's funny. Meredith, a crazy woman, leaves you and your Dad. You find Stacy, a crazy woman, and try to rescue her. It's transference, man."

Maybe, at the time I married her I was intellectually over-confident because of my education, and somehow, I thought that cognition translated seamlessly into wisdom (it doesn't). My father even tried to dissuade me getting married to Stacy. He gave me a whole speech, *at the wedding,* if you can believe it!

"It's not too late, boy. Nobody will be mad at you. All it'll be is a nice party tonight, but nobody gets married. I'm telling you, if you marry this woman, it's going to be problems for you. She's goin' to put you at odds with your family, and that's the last thing you need. Every man needs a wife, sure. But if you pick wrong—and I'll be the first to admit that *I picked wrong*— then you'll be paying for it the rest of your life. That's what I'm doing right now, son. I'm pained by the situation you put your-self in, and I know that it's on me, 'cause of the things I did. Not because I married your mom. Shit, I love the hell out of you, son, and you are who you are because you came from both me and your mom. But I wish to hell that I'd gone on and married another woman, a *good* woman, a long time ago. Not the young tail I got now, but a real woman who could've helped raise you."

Whew. That was some wedding toast.

Truth be told, though, I appreciated his advice. That was really something cool to hear from my old man—laying it all out on the table, heart on his sleeve, doing everything he could to show me (in his own way) that he gave a shit.

And why am I bringing this up now? I'll tell you why. Summer's a-kickin' off. Every summer, there's the Marivicos Carnival. And Stacy never wants to go.

So, what do I do with this recluse who happens to be my other half? Instead of speaking plainly to her: *Stacy, I can't live like this anymore; I can't contort myself to your will simply to pacify whatever insecurities have developed into monster toads from the minor pathological tadpoles of your youth. I can't stay in the house only to bandage your ego. I can't cut myself off from the world!* I just keep my mouth shut.

Well, that's oversimplifying it a little. I just don't keep my mouth shut. I think about it, ruminate on it, even, and never say anything.

The shame of it is that by the time I realized that every man must reap what he sows, my father had passed on, and I never got to patch things up with him.

Again, I'm not a big complainer. With the exception of this diatribe, of course.

As I said before, I'm getting on in years, and I don't have much patience for this wife-woman anymore. Don't get me wrong, I still love her. How can you not love someone you've spent your whole adult life with? But I'm not *in* love with her. How could you be in love with someone after their every-once-in-awhile suicide threats had now become commonplace. And the divorce threats? *Ha.* Please. I should be so lucky. I mean, I love her, I'll take care of her. But sure as shit, I'm going to the fucking Carnival this year, wife-woman or not.

CHAPTER 3

Eddie laid on his back, looking at the blue-and-orange haze
veiling a monstrously large moon. A vast stellar tapestry speckled
the sky: the grey-glow of prematurely ripe star-clusters, the
burning dots of cosmic energy dancing early and before the night.
It was a beautiful twilight.

Eddie sprawled on his dusty twin mattress—old and ratty
with thin blue and white stripes; and hard buttons, some of which
were missing. He was looking up at the sky, a nice long distance
from the Carnival camp. He found sanctuary being away from
large groups of people. His own thoughts were sparse enough
that they didn't bother him. It was the constant throng of thoughts
that pummeled his consciousness and rendered him entirely
inept. But an invasion was inevitable.

Eddie heard, like echoing voices from a distance, the intrusion
of alien thoughts. It was a noisome, anxious, uncertain collection
of reminiscences—something foreign, loud, and busy.

Abakoum stood over him, casting a minor shadow as he
blocked out the night-glow that bathed Eddie. "Eddie, my main
man. What is the happenings?"

"Hey Abakoum. I'm just—I don't know. Just laying down."

"Yes, yes, it is very important a man should relax. I sleeps eleven hour every day. Is good for body." Abakoum slapped his belly. "See?"

"Boy, I wish I could sleep that much. Sometimes I just lay awake at night and I can't do anything to fall asleep."

"Have you tries count yaks?"

"Who's Count Yaks?"

"No-no-no-no-no–*to count*; to count yaks. When they make to jump over smaller yaks."

"*Oh.* Like counting sheep?"

Abakoum let out a loud, belly-shaking chuckle. "To count *sheeps*? So stupid idea! Sheeps, they are small, Eddie! How can you make to count the sheeps when they are so small, like shitty babieses?"

"I guess," Eddie smiled. "Why yaks?"

"The yak—he is great huge beasts! He have make the beeg horns; he have make the furry furs on legs, look like rich pants; he have make the snoot—the snoot?"

"Snout," Eddie corrected him.

"Yes, yes, snout! He have make the beeg snout. Ach! Is true, Eddie—Yak is best animal for make to fall asleeps."

"I'll remember that. Thanks, Abakoum."

"Oh, Eddie! Eddie-Eddie-Eddie-Eddie-Eddie! Is Abakoum pleasure. I can to sit?" Abakoum took the liberty to do so, in the absence of an affirmative response.

"Of course."

"Would you like to make see my new tricks for tonight?"

"Of course."

Eddie smiled and sat up.

Abakoum took out two metal balls and held one in each of his hands. "Your handses, please."

Eddie obliged, sticking out his hands. Abakoum took the metal balls—they clanged in a steady and intricate melody when he tapped one against the other—and held them against the tops of Eddie's hands.

"Now you make to press *hard*, Mr. Eddie. Make press *hard*. Thirty second!"

Eddie obeyed, forcing his hands upward against the metal spheres, and held steady for thirty seconds. Abakoum then took Eddie's hands and moved them down by his torso, so Eddie's hands were directly in front of his own hips. Abakoum took a step back and circled his hands around one another; the spheres in his palms reflecting the stars.

"Try hold them down. Try hold your handses, Eddie."

Eddie tried, but his arms rose nonetheless as Abakoum continued with the circular motions. After a minute, Eddie's hands were sticking straight out in front of him; they'd gotten there, at least in Eddie's mind, involuntarily.

"Avra Ka-Davra!" Abakoum exclaimed. "How you like?"

Eddie was genuinely impressed. "Pretty fuckin' good, Abi!"

"I tell on you something, Mr. Eddie," Abakoum held a knotted, slender index finger before Eddie's face and tilted his head slightly forward, "you show me how you do trick, I show you to make mine."

"I wish I could, Abi. I would tell you." This was a lie, as Eddie would not wish his friend to suffer the same mental afflictions or physical torture that accompanied his second sight.

At that moment, Eddie heard something—a dark intrusive noise—a voice filled with thoughts battering one another in a furious tirade—the signature of Papa Marivicos's cognition. At that very moment, Papa was walking toward Eddie without either of his dwarfly *aides-de-camp*, which Eddie took to be a bad sign. Papa Marivicos's disposition was merrier with his minions at his side.

"Koumy, get out of here," Papa bellowed.

Abakoum paused for a moment before Papa Marivicos shouted, "Now!"

Abakoum hopped to his feet and fled, mumbling meekly, "Goodbye, Mr. Eddie."

Papa stroked his chin before looking pointedly at Eddie. "What's this nonsense about you not wanted to bunk up with the dwarves?"

Papa was fuming; he had assigned Eddie to the same trailer as his own tiny assistants, hoping they would keep an eye on his son.

"It's not about them, Pops. It's 'cause I can hear them at night."

"What, you can't be bothered by the little fucks snoring? It ain't their fault they got tiny tracheas—God did that!"

"No, I mean I can *hear* them. Hear what they're thinking. I don't want to. It's... it's... I just don't want to be inside other people's private thoughts. Especially when they're dreaming."

Papa Marivicos looked, for a moment, nonplussed. But he was ignited, and so he would lay into Eddie, no matter the cause. "Well, I heard you asked Beatrice if she'd help you write those... *kids*, too."

Beatrice was one of the acrobats/contortionists who performed in the adult show. She had been reasonably nice to Eddie, and so Eddie, who was barely literate, asked her to help him draft a letter.

There was a long pause before Eddie spoke. "I just wanted to know how they were doing—if they were doing okay."

"How they're doing is none of your damn business!" Papa spat out the words like venom, then kicked Eddie hard in the shin. Eddie winced and grabbed his leg. Papa Marivicos went on, laughing mockingly. "You think they want to hear from *you*? You fuckin' freak. You're no good to anybody, you hear me? Do you *hear me?* I'm the one who keeps you fed, keeps you from getting yourself killed or ending up homeless. And what do I get for welcoming you back home? What do I get for arranging things so that you wouldn't do any more damage to yourself? Treachery. You fuckin' *Benedict*."

"Pops, I'm sor—"

"Save your sorries for someone who gives a flying fuck. I don't want your explanations. I want some fucking respect."

Papa Marivicos bent down to slap Eddie in the mouth. Eddie pulled back, only for a moment, but then thought better of it, thought better of resistance, and he moved back in, coming close enough that the edge of Papa's hand awkwardly clipped his eyebrow. Eddie wanted to say *sorry* again but restrained himself.

"No more contact with them. You understand me?"

Eddie only nodded, saying nothing in response.

"Good… good."

Papa Marivicos looked around. He was back in character, his thumbs hooked into his belt loop, his stovepipe back at a tilt with sweat leaking in droplets between his eyebrows.

"I'm only hard on you because… you know I do it for your own good. Right?"

Eddie nodded.

"Good. That's good that you realize that. Now, I wanna talk about the show."

"The show?"

Papa broke character. His face dropped and his posture grew rigid. "Did I stutter, shit-for-brains?"

Sorry, Eddie thought, but caught himself before saying anything.

"Yes, boy. The *show*. I want to try a couple new things."

In response, Eddie looked up at his father and shrugged while holding his hands out, palms facing upward.

"Yeah, I know it's playin' with fire. But I think this is gonna be good. We're gonna do a new trick. Some *long-term* prediction. Prognostications, as it were."

Eddie tried a lighter tone, though he felt uneasy when he thought about what could happen with new variables in the admixture of performance and prophecy—after all, it was *his* inner realm that was being tinkered with, no matter how fragile he felt his connection with it was. "What's the idea?"

"I want you to do a lotto prediction."

Papa smiled wide, clearly introducing this new idea with no small measure of pride. Eddie was too busy calculating exactly *how* to respond without getting rough treatment in turn. It was Papa who filled the silence.

"Think about it. If you can nail the numbers, then we're in the black till kingdom come. Some newsmen'll come down and report it. People will lose their goddamn minds... lose their *motherfuckin'* minds, I say. And then we just watch the money roll in."

"Well, if I can guess—"

"It's *not* guessing, boy. You know that."

"If I can know the number before the lotto comes out, why don't I give you the number and you get the ticket with the number?"

"It's not about the money, it's about this Carnival." The look on Papa's face was ponderous and grave.

"Okay," Eddie quietly let out.

"Listen, we'll talk about it a little later. I dropped this on you on a Sunday so you could have a little time to yourself to think on it and whatnot. Yep. And I'm even goin' to let you go walk about while you think on it. Would you like that?"

Eddie nodded.

"Good... Good. That's good." Papa Marivicos smoothed his frock. "Well, you think on it a little bit. I'm going to get back to seein' that everything's geared up and ready to go for the first show Tuesday night."

Eddie fell back on the mattress and wrapped himself in the twilight tapestry as Papa's voice and footfalls echoed in his throbbing head.

CHAPTER 4

A LITTLE OVER TWO YEARS AGO

Eddie hadn't planned anything beyond leaving home. When he
first thought of fleeing, he figured he wouldn't get too far. Maybe
he'd make it to the Kayjigville town limits, maybe even hitch a
little down the road—but Papa had so many people under him,
his father would have him back on the campgrounds in no time
flat.

That's what Eddie had figured. But that wasn't what
happened.

Eddie had grown disoriented in the forest brush that ran the
expanse from the campgrounds to the closest main road. He was
lost in the foliage and couldn't find his way out for a while. Eventually, he came to a clearing with steel tracks elevated on mounds
of rocks piled high enough to form a small hillock. By that time, it
was early in the morning, and the freight trains that cut from
north to south were passing through, carrying their titanic cargo,
trudging toward industrial centers farther down the coast. From a
distance, to his left, Eddie saw one of the boxcar's bulky doors
had been slid open. He observed a man wearing bib-alls and a

tattered straw hat, his feet dangling off the side of the railway car, bottle in hand. The train was coming slow enough that the man could wave at Eddie and give him plenty of time to wave back, which is exactly what Eddie did.

And for a reason unknown to him, Eddie started running alongside the train even before the boxcar with the hobo in it had caught up to him. He picked up speed, churning his legs in cycles of raw energy until he was moving in sync with the train, which was also picking up speed.

He heard a voice, that was both commanding and comforting.

"Grab my hand—on your left!"

Eddie reached out with his left hand. The train grazed his fingers, flaying the skin of his knuckles. But before he could pull his hand back, Eddie felt a strong grip under his elbow and over his forearm. He leaned into the force of the pull while leaping off the ground. In one fluid motion, the hobo had pulled him onto the train, and Eddie had collapsed on top of his rescuer. The train picked up speed. Eddie could hear the roar of the engine and the piercing shriek of the whistle. A hand slapped him on the back—the same hardened hand that had pulled him up onto the train.

"You done good, partner. Now why don't you hop on off me?"

Eddie quickly rolled onto the dusty floor of the railway car, then examined his hand injury.

"Well, would you look at that," the hobo said, "we got ourselves a bleeder."

A tramp quartet emerged from the darkness of the car that surrounded the hobo-hero and the train's newest stowaway.

Eddie tried to sound brave, tucking his bleeding hand under his armpit. "I'm okay."

"Now, now, don't do that, son," the hobo said. "Come 'ere and let ol' Uncle Jacky take a look."

Eddie held out his hand. Jacky grasped it gently and examined it the way Papa checked the authenticity of cash bills from his

Carnival patrons, giving hyper-attention to every microscopic detail.

"I say we go ahead and disinfect that 'fore we wrap it up. Whaddya say, boy?"

Eddie simply nodded in agreement.

Having procured the consent of the patient, Jacky took a travel-size bottle of bottom-shelf vodka and removed the cap with his teeth, still holding Eddie's hand. Jacky splashed a third of the bottle on Eddie's damaged knuckles before pulling a bandana out of his back pocket. Eddie hissed at the pain, but it was momentary. Jacky wrapped the bandana tight around Eddie's hand.

"Now, go 'head and make a fist. Hold that tight—not too tight though, just enough to make sure you keep the hand covered."

Eddie nodded his thanks.

"Think nothin' of it," Jacky replied.

The other four tramps had come closer. They stood around Eddie and Jacky, who were still seated on the dusty floor. Jacky was the only one to speak.

"So, where ya headed to, kid?"

Eddie looked down at his hand, then out at the passing scenery.

"Away from here."

CHAPTER 5

The main strip running through Kayjigville is older than sin. Not the Adam and Eve variety, just in the way that it's as old as the first Pilgrim/Puritan colonies in the far north. The main road cutting through the old-town strip of colonial huts and homes is only a little younger than the settlement itself. The later generations of Kayjigville fathers decided, when they'd heard the news that the Erie Canal was nearing completion, that their town would serve as a place of rest and relaxation. The old road, Main Street, was narrow and walkable, a tack intended to keep things light-trafficked, trodden only by ladies and gentlemen and a few licensed carriages.

A couple years back, a giant hotel chain put down roots in Kayjigville and teamed up with one of the freeholders. She was a Luciferian, catch-you-next-Tuesday type, named Clara Guadali. The team's aim was to take over Main Street using eminent domain.

Thank G-d, none of that actually happened. Clara Guadali took her overlord-impulse farther south to another municipality and inveigled them to let her run and ruin their town. Now, there's nothing but a trash-strewn empty lot the size of several football fields in that unlucky ghost-town named New Sheffield. The hotel chain pulled out of the deal when the state raised taxes, rendering the hotel's pondered scheme unprofitable, and thence undoable.

The point here is that Main Street remains largely untouched by the grasping claw of modernity.

Another nice thing is that, from the end of spring and well into autumn, the Marivicos Carnival illuminates Main Street. The Carnival is (if you haven't already gathered) a big deal in these parts. People stream in from all over the state, and there's a healthy contingent of out-of-town tourists, who support a respectable bed and breakfast trade in Kayjigville (which is also regulated by the city, and which I think is—*say it with me, folks* —ridiculous).

Stacy and I even tried our hands at BnB'ing for a bit. I was opposed to having people in my home—I'm a grumpy, resentful man, very much like my father before me—but I relented after realizing that Stacy intended to permanently shroud our home in psychological darkness if I didn't give in. I said okay, but she had to do all the paperwork herself. Stacy promised it would be a her-only project, but what do you think happened in the end?

Ah fuck! Another digression. Back to Main Street.

So the Marivicos family treats Main Street like its oyster—is that a mixed metaphor or what? It drapes lights and paper lanterns, flowery cloth pennants, and sundry paraphernalia of seasonal accoutrements all over the cobblestoned street. The main thoroughfare looks nice when they do that. I defy any man or woman to walk down Main Street during the summer and not feel uplifted. With the intimacy of the street's close-quartered design and the colonials lining the prime blocks, it's the closest thing we have to a quaint European town (not that I'm grousing about how we ought to be more like our continental cousins. I like being an American, thank you very much).

It is in this festive and happy atmosphere that I take my daily strolls. And it is near Main Street where I first encountered one Eddie Marivicos. And it is when I first encountered Eddie Marivicos that the direction of my life took a decidedly more interesting one—if not a more positive one.

"But what I don't understand, Abi," Eddie said as he stopped his friend's train of thought, "is if things are so much better back home, then why are you here?"

"No, no, no, no, no, Mr. Eddie. You misunderstanded me. I am *sayings* that in Bouklafi, the situation for man is better. Not for me. I am man, yes. But I am sayings that for *man*, is better. You are man. I am man. Here—too much silly things. Who make American laws? Woman. Why? So she can make control over man. Think of this, okay? First examples: pregnant. Did you know that here, woman can make to ask for—eh, eh, how you say? *Sameem, sameem.* For the pains."

"Painkillers?" Eddie replied.

Abakoum snapped his fingers and pointed at Eddie. "*Yes.* Here, woman ask for painkeelers. And what happen when woman take painkeelers? She become fat after baby. America doctors no tell you, but is the truth, Mr. Eddie. And what happen when womans become fat?"

Eddie was silent while he contemplated. "They weigh more?"

"Keep goings."

"Uhh... they eat more?"

Abakoum gripped Eddie's shoulder. "*Walla!* Yes, exactly, Mr. Eddie. Fat womans cost moneys. Fat womans will eat all foods. Fat womans will eat *baby's* food. And then, one day... fat woman will *eat baby*."

Eddie laughed. "Oh, come on, Abi."

"Is true! Why laugh, Mr. Eddie? Think of babieses. Babieses'

"Oh," Eddie replied. He thought on it for a bit. "Do you think that's a good idea, Abi?"

"Is not about what is good ideas, Mr. Eddie. Is about what is good idea *for your bilbul*. Every man need to make woman-mouth or woman-hand or vaginas on his *bilbul*. You ask me, my friend, I says you need good old woman-mouth to make help relax."

"I don't know... I don't really have enough mon—"

Abakoum reached out placed both hands on Eddie's cheeks, applying enough pressure that Eddie's mouth contorted into something like a duck's bill. "Shh, shh, shh, shh. Abakoum take care of it, Mr. Eddie. Come, come. Let us to go make sex for whores."

"Well..." Eddie tried, but it was muffled due to his duck mouth. Abakoum chuckled and released Eddie's face.

"Wait, wait, Mr. Eddie. I must to catch my breath. Come, we sit. Come! Sit! Sit! Yes. Good."

Abakoum leaned against the brick back of the building closest to them and Eddie eased down next to him. Abakoum removed an ebony pipe from his kaftan and fished in his pockets for a light. He found a small box of matches and lit the already packed pipe, taking in so much smoke that his cheeks ballooned as though he were playing a trombone. A moment later the smoke seeped out through a slit from the corner of his mouth.

"Here, Mr. Eddie. Have some."

"What is it?"

"Is *refuah, refuah, dawa*—good for medicinals, for to make relaxations."

Eddie shrugged and took the pipe from Abakoum, then allowed himself a brief experimental draw on the bit. It wasn't anything psychotropic, nothing mood-altering, and Eddie was glad of that. He didn't know what might happen with his second sight—new abilities—if he was doped up.

"Good?" Abakoum asked.

Eddie nodded.

"Good, Mr. Eddie. Now, to give back after second smokes. Is likes the strongman say, 'puff, puff, gives.'"

Eddie took another pull and handed the pipe back to Abakoum.

"Mr. Eddie, can I ask you…?"

"Yeah, Abi?"

"Is real?"

"Is what real?"

"You know… like *sahir*. Magi, magi. *Avra kadavra*. Is real?" Abakoum inhaled deeply on the pipe, waiting for Eddie to answer.

"I… I think," Eddie began then paused. He looked from Abakoum back to the pipe. "I'm not doing anything special, Abi. It's not me."

"What you mean?"

"It's… it's…" Eddie sighed. "I don't know. Is it okay if we don't talk about it?"

Abakoum nodded. "Of course, Mr. Eddie." Then, he pressed on anyhow. "Can I make to ask *one* question?"

Eddie relented. "Sure."

Abi passed the pipe back to Eddie. "Did start it to happen when you go aways?"

Through the silvery-blue haze of the smoke, Eddie nodded. "Yeah."

CHAPTER 6

A LITTLE OVER TWO YEARS AGO

The strange car-hopping hobo who called himself Uncle Jacky—after pulling Eddie onto the railway car—told him to take a couple more swigs of the bottom-shelf elixir from the small vodka bottle. Obligingly, Eddie took more than a few swigs, then fell asleep. He woke up, more than ten hours later sweating like a pig. The sun was a hundred times hotter than he remembered it ever being. He sat up and saw that Uncle Jacky and his quartet of compadres had shed a few layers of clothing. They were happily passing around another bottle—a much larger one. Jacky was playing poker with two of the other vagabonds.

"Well, would ya look who's back in the land of the living! How'd ya sleep, kid?"

Eddie rubbed a kink out his neck as he replied, "Either really good or really bad."

Uncle Jacky let out a curt laugh. "Sure, I know all about that. All about it, for sure. Sometimes you get so deep into noo-noos that your brain can't remember where it left yer body. Fer sure. I know all about it."

Eddie heard a distant iron shriek, smelled something smoky and metallic, and felt his stomach trying to balance itself out. The train was slowing down. He looked out to the horizon, where the sun burnt furious and yellow. "Where are we?"

"Down south, m'boy. A way waaaaaays down south."

FIVE WEEKS AFTER ARRIVING A WAY WAAAAAAYS DOWN SOUTH

Eddie had been watching her since he arrived as a vagabond in this tropical swamp. He had no inkling how many alien miles he'd traveled from his home up north. But by watching her, he felt stabilized. He would leave the park by the courthouse where he and the others had encamped after disembarking from the long iron bullet that had delivered them from the relentless cold of the north. He did this every morning, just to see her.

She stood outside the storefront in the mornings. She was the first one there, but he never caught her turning the lights on or unlocking the storefront. It wasn't her store. It couldn't be, anyhow, with the way the fat old man who worked the register yelled at her.

Eddie visited the store every morning while she was working the register to buy a coffee and a bagel, but he still hadn't worked up the courage to say something to her. He couldn't shake his self-loathing. He was stupid, weak, and everything else Papa told him he was.

Eddie spent his days picking up odd jobs and dumpster-diving for stuff he could trade for spare change with the other hobos. Around noon, he would count out his precious money—precious because it bought him coffee, and every day it brought him the chance to talk to the girl behind the counter if his battered ego would comply. For the first few days, he couldn't even look her in the eye. But, if he'd been able to look up, Eddie would have noticed that the girl was also having trouble looking at him.

NINE WEEKS AFTER ARRIVING A WAY WAAAAAAYS DOWN SOUTH

They held hands and strolled along the promenade. Every time Eddie looked at Chantell, he was struck by her. In Kayjigville, Eddie hadn't seen many beautiful people. Attractive, yes. But not like Chantell. Her eyes—they didn't exist elsewhere in the world. And she wasn't overtly intellectual, which Eddie appreciated because Eddie wasn't very bright himself—at least according to Papa. And Eddie believed Papa.

It was springtime, and the bayou swelter was on. The two walked with their hands clasped together. The first time Eddie and Chantell held hands, he'd worried a lot about his palms being clammy and gross, but now they'd held hands enough that he didn't care. The incident that removed his anxiety over this had occurred a while back, when he'd tried to pull his hand away from Chantell to wipe it off, but she responded by gripping his hand tighter and not letting go. He was also finding himself more relaxed around her—maybe it was because she never yelled, screamed, cried, or insulted Eddie, or told him he was a missed chance at an abortion.

He thought he'd feel immense guilt over leaving the Carnival —that he'd feel a need, or a calling to return to Papa—but that never happened. After two months and some change, Eddie felt good. Just good. And that was a new feeling for him. One he wanted to explore. His life back home, for the first time, didn't matter.

He looked at Chantell and thought, for the hell of it, he'd give her hand a squeeze. When he did, she smiled awkwardly and leaned over to kiss him on the cheek. Eddie felt so happy, he wished he could stop time; keep this moment somewhere reachable, where he could relive it whenever he wanted.

Chantell pulled at his hand and dragged him over to a bench that overlooked the big waters, a site they settled into so that

Eddie could eat the obscenely oily sandwich Chantell had gifted him.

Chantell delicately plucked a beignet from the paper bag and handed it to Eddie on one of the drier paper towels. She licked the tips of her fingers to clean them off.

"Here. F-for..."

She hesitated, her eyes fixed on him, and then she looked down and continued, "f-for my man." Her voice was soft, and she blushed as she spoke. That's one of the things he liked best about her, is that just when he thought that he was the scared one, she showed a little bit of fear too.

"Thank you," Eddie answered, "...my woman."

She looked back into his eyes and smiled brightly, which made Eddie smile. He bit into the beignet and started chewing, taking tiny bites in swift little grabs, masticating in micro-motions. She giggled.

"What?" he asked through less than a mouthful, "what?"

"You eat like a bird."

She giggled, and then gave a piggily snort when she couldn't contain herself. He started laughing, too. Eddie paused between bites.

"You're not eating?"

Chantell shook her head. "I ate a po' boy down at Mom's."

Eddie nodded.

"Hey. How come you never say nothin' about your family?"

Eddie shrugged. "I guess, 'cause..."

He had to think about that. Eddie didn't want to make anything up or lie, so he said the first thing he thought of when he conjured up an image of Papa and the Carnival. "I guess 'cause Papa doesn't like me."

Chantell put a hand on Eddie's back and started gently tracing her fingertips along his spine, then rubbing her palm against his lower back. "My daddy didn't like me, neither," she said. There was a silence for a while before Chantell broke it. "Look, so, I'm going out the bayou to see my cousins comin' up this Friday. You wanna come with?"

Eddie nodded and smiled. Chantell leaned over and kissed him on the cheek again—Eddie didn't think he'd ever get tired of that. Chantell spoke Cajun to him. "Laissez les bon temps rouler."

"What does that mean?"

"Let the good times roll."

CHAPTER 7

Papa Marivicos was sitting in the double-wide that occupied the prime spot on the Marivicos land—close to the shitter in the shed, and within spitting distance of the lake where his fawn-dwarves, Marv and Andy, liked to go swimming. There was something very special to Papa about Marv and Andy when they were in the lake. It was more than a purity—it was a guileless, childlike happiness.

Papa had found Marv and Andy when they were little children in an orphanage. Marivicos was very old, and his family was very old, and they'd been doing what they'd been doing for a long time. One of the things Papa learnt from his mother was how to scout orphanages for talent. From the time he was only twenty, Papa Marivicos was already using his off-season time to travel around the country, bribing as he went, fattening the coffers of public officials and administrators so their greasy palms would remember the flavor of his largesse. That way, he always had access to the kids. Not in a gross way. Just in a good, old-fashioned, gypsy-like-exploitation-of-children sort of way.

Marv and Andy's mother, Patricia, had been in the circus—she was a dwarf too, of course—and had been impregnated by Tycho the Magnificent, one of the more famous little people of her day. Tycho the Magnificent was a dwarf strongman and opera singer whose primo trick was balancing a two hundred cc motorcycle on his chin while he sang "I Am the Very Model of a Modern Major-General" from *The Pirates of Penzance*. He impregnated Patricia while on the circus circuit, and then left for Europe when he got a job working at his father's actuarial firm. (It was a little-known fact that Tycho the Magnificent studied law at the University of Heidelberg before coming to America.) Patricia, heartbroken, carried the twins to term, and after Marv and Andy were born, she put them up for adoption before killing herself.

Papa often recounted the story of finding Marv and Andy. The Carnival performers remembered the tale, since it was one of the only stories that the top-hatted patriarch told that could be described as both *warm* and *loving*. But, perhaps it's better to hear it as the man himself told it, transcribed verbatim from a tape recording made by an itinerant folk historian.

PAPA MARIVICOS TELLS OF THE DAY HE FOUND MARV AND ANDY

The off-season. I'm always pissed off when it comes 'round. The Carnival is my life, you see. I don't like leaving Kayjigville; I hate leaving the grounds. I ain't happy to trust the well-being of the Carnival to the kids and cretins while I'm away. But there ain't no two ways 'bout it, I got to, got to, got *to* go and scout. That's the thing about the circus that's different from us. 'Course, there's a *million* differences—we ain't no circus. We the big leagues. The circus is where diddlers and trollops run off to get away from police and pimps. The Marivicos Carnival is where you graduate to. We're the *big leagues*; they're the *bush leagues*. And just like any big league, we have scouts. And

then we have a combine. And then we have a draft. The
difference being that I'm the man takin' care of all of it.
Papa the Scout. *Papa* the Coach. *Papa* the President of the
League. It ain't an easy gig. Heavy lies the head who wears
the crown, ya' know?

Where was I? The off-season. That's right. I don't like it,
but there's travelin' to be done. So, I went off California
way, amongst the trailer trash out past Sacramento. *But you
live in a trailer, Papa,* you say. No, my friends. I live in my
workplace. The fact that I have a double-wide don't make
me anything like trailer trash. It's like sayin' a goat and a
rhino are the same 'cause they both got horns.

Well, I'm travelin' out California way to one of the regular
places. And this sister is givin' me the tour—not a sister in
a habit, but a sister *with* a habit. She's tellin' me this and
that about how she's been on the lookout for kids that'd be
extra-special for the Carnival, how she's been putting lines
out to the foster care people to swipe promisin' young
athletes out the ghettos just in case I wanted new acrobats.
This sister was cloying, clawing, trying to get more than
her usual fee. They all try. They're all always tryin' to get
more than they deserve. But the fee is the fee. The fuckin'
fee is the fee, dammit.

Well, I was about to leave the place, having seen shit—or
not having seen any shit that I gave a shit about—when I
saw these two *tiny* little boys sittin' out by themselves in
their winter jackets, havin' themselves a game of chess,
playin' the game on a wooden board with little wood-
carved pieces. Real pretty pieces. I asked the sister, "who're
they?"

Well, she answers, "Oh, those are the Midget Twins. We're
about to get rid of them, Mr. Marivicos. They wouldn't
interest you."

Now, I don't like being told what would and wouldn't

they *didn't know*. After their custom trailer had been built, Marv and Andy returned the leftover money, accounting down to the penny in an addendum attached to the expense report. Papa laughed at—no, *with*—the boys, the littles, the gentlemen-scholars upon whom he'd come to rely—his *aides-de-camp*. He was George Washington and the two of them were his Alexander Hamilton.

On the afternoon in question, Marv and Andy opened the door to their trailer to welcome Papa, who had to take off his stovepipe hat and duck low to walk in. The whole trailer was almost like a large dollhouse: outfitted with proper appliances and furniture; shorter chairs so that Marv and Andy's feet touched the floor while they worked; shorter desks; a custom low-slung toilet (the most expensive item of all). There were easy-to-reach shelves at proportional heights holding hundreds and hundreds of carved wooden figurines. It was like Easter Island in miniature. The boys had gotten much better at woodworking since their youthful chess set days.

"Afternoon, fellas. What's the good word, boys?"

Marv swiveled around in his chair. He was holding a legal pad. "Business or pleasure, sir?"

Papa smiled. "Why don't you fill me in on what's new with you, then we can figure out what needs to be done otherwise."

Andy was the quiet one, so Marv spoke. He handed Papa a half-foot-tall wooden carving of a bearded homeless man peeking out of a wine cask. "I call it *Diogenes in a Barrel*. And Andy painted a picture of the Ferris wheel. Excellent color."

Marv pointed to a two-foot tall watercolor propped up against the window. Papa took the wood sculpture in his hand and marveled at it.

"Well, would you look at that! I love the expression, Marv. He's a sour little bastard, ain't he?"

Marv smiled a little. "Yes, sir. He's *the* cynic. *The*, sir."

"Well, yes," Papa continued.

The older man leaned in toward the sculpture to examine it

more closely, as though he might find some profundity lingering amidst the smaller sanded portions of wood grain.

"Yes, I s'pose he is. Now…"

Papa pushed his hands against his knees and rolled forward to stand, leaning in to see Andy's watercolor. "Let's see, let's see about this painting. Yes. Yes, yes, It's alright—the reds and blues. Oh, and you've got the glow coming off the bulbs! Why, Andy, this is *exceptionally* good work. Christ, boys, I don't know which of you is the more talented."

Papa habitually slapped the dust off his hat and sat before continuing. "Well, that's the pleasure category checked off. Now, you boys sure you're getting enough money? You barely take anything. Sure you got enough for your paints and chisels and gouges and stock paper. All that?"

It was Andy who finally spoke up. "Papa, we have more than enough. You give us all we need."

Papa smiled and pulled a flask out of the tattered velvet jacket he was wearing. "Well, shit, if *Andy* is sayin' it, then I know it's the gospel. Okay, so long as ya'll alright." Papa uncorked the copper flask and took a swig. "So, business."

Marv took a pen and pointed to notes he'd jotted down on the legal pad under a dated heading. He read it out loud, like he was making a presentation in an MBA class.

"First thing: Our beer distributor sent a notice that next month, prices are going up. Something about having to pay more insurance on his end. We can either switch to Lackback's Distributorship—I've already put in a call to Jer Lackback and talked to him directly—or stay with Snowman's. The difference in Snowman's old and new prices comes to seven hundred dollars a month, but he's promised free delivery from here on out. The delivery fee, though, is only twenty dollars per, so the cost differential is still more than a half-thousand dollars—"

Papa held up his hand. "Stay with Snowman. I'll talk to him. He's not gonna raise prices. He's probably just fishin' for some facetime with yours truly. I'll drop by the distributorship and see what's caught in his craw."

Marv nodded and continued his recitation.

"Second thing is seating for Eddie's show. We've had overflow the last three performances. I know you said you want to keep them lining up, sir, anxious to get in, but Andy and I have talked it over, and I'm confident we can expand the seating of the main arena and still maintain an overflow. I believe an additional seventy-five seats are a good start. But we'd suggest maintaining flexibility, which means a new tent with replaceable and inter-changeable parts. Andy spoke to a few fabricators and got thirteen separate quotes. I took the liberty of drawing up some revenue projections based on a staggered schedule of new seating arrangements. You can see the projections lined up right next to schematics showing the proposed new—"

Papa held up his hand again. "That all sounds good, Marv. As always, I put it in your hands."

Marv nodded. Then, a worried look crossed his face. He rubbed his thumbs against the legal pad, gripping it tightly and looked down instead of straight toward Marivicos.

"What?" Papa asked. "What is it?"

"There is one more thing, sir."

"And that is…?"

"Clara Guadali."

Papa made a dismissive wave with his hand and shouted. "Ach! I don't want to hear what that preening cooz has to say. Tell that rancid slit that we tabled her proposals, and if she doesn't want to get tabled, too, she'd better leave me alone."

Marv looked over at Andy, who nodded to his brother to go on.

"Well, sir, it's just that things have taken a strange turn, and Guadali seems to have come into some compromising information regarding… regarding Eddie's return and the, um… the *arrangement* that took place."

Papa exploded into a string of epithets that were austere, even for him. "Bullshit! How in the hell could that Mammon-milking rube know fuck-all about what's gone on a thousand-and-more miles away?"

Andy spoke, an event which always caught Papa's attention. "I don't think it matters *how* she found out. It matters that she knows. And she *does* know."

Andy handed Papa an opened envelope with a note inside. The language was subtle, suggestive, but clearly still indicated that its sender—the Clara Guadali in question—knew of what she spoke. Papa studied it carefully before responding.

"Well, well, well. It looks like this little bitch is a cleverer minx that we first supposed. What ought we to do, boys?"

It was Marv who replied, though Andy quickly nodded his assent. The twins rarely disagreed on anything.

"A meeting."

"It's settled then. Set it up, boys. We'll meet the cooz."

Papa Marivicos smiled slyly at the twins, who jotted a few notes without meeting his glance.

CHAPTER 8

In their quest for whores, Eddie and Abakoum found their way to a pub. And then they'd found their way to another. No Carnival performances tonight, so they found yet one more pub, until it was late into the night—much later than Eddie had stayed out since he'd come back home. They'd rocked and reeled with good feeling, Abakoum regaling his younger compatriot with new tales of an old world, and Eddie had reciprocated, telling more of his own past than he'd previously cared to share.

Abakoum finished guzzling a framboise and manically waved at the server, who sported a polo shirt and ponytail. He was gesticulating in a triangular manner from himself, to his glass, and toward her—to send out a signal for a refill. "Oh, Mr. Eddie. How I misses them."

"Wow," Eddie replied, consciously willing himself to not slur his words, "two daughters. That's crazy, Abi. How come they don't come here?"

Abi continued waving frantically until the waitress noticed him and nodded with a smile. Then, he turned back to Eddie.

"What-what, Mr. Eddie?"

"How come—how come they don't come here?"

"Who?"

"Your daughters."

Abakoum spat at his question. "Ach! They don't want leaving their palaces. They make marry to mens who are rich. And what have Abakoum? Abakoum is magicians-man, Mr. Eddie. I cannot to changing my life. They are—how you say? They are-eh, eh… when womans is not happy at how someone looks for them?"

"Ugly?"

Abakoum laughed and Eddie briefly tittered along with him. "No, no, not ugly."

"Dissatisfied?"

"N-no, what is means, distfasified?"

"Like when you accept something but you're not happy about it."

"No, no. Differences. Is like when womans is… how can to explain? Okay, here's for examples. If woman learnses something, and something is *okay* thing, not bad thing. But is no good enoughs. *Sham-sham.* How you says? *Shami?*"

"Shame?"

"Yes! When womans are thinking they are *shame* over some-things and no want to tell peoples."

"Embarrassed?"

Abakoum snapped his fingers and pointed to Eddie. "Embar-rass! Exactly, Mr. Eddie. They are embarrass of their father."

The waitress came by with a fresh round—a framboise for Abakoum and another bourbon for Eddie.

"Thanks you, my dear," Abi said, pressing his palms together and giving her an affected little bow from his seat. Eddie only nodded to her respectfully.

"That's actually the last of the night, fellas. I gotta close out your tab. You can order one more round if you want, but Teddy's going to turn off the lights soon…"

Abi waved her off, but not dismissively. "Mmmno, no, no, no, no. We ares good. Just check please."

The server bobbed back toward the bar, the length of her ponytail swaying counter to her stride.

Eddie and Abakoum sat silently for a moment. Eddie took another sip of his bourbon and swallowed, then swirled his glass and looked down ponderously at the browning amber.

"I have kids, too." Eddie was surprised to hear himself speak this confession, nearly as surprised as Abakoum, who almost spat out his drink.

"*You*, Mr. Eddie?"

Eddie nodded.

"Where are them?" Abi asked.

"I'm not sure. I had to... had to leave them when I came back."

"Mr. Eddie, are you doings okay?"

"Yeah. Sure, Abi, I'm good."

And then Abakoum pulled out the big guns. He did something so simple but effective that it was a wonder no one else ever tried it before. He didn't respond; he just looked to Eddie and waited, waited to *listen*. Sure enough, the silence made Eddie uncomfortable, and after a few short moments he spoke.

"When I was away, before I came back. I met a girl."

"Hmm?" Abakoum hummed.

"Yeah. I met a girl. She was really nice. We were together for a while."

Abakoum narrowed his eyes and let slip a modest grin.

Eddie went on. "I don't know what happened to her. I didn't wanna go back, but Papa... he sent someone down to get me. Bribed some crooked guys, and well, I didn't have a choice. Here I am. It's good though. Pete the Cat says *it's all good*."

"Pete the Cat?"

"Oh, it's-it's a kids thing. A thing the kids liked."

Liked. Past tense.

Abakoum likely wouldn't know if Eddie was talking about *his* kids or the kids in the Carnival audiences, or just kids generally.

"Yes, Mr. Eddie. *Is all good*."

In seconds that stretched long enough to bank along the curves of time, Abi must have realized there was something too poisonous in this region of Eddie's story, a dark nebula of past deeds that couldn't be effectively examined in such a place. No, this wasn't bar talk. And though Abakoum couldn't know it, the voices that Eddie hadn't heard all night started to come back. They were voices that had fallen away as the two had proceeded to get plotzed. The voices represented a cosmic burden from which Eddie had unyoked himself by keeping company with the strange, funny foreigner at his side. The fact that Eddie was so drunk but could still hear the voices scared the shit out of the boy —inebriation was usually enough to do the trick. Abi couldn't know all that, of course. But he saw enough of Eddie's squirming to know that they'd worn out their welcome at this particular pub.

"Mr. Eddie, how about we go makes continues this good times somewhere other?"

Eddie looked up from the amber swirl of his bourbon glass and cocked an eyebrow. "What did you have in mind?"

Not far from the pub where they sat, in a Victorian mansion that had seen more respectable days, two women were arguing. One was named Madam Regina; the other was named Lexi.

"You're late!" Madam Regina hissed at Lexi.

Madam Regina was a haggard woman and no amount of excessive rouge and purple lace could hide that fact of her appearance.

Lexi lacked Regina's enthusiasm for excessive maquillage. She instinctively tried to explain herself. "I'm sorry. I had to—"

Madam Regina waved her off. "Excuses are like assholes. Everybody's got one and they all stink."

Lexi giggled, not reading the moment. Regina's jibe was

"And after he leaves his presents underneath the tree, if he's done real good, I'll let him up the poop chute."

Lexi laughed so hard, the water sprayed out of her mouth and nose, onto her vanity. This prompted Fanny's laughter, and soon both were guffawing like fools. Some of the other girls who'd heard Fanny were laughing, too.

Lexi took some of the tissue paper from the sex shop bag and used it to blot the water off of her face and vanity. "Well done, Fanny. Well done."

"A-thank you vuuury much."

Lexi finished putting on her new outfit. It gripped her in a way that showed the angularity of her slim body and accentuated her skin tone. Her long dirty-blonde hair flowed down her back. She admired how the turquoise teddy caused an optical illusion that made her baby blue eyes look artificial. A beautiful monster, maybe, crafted in some teenage boy's fantasy lab. That's what she was going for anyway.

"You ready?" asked Lexi.

Fanny stood up and adjusted her boobs. "Ready as I'll ever be."

Not too far away, Abi and Eddie stumbled toward the huge Victorian house perched atop the hill that overlooked Kayjigville's main strip. Soon after they left the pub, the sounds of alien thoughts that so blighted Eddie were dulled, yet he could still slightly hear Abi thinking in a combination of bad English and some indecipherable guttural argot.

Eddie looked back at his aging friend. Abi had been leading the way for most of the night, but the night had caught up with him, and he was behind Eddie now. The gobbledygook of Abi's thoughts receded into the background as his struggle to breathe grew louder.

Abakoum took a deep breath and pointed to the house. "There she is."

"The brothel?"

"Thas is its."

The two men crossed the row of rocks that demarcated the winding road from the modest-gradated climb which led to the front of the whorehouse. Eddie securely planted himself on the start of the incline and reached back to offer his hand to Abi.

Upon being helped up, Abi let out a deep, wheezing cough and laughed. "Am not in the shapes of being a kid."

Abakoum and Eddie approached the steps leading up to the veranda. "That's alright, Abi. I think it's probably 'cause we're tired and drunk."

Both working girls and paying johns were sipping drinks and lazing about. From somewhere deep indoors came the sound of a low-down and dirty trio playing slow Southern sex-soaked ditties.

Abi was reinvigorated by the sights and sounds of their destination. He began to bellow. "Well, I hopeses you make keeped some energy, my friend. You have need it! Because now we make to put sex on womanses!"

When Abi shouted, everyone ceased their conversations and looked at them. The silence was… difficult.

Abi walked ahead of Eddie, up the steps onto the veranda, making apologies and light conversation as he went. "Oh yes, very good drinks is cosmopolitan… chhello, my friend, you are to looking the spiffy… ladieses, very good evenings to you…"

It wasn't the socially conditioned state of embarrassment that bothered Eddie, though; it was the constant thrum of the patrons' thoughts; the workers' thoughts; Abi's thoughts. All made a web through Eddie's mind, and the individual threads were impossible to follow.

…well, would you look at this heap of ratshit?…

...what the fuck are you lookin' at retard?...
...I hope my wife doesn't find out I'm here...
...have some fuckin' self-respect, look at the dirt on your fuckin' shoes...
...fuckin' old man reeks like manure and whiskey...
...look at this fuckin' retard...

And it was that word, *retard,* that popped up again and again —the *drip-drop* of water torture, a wood-pecking picus prying open the skin of a tree with its beak.

The bourbon was starting to wear off. Not that Eddie wasn't still *very* drunk. And that was one of the unfortunate pitfalls of his psychic condition, that he could get drunker and drunker, but at a certain point there would be diminishing returns, and his mind would no longer be stilled. Eddie would hear *everything*—every thought in every head—while he was sloshed, irritable, and discontented.

As he stood in the looming shadow of the brothel, the rush of others' thoughts now *really* cut through his mind, crashing into his consciousness with a rapidity that sent nausea into his guts and disequilibrium into his bowels.

Why do I have to hear?

Worse still, people's thoughts transmitted themselves through a garble, a wretched amplification, that made their inner mono-loguing sound like dumb, angry monsters. And as he staggered on his knees, buckling and now bowed, a deluge of those cuts, those woodpecker pecks, battered him repeatedly. It was the thoughts of the men that were the loudest, and the most trou-blesome—

...fuckin' cunt has no idea...
...eighteen holes, but why not more, or maybe less...
...stinks like shit...
...bill's due on the fifth, but the grace period...
...I'll tell that motherfucker who's boss, I'll tell...

...they'll know, they'll find out...

He could hear the women, too, of course:

...in Maryland until May, but he promised...
...not enough time, but she knows that!...
...car payment...
...get paid enough for this shit...

Abakoum looked down at Eddie, who was noticeably burdened by something, though Abi didn't know what. "Mr. Eddie, are you feeling okay?"

It was at that point, as he ascended the short stairway to the front veranda, that Eddie fell hard, dropping dead-weighted and sideways, slamming his head against a baluster.

CHAPTER 9

It was very late, and Papa Marivicos was not very merry—he had gone back and forth all night, asking for Eddie, but his little magical fuck of a shitbird was nowhere to be found. Feeling atypically insecure about his power over his loathsome son, he'd asked Marv and Andy if they thought Eddie had run away.

Marv replied with the typical reassuring wisdom both those little cherubs displayed. "No, sir, he's out with Abakoum. It's an off-day. I wouldn't worry too much. It's probably good for the show that he goes out and gets drunk once in a while."

It was only this reassurance that allowed Papa to endure his high-heat fury—that boiling anger that had come and taken over his body, throttling the blood in his veins.

When Papa became *truly* irritable—not just cruel as a *calculation*, not just angry as a *means*—he locked himself away in a special place. And in this special place, the old man attended to the most important business of all. He sat hunchback-statured in a grotesque forward slant, a parody of a human being, a paradox leaning over a too-short table from his too-short chair. A large, lone, candle lit the table. A flickering corona, bleeding light into the complete darkness of the rest of the room. And upon the table was a manuscript, bound in blood-leather, crimson and soaked; but not wet. The tome was impossibly drenched and dry, all at once.

It was a great hulking book; it contained more than two thousand hand-written, hand-illustrated pages. If one could see the binding of the manuscript by the light, they'd notice that the leather looked like raw hide, disfigured in places, stretched in others; bruised as a hematoma. And if Papa Marivicos were to prop the book up on its lower end it would stand up straight, as thick as it was, and one would see letters in a lost language from a lost country. And if one were able to decipher this foreign alphabet, one would see that the full name of the manuscript was: *The Book of the Deeds of the Marvelous Marivicoses*.

Papa spent the next few hours poring through the awesome manuscript. Therein lay the writ of antiquity, the hidden conjurations of the hidebound hellions of the mystical East; the great lore of the Marivicoses and all the memory and tradition kept sacred for them.

On page 777 was the explanation of the Watchers in the Sky:

Lo, find here your eons, your long-drawn dusk hour
Where turns of the clock sway no movement or power
Where a great dying slumber dreams fire to be taken
And renewing itself dies again and awakens

Lo, see eons' limbs, moved through century's ghosts
Finding new homes, and new starlight to host
The bridge with no footpath, the path with no stone

And at the very end, in an addended pamphlet, was *The Ledger of Misdeeds*, where all that was morally reprehensible and (at various times) illegal had been recorded. The volume was a tally of crimes, left for posterity. Papa Marivicos, and all those

Marvelouses who have come before him, kept score, hoping that they'd accumulated enough points to get in with their Big Man.

Not *the* Big Man. A different big man. A Thing. A Leviathan. A Beast: The Scourge and the Sorrow. The Great Deceiver. The Black Destroyer. *Chernobog.*

CHAPTER 10

Eddie's head felt like a hot-air balloon gone too high into the air, bent by the thinness of tropospheric forces. Strangely, he didn't feel the usual surge of other peoples' thoughts when he first awoke. He wondered if maybe someone had put him back in one of the far waterside tents at the Carnival. But this was not Eddie's usual cot; it was something like a hotel bed—topped with a silky laced comforter, high thread count sheets underneath, and too many pillows.

He saw her before he heard her.

He *saw* her before he *heard* her.

He normally would have heard *any* person's thoughts long before he captured that person by sight. Nevertheless, there she was, sitting by him at the bedside. A woman—a *beautiful* woman.

The woman gazed at him, concerned and curious. "Are you okay?"

Eddie felt something wet on his head. In his peripheral vision, he saw a thin birch branch extending from the side of the bed to his noggin. As he got his wits about him, he realized that the branch was an arm, and attached to it was a wet towel, pressed against his forehead. He also noticed a glass bowl on the night-stand next to the bed that contained water with floating ice cubes. *Why can't I hear what she's thinking?* "I'm... I'm okay, I think. Did I fall?"

"Boy, did you ever. You hit your head on the railing out front. Are you feeling okay?"

Eddie leaned up a little bit, looked her over, and saw that she was in turquoise lingerie. She was the most attractive woman he had seen since he'd been with Chantell. "Yeah, I'm fine. Are we... where are we? What time is it?"

"You're at Madam Regina's; I dunno, about two in the morning? Just so you know, your buddy in the funny dress and the hat, he paid me to take care of you. I have you until the morning." She said this with a smirk, pulling the wet towel off his head to check the swelling. She winced, then set it back.

"I can't hear you," Eddie said.

She looked at him and jerked her head back a bit. "What do you mean? I'm too quiet?"

"No, I mean... never mind." Eddie averted her gaze.

"Poor baby. You're just a little shaken still."

Eddie sat up and the woman pulled the towel away. She felt unnerved that Eddie was silent and still. Of course, a lot of the marks didn't talk—*at first*. But once they were in the room away from the watching eyes of the brothel girls and bouncers, they would let loose with the jabber revealing their most private, depraved fantasies.

But this guy just sat there.

"So, what's your name?" she tried.

Eddie didn't answer at first. Instead, he squeezed his eyes shut, searching, trying to activate the previously undesirable extra-sensory faculties that had so dogged him. But now, in the only moment he wanted it, he couldn't hear *anything*. Couldn't hear her thinking. Then he realized how special this moment was. It meant that this stranger, this woman, was special to him. She was special because she *was* a stranger. And, to a mind-reader, no one was a stranger.

She was not translucent, but opaque. A psychic obsidian road-block, obscuring his most useful but despised ability. For the first time in years, there existed the possibility that maybe he could get to know someone. For in the calendrically short but infinitely-felt period in which he'd been "gifted" with second sight, there was now a deliciousness to be experienced in living moment by moment.

"*Hello?* Earth to egg one. Come in, egg one." The woman became suddenly jocular.

A giddy smile crept across Eddie's face. His delight at the vanishment of his second sight sent a joyful frisson through him.

"Huh, what did you say?"

"Jesus, you really must have hit yourself pretty hard. Maybe we ought to—"

"No. I'm okay, I'm okay. I just didn't hear you. Just tell me again what you said." As Eddie spoke, he placed his hands over the woman's own, a bold approach, brought on by the infusion of felicity and nirvana that surged in his soul.

Lexi smiled—all the girls smiled, but Lexi knew that her peerless artificial smile, was better than any of the other girls' real smiles. It could make any mark feel special—though they weren't; the marks were all the same, *always*.

"What's your name?"

"Eddie Marivicos. What's yours?" Eddie replied without a millisecond of delay.

"Lexi," she said by accident. *Shit. No real names, idiot!*

"That's a great name," he gushed, "the best name I've ever heard. Sweet Lord Almighty, that is a wonderful name."

Eddie reveled in the power he felt from having to learn something new, of not having every secret thought constantly present to him.

Lexi drew back, put off by Eddie's seeming delirium, though

she couldn't say exactly why. He was as strange as the most awkward marks she'd met, but there seemed to be more to him than just common strangeness. "Oh yeah? Why's that?"

"Well, let me ask you a question, Lexi."

Lexi arched her eyebrows and crossed her arms, pensive for a moment. "Umm... okay..."

"Can you think of a number?"

Now she had a funny look, a goofy drop of the lip, a slant of the eye. "I suppose so. This isn't gonna end with me getting hurt, is it?"

Eddie laughed in a way that was over the top, absurd. "NO! Goodness, *no*. Just, just... just humor me for a minute, would'ja?"

As Lexi gave it some thought, it occurred to her—because she was, as Fanny put it, *too optimistic to know better*—that maybe this *Eddie* was just one of those stupid-happy folks who are simply delighted to know that a bucket of piss isn't a bouquet of perennials. So, she sat back and after a moment's pause, answered.

"Okay, I'm thinking of a number. What now?"

Eddie tried his *very* hardest to do anything—*anything*—to home in and focus the writhing, inscrutable energy of his *seeing*. But try as he might, he couldn't get a bead on it. Couldn't get shit. But he gave it a guess anyway.

"Are you thinking of the number sixty-seven?"

Lexi shook her head.

Eddie smiled. "Are you thinking of the number seven hundred and eight?"

Another shake of the head.

Eddie smiled wider and started childishly chuckling. "Is it four billion and two?"

There was something about the way the words "and two" came out. Something like a curious upward inflection—something reminiscent of the doltish pitch-modulation of a Valley girl. It made Lexi giggle.

"No!"

Then the oddest thing Lexi had ever seen in all her time of working in the brothel happened. Eddie broke into laughter. Like someone was tickling him. She watched him go on like this for about ten seconds, thinking that she'd wait it out, but then he just *kept going.* He writhed on the bed, and he started cackling a ferret wheeze of a cackle, some ridiculous rodent rasp. It was that stupid-funny-happy-infectious laughing that sent her over the edge. She started laughing too. And *that* was too much for Eddie. He held up his hand, motioning as if he were waving her off, the limbic language that says *no more, please, no more.* But he couldn't stop. She couldn't stop. They laughed together loudly with abandon.

Then, a loud *bump* came from the wall next to them. *"Hey! Keep it down in there! I'm tryin'a concentrate!"*

The shock of the angry thud helped them die down to the low titter of conspiring teenagers.

Eddie was the first to speak, with a smile, leaning back against the headboard. "I'm sorry. You probably think I'm crazy."

Lexi smiled, too. "That's okay. It's a good crazy, I think."

They sat quietly together for a bit. Then Lexi began to feel uncomfortable. She stood up, walked over to a wood and glass bar, picking up a cut glass goblet. "Do you want something to drink?"

Eddie nodded. He was now back to his somber self, though he still kept some delight in his heart for not hearing his second sight. "Yes. Yes, please."

Lexi poured him a bourbon. But Eddie was a bit distracted. She had an antique Coleman gas lantern. It was behind her, high on a shelf. It was mostly black with a brass knob, and a bulbous glass and mesh container surrounding the part that produced light. There was a nice handle that curved from below the glass into a downward slope. It was affixed to the lantern, but rested, as it wasn't hanging or being held.

But he wasn't just observing it like a normal person would.

"So you're a, uh... bourbon man?" Lexi asked, trying to break the silence once again.

He didn't look back at her as she spoke.

Lexi picked up a glass flute and reached for a bottle of champagne sweating frosted beads atop a mound of ice rocks. Eddie snapped out of his transfixed state and turned to her.

He winced. "Oh, don't drink that."

"Why not?" She looked back at him. It looked like he was in physical pain.

Eddie stared out the window, so far out and away that he wasn't looking anywhere at all. Then he whispered in a bleak tone, "*She* used to drink that."

"Who, *Eva Braun?*"

He was still looking out the window, and she turned away, smirking. Eddie stumbled over his words. "Please. I'll... I'll pay the house for whatever you drink, but just don't... with the champagne."

Lexi looked back at him. *Okaay psycho. What is his deal?* she thought. "Um... okay. You're the boss."

She reached into the mini fridge down to the right of the bar and pulled out a PBR, then walked back to the bed and handed Eddie his glass of bourbon. Eddie relaxed, noticeably.

"Hey, wanna see a trick?"

"Is this going to be another underwhelming guessing game?"

Eddie curled down the left corner of his lip and raised his left eyebrow at Lexi, as if to say, *coooome on.*

"Okay, okay. Yes. I would like to see a trick. Please."

Eddie smiled. He was an ever-sorrowful soul, but he couldn't help feeling, and thinking repeatedly, that he'd experienced some strange fortune to be able to find someone whose thoughts he couldn't read.

"Okay. No, wait! Don't open your beer yet," Eddie instructed.

Lexi rolled her eyes.

He continued. "Yeah, good. Okay, just hold it in front of me. Yeah. A little closer. Okay, you ready?"

"Ready."

The can of PBR opened itself in a crisp, breathy, wet snap. Lexi jumped back. "Hey! Jeeesus. How'd you do that?"

"It's a magic trick. I can't tell you that."

The can started to prematurely fizz over. Eddie yelled at Lexi. "No, no! Get it! *Get it!*"

Lexi hurried to meet her lips to the open can. She sucked back on the beer and guzzled enough to quarter-empty it. She wiped her mouth and chin with her forearm. "Okay, Magic Eddie. What's your deal, man?"

"What do you mean?"

She waved her arms around as if it was obvious. "I mean that you show up here with a guy that looks like an extra in *Aladdin*... you start laughing like a maniac because... because... because you guessed a number *wrong*... and then you start doing magic tricks. And I see you looking at my lantern, too. Seems like you really like it. I don't know. I guess you are, bar none, the *strangest* customer I've ever had."

"Oh, I'm sure that can't be true. I know the mayor comes here, and he's a *taxidermist*." Eddie took a sip of bourbon and swallowed it down before finishing. "Now *that's* strange." He looked back at the lantern. He kept doing it, too. Kept looking at the lantern.

Eddie was right: Mayor Laivid came to Madam Regina's all the time. But he had a special entrance routine where he was snuck in. Lexi had never been with him. The mayor had some peculiar fetishes, and most of the girls opted out of them. But Lexi had been working long enough to know that the mayor's visits were very hush-hush.

"How do you know that?" Lexi asked.

"Well, the girl next door is thinking about him right now,"

Eddie said, still overwhelmed at the anomaly Lexi had proven to be. Impenetrable. A secret. A mystery. She mesmerized him.

Can't read her. No, no, no, can't read her at all.

"Sooo, you can read minds?" Lexi's arms were crossed, eyebrows raised and furrowed.

"Well, apparently, not *yours*."

"Why not?"

"I don't know, and I don't care. I'm just happy not to. Something about you has—" Eddie shrugged. He took two fingers and moved them downward from a point in the air. "Something about you has dimmed the switch. I'm just downright happy not to read you. Maybe I can even turn the others off, too. So, here's lookin' at you, kid." Eddie held his glass aloft after finishing it, then asked if she minded if he had another.

"No, not at all." Lexi spoke with a new politeness. She walked back over to the bar to grab him a new drink. *Boy, oh boy, this guy's a fuckin' piece of work. Oh well. He's not hurting me, so what's the difference?* "So, how did you come to, uh, how… were you, uh, born with these powers or whatever?"

She handed him his drink and then sat down next to him on the bed.

"Well, I think it has something to do with coming back north," Eddie replied.

"What's that mean?"

Eddie turned his head again, cranking his neck toward the window, thinking of Chantell tipsy on discount bubbly. Thinking of things both easy and difficult to remember.

"Oh, I just used to be in another place. But now that place don't really exist." Eddie knocked back the rest of his bourbon, a little too quickly for him not to choke on it.

Lexi was right back on point. "Say, you know what usually makes sad people feel better?"

"What's that?"

"Fuckin'. How 'bout a nice lay?"

Without bringing his gaze back to Lexi, Eddie shook his head. "No, that's alright. But I will take another drink."

He was still looking at that damn lantern. Lexi grabbed it off the shelf. "Here," she said, placing it in his lap.

Eddie gripped the lantern, spun it around, and smiled. "This is... this is really nice. It's a nice lantern," he said. He handed it back to her, but Lexi shook her head.

"I'm giving it to you," she said.

"But-but I don't understand. I'm... I'm supposed to pay *you*, right?"

"You did. It's just, ya know, a gift. Didn't cost me anything, and you seem like the type who likes old stuff like this, anyway," Lexi replied.

Eddie picked up the lantern and held it close to his chest. His odd behavior was endearing, in a way.

"Yes-yes, I guess I do. Like old things, I mean. But, is it important to you, though? I don't... I don't wanna take something that's important to you. I still don't know why you're... why you're giving it to me."

Lexi smiled. "Yeah, that's the weird thing. I don't..." she trailed off and shrugged.

"You don't know?"

She shook her head.

Eddie ran his fingers along the glass of the lantern, then the handle. "Where did you get it? This, I mean. Who gave this to you?"

Lexi thought a moment. "I'm not sure. But I know it's mine. I don't know how to describe it. It's just always been here. I guess I thought it always would be, but you... you really like it, and so yeah. I don't know how to describe it. So just..." she sighed.

Eddie smiled at her. "Okay, yeah. I'll take it. Thank you,"

"You wanna light it?" she asked. She showed him how it worked, told him what she knew about it, and that she had a handyman at the brothel who could fix it if it broke.

They had a few more drinks before the two of them fell asleep, enveloped in the soft glow of the lantern.

THE NEXT MORNING

Eddie woke up and saw that Lexi's head was resting on his chest. He still had all his clothes on, and she was wearing a hooded sweatshirt, but her legs and buttocks were still semi-nude, peeking and protruding from the turquoise bottoms of her lingerie.

He looked over at the clock and saw that it was almost noon, which meant that he'd get a tongue-lashing, if not a good thrashing, from Papa. Eddie felt a little fuzzy, frazzled, and just a bit apocalyptic. He moved as delicately as he could, slowly sliding his left arm out from under Lexi and trying to roll without using momentum so he didn't jar the poor girl as he skedaddled. He didn't forget to grab the lantern. It was awful nice of the girl to give that to him.

Eddie carefully opened the creaky door and tiptoed into the hallway. It was dark, with no window to let any light in. He supposed that's how the brothel was meant to be set up—for privacy.

Of course, since Eddie had been put in Lexi's room while he was unconscious, he was unaware of where in the brothel he might find Abakoum. But to his surprise, Eddie walked only a few steps and found his friend sitting in a salon waiting for him, smoking a pipe and chatting up a portly and heavily cosmeticized strumpet who was laughing generously. Abakoum spoke fluidly with her, with none of the unsure stutters or syntactical mistakes of a second tongue; Abakoum had found someone with whom he shared the same native language.

Eddie made brief eye contact with the woman to whom Abakoum spoke. Abakoum turned his head in the direction the woman's eyes went. "Mr. Eddie! Good morning!"

"Hey Abi. Did-what did... did you have a good time last night?"

"Mr. Eddie, Abakoum haved wonderful times." Abi turned to Madam Regina and winked.

"Do we... should we... I don't have much cash..." Eddie's voice trailed off into a whisper.

Abakoum waved him off. "There was none worries, Mr. Eddie. Abakoum have taked care. Is present."

"Oh, Abi... you—"

"Ah, tak-tak-tak, Mr. Eddie. Now is the times of you make quiet your mouthhole. Is the pleasure of Abakoum. Take gift!" Abakoum gasped when he saw Eddie holding the lantern. "Looks like Mr. Eddie getting many of gifts today! See? You takes the gifts, Mr. Eddie. Is rude not to, so take Abi gift too, yes?"

Abi's voice grew louder, as though he meant to upbraid his younger friend. Madam Regina cut in.

"Well, I think maybe you ought to get your friend back, Aba-Cakes."

Aba-Cakes, Eddie thought. *That's a funny one.*

"Yes, yes, yes, Ms. Sexypants. I am think you is right. Mr. Eddie, shall we to go?"

"Yeah, I think that's a good idea. I have the... uh—"

Madam Regina finished his thought for him. "A show tonight. I heard it's quite the spectacle. Some real mind-fuckery, too. I'd be interested to see it."

Eddie reached into his wallet and pulled out half a dozen passes that Marv and Andy had given him for the Big Tent. Eddie tried to refuse them, saying he had no one to invite to his performances anyhow, but Papa had been standing there and told Eddie to just take the damn things and *don't be so fucking ungrateful, you stupid cockshit.*

Eddie handed the passes to Madam Regina. "Here. These are good for whenever. But, uh, just maybe—maybe you could—"

"Oh, *absolutely*, I'll ask Clarabell and see if she can come."

73

"Clarabell?"

"Your girl. The little Clarabell of the ball."

Eddie shook his head. Madam Regina frowned and let out a puff of scoffery. "Well, I suppose you know her as *Lexi*."

Eddie smiled. "You think she'd come?"

"I'll ask."

"Come, Mr. Eddie." Abakoum rose from his seat, forcefully tapping his pipe down against the edge of an ashtray so the burnt tobacco and ember came tumbling out. Then he thrust the pipe into his kaftan. "We must to make haste for the returning."

"Yeah, okay. We should go."

Abi leaned down, gave Regina a kiss on the cheek, and then turned to open a side door that led out to the exit. He clearly knew the layout of the old Victorian. As Eddie followed Abi out, Madam Regina interrupted.

"How was she?"

Eddie turned back and grinned, but Regina saw it was a smile without purity, the guilty grin of a man ever burdened and sorrowful.

"Oh, she was really nice. We had a lot of good talks."

"Did she do all the things you liked?"

"Oh, definitely, Miss. She refilled my drink and everything."

Madam Regina laughed at this, but Eddie looked confused.

"Wait a minute, boy. Did you not sleep with her?"

"No, I got a little sleep."

The Madam sighed at the realization that this fellow was a semanticist.

"No, sonny, I mean did you enjoy the sex?"

Eddie's face turned red and he looked to the floor. "Oh, well, I, uh... we didn't really do anything like *that*."

One of the woman's thick, charcoal-laden eyebrows inched up her forehead at the realization of what the young man was trying to be not-so-forthcoming about. She didn't understand why. They were in a fucking brothel. She sighed. "Ah, I see."

"Yep, yep, yep…" Eddie's voice trailed off, the volume and pitch getting lower as he repeated the word.

"Yes," a bemused Madam Regina replied. "I'll ask her about it, then."

"Great. Well, thank you very much for your hospitality. You have a wonderful establishment."

Eddie and Abi went through the door and left the peerless purple Victorian den of dedicated harlots. Madam Regina could only wonder at what she'd seen. A boy whose best friend was an elderly immigrant, and who, despite his good looks, didn't seem to know (or pretended not to know) what to do with a woman; whore or not.

CHAPTER 11

In case you haven't forgotten me, I'm still around. Chain here. *Doctor* Chain, if you please.

I really want to go to the Carnival, no matter what my wife thinks.

What's a good compromise? My father always told me that a good compromise is where *everyone* comes away only a little unhappy. So, I suppose as my marriage is concerned, I'm a *great* compromiser, because I'm more than a little unhappy. I've been stewing over this Carnival thing. I'm gearing up, getting ready to have the big rip-roarer—that knock-down-drag-out motherfucker of an argument with Stacy.

I want to go to the Carnival. I *really* want to go.

A lot of my patients have been telling me about the new gimmick they've got. Some sort of mesmerist, or mentalist, or something like that, and he's supposed to be *really* good.

Up until this point, besides meeting me, you've also perhaps gotten acquainted with a few of the other interesting folks here in Kayjigville. I'm sure some other benevolent-omniscient fabulist has kept you up to speed with a few of the other denizens I call my friends and neighbors. But now, you will have the great pleasure of receiving an introduction to the great love of my life, Stacy Thornberg. (Yes, my One True kept her maiden name. She said that *Stacy Chain* would sound like the name of a low-rent female wrestler, or perhaps even a blue movie starlet.)

There she is, sitting at the kitchen table, staring off into the distance. She's taken to these fits—well, not fits, exactly, but what else would you call a person checking out of reality? I've come to call them her Space-Time Disjunctions, or STDs. Of course, Stacy doesn't think it's very funny when I ask *are you getting another STD*, so I mostly just keep it to myself these days.

"Morning, Sweetheart," I said to my lovely, potentially STD-afflicted wife.

No answer.

"Good morning, Sweetheart," I tried again, brightening my tone, hoping she would enjoy the pleasure of my higher octave.

Still no answer. I cleared my throat—*ahem, ahem*, attention please.

"Hey, aren't you that actress, Stacy Chain?"

That did it. She shook her head and quickly came back to earth. "Oh, hardy-har-har."

"What are you up to?"

"Hmm. I was just sort of looking out at the birds, you know. Thinking to myself."

I peeked out the window. "I don't see any birds."

"Well, then maybe you're just not looking very hard."

No, I was not looking very hard. "Did you make coffee?"

She shook her head. That was another cause for resentment. I was the sole breadwinner, the fixer-upper, the jack-of-all-trades who patched things up and bought what we needed. My wife, though, does very little of that. And all I want is some coffee in the morning. Just a fucking cup of coffee, ready to go when *I'm* ready to go. Years ago, I thought I might say something. But I didn't. Well back then it bothered me a whole hell of a lot less. Once, a friend of mine asked me why I don't just say something instead of sitting quiet and getting angry at her. Well, she should *know*. Shouldn't she? I mean, do I really have to spell it out? Should I draw up a diagram and/or flowchart illustrating how *my* many obligations massively outweigh her own? Is that what I *have* to do, folks? *Is it?*

I grumbled and went over to the Keurig, spit-whispering an adolescent-petulant bromide under my breath.

"*I'm going to make some coffee.*"

"I bought you a cup."

"Well, that's... *what?*"

A delusion. She's become hysterical. Because, believe you me, Stacy most certainly did *not* go out. But then I turned around, and there it was. A white paper cup with a brown sleeve over it, and the navy-blue stamp logo of Kayjigville Coffee Makers on the side. I went over to touch the cup, to make sure that it was real. It was warm. No, it was still *hot*.

"When... when did you go out?"

"This morning. I thought I ought to go for a walk."

"You thought... you ought to go for a walk."

"Are you upset?"

Fumbling over myself, tongue almost tripping, I blurted my reply, restraining my enthusiasm, knowing that a joyous overkill might make her reconsider what she'd done.

"No, no, no, no! No, not at all. I just... no, that's no problem."

"Dark and bitter, right? Just like you like your woman?"

My heart melted. I felt a terrible shame and guilt at her comment, delivered with that polite little laugh of hers. That's marriage for you. One second, you're going over the laundry list of complaints you have about your spouse, and the next you're so deeply in love with them that you want to give them anything they want in the world. And this is where it got worse, because I realized that I had no similar gesture, no great action that would betoken a willingness to change, to renew my love. *Jesus Christ,*

I'm a fucking clown. I have to do something. *Something.* Lord knows it hasn't been easy, being with me.

"Say, I was thinking maybe I'd move my appointments today and we could work on the family tree together."

There. There it was. The family tree—a history of both our families, actually—was a collection of pictures and paraphernalia that we were putting together into little dioramas. It was also another thing that pissed me off infinitely, because I would bitch to Stacy that we had no family to pass our history on to since we didn't have kids. Over the years, I'd promised a million different times to help her with it, but I never did. That was my big *give*.

I figured that Stacy's eyes would light up, her person would glow in some holy soul ascent, and she would appreciate all that I had done for her by so selflessly offering to do the family tree. How wrong I was.

"I was thinking we might go to the Carnival. To the Main Tent. I heard the new show is really good."

And that was *precisely* when I started panicking. Why would I be panicking? Didn't I *really* want to go to the Carnival? Well, I'll you why. Because this sort of dumb luck, this unbelievable favorable turn, was a complete blindside. It's the sort of fortuity that doesn't exist, that never comes up in the lives of most ordinary men. It would be like the garage mechanic saying that your Buick blew a gasket, so they bought you a new Caddy. Or like going to the doctor for a check-up and being told you lost thirty pounds and your muscle density tripled. It would be like going to pick your wife up at the airport and finding that she'd transformed into Sophia Loren. *Gob smacked.* I was fucking *gob smacked*.

So what did I do? I played it off, giving her a peck on the cheek and an understated hug.

"Yeah, that could be pretty fun. Can I get you anything?"

"No, sweetie. I'm good."

"Alright, then. I'm going to go down to the office and open up."

Stacy smiled sweetly, without looking in my direction. "Sounds good."

I grabbed my keys from the bowl by the light switch, then shuffled my feet, thinking I might turn around and ask again if Stacy needed anything, you know, just to earn extra points and seal the deal. But I decided not to. No reason to look a gift horse in the mouth. *Not when the gift horse just told you that she wants to go with you to the Carnival.*

CHAPTER 12

Stacy and I got out to the Carnival plenty early. I offered to drive, but strangely enough the wife wanted to walk the old footpath behind Main Street and beside the river. So, we took our time taking a stroll out to the show. My beloved had taken the time (taken plenty of time) to get herself ready to go out, and I have to admit that she looked as fine as I'd seen her in a good long time. Maybe almost as fine as she looked on our wedding day. That's the bitch of the matter, the point I've been trying to drive home to her for a long time—looking like she does, we ought to go out all the time. (Yeah, I'll admit I'm a guy who likes to show off his trophies once in a while.)

She put something on her skin that made the shadows kiss the darkness on her—something that made the light glitter as it played across her ebony complexion. She wore a royal blue sundress, and I am more than happy to tell you the truth; that she looked a whole hell of a lot better than me in my shabby hush-puppies and decades-old slacks. She looked happy, but I couldn't account for *why*.

We walked down the midway holding hands when some little runt in bib-alls ran by holding a sparkler and shouting, *I made a poop in my pants, I'm da pants poopa!* He made Stacy laugh, in a high, arching reverberating way. She hadn't laughed like that in years. Me? I didn't laugh much at that, maybe because I'm a misanthrope and maybe because I just didn't know what to *do* about my wife suddenly laughing, out in public, enjoying herself like she hadn't spent most of our married life a recluse. Something in my mind told me to scream. Something in my mind told me to scream out real loud—to holler out my lungs until I was hoarse.

But why? Why would I want to do that? Because it was unfair. What was unfair? All of it. The whole thing, the whole sham, the whole damn existential clusterfuck that we wade through—me, you, my wife; microbes and nebulas, galaxies and germs. It's all so damn unfair. My wife was a beautiful woman and I was (am?) in love with her. And my wife Stacy is a smart woman—*damn* smart. So what happened that she got too scared to go out? And what happened that suddenly, she wanted to? Where is the line? Where's the cause and effect? Where's the G-d damn *reason*? Because there's got to be a *reason* for everything, right? Doesn't there *got* to be? Otherwise, it means that there was no good cause for Stacy being cuckoo for a couple decades, no good cause for tonight, and what am I to make of that? Is the whole thing a charade?

No man's success is his own. I owe it to my family, I know, I know. But what for? Why, dammit, why? And why am I thinking about all this now? Jesus Herbert Christ on Christian crutches, why even think about any of this, especially on a night like this where we're going to a fucking Carnival? Well, I suppose I'm a miserable man. A real curmudgeon. A true hater of things and people, and if I'm being honest, a hater of myself and a hater of my wife and a hater of—

"Funnel cake?"

"Yeah, sure."

I smiled weakly and bought us funnel cake, so big that I didn't need to purchase but one, and I asked for a paper bag. Like a kid again, I pulled out pieces soaked in oil and congealed white confectioner's sugar, sopping lumps of fry and dough and powder. Then I put my greasy fingers on my wife's mouth as I playfully fed her pieces of the cake.

"Quit it! You play too much!"

She slapped the arm I was using to fish out the funnel cake. We sat down together on the grass lining the sides of the midway, where the grass still grew green and hadn't been stamped out of life by millions of steps from thousands of feet. We sat down together next to dozens of other couples, most all of them much younger than us, and we necked just like the dozens of young couples next to us on the grass. Right about then, with the fragrant grass all around us, I realized I hadn't done this with my wife in years. I realized, too, that when I kissed her, she didn't kiss me back in a way that was familiar to me. She kissed me like she was another woman.

Something about that moment carved up my heart and took out a healthy chunk, hollowed me out right where the blood pours into my fucking soul. Because I knew then that I didn't know my wife. I didn't know her there and then, and maybe I hadn't known her for all the years I'd been living with her. Who was this woman, who looked more beautiful than my wife had ever looked? Maybe I'd get hitched to this woman. Or maybe I'd take her back to my place and laugh at the grass stains on our clothes and—

"Hey, let's go see the main show."

Her words broke my reverie, as she pulled back and away from my lips. "Yeah, I'd like that."

Better to do that than to think of all that was going on.

Madam Regina didn't end up going to the Carnival herself. Instead, she pawned off the gifted passes on Lexi and ordered her to go. Lexi would have gone anyhow, after what Fanny had told her about the new customer and his odd old foreign friend. A hobo magician, Fanny had called him. "Do you know who that was?" Fanny had asked Lexi, who'd responded, "No clue." Fanny informed her, "That's that telepath. He can guess things about you that nobody knows. He's the headliner for the Marivicos Main Tent."

Well, that was enough to get Lexi's attention, and she thought she might go down to the Carnival herself to check it out. Hell, she and Fanny went to the Carnival every couple of weeks during the prime season, so why not go down there for free, having these passes and whatnot?

All three of the ladies planned on going together—Lexi, Fanny, and Madam Regina. But the Madam had one of her *hush-hush* big fishies coming in that night, so she had to flake, and one of Fanny's little ones had a touch of the croup, so she had to cancel too. At first, Lexi thought she'd just fuck off on the whole thing and wait till she could go without flying solo. But her curiosity got the better of her. The guy had just been *so weird*, anti-social even, that she was deadly curious to see him in front of a crowd.

Normally, Lexi would wrap her hair in a ponytail and throw on a band shirt and some denims, maybe a windbreaker if it was breezy enough. She had a feeling, though. She didn't know what the feeling *was*, but it was feeling enough that Lexi decided she ought to—*wanted* to—get dudded up a little bit for the show. She walked out to the porch just off her studio apartment.

It was plenty warm. Warm enough in the shade, and humid to boot. So, Lexi went in and did her hair until it flowed over her shoulders and down to her waist. She touched her face up with enough azure shadow that she looked coquettish instead of like the courtesan she was. Her lashes naturally scaffolded out over her baby blues. She didn't need to touch them at all. She put on a tan sundress with tiny purple-and-green floral rose prints running up in vined vertical lines. She looked halfway between a lynx and a lion. Only she knew which one she would be tonight.

———

Eddie had managed to avoid Papa for most of the day after he'd gotten back from the brothel. Eddie was glad to have missed him, of course, and knew the old patriarch would be preoccupied with the million-and-one things that had to be done before the show. Eddie knew that the Main Tent was going to overflow; Eddie knew this not only because of common sense—the last show was close to overflow—but also because some sort of premonitory faculty had developed in him as of late, despite his knockout fall at the brothel. His ability—Eddie's tilt toward prophecy, his precognitive razor's edge sharpening with each new dawn—was now sophisticated enough, he knew, to likely grant Papa his wish to call out the lotto. *Call out the lotto.*

But it was still a crazy move. There were risks. What if Eddie was wrong? What if something happened to him, and he couldn't perform for a spell; causing the Main Tent to suffer some revenue loss, and the programming had to revert to burlesque? Or to the jump-scares of the high-flying death-taunters, sailing above the hard and net-less ground below, teasing the grim, hooded demon with his scythe? But that was the way Papa Marivicos operated. He took risks, *big* ones, and most of the time they paid off. Papa was a cruel man, but he wasn't a dummy. Cruel and shrewd and sharp as a whip.

It was almost time for him to perform, and Eddie was once again by his lonesome, behind the curtain, head tilted down to lessen the chance of his stomach sending up his puke in a bilious curdle. His head tilted downward, and his elbows were on his knees as if he were a seasick greenhorn beating back the vomitous rocking of a ship on the open sea.

He hadn't had his bourbon. Not that it was so important, now,

days, anyhow. Gots ta get yer rocks off, I think. My hope is that gettin' a little rest and reeeelaxation will up yer game."

"Yes, sir."

"Well, good. Good then. Break a keg."

Papa looked back at Eddie as though he wanted to say something more to the boy. He did *want to*, of course—he wanted to press Eddie on the lotto idea. But he didn't, making Eddie think that Marv and Andy must have gotten to the old man and told him to lay off. *All good things in their own good time.*

Eddie could picture the two dwarfish *aides-de-camp*s saying something like that to Papa. Even more, he could see that Papa would listen. Even more, Eddie knew that Marv and Andy knew that by Papa *not* mentioning something, Eddie would still act on it out of expectation. Hell, Eddie was *already* thinking about how he'd work in the lotto prediction. So, as the deep rumbling of the organ's minor-key dirge announced his imminent entry, Eddie could hear nothing but Papa's boots scraping the dirt as the old man went off to introduce his son to the throng.

All were waiting to see what the spook would come up with next—even Papa. Even Eddie.

CHAPTER 13

As Papa Marivicos prepared to make Eddie's introduction, the lights dimmed. Papa knew how to create dramatic effect, a sense of anticipation, a sense borrowed from Barnum that this ramshackle Carnival was indeed the greatest show on Earth. Flinty trash came, for theater in the round. The lights weren't just dimmed, they were *mindfully dimmed*—just enough so the spectators could only see a few feet in front of their faces, not beyond the outer rim of the dirt on the floor.

The colored lights came on first: a blue haze showcased dust motes floating in the air, coming off the floor. Purple streaks danced inside the ripples of the curtains which closed off the inauspicious hideaway where Eddie waited.

And then, a spot. A pure white spot on Papa Marivicos, so that it looked like he appeared out of nowhere. And there he stood, raggedy and robed, Bedraggled Spectacular Himself, dressed in silk and buttons and boots and stovepipe hat. Gypsy Trash. The Satanic Liberace. Looking like he'd appeared out of nowhere. *Nowhere.*

Just as Papa was getting ready to introduce him, Eddie started feeling it. The churning guts, the dropped bowels, the erratically rhythmed heart, the head sluiced with power lines of hate and fervor. Something brought him low—brought Eddie low. He couldn't stop it, couldn't stop the gravity, the magnetism. It ripped his knees down, hooking invisible fishing lines of electricity into the angles of his limbs, ripped him down to the floor. He vomited, couldn't stop vomiting, kept vomiting until he had nothing left in his knotted, soured gut but dry heaves.

MEANWHILE...

Papa Marivicos took off his stovepipe hat and spread his arms wide, reaching out to the ends of the Main Tent, stretching with every bit of energy, his wingspan sending shadows out like gales from sky. The summery heat matted his dirty, stringy white hair against his head. First, he brought his hand up past his bald pate and held it fast and slick against his head, running the edge of his palm through his greasy mane, then pressing his hair down tight.

"*Ladies and Gentlemen...*"

Even with the cliché introduction, the crowd was electric with anticipation. Papa had never felt such wild blue electricity. Invisible lightning surging through human, foot-stamping conduits, and in their awe, they shuddered with the nervous energy of children. *His* children. Papa (admittedly) felt, in a *woo-woo* way, that he was one with them.

It was his Carnival, his son. *His son*, though he wasn't very proud of the boy—an accident amid the litter of the cosmic axes of power; an *accident*, but a monetizable accident, one that summoned bolts of lightning from the sky. But it was Papa Marivicos who brought the noise, made the sound that shook the firmament, controlled the thunder. His was the voice that made the suckers quake. The suckers born every minute. Papa Marivicos, Master of Ceremonies. *Master.*

MEANWHILE...

Eddie felt as though fingers ran along the backs of his eyes, fingers laced with gunpowder—igniting and burning the insides of his orbits, flaring in excruciating bursts. That's what he *felt*. And what *happened* was that blood began to pour in drip-droplets out of the corners of his eyes, and he would have shrieked if he wasn't completely paralyzed by an alien, extra-human pain. He started retching again. Floating beads of fire-light drenched him in an impossible mercury sheath—a liquid drapery. He retched up this fire-light from his throat, a radioactive rattlesnake birthed from inside Eddie but outside the world.

Eddie could hear Papa making his introductions.

"...*come alive to cast a shadow, his premonitions carrying untold weight to sway the moons and move the masses...*"

But he couldn't will himself forward. This pain was greater than any pain that Papa could cause him.

MEANWHILE...

"*The darkly splendiferous, the spectacularly premoniscient, the singularly spectacular, and almighty-oracular: Melmoth the Magnificent!*"

Papa rolled the stovepipe hat up his arm, popped up his inside elbow and then caught the hat on his head, holding out his hands in presentation, waiting for Eddie to come out to the coda of his introduction.

At first, there was nothing. Complete silence, all the marks holding their breath, sitting still in the bleachers. Then a murmur. Then Papa looked unsure. He held his presentation pose for a few moments longer, and then, understanding that something had gone wrong... he finally moved toward the opening from where Eddie—*that stupid, weak, ratfuck*—was supposed to make some dramatic entrance.

But before Papa could move farther, a blinding light blazed

out from behind the shabby curtains that concealed Eddie. Luminescent swirls of orbiting electric pearls flew pell-mell around Eddie's body. His eyes looked like dynamite-blasted craters. Black crusted blood encircled his eye sockets. A burst of bright arterial radiation—not blood but an admixture of hemoglobin and hemlock and miniature constellations of infinite light—emerged from where the eyes were.

Were they still there? Were the eyes still there behind that grisly starry-scorched visage? Eddie was now all blood and body and fire. Billowing, coiling reams of translucent and varicolored electric terror eclipsed the body. Eddie crawled out of that infinite loop of terrorizing technicolor. Or was he floating on that unknown energy surging through him? *No. Yes. No.* He crawled on *top* of the oscillating orgy of energy pulsating from and beneath him. Then he opened his mouth, spewing a beam of blinding white light that came from within.

Papa's face was pure disgust and anger, as though this spectacular and strange transformation wasn't something unfamiliar to him, but an inconvenience still. His face turned from gnarled contempt to concern as the suckers started to scream, first the women, and then the children. Then the men rose up in a panicked fury. They, too, screamed, unfamiliar with such psychologically horrifying imagery. Papa could see that the crowd was beginning to gather itself to stampede, which would be bad for the crowd, and (more importantly) worse for business. Supernatural terror aside, that wasn't a turn that the patriarch could abide, so he instinctively began bellowing in half-rhyme, half-unreason.

"Gaze! Look deep into the radiating fury, the power of electricity!"
"No worry, no worry to account for you in the crowd"
"Though the sound and the fury, it is well and angry-loud!"

Hearing Papa Marivicos's voice in that lilting harmony of jilts and jolts stilled the crowds in the bleachers, and only a thin string of falsetto shrieks persisted in a greatly diminished chorus of panic.

"This power! This fire! Feast your eyes!"

"Long waiting, you spectators of our Carnival faith have it kept!"

"Now you are rewarded with something terrifying and great..."

With a chilling calm, Papa walked by the glittering inferno that his progeny had become, whispering to him on his way out. "There better be good reason for this, boy."

But the old, cruel patriarch couldn't read anything behind the boy's eyes. Eyes from the depths. Eyes from the ether. Eyes that *were* the ether. Eyes that were glowing lanterns, brilliant and awesome and awful.

"Jesus, Eddie, just do something good and then get out of here."

At least the crowd had turned, had calmed down. But the lights were unlike anything they'd ever seen. A gob of drunken sailors up in the bleachers slapped each other's backs and roared approval at the near-apocalyptic scene. Close to the front, old men whispered to one another, speculating on how this extraordinary special-effects feat had been achieved. A happy wave of chattering children's titters rolled over the seats.

With great effort, Eddie stood straight, extricating himself from the plasmatic electro-magnetism weighing him down. His eyes were his, but at the same time, not his. He could look out at the crowd, and he could still hear all of their thoughts. But now the thoughts weren't assailing him, weren't shredding his consciousness with an endless water-torture drip. Instead, his consciousness had shifted. It suddenly became as capacious as the sea and as complex as the whole of biological existence, allowing him to pick and analyze, stop and see every thought, every scrap of information.

Time slowed down. Or, better, time became fluid, watery, ephemeral, like it didn't exist at all. Eddie could see not only the people he keyed in on, but also their pasts, their futures, their fears and wants, their hatred and their love. If what Eddie saw could be put into simple language, one might say that he saw a mist, a haze filled with particulate matter surrounding each person.

Except for one girl. *She came. What was her name again?* As he searched his memory, the girl's name, *Lexi*, boomed out in a dual-octave blare of distorted, almost electronic noise, like a viola sent through a flanger.

Lexi sat bolt upright in her seat. If Eddie had been doing his usual show in a spotlight glow and a periphery of shadows, no one ought to have seen her in the hemisphere of dark-round where she sat. Not the case now. The dazzle of eight-hundred unknowns danced in the perceptual catch of Lexi's eyes. Her eyes were lamps that swelled with liquid fire, pearls dancing in it, orbs of microscopic lightning storms catching in and out of the brilliance. Lexi's eyes, glittering alien in themselves, alien in their reflection of Eddie's lights. The now non-existent time shared some of its fluidity with her, a one-way channel. Eddie couldn't hear her, no, but somehow, he could share himself. She tried to stand but couldn't.

Far away in the corner, in the standing-room-only aisles of dust and detritus lining the edges of the tent, where the marks stamped their boots and threw away their refuse, a doctor and his wife stood, awed by the spectacle.

Eddie stood straight up now—as straight as he could, his feet not touching the ground. The little worlds of lightning and the electric strands of fire-alive pearls swirled around him quicker, ever-quicker, ever-faster, making a whirring sound. It was a rapidly hastening helicopter sound (but without the chop of the rotor blades). It was this sound that arose over Eddie, wreathing him in a steady hum. Eddie stretched his right hand up into the air. His hand was pink and blue with smokeless fire. He traced his index finger through unseen points in the air, dragging its tip against some invisible friction, like his finger was a scalpel slicing through translucent skin. As his finger traced a line in the air, letters began to form, and the letters hung in the air, looking like

an unearthly combination of lava flow and sulfuric ignition, of
atmospheric electricity and casino neon:

L

O

T

T

O

The entire audience *oohed* and *aahed*. Some old drunk from the
back yelled out, "He's gon' tell us the winnin's!" Papa, hidden
from the crowd, smiled to himself. He was happy the boy had
listened to him after all; and why wouldn't he? The boy always
listened. Even when the nastiest bit of business had to be done,
Eddie accepted it and stood pat, or at least stood aside.

Then the crowd started rumbling. People were murmuring to
one another, men were shoving. Women clutched their children,
and even the wheelchair-bound biddies made a bid at standing up
straight, even if they hadn't done so in years.

Eddie's finger traced out the rest of the message in the air.

5

7

4

2

8

3

2

7

People started murmuring in a strange, greedy clamor. Some
mumbled to themselves in looping repetition, hardening the
memory of the numbers, whose luminescence was starting to fade
like the dying light on a firefly. And then, all at once, the entirety

of the great spectacle of lights shuttered itself into Eddie's body, rushing into him like the film of a dam breaking played at double-speed in reverse.

Papa was quick on the draw. He hissed at the boy manning the lights. "Put a shadow over 'im! Don't let 'em see!"

The lighting boy obliged, pounding the control panel until spotlights shone in a multi-directional obscurantism, wrapping Eddie's body in a cloak of complete blackness. In that instant, Papa shouted to a couple of hands nearby.

"Bring 'im in!"

Without missing a beat, the workers quickly scampered out, hooked Eddie by the armpits on either side, and dragged him back behind the stage.

From way back, Dr. Chain and Stacy watched this spectacle, breath-taken.

CHAPTER 14

When I say you wouldn't believe it if you saw it, I mean you really wouldn't believe it.

You wouldn't have trusted your own eyes if you'd seen this show. I've never seen anything like that.

The lights. It was like the lights came out of the fella. Or maybe he was a part of them, or maybe they were a part of him. I don't know how they did it, but they sure did. Whatever it is they did, they did it. Oh, what a crazy night!

For a second, while I had Stacy's hand in mind—and boy, was she ever clutching mine, squeezing so her tiny finger-knuckles bruised the insides of my own fingers—I felt like a kid again. *Like a kid again.*

Nobody ever thinks on what that really means; I know I never thought much of the phrase until this night at the Carnival. You go through life, and you do the good things, and the bad things, and you do them thousands, some of 'em millions of times, like a machine on an assembly line. Sex with the wife thousands of times, more or less.

But I can't remember, for the life of me, the *feeling* of fear, and anticipation, and excitement, and *dread of it all* that came into my being when I bedded a woman for the first time. Oh, sure, I remember it. But I remember it the way someone might remember the vague outline of a film they know they enjoyed, even if they can't remember the ending, or who died, or even what the characters were after in the first place. That's the bitch of misremembering, of forgetting the memory-excitements of being a child.

I guess I'm thinking of all this because sometimes, just sometimes, when one of those old childhood sense memories comes back, you *feel* like you did when you were a kid, with all the dumb fear and hot rushing thrill running over you.

That's what tonight's Carnival performance stirred up in me—after all the lights and pyrotechnics, I realized I could remember what it was like to be a kid again. Yes, a kid—before the world became a looping racetrack where I banked around the same curb a couple thousand times, whether I was going twenty or two hundred. And in that child-like sense memory, I felt cleansed. Not washed of all my sins, not like that. But stripped down to the basics. In the presence of something awe-creating.

The kid part of me thinks that the performance was real, and I damn to hell the adult part of me trying to ruin the fun by reminding me that such a thing couldn't be rationally possible in our world. I want to *stay* stripped down to the basics: to feel every thrill with the fear and newness of possibility that a kid feels. To feel it with *elation*. Children know what elation is before they ever hear the word. I felt that. And I also felt the holy terror, the unsureness, the lack of warranty that the crazed chaos of light wouldn't obliterate me. That is *wonder*. Or maybe wonder is the marveling before the holy terror? And after the wonder comes the *awe*, that guarantee-less exposure to something so powerful that I couldn't know just how dangerous it was. But I would find out. Oh yes, by rights I would find out.

Stacy and I waited for the crazed stampede of human animals to empty out of the tent. Most all of them, I was sure, would be headed to the closest gas station or convenience store to buy into the prophesied lotto number. We sat in serenity, waiting to come back to the land where our feet were rooted into the earth. My adult rationalism started kicking in. How was this fit of wonder *sustained*? *How*? LED lights run on tracks through a synthetic fog? Something on see-through filament wire, rigged up to light with fire? What was it?

The inner kid was still there, warring with me, so I quickly pushed those thoughts out of my mind. What a curse it can be, my beloved rationalism. No; my beloved *scientism*. Curiosity. As I gained enough of my senses back to finally stand, a huge man in a unitard with a great bristly mustache—a Kaiser mustache, stretching sideways in either direction, growing across his cheeks like the top of a beard—stood behind me and tapped on my shoulder. I looked up; the man was a full two heads taller than me.

"You're the doctor, right?"

I only nodded.

"Hmm. Good thing, then. Come with me, Doc."

I looked to Stacy, who was still expressionless, and then turned my head back to the giant.

"What for?"

He put a hand on my shoulder; fingers long enough to drape down the top of my back and sporting an equally lengthy thumb that drooped halfway down my chest. "Ain't no one tryin' to do nothin' to ya', Doc. We need *help*."

I looked back to Stacy again and she seemed to be taking it in. She nodded.

"Okay. What do you need?" I asked.

"Follow me."

Stacy and I started walking along with the giant when he suddenly stopped and turned to me.

"Just yourself, Doc."

Before I could summon up any words of protest, Stacy squeezed my forearm.

"It's okay, love. I'll wait for you on the midway. I saw a caramel corn stand. I haven't had any of that in a spell. You go ahead. I'll be alright, I promise."

I swooped in to give my wife a quick kiss on the cheek, then followed the giant out and away from the Carnival grounds, out toward the fields of darkness.

The giant led the way, and we crossed the field—it was only a couple of dozen yards away—and I walked into something like a yurt. Inside, laid up on a dirty sheetless mattress, was the main event himself—Melmoth, the light-show man. Standing in the corner next to the tent's exhaust vent was the ringmaster, Papa Marivicos, still wearing his raggedy but ostentatious garb. The giant came in after me bending almost to the waist just to fit inside.

"Need anything else from me, boss?"

The ringmaster shook his head and shooed the giant away with a flap of his hand. I stood there waiting to hear why I'd been summoned.

"What happened?" That was all I could say, though it tasted stupid coming out my mouth.

"You weren't there? I s'pose the boy's been pushed too hard too long."

"He's an employee?"

The ringmaster scoffed and let out a small, disingenuous laugh. "He's my son."

"Well, I can't really examine him here. But looking the way he is, I can't move him either. I'm going to have to go home and get some things, then come on back."

The ringmaster nodded. "Good enough. I'll have Marv and Andy take you there'n'back."

As I left the tent, I did not yet know that the winning lottery ticket had been purchased, using the numbers the light-man had predicted. By the time any of them made it to a lottery agent, they found that the number that Eddie had carved with light into the air had already been bought. That was the rule for this particular lottery—numbers were first-come, first-served. Thus, many were disappointed that they could not snatch the ticket.

But someone had.

CHAPTER 15

The day after Eddie's stellar performance at the Carnival, a red-suited Clara Guadali sat in the waiting area of Ferriman Financial, a medium-sized boutique investment firm. This was her fourteenth meeting after her last abortive attempt at beautifying some podunk municipality to which its residents were indifferent. By now, the would-be do-gooder (or goodstress) Ms. Guadali was having a difficult time securing pitch meetings, let alone successfully soliciting investors for her newest schemes.

"Ms. Guadali? They'll see you now," the secretary said flatly.

"Of course."

Clara followed the secretary down a long hallway lined with framed portraits of Ferriman partners past. One of them was portrayed standing next to Herbert Hoover, another next to Junius Morgan, and yet another next to Michael Milken. Ferriman was an old, staid firm that seemed unlikely to take Clara seriously.

But Clara was relentless. And she wanted power. And she would accumulate it, she thought to herself, no matter how long it took, no matter how many simps stood between her and that power. Her red suit said *power*. Her manly wristwatch said *power*.

Her wild wavy raven head, though, said *unpredictable,* or *human grenade,* or something like that. And that was true too.

"Ms. Guadali, please, come in, sit down."

She shared a firm handshake with one of the Ferriman partners present; a ruddy, jowly man who had no name but Ferriman. After these niceties, he undid his suit jacket with his Twizzler-red fingers and fell comfortably backward into his padded leather chair, his overhanging paunch squishing out against his white oxford shirt. The man had a full head of plugged-in ersatz hair, wavy and grey so it looked natural-ish.

Once the two were seated, Clara smoothed out her pantsuit and reached down into the leather portfolio case she'd brought with her. "Thank you for seeing me, Mr. Ferriman."

"Of course. I judge every potential investment on its merits, not solely on the rumor and conjecture that springs from a given entrepreneur's past foibles." He looked her up and down un such a way that he might as well have listed her personal past foibles, but decided, instead, on being charitable. "Whatever they may be." Ferriman spoke matter-of-factly, without a whit of malicious intent, which only made it worse.

That's just who you are. The woman known to fail. The one who wrecked that beautiful old town and for nothing. "And I thank you for that," Clara replied. Both grateful and annoyed that the elephant remained in the room.

"Can I get you anything? Coffee, water, something stronger?" Ferriman leaned back in his seat and reached, with some effort—straining as he was against the larded lateral cuts of his body—to grab his cut goblet filled a finger-full of scotch.

Clara crossed her legs, leaving the pointy end of her red stiletto directed away from Ferriman, so as to not insult him. "I'll join you, if you don't mind terribly pouring another scotch."

This was something elementary in business, a tradition, that the youth had ignored—hell, even the Ivy-pedigreed uber-brains that ran Ferriman's machinery hadn't learned it.

You always drank what your superior drank. You always drank what a potential client drank.

Ferriman gave a wide smile and swung himself upward on the momentum of his womanly ass, love-handles flapping like penguin wings inside of his shirt. It was cool in here, but Clara could see medium-grade pit stains and a dampened liner along Ferriman's suit, visible as he rolled upward.

"Not too many women drink scotch," Ferriman stated, his back turned to Clara as he swiped his bottle off the silver tray atop the portable bar top. It was only as she was pouring—slowly, with measure—that she replied.

"Let me ask you, Mr. Ferriman, what is the greatest draw in the county around Kayjigville? During the summer season— maybe a little longer."

"The Carnival."

"That's right. Old man Marivicos rakes in something like five million every season if you can believe it."

"I can. I've even met the man once or twice."

Clara Guadali was genuinely surprised to hear this. "Oh, really?"

Ferriman paused to watch Clara register this new bit of information. After a moment, she spoke.

"The Carnival makes five million every year, has made bundles of cash since Marivicos took over the Carnival from *his* father. And he's got a hold on Kayjigville, too. There're no competitors. Nothing else to nip into the nice slice of profit he carves off the town. I want to add a little competition."

"I see. What did you have in mind?"

"Well, it's awful Vanderbiltish."

"I like the Commodore."

"I know you do, sir. Believe it or not, I got the notion—the notion I'm laying out for you now—while I was sitting in the City Harbor, looking over at the marina, where I saw the *Commodora*. She's a beauty." Clara spoke softly, breaking Ferriman's reverie. She saw Ferriman shift, with some strange cast in his eyes.

"Yes, she's a very, *very* special ship. My late wife and I spent a lot of time on that boat. There's something almost magical about it."

"Something magical about the water, Mr. Ferriman. It's the *water*, sir. I read a book not so long ago whose entire premise was that those who lived near water led happier, longer lives."

"Is that so?"

"Hand to my heart, it's so. And that's why I think—I *believe*— that the proposal I'm bringing to you is something people are going to be interested in. Up and down the Mississippi, luxury riverboat cruises rake in money. The world over, open waters are rife with casino boats. I say we combine the two–an old school riverboat casino, complete with luxury staterooms. Wouldn't *that* take a chunk out of Marivicos's ass."

"Interesting."

Interesting. That's not—that's probably not a good sign.

"With respect, Mr. Ferriman, it doesn't matter much whether it's interesting; it matters if it can be profitable. And this venture can be. As nature abhors a vacuum; so does the market. The Marivicos Carnival has been on the winning side of the table, but only because there's nobody on the other side."

Ferriman raised his eyebrows. "Well, I'll admit, I like the way you've really taken the bull by the horns here."

"Thank you, sir."

"Wait a minute; I'm not done."

Clara nodded, signaling him to go on.

"It doesn't matter how good the idea is. You're a sharp one: you know what I'm going to bring up."

Clara nodded again, trying not to look defeated.

"You ruined that town, Ms. Guadali—"

"Clara."

"Fine. You ruined that town, *Clara*. The Guadali name is

synonymous with eminent domain. And in this state, that's not such a good thing."

Clara sat purposefully quiet as Ferriman continued.

"At the end of the day, you're still Clara Guadali, the evil social climber who steals property from the poor and middling classes. You see what I'm saying? You *have* to be able to see it, right? I mean—what have the other investors you've pitched said about that debacle?"

Ferriman was pretty lit, unusual given the fact it was still forenoon. He'd ramped up the drinking since his wife died, part of the reason he was redder, rounder, and more loose-lipped.

Clara sat quietly; she had nothing to say. Sisyphus had an easier go of things. *You can't have a battle of wits if there's no one on the other side.*

Clara often thought herself as a gorgon, striking her adversaries into stony silence. She couldn't help that she was smarter than everyone else, or if other people couldn't see the forest for the trees.

But it was Ferriman who delivered the final blow, which left her shaking with anger. "You're not even going to try to fight back?"

After an uncharacteristic pause, she finally stuttered. "Mr. Ferriman... this... this is a *good* plan. It is an opening. It's value investing, albeit in a nascent business enterprise—"

"A non-existent business enterprise."

"It's still value-investing. It's a small investment—thirty million to start—"

"Thirty million? Jesus, Guadali."

"For revenues of two, maybe three million, every year. And you have the boats for assets."

"What the hell am I going to do with a fleet of riverboats when the whole thing goes belly-up? Those boats aren't worth shit if they're not either on the Mississippi or floating on this fantasy old mill stream you've conjured up."

"There's more than that," Clara protested. Ferriman didn't even argue back. He simply stopped staring and took another drink, then looked down to his wrist to check the time on his *Baume & Mercier*.

Feeling defeated, but knowing she never could stop once she started, Clara went on.

"That river is a goldmine."

Ferriman glared at her. "Bullshit."

"Bullshit nothing! There's money up, down, and in that river, Ferriman. And you *know* it. I don't know how you do, but I *know* you do. Why the hell else would you take this meeting? Why the fuck am I sitting here with Old Man Ferriman, huh?"

Clara was almost hyperventilating. Her face was scarlet. When she was pissed off, she flew off the handle, and that was fine for the sack of saggy scrotal shit she called her husband, but it wasn't helpful when asking an old money patriarch to dip into the vault and fish her out a few sacks of Krugerrands.

But then, to her surprise, Ferriman smiled. And then he started laughing. He started laughing. Long and hard, hard enough that his already ruddy complexion burst into a deep scarlet of his own. He wiped tears out of his eyes as he finished.

"Oh, Jesus. Oh, my goodness, you were *pissed*. Look, I just really wanted you to fight for it, ya know? And boy did ya!"

"I... I..."

"Oh, relax, Guadali. You're right, I did know. But I'll share something with you. My late wife was from Kayjigville, and she loved that river. And she *loved* those Mississippi riverboats. I used to take her once every two years or so. I suppose you knew that." Ferriman punctuated his outburst by taking another swig from his glass.

"Actually, I did not."

"Well, all the better I suppose. Now, go ahead and tell me the rest of this business about riverboats."

Clara smiled. "Okay, Commodore."

CHAPTER 16

I stayed with the kid through the night. You wouldn't know it if you'd only seen him during his performances, but Eddie was a striking young man. A strapping young lad, or whatever the expression is. His father looked like fucking Nosferatu-on-stilts, but I suppose the kid got his looks from his mother's side. Or, who knows, maybe Papa Marivicos wasn't Eddie's biological father.

I don't know exactly what I saw last night, but I've been running it backward and forward in my mind ever since. Granted, I've been doing it unreliably, still in a state of shock-and-awe and without the advantage of a referee's pause or slow-motion button. *And I can't square my sense of reality with what I saw.*

And then there's this kid. Well, there ain't nothing wrong with Eddie now. Last night, his blood pressure went through the roof, heart beating like a rabbit's. Then at one point his pulse dropped precipitously into what might be called a cadaverous cardiac range. But after about an hour, he fell asleep and everything went back normal. No matter, I said to myself—I set up an IV for him anyhow and stuck around through the morning hours to make sure that everything was hunky-dory.

So his name's Eddie. Damn handsome, too. I'd like to think
that if Stacy and I had ended up with kids, and if one had been a
boy, then that boy would have been handsome like Eddie—a little
Roman with a touch of darkness in the body and in the soul. Or
maybe handsome like the old man, but with a less punched-in
nose and less asymmetrical tunnel-size nostrils. I'm pretty tall, but
I like to think that our son would've grown a head, the way I was
a taller than my old man.

But he'd have Stacy's eyes. And her wits. Doctor or no, my
wife's a good deal sharper than I am. And she would've been a
great mother. I just know it. In my heart—no, in my mind, too. I
see Stacy raising the boy up right and telling him to mind his p's
and q's. Makes sure he sits down and does his homework. She'd
get the teacher editions of textbooks and figure out whatever
pedagogical horseshit was current, and she'd be on-the-ball, on-
the-money, and all-fucking-over-it. And when I bitched about
how education had nothing to do with intelligence—how it was
like saying a woman without tits was actually a man and a fat
man with tits was actually a woman, Stacy would do right and tell
me that none of that mattered, that it was the *piece of paper* that
mattered, and *dammit, Doc, don't talk about titties in front of the boy.*

And I'd smile, knowing she was right, and our boy would
laugh at how many times his parents said tits and titties in front of
him, and then we'd all laugh at me and at ourselves. And this tits-
and-textbook conversation would have all the veneer of an argument, but it wouldn't *be* an argument. It would be like when little
puppies nip at one another's necks but never to injure, because
the mama dog is there to make sure it's all light and sweet.

And at the end of the night, I'd read to him instead of reading
by myself by the lamplight. I'd read him Julius Lester like my
pops did when I was a sprat, and then I'd graduate the boy up to
Mildred Taylor like my pops did when my balls dropped. And
then when he went off to school and got too big for his britches,
I'd graduate him up to Frederick Douglass and W.E.B. DuBois.

And then when he'd cooled off a little and grown up a bit, I'd give him *The Teeth of the Tiger* by Tom Clancy because—well, because by G-d, I fucking love Tom Clancy. And when his Mom came around with her Octavia Butler bullshit, I'd wink at him—it would be our secret wink, and it would tell him more than a thousand words could—and he'd read a summary of it and a few think-pieces so his Mom thought he'd read the whole book. Because he'd be *my* boy.

Yup, by rights, he'd be *my* boy, and *my* boy would be like *me*.

He wouldn't brook that sci-fi horror crap. I mean, can you imagine the kind of folks that read that dreck? And the people that *write* that shit? Bona fide fucking weirdos. But he'd read up on it to make mamadukes happy, because that's what good boys do. And then one day, when I was old and wrinkled to shit, gummy and drooly with my fake teeth and my bad knees and my limp dick (but we wouldn't talk about that, wouldn't want to traumatize the boy), my boy would show up at my door and say *hey papadukes, take a look at this. It's Thucydides, and this one's Iamblichus, and this one's Virgil.*

Yup, my boy would want to graduate *me* up to the majors, but I'd smile and shake my head and just be happy that he grew up so damn smart. I'd be like a little league coach that a pro-home-run-king still called once a month to say *I couldn't have done it without you*, and I'd obligingly say *oh, you did it your damn self.* And we'd laugh and remember the time me and his mom said "tits" at the dinner table.

Then I'd ask if the grandkids were reading the Julius Lester books, and he'd tell me they were reading Maurice Sendak because that's what his wife read when she was a kid. And I'd say that's all for the best, the grandkids being half-Jewish, and that he'd better watch out those kids don't go in his wallet while he's sleeping. And then my boy would tell me I was on speakerphone, and I'd be mortified, but my boy's wife would chime in and say, "don't worry Doc, they inherited your son's economic sensibility".

And boy oh boy would I laugh at that! Why wouldn't I? I get along real good with my daughter-in-law. Shit, I even went fishing with her old man, and my daughter-in-law's father told me about living in Israel, and coming to America, and how he kisses the ground every time he comes back stateside because dammit, he loves this country. And hell, the girl knows I love her, and I've got no problem with the heebs. Shit, I'm the one who paid for Hebrew school! And he'd be handsome, my son. So damn handsome.

That's what it would've been like, I suppose. That's what it would've been like if we'd had a boy.

This boy Eddie is a fine-looking boy. I guess it wouldn't be so bad to have a boy like him either. I bet he's sharp. I bet he's—

"Hey Doc. I'm confused."

"Oh... uh... you feeling okay?"

Eddie seemed to be in a cloudy place, a bit *out there*. "Yeah, sure. I just don't understand."

"Don't understand what?"

"Is he real?"

"Is who real?"

"Your son. The one who married the Jewish girl."

"My... my son?"

"W.E.B., or Frederick, or Lester, or Julius, maybe?"

"That's... I don't have... how did you know what I was thinking?"

"Can I ask you something?" His question came at a different angle from the others, a sharp-edged disjunct in a sea of softness otherwise.

"Sure."

"Is this now?"

"What do you mean?"

"Are we here now?" The look the boy had in his eyes

somehow crushed me. I couldn't bear what might come; another question; another moment of confused helplessness; worse, another moment of him peering behind the curtain and looking at my thoughts.

"We're here now, son. Why don't you just go ahead and rest?"

He looked up at me with some desperation in his eyes. "Will you stay and make sure I'm alright?"

I should have just said *yes* right off the bat, but I didn't. "What on earth do you think is going to happen to you?"

As if he hadn't heard the question at all, Eddie gripped my hand and pleaded. *"Will you?"*

"Yes. I'm here, boy. Nothing's going to happen to you."

Eddie nodded in response, already falling away and under in a mess of exhaustion. As he fell into his dreams, he gripped my hand tightly. I sat there for a while after he'd gone out again and waited to see if he'd loosen his hold once the sandman had come to greet him.

But he kept his grip.

The matriarch Marivicos came in after a few hours. He gave me a long, searching look. My first take on the man was that he was surly and curt. That's the way he seemed anyhow, from his sour face, from the way the other carnies tip-toed around him like he was Kong. I was surprised to find that after an initial bellicose grunt, and an unnervingly violent unfolding of an old wooden chair, Marivicos's body eased from taut to tired, and he shifted from an aural ferocity to a languid pose. He removed his hat and held it between his disproportionally elongated legs. I noticed how his eyes followed a line from his boy's face to my hand, which a sleeping Eddie still gripped.

"He fell asleep while I was taking his pulse," I lied, not knowing what Marivicos would make of the boy holding my hand. "And then he passed out from the stress. Some minor shock. That's my diagnosis. Nothing permanent. No injury, really. He's just exhausted."

Marivicos's answer was terse. "I see."

I used my other hand to point to the IV. "It's better not to move him when he's hooked up. Oh, and it's not my normal practice to sit and hold hands with an unconscious patient."

Marivicos chuckled. "No—no, of course not. Tell me, Doctor…?"

"Chain."

"Doctor Chain. Have you had something to eat?"

"No, not yet Mr. Marivicos." *I was hungry. Starved.*

"How about breakfast?"

"Oh, I don't want to trouble—"

"No, no trouble at all. It's the only decent thing we can do for you, detained as ya are, helpful as ya been."

The leather-skinned ringmaster barked out an order, half in English and half in some other tongue. Instantaneously, a few squat, ugly old maids scurried out and around the breadth of the tent.

Marivicos looked at his son almost tenderly before speaking. "We pushed him too hard."

He'd sat silently since ordering the maids to fetch whatever-these-folks-ate. I didn't open my mouth, didn't want to say anything. It's not good to talk without a reason, not a good thing to speak about things you don't know about; and I didn't even know *what* the old ringmaster was talking about yet. So, I nodded. Not assent, but the sort of body language that says *go on, old man, go on.*

"We pushed the boy too damn hard. I guess. Yeah. Yeah, that's it. Been too long, shovin' him around, goin' right fer the switch. It's the humiliation, I s'pose. Bad enough to get the switch, sure... but makin' the boy pick his own off the tree branch. I think that's worse, don'tcha?"

Marivicos fiddled with the brim of his stovepipe hat before looking to me for a response. But I still didn't know exactly what he was talking about, so I shrugged. And I felt strange, with Eddie's father there while I still held the boy's hand. And now, the boy's hand felt hot and sweaty in my own, until I realized that I was the one who was sweating.

"I got grandkids, you know. Eddie's got two by a half-black woman down south. I ain't got no problems with blacks, mind you, just an interesting aside, I s'pose. Just a way of sayin' my son's a sweet boy, doesn't care if a woman's half-black or not."

"My wife is—"

"I know all about you, Doc. I know your wife. Fine woman. Real fine woman. Small place, Kayjigville. My people been here for a long time. I was hopin' we'd be here a long time to come. I know your wife fine, Doc. Just 'cause she's not workin' doesn't mean I don't know. Smart woman, yeah?"

I nodded. That was fucking off-putting. How had this man come to know so much about *my wife?* But it was a small world, after all; and, looking at this kooky crackpot, I figured it best to save my energy for whatever strange directions this conversation may take.

"Yeah. Sure'nuf. Smart woman. My woman was smart, too. She's not around."

This time I didn't even nod. *What does he want?*

"Eddie loved her, I guess. Not my woman—never knew his mother. Would've loved her, o'course. Loved that half-black down south. Sure he would'a been a right good husband to her. But I couldn't let him stay down there all by himself, without the family. Family's everything. We're a clan. The Marivicos Clan. You understand?"

I fumbled for words, trying to find some insight into what he was thinking at this moment. When I finally heard myself speaking, it sounded like a cliché, an automatic shrink question when a patient was stubborn, or hard to read.

"Where are your grandkids?"

Marivicos laughed, but it wasn't in good humor. He laughed with sorrow and incredulity, maybe surprised at himself, maybe hurt in an odd moment of self-reflection.

"Ah, my little octoroons. They're beautiful. Boy, Doc, I tell you, Eddie carries the same blood his mama had. It's that magic blood. Don't matter 'bout the father or grandpappy, that magic blood makes bee-yooteeful babies. Made Eddie a handsome boy. Made his little baby octoroons just about the most angelic little things you ever done seen."

"Does Eddie ever get to see them?"

This time it was Marivicos who was silent. He just sat, with arms crossed, his stovepipe hat tucked under and behind his right armpit. Then he gave his head a vigorous shake.

"Well, maybe that's part of it," I offered.

"Part of *what*?" His demeanor changed; but I've seen it all, and little scared me (beside the fact that his broad, hunchbacked shoulders were blocking the only exit). I decided to shift my line of questioning, hoping to carefully suss out how deep the rabbit hole of abuse went.

"Can I ask you something?"

"Sure," he said. But the way he said it, the way he shaped that "O" made the word sound like "shore".

"Does Eddie ever lash out at you? Has he ever yelled back at you, done anything—misbehaved, anything like that?"

"Well, no. Not really. He ran away the one time, but… nah, Eddie ain't like that. Stupid as all get-out, hard to train, but he's not insolent just for being insolent's sake."

Hard to train; stupid. Fucking hell. "I see."

I lapsed into silence. Suddenly, it felt good to be holding Eddie's hand. Then Papa broke the quiet.

"Well, come on now, Doc. Tell Papa what yer thinkin'."

I was about to speak when the squat old maids swept in through the slit entrance of the tent. They unfolded and plopped down the legged table-stands, the kind you eat TV dinners on, and set down small rectangles of cloth and lace napkins, silver cutlery and a crystal glass—a full set for eating on each of the two fold-out tables. The cutlery and the hand-glazed cups looked old and fragile and fine; and the lace napkins, though ragged and moth-bitten, also looked of some fine vintage. I nodded to the women and expressed my thanks, but they didn't acknowledge me. Another set of squat old maids came sweeping in after them —one of them poured what looked like grapefruit juice into our glasses; the other took a two-pronged serving fork and started serving us from a disposable aluminum tray. The food looked like eggs cooked sunny side up with marinara and peppers in it.

"Thank you."

But the old maids either didn't hear me or pretended not to. *They're not allowed to.*

"I got a touch of the 'shine put in the juice. Hope you don't mind."

"No, that's fine."

Marivicos picked up his glass and held it aloft. I picked mine up too, and he forcefully clanged his cup against mine, hard enough that I was surprised our glasses didn't break.

"To good women. Am I right?"

"Yes, sir." I'm going to be honest, I waited for him to drink first. I don't know if it was the sleep deprivation, or knowing he was a complete shit to *his own son.* As I said, I'm not typically wary, and as a professional crazy-fixer not much intimidates me, but this... human colostomy bag unnerved me enough that I had the urge to become a sixty-four year old Usain Bolt and get the *fuck out of there.* But there was a son, not mine, but not his by right, sitting with me. Kid needed me.

"Go'head, now. Eat, eat."

I picked up a silver fork and took a small bite of egg, a small bite with the smallest bit of mystery sauce hanging off the brown-crisped edge of yolk. I was surprised to discover that it was good. *Damn good.*

"Interesting question you put to me, Doc. *Real* interesting. Now, I don't know exactly what's wrong with the boy, but he ain't actin' right as of late, gettin' sick and whatnot. You know, pukin' and all that. Ain't seen nothin' like this though. Worst he's been, I tell ya. Well, I think that some of what's happened might be on me. I might have given him an extra shove," he looked off to the left, "figuratively, course. But I don't got the foggiest of how to fix it. Tell me, Doc... you acceptin' new patients? Off the books, of course. I think you understand that my boy's condition is... unique. You'd be generously compensated."

I quickly swallowed my bite of egg before answering. I wanted to help the boy, obviously. I didn't want to let on to Marivicos that I was a psychologist, on the off-chance that he knew what that job entailed, so instead of puffing my chest out and proudly proclaiming my jack-of-all-trades bullshit, I just said; "Yes, I'll help you with your son, Mr. Marivicos."

"Smart man, doc."

"As smart as the next fella."

"Oh, that's rich. A humble doctor. Now I *have* seen everything."

I smiled at that. I couldn't help it. I'm not above taking compliments from the human equivalent of the creature from the black lagoon. Maybe that says something about me, but now isn't the time to delve into my own psyche.

"Well, Doc, I sure appreciate you helpin' me out with this Eddie situation."

I took another sip of the moonshiner's Mimosa. "Of course. When shall I start?"

We then worked at the pace of previously mentioned athlete to determine setting and plan of care.

Off the books, of course.

CHAPTER 17

LATER THAT NIGHT

A very strange building a few miles outside of Kayjigville housed The Pony Express. No, not the fabled nineteenth-century courier service that was the horseback-era precursor to USPS. The Pony Express, in these parts, was an off-books casino (that's putting it charitably).

Here's how The Pony Express came to be more than a century ago. Through some pork-barreling, a former Postmaster General constructed an addition onto his own bizarrely built mansion. The building itself was gothic, steepled, but incredibly strange: it went up seven stories into the air, each story incrementally smaller than the one below it, like a weird ziggurat transplanted from some ancient landscape. At the very top hung a crow's nest, as though the mansion was meant to be captained by some latter-day Long John Silver. The pork-barreled addition was a single-story cavernous open space, lined along the walls with bowed steel girders and intricately carved wooden booths.

Fast-forward to present day. The Rizzos fell into ownership of The Pony Express. The Rizzos were a mafioso family. They were

localized, somewhat greasy, but in a small-time way. The mansion
became a private club for the new owners and profiteers of The
Pony Express Casino, a place where they could get a little rest and
relaxation, bring their goomas (that's contemporary Latin for *side-
piece)*, and where book-cookery and tax evasion could be
discreetly carried out. The casino was accessible to all, while the
mansion itself was not.

Inside the casino were huge green boards all along the walls,
rows and rows of television sets strung up along the sides and
wired down from the ceiling, craps tables, a caged box where
chips and money were kept, and even facilities for drink service.
Food was served, but it wasn't good—you'd be better off sticking
to the free peanuts and pretzels sat out next to the black plastic
ashtrays. Most of the high-rolling dicks didn't come into the Pony
during regular business hours, but they got the place to themselves later. After hours, they came scuttling down from the
mansion wearing sharkskin suits and their gators, *bouffants*
coiffed-up with oil, wrists and pinkies dripping with bling.

This was the first nightshift Lexi was scheduled to work,
serving the high rollers, the big swinging dicks. But first, she had
to do a little wrangling with Regina to ensure her shift at the
brothel was covered. Being moved up to the gangster-hour shift at
The Pony meant opportunity. It meant having the ear of a man
who might make a difference in your life, guys who could do you
favors. When you lived above a garage and worked in a whorehouse for most of the week, the allure of *favors* was powerful
indeed.

Lexi wasn't crazy, though, about the outfit she had to wear.
Fanny knew the ins and outs of the black trades and the night
markets, and she'd warned Lexi to expect to give out free handies
and hummers to the geriatric gangsters. Well, what was the difference? It's all a confidence game. None of it's real. Money may be
worth more or less than the paper it's printed on.

But it's the spirit of confidence that counts. Wafting in and out of Mammon's multitude of mediums, sometimes paper cash, sometimes coins, sometimes plastic chips (which could be worth thousands, and in some places, *millions*). But a medium is always just that: a ghost, a specter of specie, an apparition of some *thing* that was money, some construct created long ago to help folks get along without having to give up a goat or a daughter whenever they wanted to buy a sandwich. A couple millennia ago, it was clay tablets imprinted with tiny little triangles. Today, it's a greenback with a little counterfeit strip run through it.

None of it was real.

So, what did it matter if Lexi received some paper or some tiny plastic circles, or the benefit of some insider information, or the support or backing of some feeble mobster—in exchange for her person? It's all the same. None of it was real. It wasn't money. It was confidence. Still, she really didn't like the outfit. It was something a trashy cocktail waitress might wear, or maybe a low-rent playboy bunny.

When she got to The Pony Express, Angelo, the manager, was in the parking lot looking over a clipboard with a pen while a couple of different delivery trucks pulled in.

"No, no, that doesn't go in through the front... what the hell are you doing... there's a carpet that way."

Lexi walked up to Angelo and waved. He was a nice enough guy, Angelo was. He just took his job very, very seriously. There were worse things. When he saw her, he had a not-so-good look on his face.

"Hey, Ang. What's good?"

"Lexi... you're a bit early aren't ya?"

"The early bird gets the worm, they say. Not that you're a worm, or, like, that anyone else here is a worm. I'm just saying I figured it's a good idea for a gal to show up early on her first—"

"Don't put that shit over there! What are you doing? Fuckin' fuck my life!" Angelo slapped his pen against his clipboard and turned to Lexi.

"Listen, Lex, I'm real sorry, but we're cutting back your shift. I don't ever give out shifts without knowin' they're to be had, but word came down from Tommy himself. Wish it weren't that way, but it is."

"But-but… Ang, I switched my shift at Regina's to get a cover for tonight. I could be *earning*, man, but I'm here."

Angelo turned away briefly. "Hey! Hey, asshole! Does that look like the fucking loading dock to you? Is this your first day?"

Just as quickly, he pivoted back to Lexi and sighed sympathetically. "I know, Lex. *I know*. But that's what it is. You know I'm not the boss, right? I mean, you *know* that if it was up to me, you'd be up to work tonight. Right?"

Lexi nodded.

"I'm sorry, Lex. Sometimes this shit happens. And I can't tell you why it's happening, but just know it's a good reason. When someone in the mansion calls an audible, I just go with it. I'm not the quarterback."

"Ang… I know. I'm-I'm just disappointed. I believe you, dude." She looked down at her feet and kicked the dirt.

"Ah, shit, Lex, now I feel bad. I moved you up, too. You weren't next on the list, but I put you in. Maybe if I'd waited, just till your number—"

Lexi waved away his concern with her hands. "No, no, come on. Ang, I'm okay, really. I was just surprised. It's like when you go to the video store and everyone's bought out the new movie."

Angelo laughed at that. "Yeah, okay Lex. I feel you."

"Well, I'm going to go home then, anyway. I need a night to myself, so it's not so bad."

As Lexi turned back to head to her car, Angelo stopped her.

"Wait. Listen… there's a big bad shindig coming up in a couple of days. I can't make any promises, *but*… if you show up in a sundress or something not so… prostitute-y, I can probably get you in."

"Prostitute-y?"

Angelo laughed. "Am I wrong?"

Lexi smiled good-humoredly and thought to herself: *you're not wrong, Walter, you're just an asshole.*

"Okay, Ang. I'll be there. With fucking bells on."

As Lexi walked back to her car, she heard Angelo yelling at somebody else.

"Jeeeeesus. Who the fuck gave you this job?"

Lexi pulled into the parking lot at Madam Regina's and went in to sit at the bar. She was obviously off-shift, but she was hoping that maybe by showing up she'd be able to take her room for the night and earn a little surprise scratch. But to Lexi's surprise, when Regina walked by, she just gave Lexi a curt but polite "hey, Lex," and kept on.

She must have something else on her mind. Usually, Regina would ball her out, accuse her of playing fuck-around, and then yell at her in front of the other girls (if not the marks). The lights above the bar were the only ones on—it was early, yet—and Jayjay stood behind the bar making micro-adjustments to the shot glasses. Natural enough, being the obsessive-compulsive he was.

"Whaddya say, Jay?"

"Hey Lex. What's good?"

"All good. All good in the hood. You got any freebies for a poor workin' girl?"

Jayjay smiled. "Always. Hey, I heard some *crazy* shit about the Carnival."

"Oh yeah? What'd you hear?"

He poured two shots of vodka into a tall glass he'd scooped rocks into, then sprayed some club soda into it, remembering that Lexi never wanted a lemon. As he slapped down a drink napkin and sat her drink on it, he continued. "I heard that there's a motherfuckin' devil on the stage, girl. What'chu say?"

Lexi laughed. "I don't know 'bout all that. But it was a hell of a show."

"Oh, you was *there*. I see, I see. Gimme the lowdown."

"No lowdown. Just some pyrotechnics. Laser lights and stuff."

Lexi fished a painkiller out of one of the pockets of her denim jacket and popped it in her mouth before washing it down with her vodka and soda.

"Nothing supernatural Jay. Just 'cause these townies never seen a couple of flamethrowers and a colored light reflected through a couple mirrors... I saw the same shit at a Salty Sweets show when I was a teenager."

Jayjay clicked his tongue and teeth. "Mmm-hmm."

"What?"

"Nothin'."

"Oh, nothin' my ass. I know what that *mmm-hmm* means."

"Whatever, Lex. Now you just bein' belligerent and shit."

She took a sip and averted her gaze to look off into the hazy unlit reaches of the barroom. "Yeah, I guess you're right. Sorry."

"That's alright. Like my ma used to say, 'you can be butthurt so long as you be nice about it.'"

Lexi laughed. "Your mama sounds like a smart lady."

"Nah. I love my ma but she dumber than paint."

"*Jayjay*! You're terrible."

"Only way to be. Listen, I'mma go check the taps, you okay here by yourself?"

"Why wouldn't I be?"

"Jus' askin'," Jayjay said and looked down at his knuckles.

"Jayjay."

"I was jus' askin'."

"*Jayjay*."

"Alright, alright. Some dude was around askin' for you. He jus' seemed a lil'bit..."

"Weird?"

"Yeah. Yup. Weird. Not dangerous or nothin', jus' weird."

"I think I'll be alright, Jayjay."

"Kay. See you inna minute."

Lexi nodded and looked down at her drink. She dipped her index finger in and swirled the ice around a few times until there was a little tranquil cyclone running around in her glass. Then she licked the tip of her finger and watched the drink swirl around some more. She heard something move in the corner, heard wood shuffling, or maybe a something brushing up against a table, and she gave a start.

Lexi stood up from her stool and whipped around, looking toward where the sound came from. She heard another wooden creak and shuffle and saw shadows moving against shadows. As slowly and discreetly as possible, she leaned over the bar top, grabbed a towel, then slipped a large glass tumbler inside.

"Anybody there?"

No answer. She moved closer to the shadows in the unlit ends of the barroom.

"Hello?"

Suddenly, a pale hand reached toward her and she immediately smacked it with the towel-wrapped glass down hard. A weak "aaagh" came spluttering from the target's mouth. She then used the glass as a battering ram, connecting a blow to the face of the shadow-man, before her shadow-cloaked, would-be-assailant fell to her feet.

It was Eddie. The weirdo. The one from the other night. The main attraction. She'd knocked his daylights out.

"Well, *shit*. Perfect. Juuuust perfect."

Eddie's eyelids fluttered, and he looked around. He was in a room similar enough to the one he'd woken up in the last time he was at the brothel. There were tiny little variations in the wallpaper pattern and placement of the bar, but mostly it was the same. He was even laid up in the same spot on the bed, with a towel on his head again. The girl was sitting, waiting for him to wake up, also in the same position. The same girl who had gifted him the lantern. But now she was wearing jeans and a t-shirt. Her denim jacket and a pair of spiked heels sat on the chair behind her.

"You again, buddy? You keep doing this and it's going to become a habit."

"I... I'm sorry. I just—"

"*Kidding.* I'm just kidding. But really, what were you *thinking*?"

"I just... I don't know... I just wanted to come by and say hello."

"Do you think that maybe waiting in a part of the bar where I could *see* you might've been an okay idea?"

"Well... yeah. Looking back, now that seems like it would've been a better idea."

"*I'll say.* I knocked you good, sweetheart. You're lucky your boy's in tight with the Madam. She let me take you here into the big shot's room."

"Oh."

Lexi looked him up and down. She couldn't decide if he might be good-looking if he wasn't so goddamn *strange*.

"Well, pick your jaw up off the floor, cowboy. Everything's fine *now*. No pressure neither. You just relax her a minute while you collect yourself. Get your bearings and whatnot."

Eddie nodded.

"So. That was quite a show the other night."

"You were there?" Eddie asked hopefully. Then he cringed a little, imagining that the show was probably a fair source of embarrassment for him too.

"Yes, indeedy speedy. You know, you play the slack-jawed yokel pretty well, but you must have *something* goin' on upstairs if you could put on a show like that. What's your trick? Sparklers up the sleeve? Flamethrower in the pants? Douse your hair in chemical product and then set it on fire long enough to singe?"

"Uh-uh. No. I just see it happening."

His candor was unsettling. *Does he believe he did the things that people think he did?*

"Well, how'd you do it?"

Eddie only answered with a puzzled look, and Lexi spoke soothingly.

"I know, I know—trade secret. Don't worry, you don't have to tell me. How's your head, cowboy?"

"Fine, I think."

"I'll be the judge of that." Lexi lifted up the towel and took a look. "No gash or anything, but you've got a hell of welt. You're lucky Jayjay buys those mega-shit no-breakers in bulk. You're not the first guy to be on the ass-end of a failed glass smash here. Them shits are *strong*. Anyhow, I think you'll be alright. Though between tonight and the other night, you might have migraine headaches until, like, the end of time."

"I already have migraine headaches."

"Well, all's well that ends well."

"What?

"Never mind. You wanna drink?"

"Sure."

Lexi walked to the bar, grabbed two cut glasses from the top and poured them drinks. She was off duty; so she poured herself a real one. This was a routine she'd repeated thousands of times— off the bed, on to the bar, pour the drinks. She returned with the two three-finger-pour portions of bourbon. After she handed Eddie his glass, she sat on the bed next to him and stared.

Usually, a man whose eyes lock with a pretty woman can stand the stare a moment or two, not much longer. Usually, when a pretty woman fixes her eyes on him, the man will either turn away or hurriedly say something foolish to break the silence. But Eddie stared back at Lexi. She had the feeling, too, that he wasn't really looking at her, but looking beyond those eyes and through into the very seat of the soul at the pit of her existence. Eddie didn't look away. He was a peculiar man, who, Lexi figured, required peculiar handling. So, she tried talking to him the way she might interrogate an animal locked behind a cage at a zoo.

"What are you thinking of?"

"I don't want to say."

"Why not?"

"Because it's hard enough."

"What's hard?"

"I don't know."

"You're not being very helpful."

Eddie's voice dropped with a somber cadence. "I'm sorry."

"Why are you apologizing? You haven't done anything."

"I think... that's what I'm sorry for."

"What do you mean?"

"To hear you."

Lexi was confused. "What?"

"I was trying to hear you..."

"When? Just now?"

"No, before. When you asked what I was thinking."

"To hear me?"

"I couldn't. I can't, I mean, I still can't hear you."

"But we're talking."

Lexi seemed confused. Then Eddie tapped his temple with his pointer and middle fingers.

"Up here. I can't hear you up here. That's why I came back."

"Because you can't hear me."

Eddie responded, "Yes."

Lexi echoed his word, completing the bizarre cycle of solemnity and bewilderment. "Yes."

They sat for a while, sipping their drinks and staring at one another. The gaze grew. An invisible smoke of swaying lust, one that neither of them could admit to. It was a gaze of improbable length, and they dared not look away. Lexi was thinking that maybe, only maybe, she might like to kiss him.

Eddie moved forward quickly but not clumsily. He was not in a jarring hurry, nor was he anxious; he was simply determined. He moved, and he kissed her. Gently. On the lips. No tongue (he was not that bold).

By this point, Eddie was bright red, flush with an inborn modesty that brought embarrassment after any boldness. Lexi was lost in her head: she was staring at Eddie in wonder, trying to process the divide between the boy who had just mumbled to her and the man who had just kissed her. Her mind fell into separate spheres of conscious thought, one part for the involuntary lust— another part for the angry guardian admonishing her not to kiss customers outside of business hours, and certainly not for free. As he drew back in and placed his lips against hers, Lexi felt her angry guardian diminish to a shadow, weak and ineffectual.

When Eddie tried to pull away, Lexi grabbed him by the shirt and yanked him back against her. When she shoved her tongue into his mouth, she thought she heard him yelp.

CHAPTER 18

Clara Guadali was one tough broad. Her father had told her as much.

Giuseppe Guadali had loved his daughter Clara immensely, in his own way. It's just that his own way was highly inappropriate for a father. He mostly always behaved. Although, sometimes he would lie behind her without wearing his briefs. But when Clara turned twelve, she asked her father to stop coming in naked, and Giuseppe had obliged her without objection.

At the time, Clara thought that his willingness to wear underwear was the hallmark of an eminently reasonable man, of a caring father. When she grew up and discovered that Giuseppe's nighttime visits to her bedroom were strange and maybe a bit predatory, she decided not to talk about it to anyone. Even before then, she knew there was something strange about it, so she decided she would keep it to herself. It was a *secret*. And the thing about secrets is that there is some mystic instruction that comes along with a secret, some invisible voice whispering *this is private, this is shame.*

Secrets are mystical sources of shame. So, when she came upon a *secret*, she was excellent at guessing the fuller extent of the story *behind* the secret. And that was what gave her *leverage*. And *leverage* could transform into *power*. So, Clara reasoned, shame *was* power. Which is why her father always said she was a tough broad.

Clara Guadali's husband had cheated on her, and that brought her shame, took away power. She ceded power to him. Why did she do that? *Why did I do that?* Clara wasn't one to cede power. But she had. Difficult to say. Why was she thinking of this now? Maybe because she was meeting with a man who had power, and so must be well-versed in the uses of shame. *The uses of shame.*

She had come alone. Why wouldn't she? Clara wasn't a mogul. She wasn't anything now. Once, Clara Guadali had been upwardly mobile, a successful status-seeker clambering aboard the great *U.S.S. Jones*. But the fall from grace, from favor, had brought her down to Earth. Ah, the shame of her failure, the loss of her power. If only those ignorant hicks had understood what she was trying to do. If only…

Clara sat, waiting at a fold-out feasting table with a red and white disposable tablecloth laid over it. She looked at her wrist-watch and saw that the man who was supposed to be on the opposing side of the table was late. Clara thought about this—a power move, a matter-of-course for hard-bargainers, for setting the tone. She could wait. It mattered little to her whether Mariv-icos was one minute late or one hour late; it didn't change her prerogatives or her tactics.

Finally, Marivicos marched in, his miniature assistants on either side of him. They sat down across from her. Marivicos rested his elbows on the table and interlaced his fingers, squeezing at the knuckles. *He's already irritated. Good.*

"Mrs. Guadali. How can I help you?"

She didn't speak. Instead she reached down into her briefcase and pulled out a manila folder. She opened it, revealing a picture of a girl—lighter shade of dark, wavy hair like straw and gold and dark honey. Clara slid the folder toward Marivicos, then tapped the long manicured nail of her pointer finger against the face in the photo.

"That's your son's wife. Daughter-in-law, you might call her."

"What about her?"

Clara clicked her tongue against her teeth and hissed in her best Sinister Sister cadence. "You're a cold motherfucker, Marivicos."

"Oh yeah? How's that?"

"I think you know well enough. But if you want to go through the motions, I'll go through the fuckin' motions."

Marivicos only smiled at her as she continued.

"If you want to play dumb, fine. But if you're smart enough to know I got you by your fuckin' stinking sack, then we can cut out the bullshit and get down to business."

Had she started too strong? Negotiation was about the mutually acceptable stasis of unhappiness: compromise. Start off your partner too sour, and you're not going to get to equilibrium. He stayed silent, still smiling. *Shit.*

"You had her killed," she accused.

"Did I now?"

"You deny it?"

Marivicos, still smiling, now started laughing. This confused Clara mightily. The two little dwarves on either side of him said nothing, only sat there stone-faced, staring not at her but straight through her. Marivicos started laughing louder until finally a hacking, wheezing ratchet cranked and croaked his grey airbags and he had to stop. He still said nothing back to Clara. Instead, he pulled out his own manila folder and slid it across the table to Guadali. *Shit.*

"What's this?" she asked.

One of the little ones answered her instead of Marivicos. "It will become clearer if you look at the contents of the folder."

Clara took the folder. Her finger fluttered ever so briefly, a whirl, a loop of unconscious erratic tic-tic-ticking. Yes. *No control.* For a moment, she tipped her hand. Yes. *They saw. That* they saw mattered little, though, once she got ahold of herself and opened the folder. There were pictures inside. Glossy, professional-sized pictures. Grainy printouts. Lots. Lots of pictures, from many different vantage points—and from several human and mechanical perspectives; meaning *un*secret. Pictures of tampering, of gas canisters, of clumsy henchmen. Pictures of water supplies—tainted. Pictures of secrets. Pictures of leverage (against her). Pictures of power (over her). She looked them over. Looked at them calmly, sure; controlled her breathing sure; but it didn't matter. Clara could argue, disavow, hem and haw, but she knew the cards Marivicos was holding.

Marivicos didn't speak a word. He was just smiling. Smiling wide. *Grinning like a fuckin' fool.* Fool or not, he had her. They both had dirt, but Marivicos's against her was damning. All she had was proof that another relative existed and Papa was trying to keep it a secret. Marivicos, on the other hand, had evidence—tangible, viewable, forensically sound, proof-positive evidence—of her misdeeds. No, of her *crimes.*

Marivicos leaned over and whispered something to one of his *aides-de-camps*, who smiled in turn. Finally, at long last, the old carny-patriarch spoke his truth to Clara.

"You know, this ain't my first rodeo. People like you... they come and go. All ya'll got yer plans. But I've been here for a long time. And I'm going to be here for a long time. Ya' get me?"

Clara didn't respond, but she saw something darkly glimmering in Marivicos' eyes. Not a twinkle, but the glistening shadow of a soul-sick abyss.

"Do you get me?"

Marivicos screamed these words, repeating himself as he slammed his fists on the table. Clara didn't know why, or how it had happened, but she was by now absolutely terrified. She suddenly felt very sick, the edges of her vision blurred not by the limits of her peripheral vision, but by some unfamiliar, awful malady that wasn't, well... *human.*

"Y-yes."

Marivicos smiled and steepled his fingers again.

"Good. That's real good, Ms. Guadali. Now I reckon you got business plans here. Am'I'right 'bout that?"

She nodded without saying a word.

"Yeah, I thought's much. Woman like you don't come to a feller like me jus' to blackmail. That's petty stuff. Small ball, bush-league nonsense. Naw, you got herself *aspiration*s. That's right. fellas, *aspirations.*"

With that declaration, Marivicos turned in a rickety rusty rotation to look at one and then the other of his little consorts, whom he now spoke to, while making it clear he really meant his message for Clara.

"She got herself some *aspirations.* Well, that's all fine'n'dandy, Ms. Guadali, so long as you keep your *aspirations* out of my finely tuned seasonal Carnival business, thank you vury much. *Pfft.* Aspirations. You keep'm to yourself. Mind your side of the street, know what I mean? Keep your hand out my pocket and keep your nose clean. That's my advice."

But it was Clara who replied, her voice scarcely above a whisper. "*Missus* Guadali."

"Sorry now, what was that?"

"It's *Missus* Guadali. Not *Miss.*"

Marivicos laughed.

"Yeah, well, we got them pictures too. Seems that nuptial appellation carries a little more water with you than what it carries with yer husband. If you take my meaning."

Marivicos smiled wider. *Awful. Evil.* Then he continued. "We done here?"

Marivicos spat these words rhetorically, then he stood up and walked away. Just before he exited through the slit in the tent leading out to the main acreage, he turned around for a parting comment.

"You can keep the pictures, by the way. I can always get more."

ACT II

"The awful thing is that beauty is mysterious as well as terrible. God and the devil are fighting there, and the battlefield is the heart of man."

— FYODOR DOSTOEVSKY, *THE BROTHERS KARAMAZOV*

CHAPTER 19

TWO YEARS AFTER ARRIVING DOWN SOUTH

How did he find me? How did he know? How could he... how could Papa find out?

But, of course, Papa always found out. That's why he was Papa and Eddie was Eddie. Just as the world was round and the sky was blue. Just as folks rubber necked out of half-cracked windows when a jack-knifed trailer was blazing on a turnpike. Just like those church-ladies who thought every man a rapist. Just as drunks always headed down and not up. It was the way of the world. The world's got a way, and that's the way. *Of course he'd found him.* Papa always found out.

Now Eddie was in a room, waiting. Some cavern. Some creaky, wet humidor of horror. Underground? Maybe. In a basement, at least. Houses in the bayou didn't often have basements. Not many at all. But Eddie was in one of them. Wasn't cuffed or nothing, wasn't bound. But his eye was swollen something awful, and his head had been cracked nice and good, and there was a pancake of brown-red dried blood matting his hair.

There was a clock on the wall, but it didn't much matter since it was obviously broken. The second hand trembled between the third and fourth second as though it was terrified to take a step forward. One little click. That one little click was too much for the second hand, so it was trapped in the purgatory of indecision until a higher power intervened.

Where were the babies? That's what Chantell called the little ones, and that made sense. The oldest was twelve months old, and the other was two months, and they still shit their pants and cried a lot.

The door to the room creaked, clicked, hissed and moaned. Metal scraped against metal until the door opened. A cop entered. Big pot belly, trooper hat. The top buttons of his shirt popped open to expose a soiled undershirt thick with bayou dew. The cop walked in and sat down across from Eddie. They were at a stainless steel desk, sitting on stainless steel chairs, exchanging stained, steely glances with each other.

Eddie felt guilty, though he didn't think he'd done anything illegal. Chantell had told him he had rights. She'd said that a man's got rights. A grown man can go where he likes and do what he likes so long as he don't hurt nobody else. But that's not the way it was. Because the odds were fixed, and the house always won, and Papa always found out.

The trooper broke the silence in the cellar. "You know why you're here, boy?"

"Time to go home?"

"Yessiree. Time to go home, boy."

The cop reached into his front pocket of his uniform. The pocket flap was lined with yellow-gold over a deep navy flap, while the rest of the uniform was a light blue-grey. The front pocket sat right above a canoe-crescent of manboob sweat. With his stubby, sweaty sausage fingers he grabbed a pack of Reds from the flap-open pocket, picking two out, which he waved under Eddie's face.

"You want a smoke?"

Eddie shook his head.

"Suit yourself." The fat cop lit up and took a long draw. He sighed and expelled a blue-grey vapor through his nostrils. "Well, boy, this ain't a fine part of the job, but it's a job that's gotta be done anyhow."

"Where are my babies?" Eddie surprised himself as the words tumbled out of his mouth. He sounded feminine, he thought. When Chantell asked for her babies, she sounded similar. That's what Chantell called them—my babies—and Eddie just didn't know what else to call them by. But they weren't with him, and he didn't know where they were, and they were still his babies.

"Your children are wards of the state, son. You ain't got the particulars for legal guardianship, and y'ain't got the... social skills... to take care of 'em."

"What about my..." Eddie searched for the right term but could only settle on the closest word he knew. "Wife?"

The fat cop laughed. "That little hi-yaller whore ain't your wife and you know it, boy. 'Sides, she's gone. Resisted, that's what she did. Had to be put down."

"Put down?"

"She's dead, son. Dead as a doornail."

Eddie thought he should be choking for a breath of air. His chest should be tightening—gripping his heart in a steely vise. His knees should go weak and wobbly and the rest of him should be numbed to the point of truly being dumb. Numb, dumb, numb. Any and all of those things one often saw on the TV—but that's not what he felt. Instead, he felt relief. He felt a terrible sadness, too, but he wasn't aware of that, because that sadness was stuffed down deep in his bowels, hidden in dusty corners of his heart and head, places that could escape his dread.

Can't let myself feel it—no, no-na-no-na-no, no.

Relief. Yeah. He'd always known this was coming. Coming down the pike, sir, yessir! Always knew it was coming. Papa always found out.

Can't let myself feel it—can't let myself feel it—

He kept telling himself that Papa always found out.

Time warbled and swam in and out his bones, and his eyes swam in and out too. A couple of seconds? A few minutes? *Pound-pound-pound.* His head. Head hurt. Blood not caked; fresh blood. A smell that was rotten, acidic. His own sick. His own blood. His head pounding.

Pound-pound-pound.

Papa always found out.

The fat cop was behind Eddie. The fat cop's stubby digits were gripping Eddie, by the hairs, by the hairs, by the hairs of his head, slamming his head into the stainless steel desk—*pound-pound-pound*—slamming Eddie's head into his own sick, slamming Eddie's head into his own sick and his own blood. The fat cop pulled back, hollering something—Eddie didn't know what. The holler, the bellow, muffled, coming from another room?

Pound-pound-pound.

"D'ya fuckin' hear me, boy?

And then a silence and the bells and the whistle and the stringing beep cutting one unending tone into his head.

"Now yer' gonna sign this, boy. And we're gon' clean up yer' mess. Yer' pa demands it, you gon' do just what he say. Go 'head now, boy! Make your mark."

"Fuck you," Eddie said.

The fat cop laughed, and the voice was inside the room with them now. "Son, now I'm gon' learn you somethin' now. I'm gon' learn you somethin' real good."

It was a few more hours? Days? Weeks? But Eddie came around to his captor's perspective. He signed the paper, even if he couldn't read what it said.

If he could have read it, he would have understood that he was signing away the rights to his babies. And if he would have known that, he still would have signed it. Because Papa always finds out.

A FEW WEEKS LATER

Eddie smelled shit and hay. There was a wobble and a steady churning sound like a train on rails. Eddie didn't like much about his situation, but he did like that sound. It comforted him to hear something familiar. There was light, but only a little, coming in though a vertical slat. It was a burning light, one that caught in his eyes and in his breath. The light was in his breath.

He had been in here for hours? Days? Weeks? And the smell hit him hard, and then Eddie was there in his sick again. And in his shit, and probably in his blood.

He was sore all over. His whole body, but especially his head. He touched his temple. Something popped, then something warm splattered on his hand, and his head felt a little less sore, but then something smelled because of all that. The sick came again. It was terrible, terrible, terrible. Too terrible, that smell. But he couldn't do anything about it.

He also could do nothing about the odd, odious thoughts (or sounds) that roiled through his mind. They were not his own. He did not recognize the shapes or sounds of them, but he understood that they were voices, and that now, he was different. A memory of something he had not experienced—a black void, immeasurable plumes of stardust. He was either insane or an aberration. Either way, something was wrong with him. But no one would help. Certainly not Papa. But Papa would find out. Eddie knew this. It was an indisputable, foul fact, omnipresent throughout his life. Eddie wanted to scream. It was so loud inside his skull, which housed a once-innocent mind, now flooded and corrupted by insidious sounds, thoughts, words he did not know and would never think to put together. He curled tighter into himself. He hummed. He spoke. He did whatever he could to stop that chatter, but it never ceased.

After a few hours, the sounds of the track and the steady churning burned down to a low rumble, louder but an octave lower. The slats of light cut against his eyes and his body burned a little brighter, and he heard something sliding and rumbling, something like a big door. He heard rustling, and feet, and breathing. And then the sound of wood or metal, or something, rustling and bumping, a sound like it was in his head. Intrusive thoughts poured through his psyche; voices that did not belong to him. A loud creaking, and a breaking. Wood snapped. The light flooded in, blinding him, and Eddie finally smelled fresh air.

He saw the silhouette of a gangly, long-limbed, malevolent mad-hatter. A cacophony of angry rambling and growls invaded his perception as he tried to get his bearings. He was home now, he knew. And after a little while, with his eyes adjusting to the blinding light, Eddie saw his exact location, too. A wooden crate, inside a boxcar, on a train. Maybe even on the same line that had taken him down south. The silhouette ambled, clarified, and then it was him. Papa. Who always found out.

Papa Marivicos smiled. But he wasn't happy. It was a beater's smile: the maleficent grin of the mad. Still, he smiled—*smiled, smiled, smiled.*. The raucous inner monologue of an enraged madman preceded Papa's spoken words, but Eddie couldn't pluck out anything concrete from that slew of noise pollution. The words Papa *said*, though, those he heard loud and clear.

"Welcome back, son. Where, oh where've you been?"

CHAPTER 20

That magnificent suit-with-pointy-coattails-wearing-hat-tipping Slenderman with a face allowed me to look after "his son". I hate to refer to Eddie like that without air or text quotes. Not that text was truly under consideration. Session notes are out of the question, unless it's about physical checkups. Those are always one-hour check notes—*Patient is resting with eyes closed. Heart rate 77, resp. 17. BP 90/71,* and so on—I just omit the psych evaluation (or whatever the fuck it is I'm doing). I cover my ass any way I can. The CYA method. It's wildly popular for most humans.

Excuse my profanity here. I'm not prone to that often. As I said, I'm not a big complainer.

I think it's completely outside the realm of possibility—absolutely positively impossible—that the kid had any clue what I was thinking when he woke up in that tent. I was so lost in thought that I must have been mumbling; blabbering like some schizoid lost in a delusional world, because that's exactly where I had been. That's the truth of the matter—he probably just heard my babbling. Still, there was something special about that night.

Anyway, nothing throughout the sessions indicate that he can read my mind. That would be insane.

During the first session, I had a difficult time drawing anything out of him—like pulling teeth from a duck. Honestly, it was hard to practice as a doctor instead of a friend, which wouldn't be very professional. You can't treat patients like your friends.

"Hey bud, how are you feeling today?" That was the first thing I said to the kid. First thing.

He didn't say anything, and I began to realize this kid was going to be tough to work with. As I thought that, he slumped down in his chair and crossed his arms, still staring at the mat beneath his feet, which was as dirty as my car was old. (It wasn't that I couldn't afford to purchase a new vehicle; I made a decent living. There just wasn't anything wrong with my current one yet; plus, it was a Fairline, a *classic*. Why replace something that functions? I think I took that attitude toward my wife, whether she functioned as advertised or not. She did not; recent behavior notwithstanding.)

So, I took the approach appropriate for difficult patients. There are many kinds of difficult patients, but I mostly encountered the floridly psychotic, or the stonewallers. Eddie fell into the latter category—I expected as much. Perhaps his old man smacked him around a bit or who knows what else. Those abused kids don't talk at first—if they ever talk at all.

I suggested to Eddie that we go for a short drive in the countryside—he didn't object.

I didn't say shit to him at first—just drove. He didn't appear to mind the silence. I surmised that he likely preferred it. This drive wasn't some psychological tactic on my part; I just felt for the kid. My old man wasn't the greatest friend to me (as I've said before, he loved me in his own way).

It was that thought that led me to an opening. Had to do it. Unethical as shit but something told me to do it anyway.

"My old man, Pops, now he never really drove me around like this." I went on and rambled some nonsense that was true, but it was nonsense anyway for a bit. Bitching about my father's... rougher side. I even told Eddie about the wedding toast. "Ain't that some crazy shit?" I asked him. "I know there are worse fathers out there..."

I thought maybe that would do it—give him an opportunity to talk about his pops. But he just grunted. Calling him a kid was accurate, I guess.

As I was driving him back to the Carnival grounds, I pulled a lot of that standard old-man-shit. "Oh that strip mall used to be a whole lotta nothin' thirty years ago. Open space, far as you could see, but they turned it into a haven for vapid losers." Maybe I revealed too much of myself. Maybe I was a jerk.

Despite my distaste for the mall, we did make a pit-stop for ice cream there.

The rest of the drive, I ruminated on whether I was actually a jaded jerk. Had I made a good impression? Or would I just be another bitter old man in his life?

I pulled the car over on the shoulder near the grounds. Kid said he could take it from there.

"You're a g-good man I think. I'll tell Papa about how you took my blood pressure and made sure I ate all my ice cream. I'll tell him that."

I was damned shocked when he spoke, and damned shocked at what he said. Kid was assuring me that his dad wasn't going to take him away from the sessions. Well, he wasn't lying. I did take his blood pressure. I did make sure he ate all of his ice cream that we got from that strip mall, home to the vapid and preened.

He didn't read my mind, I was sure of it. He walked off, into one of the Carnival tents without another word.

Things had been going well between Eddie and Papa. That was rare. Sure, it had happened before, but whenever there was a lull between bouts of punishment—and nearly *everything* Papa did was punitive—Eddie started to get nervous.

Some people lived their lives this way. The lingering question, the existential question that appeared, again and again, was *when will the other shoe drop?* Some people lived this way for so long that it develops into their defining pathology. Surely, you know a man, or a woman, or *someone* who has built an entire life around destroying before they've been destroyed. These folk are the embodiment of human brushfires, of controlled burns that clear away the foliage of friendship. Self-sabotage, you might call it. Self-hatred, maybe. Fear? Certainly. Yes, *fear*. Fear that rests in the reptilian cockpit of the mind. Fear—that old deadhead sitting in waiting, fallow and boneless, holding breath as the airship called life coasts higher and higher before its final plunge to the cold blue finality of the ocean.

Eddie felt something like that. That kind of fear.

His fear, he thought (or didn't think so much as *know*) came about because Papa started giving him some freedom, some leeway, some money and some time—his *own* time; Eddie's time. And that made him nervous.

Eddie had a car now. When had that happened? Of course, he didn't drive it. Abi drove the car. Or Lexi did. Doc Chain never drove the car, though. As Doc put it, he liked his Fairline just fine, thank-you-very-much. But still, the car was *his*—Eddie's. Or maybe it wasn't? Eddie had no idea whose name was on the paperwork. Eddie had no idea about insurance. But then again, those were just words; words on paper that didn't mean anything. Yes, the car existed. And when Eddie walked over to it with Abi, and when he and Abi got in the car, they drove somewhere and Papa mostly didn't ask, and (it seemed) mostly didn't care. The car *still* existed. It was freedom. Freedom was rare, unusual. Freedom was the first foot down.

Over the last three months or so, Doctor Chain had told Eddie to try and avoid tripping himself up. *If you have a bad feeling, find a place where you can be alone. Go there—make it your home.* That's what Eddie had done. Because the voices were still there. And there wasn't shit Eddie could do about it, there wasn't shit Doc could do about it either. The only relief was when Lexi was with him; he still couldn't *hear* her. Still couldn't know what she was thinking.

A quiet place, to be alone? Eddie could find that. It took a minute, but Eddie could find it. It turned out to be Madam Regina's.

Abakoum was the one who took Eddie there. Abi and Madam Regina had some sort of *something* going on, what with all the time the two of them spent together. After all, Abi couldn't afford to go to the brothel as often as he—as they—did. But they didn't always go there for the usual reasons. Sometimes when he was there, Eddie ventured out to the veranda, where the other marks were, and performed some small-ball illusions.

Of late, the three of them—Eddie, Abi, and Lexi—had been spending more time together. Usually, if they were all free, Abi would drive Eddie to go pick up Lexi at her place. And that's where they were now.

Eddie didn't know how he felt about Lexi. Sure, he knew well enough what he *liked* about her. But he didn't know what she really thought about him. Eddie found respite in that fact. Most of the time. The rest of the time, it was maddening. He had ridden through the wave of infatuation that came over him when they'd first gotten to know one another. And now he felt they were on some even plane. But where lay the line between him and his cryptic companion?

This time, when they picked her up, Lexi yelled playfully at the two men as she scurried down the steps from her garage-top studio.

"Eddie and Abi! The madmen strike again!"

Abi replied with a smile, in his usual fractured English. "*Koor wadaan*, Lex. Am I's the picture to health? Looks upon we, Lexi. Men are mens!"

Eddie was laconic, as usual. "Hey Lex."

It was an old convertible. *Very* old. Lexi hopped the backseat of the droptop like an athlete overcoming a hurdle and plopped down with a surprisingly silent *whoosh*. Like that old shot of Marilyn Monroe over the sidewalk grate, her sundress flew up, allowing Eddie a brief peek at her panties. Lexi caught him peeking, and he blushed. Nothing was said, even though she smiled (mostly to herself). Her eyes reflected the waning sun and the purple-orange blend of the dusk.

"So, where we goin', guys?"

"I have make very important date on Miss Regina."

"Oh yeah? So what does that mean for the two of us, Eddie?"

Eddie only shrugged in response.

Lexi smiled. "Well, I'm sure we can think of something."

Eddie blushed.

Lexi tapped the headrest of the driver's seat. "Say Abi, why don't you teach Eddie to drive?"

"Ah. Because Mr. Eddie have not wanting to learn to drive."

Lexi looked at Eddie, puzzled by this announcement. "Why not?"

Eddie shrugged again.

"Uh-ohs! Are Lexi going make to Mr. Eddie drive? This is a-stranges, my friends, here in America. In my country—"

Lexi laughed as she interrupted. "The men make the women drive?"

"*No*. Thas is ridonkulous. Womenses *offer* to drive mens. Is great honor."

That gave Lexi permission to get a little more intimate with Abi, at least conversationally. "Oh, *is it* now? You know, Abi, I'm thinkin' now that I don't know very much about your old country. Do you miss it much?"

Abi's driver-side arm was perched on the sill, his passenger-side limb swishing around the steering wheel in a neat turn. He scrunched his nose as he answered her. "Some things are I miss, yes."

"Like what?" Lexi hunched over expectantly, planting her elbows on the shoulders of both the passenger and driver seats.

"I misses... hmm, I will think... I misses... ach! Yes, rememberings! I miss movies."

"But can't you go to the movies here?"

"Is are different here. In Bouklafi, cinema is make run by Uncle Harif. Harif Cinema is best in all Bouklafi. And Harif Cinema make play Bouklafi movie that canno seeings here. Best movies. And Harif Cinema make to serve baklava to eat while see movies. *And*, Harif Cinema own by Uncle Harif, which is means that Abakoum watch for free. Very good cinema. I misses Bouklafi movie. Is movie are of my childhoods."

"Well, like what kind of movies? Action-adventure, fantasy–"

"Ach! No fantasy! Fantasy is movie they showings at Durkat's Cinema. One time they make police on man who pound himself in cock for in fantasy movie. Harif Cinema is no like fantasy movie place."

Lexi giggled. "Abi, not *that* kind of fantasy."

"Whas is other fantasy?"

"Like... you know, like, um—"

At this point, Eddie cut in. "Like *Lord of the Rings*."

"Abakoum not know this movie."

Lexi couldn't contain herself. "*Really?* Well, what about *Star Wars*?"

"No. Not know this movie."

"Oh, come on! Well, how about *Harry Potter*?" Lexi said with playful incredulity.

"Never hearing."

Lexi shook her head. They sat quietly for a moment. Then Eddie spoke up.

"I don't suppose you've ever seen *Meteor Man*?"

Abi thought for a second before replying. "Is movie with Robert Townsend?"

Eddie was surprised he knew. It was, however, a deep, mixed confusion; equal parts astonishment and happy surprise. "Y-yeah. Yeah, that's the one."

"Mr. Eddie, Abakoum have many ignorant thing he not know. Abakoum not know *Ring of Lords* movie, no. Abakoum not know *Hairy Porter*, no. But you make say Abakoum not know *Meteor Man*... this are ridonkulous. Robert Townsend he great black-person actors. All persons in Bouklafi know Robert Townsend. *'Have you seen Meteor Man'?*"

Abi wound up his declamation with a surprisingly spot-on imitation of Eddie's northeasterner accent. "No, Mr. Eddie. And Abakoum never make shitpants, either."

There was a brief silence until Lexi chimed in. "Wait, Abi, I'm confused. So, you *have* seen *Meteor Man*?"

"Of courses."

Another brief silence.

"*And* you've shit your pants?"

"Well... not today."

They all laughed before Lexi asked another question. "Were you ever married, Abi?"

"Yes. One time."

"What was she like?"

"Ah, my wife. Abakoum's wife was are beeeeooootiful womans. Big hips. Big *tzitzim*. She have had eyes like yours, Ms. Lexi. But have eyes are *much* bigger. Like little poopy."

"Poopy? Are we back to shitpants, Abi?"

"Yes, have eyes bigger much like little poopy," Abi ignored Lexi's comment, adding a little pant-sound and a playful yip for good measure.

"Oooooh, you mean a *puppy*. Puppy-dog eyes."

"Thas is what are said! Poopy eyes. She have had big poopy dog eyes. Like big, adorables *poopy... POOPY.*"

Lexi giggled so hard she nearly choked. "Where did you meet?"

"Abakoum's mother have introductions us."

"How old were you when you got married?"

"Fifteen."

"Jesus! She was fifteen?"

"No-no-no-no-no-no-no. Thas is ridonkulous. *Abakoum* have been fifteen. Abakoum wife have been twelve."

"Oh," she answered, "that... makes... uh... much more sense."

Lexi realized they'd be at Madam Regina's before long, and she needed to get dressed for the occasion. Without a word, she started fishing through the sundry junk in her oversized purse, finally retrieving a balled-up nesting-doll of plastic bags. She started pulling one bag out of the other until she got to ground zero of the mess, where she kept her royal blue dress.

Unashamedly, she pulled off her tank top as Abi and Eddie modestly kept their eyes forward. Eddie, though, couldn't help furtively peeking when and however he could, and Lexi smiled at that. She undressed down to her bra and panties and slipped on the dress, then earrings, then a necklace. She continued her makeover with the application of much powder and shadow, and finally by switching out her hushpuppies for harsh-heeled pumps.

During this whole transformation, Eddie looked at Abi, who was smiling. Then Abi and Lexi looked at one another. Lexi turned around and pulled at the backseat armrest, behind which was an opening into the trunk. She felt around until she found what she was looking for, an indigo sport coat with a faint almond window-pane pattern cutting through the blue. She handed the jacket to Eddie. "Here, put this on."

"Why?"

"Because we're going somewhere."

"Uh... *why?*"

"*Because*, Eddie, we can't just hang out at the house the whole time." (Lexi's euphemism for the brothel was *the house*.) "And because we never *do* anything."

"That's not true. We do plenty of stuff. Like... like... you know, like talking."

"Eddie, you're goin' to hafta' pardon me if I'm not fully satisfied with your skills as a conversationalist. Besides, you can't just keep a girl in the bedroom her whole life. You gotta' take me out, parade me around."

Eddie knew Lexi was being playful, but he enjoyed when she talked about him like this, as if they were together—the way that a normal woman might complain to a normal man with whom she was in a relationship. But all he could proffer was a monosyllable.

"Oh."

Lexi shook her arm playfully in Eddie's face, still holding the sport coat.

"Now put it on, handsome."

CHAPTER 21

Abi pulled up to the edge of the grass along the large plot of green acreage upon which The Pony and its mansioned annex sat. Lexi got out of the car and slammed the door behind her.

"Well, come on now, Eddie. What're you waitin' for?"

Eddie looked like a deer in the headlights. All he could do was turn to Abi with a helpless bleat of desperation leaking from his throat. "Abi, you're not coming?"

Abi responded by waving Eddie toward him so the younger man would be leaning down next to him. Then Abi whispered, "No, no, Mr. Eddie. Abakoum have going see special lady. Go, Mr. Eddie. Go and to have good times. Life is make very shorts, no?"

Eddie nodded in response.

"Yes, is make *very* shorts. Go now. Go make to good times with lady." With that, Abi pulled away, leaving Eddie to nearly stumble where he'd only a millisecond before been leaning his full weight on the car's window ledge.

Lexi chimed in with a mock shout. "Nobody's gon' save you now, Eddie. You've got no options. You're just gonna' have to take me to this party."

Eddie, now wearing the sport coat, adjusted himself and shook a bit, hoping that a little shimmy would make him feel more comfortable.

It didn't.

Lexi must have gotten tired of waiting: She grabbed Eddie forcefully by the elbow, almost like a reprimanding schoolmarm, and yanked him toward the streaming line of glittering party-goers filing into The Pony.

They walked across the grass, Lexi leaning and pulling down on Eddie's arm as an anchor of support—after all, it was tricky to be walking on dewy grass in the evening's encroaching darkness. The two of them soon closed in on the snaking crowd of criminals and courtesans, politicians and puffy-lipped trophies, and made toward the end of the line.

A voice bellowed over the ambient chatter.

"Indominus Lex!"

The voice belonged to a man in a black peak-lapel suit. The guy was a looker, which would have bothered Eddie if he'd thought he had the right to be bothered. But by nature, Eddie felt himself entitled to nothing.

The man yelled out again. "Come on over here!"

The man donned a black fedora, revealing an over-thick head of a nightmare-black mane, slicked back with pomade or maybe axle grease. He wore gaudy pearl and diamond cufflinks that shone out of the eyelets of the French cuffs of his also-black shirt, opened to three buttons down. He wore monk-strap patent leather shoes— white as a wedding dress. Draped around his neck and down to his lapels was a white cashmere shawl.

"Bobby!" Lexi called to him in response. She ran into the man's arms; he swung her around and planted an aggressive kiss on her lips. She pulled away, friendly enough, and slapped him on the chest. "Behave yourself!"

Lexi turned to Eddie. "Eddie, this is Bobby, Bobby this is Eddie. Eddie works at the Carnival."

"Works at it? I heard he's the *main event*. How you doin'

chief?" Bobby smacked Eddie on the arm, almost a little too hard for Eddie's liking.

"Good. Nice to meet you." Eddie held out his hand, but Bobby smacked it away and sputtered.

"Get outta here! Nah, I'm jus' playin', son. Come on, I'll get youse inside."

Eddie had never done the high-class, well-to-do thing, especially when it involved large groups of fancy people. Never been at a *fundraiser*, whatever that was. Weren't all businesses fundraisers? Did having a job make a *person* a fundraiser?

He looked up at the billowed and curved banner. It was spotty with beaded red letters. Lexi looked from him to the sign.

"Eddie, it says 'Equus Africanus Asinus Trust Annual Charity Ball'."

"What's that mean?" Eddie asked.

"Oh, it's a donkey charity," the new guy answered.

"It says 'donkey charity'?"

"No... is the sign hard to read? Maybe I oughta' fix—"

Lexi leaned over and whispered in Bobby's ear. Eddie knew exactly what she was saying to him; Eddie knew she was telling Bobby that *Eddie can't read too good* or some-such variation of that. But it wasn't *untrue*. Sure, he could read letters here and there, and he'd picked up numbers pretty good from an abacus and going on purchase runs with some of the carnies, but at the end of it, Eddie was still, undeniably, illiterate.

Bobby waved his hand at the sign in a swipe, like it had insulted him—insulted his friend. "Don't worry 'bout it, Ed. Sign's stupid anyhow."

Eddie replied with a polite smile as the group headed to the double-doored entrance.

Once inside (apparently this Bobby character had the kind of clout which allowed them to skip the line), Bobby suggested drinks, to which Lexi replied with a bubbly "oh yeah!", while Eddie only nodded.

"Be right back." The dapper young man took off toward the bar.

"So, Eddie, what do you think?"

Eddie looked around a bit, taking everything in. "Pretty fuckin' cool."

Lexi giggled, snorting a little. "You're funny."

"What, why?"

"I don't know. Just the way you say things sometimes. It's like you're just saying what you're thinking. Sometimes you just keep to yourself and don't say a lot at all. But that's good, you know? People talk too much. *Especially me.* But you don't. Unless you do, and then you only say what you're thinking."

"Isn't that what everybody does? How could people say something unless they thought it first?"

"No... I mean yes... I mean... it's not exactly like that. People will think of something, then they look around at the people they're with, then they decide what they can't say around those people, and *then* they say something. Most people."

"Sounds like a lot of effort."

Lexi shrugged. "Maybe, but that's how everyone does. They do it so much that they don't even think about it anymore when they do it, and they just filter out the shit they think they shouldn't say; they do lickety-split and lickety-splat."

"But I don't do that."

"Nope."

"How do you know? I mean, you can't read minds."

"Neither can—oh, wait, never mind. I don't know, I guess you'll have to trust that my high regard for your straight-talk is what *I* really think."

Eddie paused, seeming to concentrate with great effort. "It's confusing."

"Everything's confusing, sweetheart. That's why it's better not to think."

Without another word, Eddie and Lexi started strolling

around, people-watching. Lexi pointed at a woman wearing a furry hat, something akin to a Hasidic *shtreimel*, or like a Cossack's winter cap. The woman was wearing diamond earrings with gems so large that they stretched her earlobes, making her look like a drummer in a hardcore band. Lexi couldn't resist commenting.

"Take a look at this one. What do you think *her* deal is?"

"I'm not sure. Maybe she's a rich lady?"

"Close, but it's a little more than that."

"Oh, yeah? What, then?"

"Her name is Fanny Fuzzman, and she's the heiress to the Fuzzman Furs and Britches Royal Fur Company. They're the largest manufacturer in the northeast of squirrel-fur coats, hats, and all other fashion accessories."

Eddie chortled. "Nuh-uh. Are you serious?"

"Of course not. But it sounds like it could be true, right?"

"You're ridiculous."

Lexi couldn't resist pinching Eddie's ass as she replied. "Oh, you love it. Listen, I'm going to go tinkle. Keep 'dat ass here in case I want a bite when I get back."

Eddie's face turned red, but before he could reply Lexi was already out of earshot and headed to the ladies' room.

As soon as Lexi was more than a few strides away, the voices started coming back to Eddie. And they were louder, closer than they'd been in—well, maybe forever. There were too many people packed in too small a space; there were hundreds of people, all within a few yards of him.

Hundreds of people with thousands of thoughts. He heard them all—the thoughts they thought they had, the thoughts they thought without knowing they were thinking them. He heard the sub-linguistic grunt and babble of primeval meanings circuiting through people's minds. It was like looking at a translucent animal and seeing its blood-veined innards. Eddie heard memories, some forgotten, most just rattling around the emptiness of their heads.

And all this hearing *hurt*. It hurt very badly.

Eddie started to stumble. His vision blurred; his head was overcooked, overdone. His... everything was burning. It was an ineffable pain, a pain beyond pain, a feeling both physiological and metaphysical. Eddie stumbled to the ground as the words and thoughts of others assailed him. Standing was not an option now.

"You okay, kid?"

Eddie looked up from the floor, where he was lying on his back. As his eyes focused, he saw a white-maned man in a midnight blue Mayfair suit. The silver fox bent down to Eddie, as if to conduct an examination through the gold Montblanc glasses tilting on the perch of his nose-tip. Then he hooked his own arm under Eddie's pits.

"You look a little green around the gills, chief."

Eddie could still hear all the other voices, but the concern of this blue-suited silver fox with the gilt glasses gave him some brief respite, and Eddie managed to nod and attempt a wave, albeit unsuccessfully. The white-haired fellow snapped his fingers and two younger guys in pinstripe suits ran to take over the hauling of Eddie up by his underarms.

The two jamokes dragged Eddie over to a curtained-off booth —a makeshift private area with a table and chairs inside. They plopped him down in one of the chairs as some of the partygoers looked discreetly over their shoulders, others flagrantly rubber-necked, assuming (not unreasonably) that the silver fox and his two henchmen had a world of trouble imagined for poor old Eddie.

But that's not what happened.

"Hey, ain't you Melmoth the Magnificent?"

Lexi couldn't find Eddie anywhere. The party was in full swing, and even in a place as big as The Pony, the punters were jammed in tight as a camel's arse in a sandstorm. Abi had told her that Eddie going out and about in public wasn't a bad idea in and of itself, but that because of Eddie's *condition*, it'd be best if she kept a close eye on him. But now he was lost.

Lexi started panicking. She pushed through the crowd, ignoring the chiding of old biddies and the odd catcall from the drooly old wolves who'd made it out of hearing range of their wives or goomas.

"Bobby! *Bobby!*"

Lexi waved at Bobby, who was chatting up a skirt in heavy mascara and a return-to-the-store-the-next-day getup. Bobby nodded to Lexi, gave the skirt a quick peck on the cheek and came back to her, holding two drinks in a crisscross of the fingers of one hand, and his own drink by the stem in the other hand.

"Lex, sorry... hey, where's your friend?"

"I don't know. Jesus, *I don't fuckin' know!*"

Bobby cocked his head and his eyebrow. Double-cocked. "What's wrong? What's wrong with you?"

"He's not supposed to be *out*, Bobby. He's not supposed to be—"

"Hey, hey, take it easy. He's not a kid, right? He prolly just had to pinch a loaf or somethin', didn't want to tell you he had to squeeze one off, so he went out when youse wasn't lookin'."

"You are so fucking charming, Bobby."

Bobby took a sip of his Whiskey Old-Fashioned before answering. "I'm not the one throwing a shit-fit, baby."

"I have to *find* him. He could get in big trouble if something happens."

"With that *mezza fanook* ? What trouble's he goin' to cause?"

"Ugh. You're being an *asshole*, you know that?"

"Whoa, whoa, whoa, just back it up. Back it up a second,

sweetheart." Bobby's inflections were becoming more mocking than playful.

"I'm not your sweetheart, *Robert*. I'm the *mezza fanook's* fuckin' date." Lexi was fuming.

Bobby smirked. "Oh yeah? How much you chargin' him for the pleasure?"

Lexi slapped Bobby's drink upwards from the base so that it splashed all over him.

"You fuckin' lousy gash! Get the fuck outta' here, you gutter fuckin' cooz!"

As Bobby reared back to cuff Lexi a good one, a big meaty jamoke paw caught his arm before it even came around on the downswing.

"Hey Junior. The old man wants to see you and your friend."

CHAPTER 22

The last couple of weeks have been some of the best of my life.
Something clicked. Something *happened*. I don't know what it was,
and I don't really care.

Stacy is a new woman.

Who knows why it happened? They say don't look a gift horse
in the mouth, right? Well, I'm not. But I am staring out into the
future, and the motherfucker seems to be a road paved with
golden bricks. We have been out almost every single day over the
last couple of weeks.

She's out-and-about, thank you very much.

Maybe I said something nice to her, but I don't remember it.
Or maybe there was something irritating, or just downright shitty,
that I'd been doing for all these years of marriage, and I stopped
doing it without being aware. But when I think on it—and I mean
when I think really hard on it—I still come up with nothing.

I haven't done anything special, nor have I changed anything.

Regardless, Stacy is up for living life in a whole new way. She
leaves the house and does the grocery shopping. She went out
and got some pick-up hoagies for dinner. We put on *The Mouse*

That Roared, and we laughed and laughed. And then we fucked on the couch. After that, we just laid there, in our sweat, our fluids staining the couch (and some oil and vinegar from the hoagies, along with a nice dusting of crumbled BBQ chips), and we talked about how Stacy loved Peter Sellers movies when she was a kid, almost as much as she loved old kung-fu movies.

Tonight, we got dressed up for the first time in a long time. Sure, we'd donned the duds once or twice over the last few weeks to go to a nice restaurant, but tonight we were dressed to the nines, to the tens even. Full dandy and shit. We were going to The Pony for the Equus Africanus Asinus Trust Annual Charity Ball. I had nothing to do with the annoying length of the name. I'd have settled for something far less grandiose, like: The Fucking Party.

It's not a cause I'm particularly invested in, but I am interested to go to The Pony, because that's where Cold Rob Rizzo (AKA Bobby Business) runs numbers and makes kings (or slices their heads off), and I've never seen a real gangster in person. Shit, I sound like my brother, G-d rest his soul, firing off, speculating, grabbing the ass end of a rumor and spanking it until there's no truth left.

Of course I don't know that Rizzo's a gangster, but I'm excited anyhow. Hell, I'm one of the only doctors in Kayjigville, and I never get invited to shit like this. Once upon a time, maybe, but once Stacy turned full shut-in and I couldn't show up, there started a decades-long cessation of social event calendaring.

But the Time of the Social Troubles is gone! The Era of Boogie-Woogie is at hand! Don't you move a peg! Now bitch, shake that leg! Shit, I shouldn't even be thinking about that—the past, the bad things, the regrets and resentments, and so on—especially now that we are out! Out and about, my friends. Out and about. Shake that motherfuckin' leg.

Never mind all that. Here we are now—The Pony. Another good night for me and the lady.

MEANWHILE...

Papa pulled out the book. *The Book of Deeds of the Marvelous Mariv-icoses*. Heavy secrets. A cipher. Thousands of bloody hours put into the fire. Thousands of bloody hours put into the dirt. The soil of what's been closely kept. In it, conjure and sin. Dirty and spoiled. Fertile and something-somewhere between good and evil. That was all in the book, and Papa pulled it out.

The Book was crying. Bloody tears. Bloody beads rolled down into the soil, staining it red. Papa's fingers, his devilish finger-bones turned the pages slowly, slowly. His long dirty nails, those sharp blades of keratin tapered into needle points, cut through the vellum.

Hands, hands cooked clean until they were bleached like white salt-flats with cracks running through their desert terrain. Hands the color of the crack-horned cow's skull, marking off the entrance to some gold miner's ghost town. Some color like that. Human hands, maybe. But just maybe, only maybe, and no more than that. Because the eyes can play tricks on you.

When Papa's ungodly-white finger bones touched the bloody, tear-stained, living pages of *The Book of Deeds*, something stirred in the spirit world. It was something Papa Marivicos had been hearing about his entire life—heard it from his uncle who reared him up from a pipsqueak, heard it from his dirt-mouthed Roma grand-aunt—heard it from anyone with the Marivicos name; Papa heard the Uumen. It was calling to him.

Uumen. Words of perfect harmony when seeded, perfect dissonance when needed, perfect concordance once deeded. That's what they used to say, anyhow. Uumen. The perfect sounds that weren't sounds. The ways of saying things with a precision that could make portals rip open and stars die on their way to being born. Uumen, the holiest (or unholiest) of words.

The Book of Deeds was writhing, its crimson covering melting, seeping into Papa's marrow. Letters lifted off of the page and danced in a cold part of the universe, where there is no time or space but only the dense immateriality of metaphysical evil, breeding, spawning, hovering. The letters danced in the air and turned to ice that stuck into Papa's paper-thin skin and through his veins.

Uumen. Indescribable words, but Papa could speak them now. He could use them, the Uumen, as he liked, to contort the will of others, to distort the veil of reality as Papa short-circuited the energy that underlay it all.

The mantles of ice that now surrounded him allowed perfect movement and no movement at all. This was the moment right before the moment, the precipitating pre-check before the launch. His arms shimmered like interstellar ice grains, their veins populated with cosmogonic nitriles and ester, the old words, the first words. When Papa spoke the sounds, the ineffable unholy (or holy) formations flexed and bowed like frozen glaciers of particulate sailing past a supernova, exploding into frozen heat. No one can describe it, as it truly was, because it's not the sort of thing that goes into standard language, common tongue.

He had to admit to himself, Papa did, had to admit that Eddie had been the key to it all.

Eddie had been brought low by Papa and then brought back to Papa and then had brought out of Papa the Uumen. Papa Marivicos had tried many times before—many, many times—to conjure and wail those terrifying words in their sonic-shaking warble. But the words had never been more than garbled stuttering on his lame tongue. Nothing but impotent syllables until Eddie came back, house-broken and soul-starved. And when Eddie came back, and his fits started, Papa knew it was all real. Papa stopped pushing and fiddling, he just waited.

When the time's right, the time's right.

Then one day, it worked. That day, it worked. Papa opened *The*

Book of Deeds, and it worked. The Uumen. And since then, Eddie wasn't the only one with a little something new to swing around. Papa had something new, too.

Papa had a brand-new bag.

CHAPTER 23

Stacy was shining tonight.

Really, she was. It was like the way things used to be, when we were young, and I would just tag along to cocktail parties and ball-and-gown ditties. How could these long years have stripped from my memory something so powerful and familiar: her poise, her social grace, her dance-floor dazzle? I had forgotten. I had completely forgotten how well Stacy could work a room.

We'd scarcely entered The Pony when Stacy started waving to a couple she recognized from those remembrances of things past.

"There they are!" she said to the couple. She placed her hand so gracefully on my arm when she leaned in to tell me who they were. "Honey, this is Mr. and Mrs. Klostenburg. They own that lovely art gallery on Main Street—you know, the one with the watercolor of the wooden head eating the sun in the window? Oh, I just love that piece. Whose work is that?"

Mr. Klostenburg was fussily pressing his spit-licked thumb against his four-in-hand in a futile attempt to get a wine spot out. But he was apparently paying attention. "I think it's... er, uh... I think... Freddy Something-or-other?"

Mrs. Klostenburg rescued him by cutting in, as wives will. "Freddy Bess. Very strange fellow, but a marvelous artist."

"Stacy's an artist." I couldn't help cutting in myself, blurting out as a proud husband will, though Stacy was quick to demur.

"Forgive my husband. He's fond of hyperbole. I'm a dabbler. Maybe not a dilettante, but certainly a dabbler."

Still fiddling with his necktie, Mr. Klostenburg replied. "The habits and hurdles of the habitués of the art world are neither here nor there, my dear! But it is instead, the noble striving, the—"

As wives will, Mrs. Klostenburg cut her husband off. "Karl's trying to say it doesn't matter what you think of yourself or how much time you put in. Art is art separate from all that."

Mr. Klostenburg continued to blot his tie with his thumb, almost to the point of distraction. "Indeed! Art for art's sake! Art for art's sake! They forget that, they all do. That's why we opened the gallery. It's not a moneymaker, you know."

His wife agreed. "Oh, no, no, no, no, no, no, it certainly is not. Not a moneymaker."

Stacy ramped up the conversation more than a few notches, to the extent that it seemed strangely out of place even at The Pony.

Mrs. Klostenburg asked for clarification often, even though Stacy's statements were clear as day, at least to me. She was obviously out of her element, but Stacy continued, unabated. She seemed buoyed by the sudden realization that she was making sense despite her bombast. She was like a high-school girl discovering a thesaurus for the first time.

Mr. Klostenburg wasn't looking at the wine stain anymore—he was still holding the tie between his thumb and forefinger, sure, but he wasn't looking at it.

Stacy paused politely, awaiting a natural reply from her conversation partners, but no one chimed in, so she continued, knowing how her nature abhorred a vacuum. She surprised even herself with the reach of her metaphors, no matter how trite they sounded to her listeners.

As Stacy's crescendo burst into a climax, the Klostenbergs started at her with frozen expressions, as though paralyzed by a passing gorgon.

Stacy smiled and tilted up on her heels to kiss me on the cheek when she wrapped up her essentially one-sided conversation with a couple who tried too hard if you ask me. Sometimes I wondered if it frustrated my wife to be the smartest person in the room. Hell, the couple was obviously pretending to understand her metaphors; to argue her philosophizing. I was dazzled.

I smiled, happy to be Stacy's arm candy, just happy to stand there on mute. Another lull, so I decided to fill it with a toast, raising my glass. I was beaming with pride and a sense of smugness that shouldn't even belong to me but hell, I had caught the world's most clever, and beautiful woman. Tonight, it was a privilege to stand at her side. Oh how I almost longed to turn back the clock to appreciate the best parts of her instead of loathing the worst.

Just then, out of the corner of my eye, I thought I saw someone who looked very much like Eddie. The figure was being pulled along by his arms by two finely-tailored hulks.

I leaned over to Stacy and whispered, "Honey, I'll be right back."

She dismissed me with a smooch and a wink.

MEANWHILE...

Papa was still perusing *The Book of Deeds*. Peering darkly into its pages, he finally laid his straining eyes on the woman he'd been searching for. Papa had sought her out before, but to no avail. This time, though, it was much easier to find her. Simple, even. There she was, glittering on the page, the ambient glow of her features pulsing through the page. He wondered, Papa did, if she would feel something if he touched her image on the page. A small querying wonder turned to a malicious thought: *if I jus' squished her on paper... I wonder if she'd crumble right there'n'front of 'em all.* He almost did it. Papa wanted to do it. But he'd come all this way, waited too long. Papa had only just learned how to work the Uumen. Better to just do it the way he was supposed to.

Thus self-assuredly, Papa picked up a folded paper sealed with wax. He'd done it all correctly; used a quill pen and a blood-ink fusion, written carefully and neatly in the old script, the old tongue. Papa cracked open the seal of the folded paper and spoke the Uumen with careful precision.

"S[...]n...R[...]ye." (To describe the sounds using our conventional twenty-six-letter alphabet is impossible.)

As if by magic (which it was) the blood-ink inscription raised itself off the folded paper and leapt into the open book, wrapping itself in crimson coils around the moving images of the woman in real time.

Finally, Papa closed the book.

And he waited.

Well, I was right. It was Eddie.

I was happy to see that my other suspicion was wrong. Dead wrong. They weren't doing anything nasty to him at all. They were helping him. Well, not so much they; the big cheese himself was helping Eddie.

It took a minute, but I managed to successfully explain that I was Eddie's physician to the duo of suited bears standing guard at the private area.

By the time I got inside, I was surprised to see that Eddie was much more animated than he previously had been. The biggest surprise, though, was that Bobby Rizzo Sr. was sitting face-to-face with Eddie, and both of them were smiling. Eddie's voice was that of a little kid being tickle-tortured.

"No more, no more!"

"Aw, come on! You can't hold out on a fan, Melmoth."

"My name is Eddie, Mr. Rizzo."

"Okay, Eddie. But then you gotta call me Bobby."

"Mr. Riz... okay, Bobby. But I'm givin' away the whole show. There's gonna be nothing left when you come to see it!"

I stood and waited—didn't want to interrupt, of course. I'd pass the time in the wings till they noticed me, like a patient night-shift pancake-house waitress.

"Last one. Last one, Mr. Rizzo—"

"Bobby."

Eddie laughed awkwardly. "Bobby. Last one, Bobby."

"Okay, okay, okay. Here it is. Where did I go on my honeymoon? Nah, that's too easy. Let me think of a tough one for ya, kid."

"How about a trick instead?"

Rizzo's eyes widened, the creases under his white mane crinkled and crumpled together in a lattice of leathery tan. "A trick, kid? You mean a real, good, serious magic trick?"

"Yessir, Mr. Rizzo."

Rizzo was slurring by now. "Fuckin'-A, kid. Lessee it."

"You got a C-note, Mr. Rizzo?"

Rizzo raised an eyebrow. Eddie held his open palms out to his side, gesturing innocence. Rizzo shrugged and snapped his fingers. Almost as a reflex, one of the jamokes pulled out a hundred-dollar bill and handed it to Eddie.

"Okay, Mr. Rizzo. Here goes—"

"Sleeves, kid. Come on."

"Sleeves?"

"Come on, kid, roll up the sleeves so's we knows there's no trick."

"But it is a trick."

"Yeah, but so's we knows it's not a dirty trick. You know what I mean." Rizzo slurred a bit, but not so much that his words lacked clarity or connectivity.

"I'll do you one better."

Eddie flashed the hundred-dollar bill and asked Rizzo to hold it. Rizzo's face waggled and creased in more than one place. "Well, alright. Now we's talkin'."

"Go ahead and take a look at it. Make sure there's no, you know, invisible strings or nothin'. No dirty tricks."

Rizzo turned the hundred around a few turns, taking an inordinate amount of time inspecting his own money, play-acting along with the routine. "Okay, kiddo. My money's clean as a whistle. Like always." He attempted a very not subtle wink.

"Now hold it up so Franklin's face is towards me."

Rizzo obliged.

"Now make sure you got a good grip on each side. Got a good grip?"

Rizzo nodded.

"Okay."

That's when things started getting supernatural—not just magical. Eddie's neck started to throb, the veins bulging like overtaut strings on an instrument. His face dipped down between his knees and a moan emanated from somewhere within his folded body. It was a moan from within and without, a sound too alien from human physiology to come from Eddie.

Eddie's elbows shot outward, his palms bore down on his knees, as if some invisible force had flayed his inner arms and forced them into a contorted bow.

Eddie looked up—and it was in that moment that I saw the sharp points running the gum-lining of the boy's mouth, saw the kid's teeth made of ivory and splattered neon organ-matter. In that instant, Eddie's eyes glowed green—shattered green glass with light filtering through. As his arms shot forward, Rizzo gave a start; his two goons almost went for Eddie, but they decided not to—for fear, only for fear.

Eddie's hands straightened out, rigidly flattened, palm facing palm a foot apart, like two sides of a vise. Eddie pulled his palms farther apart, as his eyes burned brighter. As he did, the hundred-dollar bill in Rizzo's hand lengthened horizontally. Then the bill shimmered; its pallid green-grey swirled and reformed as the bill grew wider and wider, until finally, the bill separated and became two. The hundred-dollar bill became two hundred-dollar bills. Rizzo looked down. He was now holding two C-notes, one in each hand.

Eddie fell from his chair. It was at that moment that I ran to him. I made a dash, but it wasn't fast enough to catch him. He conked his head real good this time.

Rizzo was still staring at the two separate hundred-dollar bills when another of his jamoke-heavies came rushing through the curtain. This new bruiser had his hands spread sideways to separate two figures (a girl and a guy) who were locked in heated combat. The girl was Lexi, and the guy looked like a younger version of Rizzo, but with greased black hair and considerably poorer taste in clothing.

As Lexi and the grease-head incoherently screamed at one another, she swung her handbag to try to hit him, but she missed and bonked the jamoke instead. The handbag's clasp scratched the big fella across the face real deep, releasing a spray of blood that spattered both onto Rizzo's face and all over the greasehead. Immediately, the greasehead started vomiting a puddle of champagne and red gravy that splattered all over the ground.

Rizzo wiped the blood off his face and glowered at the grease-head with cold, angry eyes. Three more big jamokes ran into the small area. The tallest of the three walloped Lexi while the other two got into an altercation with a couple of drunks who wanted to gawk. All of them were locked in a balletic union of violence.

With Rizzo screaming at him, the greasehead reached inside

his jacket, pulled out a pistol and took aim. Rizzo charged the black-haired clown that I presumed to be his son, while the jamokes charged Rizzo in an attempt to stop him from getting himself shot. In all the confusion, Lexi reared back with her handbag. She was clearly aiming to bash greasehead, gun or not.

But all that became irrelevant. Quickly.

Good doctor that I was, I was still holding Eddie's body, which mysteriously vibrated under my touch. I could feel it hum. Then, an aqua-colored plasmic echo of Eddie—or, a physical foreshadowing of Eddie?—shot up to its feet and stood ramrod straight. Without a beat, Eddie's still bent-over body pulled up and rocketed into the floating blue imitation of his own body. Eddie shuttered into the same place as his ethereal doppelgänger. When this happened, I heard a loud boom—a cross between a lightning crack and a cannonade.

Reflexively, I squinted hard and covered my ears. My mind was telling me I was going to die in some sort of cosmic explosion.

After a second or two I realized my balls weren't caught in my throat, and my face hadn't melted off. I opened my eyes slowly, peeking through the spaces between my own fingers like a kid at his first horror movie. It was then that I saw Eddie; but not Eddie.

It looked like Eddie, but his body was transfigured. He shone like a sun made of an indescribable light. In the shape of a human, sure. With eyes and limbs, sure. But with opalescent strands of flickering jewel-fire running mad circuits through a crystal-clear sheath of glass skin. Everyone in the room except for me and the elder Rizzo were frozen into place.

"Hzzzzt. Hrrrrft. Hzzzrrrrrft."

A sputtering sound like a transformer shorting out. Or maybe it was Eddie speaking. I couldn't say for sure; his mouth had disappeared. But then I did hear him. I heard his voice, inside of mine. What I mean is, I was speaking, out loud, to myself, but I didn't know what I was saying 'till I heard it. I said—Eddie said, "Get Lexi and wait for me outside."

I listened to... myself? Eddie? And I grabbed her. When we'd rushed out of the curtained enclosure, I could see that everyone in The Pony was frozen still, like figures in a wax museum. Lexi was crying.

I couldn't see Stacy, though.

Where was my wife?

ABOUT 15 MINUTES EARLIER

Stacy couldn't control herself. She didn't know how or why, but this wash of compulsion had come upon her again. She felt controlled. Like a marionette, maybe. Or an empty container. A puppet with a storage bin.

She was on the cool grass, out back of The Pony. She'd cut around from the kitchen port after bumming a cigarette from one of the caterers. She didn't smoke, but she took the square and burned it down to the filter, biding her time as she slowly snuck away from the caterers' chatter and toward where the compulsion told her to go.

A tall sickly-looking goon was standing sentinel at the tower-tiered ziggurat of a mansion that sat beside The Pony. Stacy felt sick, sour, like her stomach and her bowels were sure to shoot out of her. She picked up a rock from the ground and chucked it through the darkness where it clanked against something. The tall sickly sentinel followed the sound and walked off the back veranda.

The compulsion told her to move quickly. She ran in a hiccuping hitch-step up the stairs and tried the back door. It was locked. She turned and saw the goon coming back. The tall gangly sentinel came closer and closer, until he was in her line of sight. He smiled creepily at her, coming closer and closer still. Stacy felt an animal terror grasping at her spine, at her guts.

He was now standing almost nose-to-nose with Stacy. Well, not nose to nose exactly, what with him being about two heads taller. He stared down at her, then scoffed. "You're a little late. I can't give you more than fifteen, maybe twenty minutes." He produced a large old-looking iron key and unlocked the door.

She scrunched her nose. A firefly flew by. She didn't understand. But she didn't have to. The tall gangly sentinel stepped aside. She turned the doorknob and walked in. Stacy didn't know what she was looking for. But she didn't need to. The feeling would tell her. The compulsion would tell her.

MEANWHILE...

Papa's ether-loaded icy hands played a soft sonata through the winding trails of the crimson ink in *The Book of Deeds*. The volume was closed, yes, but now a smoke-visage of a hologram-like figurate danced over the bloody cover. Papa's bone-fingers controlled the luminescent phantom-ballerina as she danced across the cover of *The Book*. The ends of the crimson trails, looping and winding on one another like a cut live-wire, flailed but still remained as they were—strings guiding a marionette.

CHAPTER 24

Clara Guadali was sitting in the finely furnished penthouse office at the pinnacle of an oval-topped glass edifice. Ferriman had paid for her to set up shop there. Everything was riding on the *Commodora* deal going off without a hitch. *Everything.*

Clara was thinking of her father. *You're a tough broad,* he'd always said. And she remembered what he'd done to bring home the bacon. He'd told her that it was preferable not to break the law; but if you weren't found out, then you weren't really a criminal. Clara remembered the beef they'd finally caught him on; real small-ball stuff.

Tax evasion. Wire fraud. Mail fraud. Those were the ones they got you on if they had nothing else. That's how they got Capone. That's how that turncoat in New York brought down his own people.

He'd been doing it for years, her pops.

Vouchers.

Distributors gave vouchers. You paid for a certain amount in a shipment, they sent you double the supply of whatever you bought—rubber buckets, brooms, other shit in Mr. Guadali's hardware store. He would keep the vig, the double-supply, and sell it after things cooled down. Sell it, pocket the cash, and spend it on, say, a swimming pool in the back of the house for the kids.

He'd done so much worse, Clara's old man. But in the end, they still got him, even if it was for a chump change side racket. By the time he got out of the clink, the businesses had all failed and the money was gone.

So, Clara had an aversion to the illegality of what she was doing. But after her eminent domain debacle, this was it. This was her last chance to get out of Dodge.

Clara found a few of Marivicos's carnies who were in fiscal peril—mortgages ready to default, vehicles on the cusp of being repossessed, debts to loan sharks. She bought up their debt, which required taking a second mortgage out on her own house, a nice little Victorian that her prick of a cheating husband was on the hook for. Then, she called in the first account.

And—in a cosmic, karmic coincidence that made Clara nearly squeal with joy—it was the strongman who held the largest debt. Clara found out where the big guy drank and showed up for happy hour. She bought him a few drinks, got him tipsy enough to start bitching, and then she gave him the low-down on the situation as she perceived it. Clara felt nervous as she was dosing the drunk with veiled (and probably idle) threats, but she carried it off with conviction.

The strongman caved, weeping so intensely that snot rained down in globules into his handlebar mustache. She forgave him his debts in exchange for certain services—to wit, the strongman would give her inside information on Papa Marivicos, and he would act as her muscle as she searched Kayjigville for debtors she could draft into her service.

After that, it was just a matter of having the strongman crack some heads. Pretty soon, she had a lucrative collection racket. Clara collected on some loans; and forgave others, in exchange for favors, of course.

For the most part, any information she got on Marivicos was

useless. The man was deliberately obscure. And he was good at it. Clara was reaching the outer limits of exasperation when an idea dawned on her.

She ordered one of her newly acquired peasants to place a camera in Marivicos's trailer. It wasn't long before Clara came upon some very useful information.

"He's prayin'. Sumthin' like it, anyhow."

The man sitting in front of Clara irritated her. He was a maintenance man for the slot machines. Strictly speaking, he didn't work for Marivicos. And he always came, hat in hand. Literally. He'd sit down, take off his trucker cap brimmed with dried sweat and twist it in his hand. Irritating.

"Why do I care if, when, how, or even *why* Marivicos prays?"

"Well, it ain't reg'lur prayin'."

Clara rolled her eyes at this revelation. "Maybe it'd be better if you got to the point."

The man took out a pack of cigarettes and held it out as an offering to Clara. "You wann'un?"

She shook her head. Clara was about to yell at him, to tell him to get moving or get out, when she noticed the pack of smokes was shaking uncontrollably. The man was trembling something awful.

"Listen, take a minute to gather yourself, alright? There's no rush. You're here now, and that's what I need. Someone who can help me. Now, do you think that's something you can do? Can you help me?"

The man nodded, still fidgeting with his hat.

"Good. Just take a minute to gather your thoughts. I'll get you something to help you relax. Would that be alright? What's your name?"

"Norm. Marcus Norm."

"Do your friends call you Normy?"

"Some, yeah."

He seemed to be softening up.

"I can call you Normy, can I?"

He nodded. Clara reached under the desk and opened the small refrigerator. She grabbed a Coors and held it out across the desk.

"Normy, how about a beer? That'd go well with your smoke, wouldn't it?"

He nodded and took the beer in his hand. "Thanks much."

Normy opened the beer with his trembling hand, though, Clara noted, his hands shook a little less than they had before. He drew on the cigarette and exhaled the smoke through his nose as he spoke. His voice, too, was shaky. And slow.

"I been bringin' slots 'n fixin' the machines Papa's got fer' somethin' goin' on thirty, thirty-three years now. I run the wires up'n behind the trailers. Anyhow, Papa likes fer' the wires be run into a control room. Control room's in a bigger cabin next to another room. I ain't known what's in the other room. This las'-time, though, I pull off this'ere panel right next to the breakers—not the distribution panel, different 'un—and I sees Papa in there. He's got himself a book on out in front of 'im, but it's got, uh... it's got, like... like a woman dancin' on it."

"A picture of a woman dancing?"

"No. No. I look'nside through the panel—he can't see me no-how, cause the room behind me was darker'n hell, he couldn't'a seen no light come through behind me 'cause there weren't any—and I sees he's got a lady dancing on top'a the book. Like a real lady, but tiny'n kinda' like smoke."

"An apparition, kind of?"

"Say what?"

"Like... a ghost?"

"Yeah, like that. A 'perition. So I see the 'perition, and he's pullin' at it with his fingers. He's makin' the 'perition do things."

Clara nodded, urging the man to continue. Though he spoke matter-of-factly, she detected reluctance from him. She had to be gentle. "What kind of things?"

"Well, first the 'perition's talkin' to some big'n'tall feller. Couldn't see for naught where'n they was talkin', but I recognized the breaker next to where'n they was talkin'. It's over at the old mansion next to The Pony. Old mansion, y'know."

"I know it."

"Yep. Well, next day I drive out The Pony. I go in, have myself a drink, play the tables a little. I'm walkin' out after a few 'ars, an' I sees the tall feller gettin' worked over right good by a coupl'a other big fellers." He paused, lit another cigarette with the butt of his current one. "Now I ain't one to get involved, and it ain't rare fer the fellers at The Pony, roughin' up some'un. I just put my head down, and the other fellers don't care much, you know?"

"You think there's a connection between what you saw on top of Papa's book and then the big guys beating the other... 'feller'?"

"Yes ma'am, that's what I was thinkin'."

"Interesting." Clara thought on it a moment. "Do you think Marivicos was watching a surveillance tape?"

"Well... I had the thought myself, but then I sees somethin' else made me think otherwise."

"Go on."

Normy's hand started to shake again. He reached down to the open cigarette pack and fished out another square, lit it, and took another sip of beer. His hands started shaking once more. "Papa was talkin' and he said some words that ain't sound like words."

"What do you mean by that?"

"I seen 'im. Seen his hands changin'. They turned int'a somethin' like ice. But had colors on 'em, too. Like glowin' coals or somethin'. And they was bigger, too. When he spoke, the words were... well, I dunno what t'say they sounded like."

Normy paused for a moment before continuing.

"My uncle worked the slaughterhouses. Once they had a litl'un he wanted to take home. Day my uncle comes 'round to pick up the calf, they got it strung up the air rail already. They ain't hooked the calf in'ta the rail right, and it was too short, too

179

lil', and the door'n the slaughterhouse was only halfway open. Calf comes 'round on the rail, gets snagged up on the door. Now, that air rail is mighty strong. So the lil' thing gets ripped open. Hear the bones crack, the stomach and evrythin' inside rip and squish 'round, fallin' down on the concrete. And the calf yelled and shrieked somethin' awful. I ain't never forgot that sound, and now I sho' won't."

"That's the sound you heard?"

"Same sound, just 'bout. Only sound I can compare it to."

Clara didn't know what to think. The man talked crazy. But his eyes weren't lying. To her, there were a couple of different takes on what he was telling her. One way to look at it was that the man maybe misheard something and/or got tricked by his own eyes. That seemed likely enough. The other thing—the other maybe— was that he was mixing up some things that were true with a nice dollop of superstitious fear. Now, that wasn't so bad a thing, so long as she could sift through the chaff and get at the wheat. That's what her whole job was after all, wasn't it? That's what any successful enterprise entailed, didn't it? Separating the bullshit out.

There were a few other things she'd heard about within the last couple of days. The mechanic who was indebted to her for his business loans serviced the vehicles for Rizzo and the other heavies who ran The Pony. The mechanic had told Clara that Rizzo's son, Bobby Jr., had been loudly harping on how he was going to put whoever stole some-amount-of-money into the ground. So, there was that, too.

"Do you think you'd recognize the woman if you saw her face again?"

"Oh, I know 'er well enough, ma'am. That lady is the doc's wife."

"What's the doctor's name? Or hers?"

"I know 'er name. Shit. It's on the tip'a my tongue."

But Clara didn't need Normy to finish. Being an enterprising and prudent strategist, Clara Guadali had already familiarized herself with most people who were trapped within Papa Marivicos's orbit. One of them was undoubtedly the woman whose name Normy was trying to remember.

Stacy Thornberg.

CHAPTER 25

Well, she's back, folks. Mama's back in town.

I was worried for a minute there, what with the two of us getting separated during the Eddie apocalypse at The Pony, but leave it to my good-old-fashioned crazy-pants mama to make a stupendous return. Just a little while ago, she began emptying—and I mean *emptying*—all of the kitchen cabinets.

"What are you looking for, Stacy?"

She didn't bother to look up at me. "I had something important here, and now I can't find it."

Your marbles? Did you lose your marbles?

"What can't you find?"

"It's... a thing," she replied.

"Okay. Well, that's sort of vague. What does said *thing* look like?"

A few old boxes of mac-n-cheese spilled out of the cabinets with a *clack.*

"It's just a thing."

"You're acting strange." As soon as the words left my mouth, I regretted them. Because everything that Stacy had done for the last few decades had been strange. But I hadn't said anything at all then, so why say anything now?

"I am not acting strange." Stacy leaned half her body into the space under the sink, reaching back behind the pipes and feeling around before asking for a flashlight.

"Look behind the wet wipes," I suggested. You see, I still wished to assist in her venture, though I felt a sort of helplessness. This was rare. I helped people for a living, but at that moment there was that rare feeling—and I'd had it a few times before—that she couldn't be helped. This made me instantaneously ashamed of myself.

She jolted out from under the sink, scraping her shoulder against the wood, hissing from the scrape. Like the wood had borne into her flesh like some sort of welder's torch and split it open. I imagined the wound itself hissed, as that wasn't a sound my wife made. Must have come from somewhere else. Now *I* was the one having crazy thoughts.

She walked with a deliberate stomp-stomp-stomp that sounded like a fat lady wearing clogs. That was her angry walk. I trailed behind her, giving a wide berth, not wanting to piss her off more than she already was.

"I can't find the flashlight!"

I watched her rummage ineffectively through the pantry. She obviously didn't know its contents as well as I did.

"Behind the wet wipes."

"You said that."

"Just trying to help."

Stacy ignored me and continued searching. "Found it!"

Brandishing the flashlight, she breezed past me in the hallway, knocking into me like I was an anonymous airline passenger blocking the way to her window seat.

"Listen, I'm a little uncomfortable with you destroying the house because you can't find a-a... thing."

She crouched back down under the sink to shine the flashlight behind the pipes. "I can find plenty of things. I just can't find the thing I'm looking for."

"Very clever. You know what I'm talking about, Stacy."

She sighed and pulled back out from under the sink again, this time nailing the back of her head on the wooden frame. "*Shit!* It's a goddam envelope you fuckin'... *fuck!*"

"Maybe that wouldn't happen if—"

"Shut up! Just *shut the fuck up,* would you?"

She was furious. Her lip was trembling. She looked like she was either about to cry or purchase a gun and shoot me in the face with it.

I threw my hands up in frustration. "Fine. You find your envelope. I'm going to go check on Eddie. Is that okay?"

She didn't answer.

"I said is that okay?"

"It's fine! You know I think it's fine. I like him. Go take care of him."

Stacy stomped past me on the way to the stairs.

"I just wanted—"

"Go help somebody who needs it, you fuckin' busybody."

I was too stunned to reply. I was too stunned to do much of anything except stare at the empty space my wife had just occupied.

After a few seconds I heard a door slam.

In an almost desperate state, maybe having something to do with denial that my amazing, charming and brilliant wife had transformed, almost within seconds, back to a shriveled (albeit a bit more attractive than the literal form) dried out nutcase, I went searching for Eddie. I could have done a million other things, some probably more psychologically beneficial to me. Instead, I drove my bifocal-glasses-hanging-half-out-of-my-math-teacher-shirt pocket-wearing old ass (was I not only old, but a nerd to boot?) to the Carnival grounds. I put on my new hiking boots as I got out of the car. I wandered around for ten minutes or so, searching for Eddie. I was just about to call out his name. (I was no intrepid wanderer out here; I'll have to admit. After actually seeing what was behind the curtain, this place made my skin crawl.)

Eddie just kind of... materialized. Not in the supernatural way. Nah, nothing like that CGI looking way he appeared at The Pony. I just turned around and he was standing there. It wasn't really that interesting. I'll admit sometimes I don't know what I'm on about, or why, but here we are.

"Hey, son. Stacy was just letting all the marbles loose from the Chinese checkers sack and I needed to get out of there," I chuckled. I truthfully didn't know what I was doing there. I wanted to talk to someone, but this kid probably wasn't the person to talk to about my problems. Still, it's not like I didn't want to know more about the pale, sometimes-unnaturally-illuminated kid that stood before me.

"Doc." He nodded and gestured in the direction he presumably wanted to go. Eddie navigated the campgrounds as easily as you'd expect an inhabitant to do. I suppose I wasn't expecting anything different. I wasn't expecting anything.

We ended up on the hood of some old car, much farther out, a more appropriate challenge for my boots. He waited for me to speak first as he always did. I just didn't know what to say, and I was shaken up. I wouldn't tell Eddie that, of course. You don't tell your... patient? Friend?

I had talked to him several times at this point. We'd had our therapy sessions, of course. That wasn't the track we were still really on, but here and there. I just wanted to know the kid at this point. However, I know he thought more than he spoke. I proceeded to talk to him, and maybe I shouldn't call it talking. It was more like very awkwardly interacting with him.

Look, not only was my wife donning a figurative straight jacket (unfortunately, someone had cut the restraints off it, even if it only existed in my imagination) but this kid had also... *glowed* recently. And that isn't even the right word for what I saw him do. I didn't know what to say. Thing is, I can babble nonsensically and incessantly for hours, but forming a genuine expression of thought into dialogue, well, that was hard to do with Eddie for some reason.

"Thanks for droppin' by, Doc."

I felt my shoulders slump in a good way. The corners of my mouth started to turn up into a grin.

He was happy I was there. He smiled, a little, anyway.

As we sat on the car and I was wishing I could have the kind of effect that hobo from *way, waaaaay down south* had on the kid. He spoke of said hobo in three words, and fondly. As a matter of fact, I believe his exact words were: "He helped me."

But I'm not an alcoholic hobo. Now I'm not going to say I never considered such a lifestyle. Who hasn't? Just run away from everything and chug some cheap gin that burns the hell out of your insides and might kill you later on; but really, who cares? We all get sick of life here and there, right? I can't deny this fact. It's a right of damn passage, for G-d's sake, to want to run away from everything. Patients are candid about that.

Eddie ran away from everything. Can't say I blame the kid, after piecing together his situation at "home." Which he never called it. Eddie had no home. "Papa calls it a Carnival. Don't call it a circus." The man was a gatekeeper of words, apparently.

And then I realized that his *keeper* had been less of a father to Eddie than that hobo. Papa Marivicos was less than nothing and had the same amount to give. Picking on words, even. I must have showed disgust when Eddie talked about Papa. Which was just a few words at a time. Once, he had looked at me and said, "I have to stay with him."

Prisoner, or Stockholm syndrome? Both.

Out of nowhere, the kid says, "He's my dad. Don't like him though." He looked around. Not *looked* so much as tilted his head. As though he knew the sound of Mr. Marivicos's pointy thrift store shoes slipping around in this area. He was listening.

I ignored this, wishing I could ask.

"Doc, I really can read minds. You don't have to believe me. But I can tell you some stuff."

He put his hands together, then took the fingers of his left hand into the clutches of his index finger and thumb on the other, measuring each over and over as he spoke. Not a common move but it was something much like a small child would do. I kicked myself for never giving Eddie a deck of cards to shuffle, something to fidget with while we talked. Kids hate eye contact sometimes.

"Well, you know you can tell me things, Eddie."

"I-I had a woman?"

I nodded, hoping he'd say more. He did.

"Chantell. We had two babies. Well, before they found me and brought me back."

"Where are they now?" I demanded. Not from him, almost asking G-d the question. Demanding some explanation. This sure as hell couldn't be a good thing.

"Police found me. Well, Papa did. He sent the police. They took our babies. Mine. Chantell... died."

Oh was that all? What should I ask then? *And how did that make you feel, Eddie?* Or, *oh shit, two missing kids, how's that workin' out for you?* I was about to cry for the kid; I had a hard time forming a reply to that bomb he dropped.

So I said the absolute smartest thing, the most genuine thing that made perfect sense, the most original, brilliant thing I could come up with. I said, "Oh."

Eddie made some kind of noise that sounded close to a chuckle. "I know you're sad. You don't have to say anything. You help me too, Doc."

I think that was all I wanted.

Why couldn't I keep him?

3:37 AM, EARLIER THAT DAY

"You think this ticket is the real deal?"

The asker was a graveyard-shift parking attendant from the too-hip saloon that had just opened up a spell down the river. The driver sat quietly next to him in the car. His taciturn nature was common among career criminals. The driver also owned a modest flower shop. That's how the two of them met.

"Didn't get too good a look," the florist answered. The ticket was inside an envelope, and he wasn't about to take any shit from Guadali for sneaking a peek.

Between passing words, the car was silent. Only the droning roll of rubber running fast over the pavement, the staccato peck and pock of an odd divot or dot in the road, interrupted the lull. Both listened and watched for traces of authorities. Distant sirens. Flashes of lights that deviated from the usual ambiance of the town.

"Did you ever dream about winning the lotto? As a kid or anything?"

"No," the florist replied.

"Really? Not even once? You never thought to yourself, well I'm gonna buy that cause I got the winning ticket?"

The florist sat quiet for a moment. He looked like he was considering the question, mulling it over.

"No."

More silence.

"You know, you're a pretty quiet guy."

The florist stared straight ahead. "Some people say that's a good thing."

More silence.

The parking attendant grinned innocently, then continued his interrogation. "Is it because you had some trauma in the past, so you've become hardened by that experience, and you've lived your life meeting opponents without flinching, but there's a part of you that's missing, and so you're just waiting to meet the right person to open your heart to?"

At this pronouncement, the florist stared back, then finally cracked an almost imperceptible smile without saying a word. The parking attendant angled himself into the silence, like he was nestling a sleek sedan into a tight space.

"There it is! I knew there was something behind that ice-cold veneer."

The florist's replied flatly, "Well, what can I say? It was funny."

More silence, then the florist added, "When I was a kid, I dreamed of writing movies."

The parking attendant replied with spontaneous but genuine surprise. "Really?"

"Yep. I saw *Conan* in the cinema. I couldn't believe they could make something like that."

"You couldn't believe they could make a movie starring a bodybuilder who kicks ass the whole time? That sounds like it's on you, my man."

The florist smiled. "No, a movie with mythology and thrills and…"

"And?"

"And James Earl Jones."

"There it is! A Joneso-phile. You want a smoke?"

The florist shook his head.

"So what happened? How'd you end up—?"

"Becoming a thief?"

"Yeah. That, too."

"Dad died. Had to go to work."

"Oh. And later?"

"I thought about that. Said to myself there'll be a day. Never came."

"Because?"

"Because the world's got an appetite and we're all on the menu."

"Huh."

More silence.

Then the parking attendant spoke. "I'd piss it all away."

"Sorry?" the florist said.

"The money. If I won the lotto. I'd buy boatloads of booze, coke, a couple of broads, and a house to burn it all away in. Maybe a couple cars—a Bentley, a Jag. Might travel a bit, too."

The florist smiled once again. "I guess some travel couldn't hurt."

"Where would you go?" the parking attendant asked.

"Brownwood, Texas."

"What? Why?"

"That's where Robert E. Howard is buried."

"Who the hell is Robert E. Howard?"

"He wrote *Conan*."

"The movie…"

"No, the book."

"Okay, so just to be clear, in this hypothetical scenario: you win millions and millions of dollars, more money than you'll ever see in your life, more than enough money to go anywhere in the world, first-class, and you would go to Brownwood, Texas to visit the grave of the guy who came up with *Conan the Barbarian*?"

The florist sat quiet for a moment. He glanced at the ticket that his newly minted criminal compatriot held in his hands. The ticket Guadali had them pinch.

"Yeah."

"Well, say what you want about the strong-and-silent type, but you fellas certainly know how to dream."

CHAPTER 26

"Wow-wow. She really is a beee-yooot!"

"Yessir, she is."

The design-and-build team walked Clara Guadali and Mr. Ferriman through the grand floor of the *Commodora*, where all the tables and bar tops were already set up for a river-bound paradise of gambling and boozing. While Ferriman towered above the two members of the design team, Clara barely equaled their height, even in her absurdly high heels.

"Is she safe?" Ferriman asked, regarding the boat.

"Me and my firm have been designing these ladies as long as you've been alive, or near it. I think I know what I'm doing. Yeah, she's safe," the engineer replied.

"I guess I have to ask, that's all," Ferriman said with a slight chuckle that rattled his jowls.

"Fair enough, sir. It is your money, after all."

Ferriman directed his next question to Clara. "When are we launching?"

"You don't read the local paper?"

"Not if I can help it."

"How about this Friday?"

"Friday? Really? Friday?"

"Yes, sir."

Ferriman turned to the engineer for confirmation.

"She's all ready to go?"

"Stem to stern, she is. Been checked about a hundred times over and a hundred times more. Mrs. Guadali here has had the crew onboard, and we talked with the Captain. He feels good about it. Knock on wood, should be ready to go."

Ferriman nodded and knocked his knuckles against the gang-plank. "Friday then."

Finally, he turned to Clara to compliment her. "Nice job. Ahead of schedule and under budget."

"Under promise and overdeliver, sir."

As Eddie was walking to Dr. Chain's office, he took small bites from a Granny Smith, sucking his teeth and curling his lip every time the sour-sweet taste flushed his mouth. He rounded the corner, where some kids were circling around one another as they threw small pieces of chalk at a designated target. It looked like some kind of game, but damned if Eddie could figure out the rules.

Drawing closer to Chain's house, he saw a familiar figure smoking a cigarette and leaning against the front-passenger side of an old Deville. Eddie's face sank into a worried frown. No, that's not him. Couldn't be. But sure as shit, there stood Bobby Rizzo Jr.

It was hot out, but Bobby wore a dark suit anyway. From the way Bobby leaned on the Deville, Eddie could see that he was wearing dress socks, too. Bold for an unseasonably hot summer's day. Eddie wondered what the man was doing there in the first place, then he moved his hand for a wave, but some impulse, some fear, convinced him not to. Eddie just kept on his way to Dr.

Chain's. Who knows? Maybe he wouldn't even notice Eddie was around.

But Bobby Rizzo Jr. noticed. "Melmoth the Magnificent! How you doin', bigshot?"

"I'm pretty good, I guess."

"'I guess'? What the hell kind of answer is that? You're either good, or you are not good, my friend."

They were close enough now that Eddie stopped to converse. "What're you up to Bobby? Visiting a friend around here?"

Before replying, Bobby laughed and curled his lip in a sneer—a confusing, severe contortion of his face. "No, no friends around here, Eddie-boy. I'm here to talk to you, pal."

"Talk to me? Why? I mean, what for?"

Bobby looked around for a moment to see if anyone was nearby, to see if maybe the doctor or his wife could see him and Eddie having their little chat. No one was around though—lucky as he was. The street was empty, even in the late morning. Bobby flicked away his cigarette and slowly walked past the floor-pointing chevron symbol on the Cadillac grille. With a flourish, he opened the passenger door, walked over to the driver's side, and climbed into his Deville.

He looked toward Eddie and gestured for him to follow. "Hop on in."

Bobby started up the car. Louis Prima's *Sheik of Araby* was playing softly on the radio. He clicked it off.

Eddie only stood there and stared for a moment, not knowing what to do, not knowing what was going on. Bobby rolled down the driver side window.

"Well?"

"I... I have an appointment with Dr. Chain."

"You're early."

"But what if we don't get back in time?"

"Eddie-boy, when you hear what I have to say, you'll understand that the doc would probably want you to join me for this ride."

Bobby plucked the cigarette from behind the back of his ear, rested it on his lips, and lit it. He blew out the smoke. "Come on, sweetheart, I ain't got all fuckin' day."

Eddie wanted to say no and simply walk away, but his feet were already moving toward the passenger side of the Deville. Something in him just couldn't say no. Oh, well. Just another bad decision. Just another foot-first stumble into the bullshit machinations of exploiters. Just another day.

Eddie climbed into the passenger seat, closed the door behind him, then buckled his seatbelt. Bobby saw this and scoffed. They drove off.

At first, they sat silent in the car. Bobby smoked his cigarettes one after another and hummed along with the radio. Eddie stared off and away. Finally, Bobby broke the conversational silence. "Lex really likes you, you know."

"Yeah, she's great."

"Is she?"

"Well... yeah. Yeah, she is."

"What's so great about her?"

I can't read her mind. "I guess her sense of humor."

Bobby laughed and launched into a diatribe.

"Women don't have a sense of humor. They're always getting pissed off at us for our sense of humor, Eddie-boy. Women are the reason there was prohibition. Women are the reason they made Reefer Madness and why I have to hire new employees every coupl'a months because my guys are going to the pokey on some dimebag-bullshit rap. Women wouldn't know funny if it came up and bit them on their fuckin' cunt. You want to know funny? Andrew Dice Clay. That guy's funny."

Eddie didn't respond. He just waited. Eddie knew what type Bobby was. Bobby was a talker, not a listener. Bobby was angry, and probably more than a little spoiled. Bobby was a ladies' man, and paradoxically—but not paradoxically enough so that it was an uncommon thing—a misogynist.

To wit, Bobby hated women.

After Bobby's outburst, they drove along in silence. They spent some time, curving here and there along the winding roads, and Eddie started to recognize little familiar things—patches of grass, pieces of rock, protrusions of branches—and put together that they were headed back to The Pony. He felt some relief. He could use a drink; being in the car with Bobby was painful. Listening to Bobby's consciousness was like hearing baboons screeching and fucking each other.

The abhorrent thoughts rolled through the car, through Eddie's mind. The urge to impotently plug his ears was strong. No matter what he did, there was no escape from Bobby's horrendous musings, and the background thoughts, and the background of the background thoughts. This man's mind was a mishmash of misogyny and putrid fantasies. One of them, Eddie didn't want to hear/think/entertain. It stabbed him right in the heart. If Lexi was a breath of fresh air, Bobby was a plastic bag tied tight around Eddie's neck. And when Bobby thought about Lexi, Eddie couldn't breathe.

Get ridda this motherfucka here. I'll get that bitch to suck my dick real nice. She gets a taste-a Bobby Jr., she ain't gonna want his shriveled dick never again.

This was Bobby. This was Eddie's curse—he would always know who people really were. And there weren't many good ones. Bobby's curse was that he was a fucking dumbass. Eddie's hands were balled into fists. It took all he had not to knock Bobby's lights out.

But that treatment was far too good for someone like Bobby. Eddie vowed that wouldn't be doing the Rizzo's any favors.

As they nosed into the gravel-rock circle of driveway off to the right of the mansion, Eddie could hear Bobby thinking to turn right. That's when Eddie realized they weren't there for a drink.

The last couple weeks of work had been good for Lexi. She didn't really enjoy the physicality of the acts she was asked to perform, but she liked talking to many of the marks, and she was happy to have met Eddie.

There were other marks, too, that she liked well enough. There was that Kraut who always came in on Tuesdays—Andreas by name—who liked to talk about engineering. Lexi liked talking to him because he knew all about bridges, which she found to be fascinating. Andreas regaled her with stories about Washington Roebling and the Brooklyn Bridge, how the bridge could grow or shrink about three yards of height when it was summer or winter (or just depending on the day), how Roebling didn't have the benefit of knowing aerodynamics and how it was pure kismet that the Brooklyn Bridge was designed in such a way to minimize weather beating down its integrity. Bridges were cool.

Andreas was cool.

And she felt bad for him, for Andreas, who was lonely and old, and who missed his wife. They always had a nice talk for about fifty minutes of his allotted hour before Lexi reached over and jerked him off (that's all he ever wanted). After he came, Andreas would let Lexi clean him off, looking away from her all the while, unable to meet her eyes. Then, he would quickly get dressed and leave, barely saying anything; except right before leaving, when he would mutter something—*entschuldigung*—that Lexi couldn't understand.

There was something about Eddie, though, that Lexi liked, but in a different way from the others.

What could it be?

Lexi had male friends, sort of. Guys she worked with. Bartenders, bouncers, or guys around her age she saw in places she regularly went to, like the grocery store or the pharmacy. But she never really went out to do stuff with them.

Eddie, though, liked going places. More specifically, he liked going places with her. Maybe those places weren't what she had in mind when she'd first met him, but she learned to enjoy the solitude and quiet that the very few places Eddie liked to go had to offer.

And he was easy. Eddie was a go-along, get-along kind of guy. Sure, he drank too much, but that was really because of his condition. What Lexi liked best about Eddie was that he liked going places far away from people. She'd taken him to the old abandoned lighthouse about a half-hour's drive away, where the river flowed out into the ocean. When she asked him where he wanted to go, Eddie would often suggest the lighthouse. It was quiet there, and peaceful, and because the road ended a long ways away, so you had to get out of your car to walk to the lighthouse —there were never any other people there. Eddie liked going to solitary places. And sometimes, they could just sit together, without talking, and stare out toward the ocean.

It was the last time they went that Lexi had felt a change in her heart. They were sitting out on the clearing in the brush next to the cliff that kept the lighthouse. It was twilight, and the purpling oranges and reds of the sleep-weary sun casted a beautiful glow over Eddie's face. She examined him; he seemed completely at peace. And then, one of those transformations happened—a transformation of thought she could feel in that very moment—where she saw the muscle in his shoulders. She saw the older-than-age weariness of his eyes, and she felt a change in blood and a flood of feeling while staring at him. There was something uncommon about him. And sitting there, watching the sun set, she suddenly became very excited about her Uncommon Eddie. Eddie, who was too sweet to not be nervous, but managed to perform in front of thousands of people. Eddie, who couldn't read very well at all but spoke with fluidity and candor. Eddie, who seemed to enjoy all the things about Lexi that most other people thought were bad.

When they were alone at the end of the river, they could see the horizon looming as a call-curtain on the whole of existence. It was at that special hour that Eddie would speak, when the colors of the sky were awesome enough to stir something in Lexi— something sublime, something worshipful—that she didn't know existed. The last time they were there together, he spoke for almost four hours. Eddie spoke till the purpling sky receded, until the broad sweep of stars unrolled across the Great Domain, so bright and shining they looked close enough to touch.

She asked him if he could start a fire, and he did one of his magic tricks and lit one without matches or fuel or anything. After the fire got going, they lay back and looked at the stars, and Lexi pointed at constellations and gave them silly names, and made up stories about them, which made Eddie laugh as hard as she'd ever heard him laugh. And when Lexi started feeling drowsy, she put her head on Eddie's chest, and Eddie tightened and became conscious of his own breathing.

"Don't worry about me. I like the sounds you make. I wanna hear your heart beat at a normal rate," she'd told him.

So, Eddie relaxed, and Lexi fell asleep with her head on his chest.

Still, she worried that he didn't like her like that.

Eddie never wanted to fuck. He never came on to her. One night they were out by the lighthouse and Lexi was in a pissy mood. That prick Bobby had showed up at work and badgered her about going out with him again. (Lexi was struck with terror when she thought of the possibility of Bobby coming to the brothel as a paying customer so that she might have to fuck him, or worse, suck him off.)

That night by the fire she felt a desperation, some existential despair, and she became angry at Eddie for not making a move in such a perfect setting.

So she threw a fit and walked away from the fire, knowing she was being petulant—maybe even a bit calculating. She wanted intimacy, some physical proof that the affection she felt was mutual. He wasn't a normal person sure, but most humans have those basic primal motivators that are found in the animal kingdom—get food, and (most importantly under the circumstances) fuck.

"What the fuck dude, why won't you touch me? We've been hanging out for a while now. *Hell*, we've been dating for a while now, and I'm not really a dating girl, Eddie. Do you just wanna be friends? Is that it? 'Cause I have enough friends. What are we? Do you even care about me at all? Fuck!"

But it didn't work, and then she felt bad, guilty. Eddie stood there with his hands at his sides, looking down and away toward the cold, cold ground. He paused for a few moments as if he was deep in thought, and then looked her in the eyes. Eddie took her by the hand. She tried to pull away, making like she was revolted by his touch, but of course she wasn't—he gently led her back to the fire, and guided her to sit down by softly pressing down on her shoulders. She obliged, and he picked up the blanket she'd brought along and wrapped it around her shoulders.

Eddie sat down next to her, and finally spoke. "It's okay if you're upset. We can go back if you want." He turned his gaze away from the fire.

She looked into his eyes and saw that he was staring into hers. She leaned over and kissed him, wanting much but expecting little, and was more than surprised when he reciprocated, with passion, with tongue, with his hands on her body.

When they arrived at The Pony, Bobby brought Eddie into a small windowless room filled with television monitors, keyboards, and sundry other control panels and modules. A bespectacled elderly man with frizzy side-bushes of salt-and-pepper hair flicked switches and pressed buttons to pull up something Bobby had asked him to display on the largest of the many monitors in front of them. When the old man had found what he was looking for, he nodded to Bobby.

Bobby turned to Eddie with an unsettling smile. "Now Eddie, you're gonna wanna watch this."

The old man pressed a button, and a grainy video started playing. A large safe, tall as a grown man, came into focus at the center of the screen. The safe had a large bronze turning wheel on its door. After about ten seconds, a woman in a form-fitting cocktail dress walked into the frame and approached the safe. She was dark, very dark. Even looking at the back of her head, Eddie got the feeling he recognized the woman from somewhere. He heard what Bobby was thinking—*wonder what this fuckin' mezza fanook's gonna' think now that we got his doc's moolie wife dead to fuckin' rights.*

Eddie's stomach knotted up as continued to watch. It was indeed Stacy Thornberg on that screen.

In the video, she reached out to the turning wheel on the safe and laid the tips of her fingers on it. Even in the grainy picture, you could see another character: the light. It wasn't just your normal, everyday light. It had a life of its own—brightening, igniting, transforming—becoming a sort of controlled burn that didn't behave like it was affected by the air or anything else. Fire with a purpose, a fire that shot forward in waves. The luminescence rolled off Stacy's fingers and consumed the wheel of the safe, shooting off sparks in huge crests of bright showery light.

Weirdly, Stacy's hand didn't seem affected by what must have been blistering heat. Eddie could see her head tilted back, stretching far enough that even on the grainy, low-res screen, he could make out her contorted neck snapping backward. Far. Too far. So far that he could pinpoint Stacy's eyes. Her jaw opened wider. Wider, wider, wider—until it became elongated, popped out at the joints, hanging large and long—an alligator's jaw in fleshly color. The top row of her teeth were visible, that's how far back her jaw stretched. The rest of her mouth was blurred, but it was clear that something was coming out of it.

Eddie couldn't say what it was. It was too hard to see. But maybe no one could. Not even some G-man intelligence expert peering at the video with forensic and analytic tools to crop and enhance the picture. But it appeared to Eddie, as though a gangly knotted pair of arthritic arms emerged from her gaping maw. He couldn't be sure since he couldn't see clearly, but what he could see were these little bent sticks coming from her mouth—sticks that were bleached colorless. Attached to those sticks were bleach-bone hands, which reached through the fire and sparks of Stacy's hand, gripped tight around the melted wheel, and yanked the door right off the safe, as if it were weightless. One of those spindly hands then reached into the safe, and the man who controlled the playback paused it at the very moment the woman removed what was in the safe.

A simple envelope, from the looks of things. Or a letter. A piece of paper. Something that would seem of such little consequence that Eddie couldn't fathom the ferocity Bobby Jr. felt and displayed over the matter.

It was Bobby who broke the silence. "That's enough."

The old man pressed a button to stop the video playback—all that remained black-white-gray static dancing to a melody of white noise. Even in the dim light the static screen cast, Eddie could see the old man's face was pale with a thousand-yard stare.

"Yo, Eddie boy, what the fuck was that? Let's put aside the *Alien* shit, 'cause I ain't got the time, and I don't wanna know, if you wanna know, you know? But what I *do* wanna know is this: What do you think of ol' Dr. Chain's wife making her tee-vee debut. You think she's got what it takes?"

This was bad. But there was always a way out with guys like these. Because they liked to give you a way, they liked to set things up so they could be paid back, so they could exploit you. People like Bobby dealt in "favors". And Papa had said favors were more valuable than gold. Well now Bobby had something that Eddie didn't want to get out. Eddie liked Doc. Jesus Christ; it would kill him if he knew…

"What do you want from me?"

Bobby continued to grin like the Cheshire cat. "Well, you know what was in that safe, Eddie-boy? Can ya' take a wild fuckin' guess at that?"

Eddie said nothing.

Bobby leaned in so that he was less than two inches from Eddie's face. Bobby's face was red, and his chest heaved with angry breath, his lungs breathing angry air, and Eddie didn't need to hear what Bobby said next, because Eddie could hear and see it in his mind.

Still, Bobby screamed, "THE FUCKING LOTTERY TICKET! THE WINNING FUCKING TICKET YOU DUMB FUCKIN' CUNT-FACED MUTANT PIECE OF FUCKIN' TRASH!" Bobby stepped back, took a few breaths. The wildhorse trampling of thoughts racing through his mind slowed to a gallop.

"I didn't put it in there, if that's what you're asking. And I didn't send anyone or any... *thing* to steal it," Eddie said.

"Oh, we know that, Eddie-boy. Well, at least we know you ain't put it there. Ya see, *we* did. That's the Rizzo's money right there. That bitch stole money from the Rizzos. That shit don't fly well in this town, Eddie-boy," Bobby said, a bit calmer. It was better than the screaming out loud while screaming inside his head. That kind of thing caused Eddie a visceral suffering, and it took a moment for him to get his bearings.

Eddie regained his composure and processed what Bobby had just divulged. "Why didn't you just claim the prize if you had the ticket?"

Bobby's greasy grin returned. "It's called *appearances*, Eddie-boy. The Rizzos publicly collecting a fortune? That brings attention. That brings heat. We were workin' out the details until that fuckin' she-devil fucked everything up."

During Bobby's explanation, Eddie realized he really did not give a shit, and regretted asking. He refocused, remembered where he was, and why. Eddie asked him a second time, "What do you want from me?"

Bobby's smile morphed from unsettling to evil as he pulled out a printout and a catalog. At the top of the printout was the word *Equibase*. The catalog was titled *The American Casino Guidebook*. He held them up in his hand as if he were showing Eddie a newly invented piece of machinery. There were loads more books and printouts behind him, too.

"Eddie-boy... I want you to pick me some winners."

CHAPTER 27

Clara Guadali was happy.

Eminently happy.

She slid open the main middle drawer of her desk and looked down at an envelope that a florist and a parking attendant had recently delivered to her. Its presence, here, in her office, was a source of unutterable warmth and comfort. It showed that Marivicos had been fucking with the wrong woman. He wanted to shove her malfeasance in her face, threaten her (although to be fair, she had tried to extort him first). She could play dirty, too. Eddie—or, Melmoth the Magnificent, wherever the fuck Marivicos got that stupid name from—was Papa's prize. It was the kid's lotto trick that had sent Kayjigville and the state into a tizzy. Well, she'd stopped that alright. Whatever he had planned for the lotto ticket was now jeopardized by the fact that Clara had her underlings procure it.

Everything was going swimmingly for Clara Guadali. She liked that word. *Swimmingly*. Fluidity. Motion. Rivers. Graceful flow, Point A to Point Z. Ballet. Dance. *Swimmingly*. Clara was the businesswoman embodiment of all those things that took outside force and transformed it into a seamless momentum of beauty.

Had there ever been a cleverer person? Probably not, she imagined.

In two days, the *Commodora* would be out on the river, plying the tides and reaping the catch. Over the course of a few months —maybe even a few weeks, depending on whether Marivicos had some reserves to get him through recessionary times—Clara Guadali would be standing over the economic corpse of that foul, nasty old man. She'd come to learn one more thing about debt-collecting—that it was not only an excellent means of bringing in supplementary revenues, but also a field she took to, also with graceful flow.

I collect debts swimmingly.

Plus, the information she received from her debtors was at least as valuable as the money. In all likeliness, Clara would keep up that little enterprise, even long after Marivicos was gone. She even admitted that she enjoyed it, delighted in seeing Papa's own strongman barrel his hammer-hand fists into the soft guts of the cheapskate do-nothings she collected from. She enjoyed it mightily.

It was a glorious turn in the great story that was Clara Guadali's: A modest, stunningly beautiful genius from humble origins—just a racketeer's daughter—tries to enlighten the benighted yokels of a town by transforming their undeveloped housing stock into marketable commercial real estate. Granted, those yokels still lived in those houses, but that was just a trivial detail. Admittedly, after being spurned by said benighted yokels, Clara Guadali floundered for some time. All appeared lost. But then, like a phoenix from the ashes, she rose up to smite the mightiest adversary of her day, one Papa Marivicos. And then, from that day on, Clara would soar up through the ranks of the plutocracy, until one day she was governor, and then president. Maybe she would appoint herself to the Supreme Court— but thinking about that now was putting the cart before the horse.

Yes, it was all coming together. Swimmingly.

The phone rang. Clara resented having her dreamy self-aggrandizing reverie interrupted, but the work line was the work line and business was business, and while business was booming she answered calls. One day Clara would get a secretary. But that day had not yet come. Soon, though, it would.

She picked up the phone.

"Miss Guadali. I need to talk to you."

It was the strongman.

"Okay, talk."

"Not over the phone. I have some important... some important... uh... important news... something important to tell you. Can't say it over the phone. I need to meet. Right away."

Clara looked down at her planner. "Well, how about tomorrow afternoon, say around—"

"No. You don't understand, ma'am. I need to meet you right away. Tonight."

Clara rolled her eyes. *Fucking idiot.* How many people did she have to tell how to do their jobs? Well, that was the price of genius, the price of success. The sad reality of excellence in leadership; heavy the head that wears the crown. And maybe it was the case that the strongman really did need her help. Better safe than sorry; discretion is the better part of valor, etcetera, etcetera.

"Okay, tell me where."

"The boat."

"Fine. I'll be there in an hour."

———

Abi heard a slight commotion. It wasn't unusual in the Carnival for a commotion to happen. However, this time, something in Abakoum's gut twisted, knotted. He felt the same way he'd seen Mr. Eddie feel when he got sick. Still, he snuck around the back-side of the tent and opened the flap ever-so-slightly. He didn't want to go in.

Not everyone was gathered inside the main tent, but there were enough folks present that all wondered what it could be about. The last time Papa had had a meeting this large it was because one of the trapeze artists had fallen after doing a no-net routine. But that had been years ago. Abakoum wondered why he'd not been invited. This was all so strange.

The strangest thing was that there was a whole new set-up crew. Big fellas, too. Some of them looked pretty worse for the wear. Some of them were very tall. All of them had scars and fucked up teeth. They looked like mercenaries. The horror of their physicality was only accentuated by the contrast between their grizzled forms squeezed into the yellow shirts that the showtime-crew wore.

Strangely, there was someone up in the back at the control console, working the spotlight. The lights went down and it was pitch black in the tent. Many whispered; a few of the acrobats squealed. Then, the spotlight turned on and caught Papa Mariv-icos standing smack dab in the middle of the circle. He had mate-rialized too quickly for nature, so a few of them gasped.

What the light revealed was the same man Abakoum had seen every day for several years. Yes. The same man. Only he seemed taller. More imposing than before. His eyes were sunken, his skin paled, and even his signature stovepipe hat appeared to have withered. This man was the same, but not the same at all.

Behind the assemblage, there was air in near-imperceptible motion, minute fluctuations in heat and wind, the body heat of the yellow-shirted mercenaries closing in behind them.

Papa spoke.

"Thank you all for coming here tonight. Although, I admit, I am your employer, so it ain't very likely that I'd ask, and you wouldn't show."

A few sycophants let out light but unnaturally flattering titters.

"Anyhow, I want to talk to ya'll about a problem that affects all of us. Or, really, about a concept that we must consider, and honor, if we're gonna carry the grand tree-dition of this Carnival into the future. And that concept is *trust*."

A few more whispers, a few involuntary quick-shunting inhalations, and the invisible air and wind-heat of the mercenaries coming in even closer. Abakoum leaned in just a bit farther. Just enough that Papa could catch his eye staring. If Papa knew where to look. But Papa was focused. He was in full-swing showmanship. Abakoum could hear this in his boss's voice.

"I'm sure that many of ya'll think that I've been mighty hard on ya. Hell, I know it. I don't dispute it, even. My father was like it. Grandpappy was like it—hard, you know. Everyone in the clan seem to've been that way, except for ol' soft Eddie."

Did this have to do with Eddie? Abakoum had not seen him there. No. No, this was something else.

"Well, recently I've become sort of... how would I put it? Lax about keepin' everything in line. Missed dottin' a few i's, neglected to cross a few t's, as it were. Figured things were goin' well with this show my boy's been doin', and why not let folks enjoy themselves?"

Papa nodded up at the spotlight operator. "Well, I believe that I have been mistaken in choosing to be so accommodating."

The spotlight crawled away from Papa and up the side of the tent, briefly passing over the creep-curved grin of a half-toothless hulk in yellow before the pale circle of light found its way up to the top of the tent and then toward the very center. It took a few moments before they all understood what the spotlight had chosen as its object of illumination.

Two naked, mutilated bodies were swaying from the very top of the tent. They were hanging by their necks.

Nary a gasp nor groan was uttered for approximately five seconds. Then women shrieked and men bellowed. Quickly, though, the yellow-shirted mercenaries fell upon the assembled performers from behind, holding knives to their necks and restraining any of those who might be threatening enough to harm Papa or strong enough to escape. The mercenaries forced some of them to their knees. Strangely, the others kneeled, too, as though an invisible string had been connecting them all.

Abakoum wanted to run, to look away. But out of flight, fight, or freeze—the instinct that overcame him was to stay still. Play dead so he didn't end up that way.

Papa's disembodied voice floated into the black air, the only light being the spotlight still cast over the two lynched bodies high above. It was the contortionist, Beatrice, and her partner. Some of their fingertips had been chopped off, the whole digits that remained had their fingernails removed. Large gashes, not quite knife wounds, but jagged rips, opened through their abdomens, revealing viscera dangling from their once-taut bellies. Their feet were chopped off. The male's penis had been cut off and shoved into Beatrice's mouth, and her vagina looked like it had been worked over with a power drill. Papa's disembodied voice rang out, shrill and eerie into the otherwise completely pitch-black tent.

"I HAVE LEARNED MY LESSON. I have been too kind. For too long. Now, this Clara Guadali has some of ya'll by the balls. I'm sure plenty of ya are familiar with Miss Guadali, yes. Ya'll spied on me, conspired against me, conspired against this family. Miss Guadali duped you to betray your own damn *family*. Now, I am not an unreasonable man. I am willing to grant exemptions. We are a *family* here. Don't ever forget that. The Marivicos Carnival is a family. And in families, the kin learn to forgive. Maybe not at first, maybe not completely, but they do forgive. I am a very forgiving man. Wouldn't ya'll agree that I am a forgiving man?"

A murmur of sobs and choked yeses lightly pattered through the blackness.

"Yes, I am. Because I am so forgiving, I am gonna forgive a certain number of people here. But only if they admit what they

did. And only if they repent and confess by naming their...
whatchacallit... co-conspirators."

None of them could see, but Papa was grinning as wide as a
twenty-lane highway.

"Now who's gonna be first?"

Marcus Norm was shaking and trembling something fierce.
That, combined with him ferociously twisting his trucker hat in
his hands, caught some unwanted attention.

Papa bent down to speak with him, his brow flattened into
something that appeared almost compassionate. "Normy, Normy,
Normy. Thank you for joinin' us tonight. I know that ya think
you're just a lowly contractor, but you are a part of this family.
Normy, ya look like you seen a ghost, you look straight...
unnerved. Tell Papa what ya done."

"Mr. Marivicos... sir... please, I din't mean to cause ya no trouble." Tears formed as Normy went on. "My girl's pregnant again,
an' what I do here don't always pay all them bills."

Papa tutted at Normy and with the back of his bony spindly
hand, he caressed the man's sweaty head.

"Go on, Normy. Go on, tell Papa who else you workin' with
here," Marivicos rasped softly.

Normy pointed to the strongman and another carnival worker
he had spotted during his outing to Clara's office. "Mr. Marivicos... sir... I'm as sorry as I can be. I swear on muh pappy's grave,
sir. Please."

"Thank you Normy. I thank you for thinkin' about your family
at home, and here, and doin' right by me."

After about an hour, Papa Marivicos had learned everything
he needed to know. When he felt he'd gotten all the information
he was going to, he had his mercenaries kill the rest of them, the
confessors too. Only Normy remained.

A mercenary had one hand clamped on Normy's hair, the
other hand pressing a large Bowie knife against the man's throat.

Papa stood in front of his captive, looking down at him. Normy could barely speak though the sobs.

"Papa... sir... pleas—"

The merc deftly sliced through Normy's throat and jugular. As the merc let go, Normy grasped the huge wound on his neck, trying in vain to stop the bleeding. Papa smiled as he watched Normy squirm for about twenty seconds. Until he didn't squirm anymore.

Abakoum felt the burn of bile rise in his throat. He could take no more. No, no more. Please no more. Please.

He ran away from the tent, holding his stomach, as though he were the one who had been disemboweled. In a way, he felt that he had been. Those people were human. They were his friends. His family. And now they were guts spattered against a colorful tent. Blood pooled on the floor. Dead. Gone. Tortured and murdered.

Abakoum could hold in his sick no longer, and before he reached his tent, he retched every last solid and liquid from his gut. When he had nothing left but air to painfully heave into the trash, he lay down in his bed.

He curled up in the fetal position, shaking, shaking, shaking. Tears streaked his face.

"Allah, help Abi," he whispered.

He hugged his knees to his chest, even though it hurt.

"Ama. I want my Ama."

"Hello?"

Clara approached the gangplank of the boat and paused before boarding. All the lights on the deck were off. The only sign of life was a faint glow coming from deep inside, on the main floor of the *Commodora*, where the play tables were.

Fuckin' idiot doesn't know how to work a light switch.

Clara walked on deck and tried to make out the shapes and curves of the *Commodora*. She thought she knew the ship well, but now that she had to feel her way around in the dark, it was a mite more difficult. She squinted, trying to pinpoint places along the boat using the dull shine of the moon, and the very dim light that emanated from within the riverboat. Like a *'perition*. Clara smiled. *Fuckin' dolt.*

It took a little less than five minutes (it felt like twenty), but she made her way to the starboard-side door adjacent the captain's helm and felt around for the lever-handle to open it. She felt the cooled iron frosted from the oddly chilled air, pulled the handle, and walked in. Once inside, Clara saw the light more clearly—she briskly but carefully trod toward it.

Through the glass of the gaudy gilded French doors, Clara could make out an outline of something—or somebody. It looked like a hump of reddened flesh bound up in branches. As she drew closer, it became clear that it was her spy, her second, her muscle.

The strongman was bloodied and broken-boned, tied tight to a chair, squirming and straining to break free.

This was a setup, and she had walked right into it. *Goddamn it, I'm smarter than this.*

Confidence waned within her. She'd lived a life surrounded by deception, treachery, evil men and women. Clara assumed that, when confronted with such imagery, she would remain the calm, cool warrior she knew herself to be. Still, her hands shook as she opened the doors. Her heart picked up its lackadaisical pace and morphed into something akin to a big bass drum at some metal concert. She shook it off. *Shake it off. That's what you do. You do it swimmingly.* But the only thing that swam was her vision as she walked in, hesitant but not wanting to show it, and the picture became much clearer.

Papa Marivicos stood there holding his stovepipe hat in his bony hands, with a small crew of large men behind him. Papa was smiling; a mutant smile, crooked and cruel, curved too high up toward the thin drapery of the sickly skin hanging from his cheek-bones. He looked different from when Clara had seen him last. Sicker. Stranger. Blued patches of skin centered in planet-rings of dead yellow circles. Purpling veins bulged around his eyes and lips, thin and stringy and—in Clara's mind—screaming to be punctured. He seemed taller, his limbs longer, his forehead larger. It looked like his teeth were bleeding indigo. And they were sharp. Papa's voice rasped as he spoke.

"Missss Guadalini, I'm gonna assume you know what this is about."

Clara attempted to think of a clever retort, but it wouldn't come. She couldn't even produce the words to correct the way he garbled both her name and title. Those things mattered less to her. Suddenly. Suddenly a lot of things mattered less to her. She was grateful for the lack of full-blown fluorescent lighting, otherwise Papa would detect the hummingbird pattering of her heart. But something within her told her that maybe, just maybe, he already could. She steeled herself.

"I do."

"Well, that makes things easier, at least."

"What are you—"

"A-tut-tut-tut-tut-tut, Clara. You don't mind if I call ya Clara, do ya? You see, Clara, I fear that your... *aspirations* have gotten the best of you. Do ya think that, Clara? Do ya think that things have gotten away from ya? Do ya think that this state of affairs... do ya think it's becoming a little... *untidy* for ya?"

With every breath, a ratcheting and wet croak-click-clack-click-croak oozed from Marivicos's respiratory system. Every time he breathed in, it seemed like his eyes grew larger. That indigo fluid leaked from his teeth, pouring forth and crawling against gravity, an indigo alive and infectious swarming over dry-white teeth. He took long pauses in the middle of speaking as he walked circles around the bound strongman—he placed his index finger on the strongman's head, smearing the blood around on his scalp.

Marivicos (or whatever that *thing* was) orbited his hostage like he was the center pole of a merry-go-round.

"Ya know, Clara, you strike me as the kind'a woman who does her research. Would I be right in saying that... saying... that you do your research?"

Clara nodded, though she wasn't conscious of doing so. Only moments before she'd arrived here, she felt like wrought iron. Hard as nails. She'd never guess, though, what grotesqueries would warp a man to deathly ruin, what corruption of blood and soul might turn a man into a devilish... thing. She closed her eyes momentarily and opened them with what she hoped was a steely gaze as her tormentor continued his diatribe.

"Yes, yes... indeed. I thought as much."

Papa walked away from playing ring-around-the-rosie with the strongman's head as the henchmen approached his quarry with ropes and chains in hand. After several moments, he resumed his soliloquy.

"I think that in this case, however, your research leaves *much* to be desired. You see... there are things you can't find out about me... things ya don't know..."

The henchmen tied rope to the strongman's extremities, looping them hard and tight, knotting the ropes around his ankles and wrists; his neck and his waist.

"I know I look young, Clara, but I am in some ways older than anything you know of. Clara, I want you to remember that. Can ya remember that... Clara? Can ya? It's very important to me, you see... *very* important. Because I wouldn't want ya makin' mistakes, Clara. I wouldn't want ya to let your aspirations get the best of ya... Clara."

The henchmen tied the rope into a lariat loop, using padlocks to attach the knot to the large coiled chains on the floor. The chains trailed in two directions, outside the windows—on both the port and starboard side of the room.

"Because of your ignorance, Clara, I'm gonna cut ya a break.

I'm gonna... you see... I'm *going* to cut you a break on this one. If only because... you don't know who you've been tanglin' with."

The henchmen finished tying their knots and securing their padlocks. Marivicos briefly looked behind his shoulder at the oldest of the henchmen, a burly giant with grey mutton chops. The giant gave him a nod.

"But I can't let ya get away scot-free. No, no, no, no, no, that wouldn't be fair. You run a business. You understand. I know about your little... loan business, too. Well, I suppose I know everything now. You understand, then. You understand that a businessman must keep *control* over his employees."

Clara couldn't imagine why, but she let slip a retort. "I'm not your employee."

"*YOU ARE WHAT I SAY YOU ARE!*" Marivicos roared. It sounded more animal than human.

Papa turned around and made a thumbs-down gesture to the henchmen. One of them muttered something to the others in a language that sounded Eastern European but weirder—maybe Finnish? Clara could make out that they were discussing something heavy on the boat.

Clara heard two loud splashes on both sides of the ship. A frenzied *tip-tip-tip* came from the chains as they rapidly uncoiled and escaped the room like two nimble serpents. There was a loud snap, followed by warbling like a Jew's harp. The ropes became taut and vibrated like guitar strings for only a millisecond, before snapping tight and straight. The strongman's body was violently pulled in two different directions.

Clara wanted to look away, but it was too late. The brute force ripped off one of his arms first. He screamed bloody murder. Two of his feet were shorn from his legs. The strongman screamed as loud as he could, a terrible sound—the sounds of terror when one realizes they are moments from death—until, finally, the last rope pulled on his head, stretching his neck for just one moment before the loud pop of his vertebrae breaking resounded throughout the boat. The rope made for a grisly decapitation and did not carry the head outside the window with it. The disembodied head slammed into the wall, then plopped on the ground. It rolled a couple of times before stopping; the man's lips twitched a few times and let slip a stifled gurgle. The life thankfully, finally faded from his eyes.

Clara couldn't look any longer, but she could hear the chains and ropes finish pulling body parts along the outside deck into the water, until finally there was silence. On the seat where the strongman had been bound, there was no evidence of a human being—no evidence other than the large puddle of blood pooling beneath the chair and the industrial-mop-wide streaks of blood streaming all over inside of the room, and likely all over the ship's outer deck. And of course, the battered, bloodied head resting near Clara's feet.

Clara felt as though she was about to retch but was able to control herself. She had come from a family where violence and small-time mob schemes were common, but she had never witnessed anything so cruel, so violently grotesque.

Papa laughed. He laughed hard. Hard enough that he started coughing, which then dissolved into a pneumonic wheezing. He turned to the henchman, the one with the grey mutton chops.

"You weren't kidding, Rajik, that was a good one."

The mutton-chopped brute smiled as he picked up the strongman's head and chucked it out of the window. A muffled splash followed.

Marivicos turned back to Clara. "Miss Guadali, I take it I've impressed upon you the extremity of my desire to keep you out of my business."

Clara nodded.

"Good. Good. Now, will you be so kind as to go retrieve *my* lottery ticket?"

Eddie turned the knob on the lantern. He liked to sleep with it on at night. Somehow, it made things quieter. Or he felt it did.

Lex was busy working. Eddie didn't know where to go. Without her, the nagging noise of everyone's thoughts, feelings, memories, desires, imaginings—it was an outside influence, but it sure felt like psychological warfare.

So, when Lexi was unavailable, Eddie tried his hardest to hide in his tent, far, far from any noise. Still, he could hear mumblings. But they weren't loud enough to keep him up at night.

Since Lexi had gifted him the lantern, Eddie felt that the calamity of sounds, the barrage of nonconsensual soul-bearing—it died down. When he turned the brass knob of the lantern, when he lit it, he felt... different. Better in a way he was unsure how to explain even to himself.

So his bed and the tent had become somewhat of a substitute sanctuary for him when Lexi was absent. That's where he was when a soft voice emerged from outside his tent. "Mr. Eddie?"

The same sensation came over him as when he'd met Lexi: Eddie hadn't heard Abi approach. He was confused by this. Relieved, yet again, but confused. Maybe his abilities were weakening. Maybe his superstitious belief that a physical object helped him was just that—a superstition.

"Yeah, Abi. You can come in," Eddie said. He sat up.

The tent flaps parted, and a beaten-down man entered the tent. And that's when the feelings rushed at him. He couldn't read his friend's thoughts, or pick out phrases, but there was something in Abi's mind that was so painful there weren't words for what he felt.

"Abi, are you okay?"

Abi smiled. "Mr. Eddie, no pretends you cannot knows this," he said. His smile was sad. He groaned as he sat on the stool that served as a nightstand next to Eddie's bed. The lantern was on the ground in front of Eddie.

"But I *don't* know," Eddie said, trying to hide his happiness when his friend was so sullen. "I can't hear anything. But I feel something, and it's not good—"

"You no hears Abi's inside mind?"

Eddie shook his head.

"What has happened so you not hears me?"

Eddie shrugged. "You know I can't read Lexi's mind. I don't know. Maybe I'm losing the whole thing. I hope."

Abakoum nodded. "I hopes so, too, Mr. Eddie. Abi knows Mr. Eddie no like it. It hurt Mr. Eddie. Abi wants no hurt for Mr. Eddie."

"Thanks, Abi," Eddie replied.

Abi seemed to not know what to say. Eddie detected a reticence and a fear from his friend, but nothing more. But he didn't want to press him. If Abi wanted to tell him, he would. That's how normal people worked, wasn't it?

Abi chuckled and picked up the lantern. "Nice gift from nice Lexi lady, yes?"

Eddie wanted to explain to Abi that Lexi was good, and that because Lexi was good, she had given him the lantern. And he wanted to tell Abi that he thought the lantern maintained some of Lexi's goodness. He tried.

"It-it… It's nice, yeah."

Abakoum smiled wide. "Yes. Is very nice. Is very light. But you, Mr. Eddie, you have… eh… you have… ah! Abi cannot thinks right now. Mr. Eddie love lamp?"

Eddie sighed. "Yes, Abi. Mr. Eddie loves lamp."

"Is okay! Abi love things that aren't peoples, too."

"Thanks."

"Yes, yes, is true," Abi said. He gently spun the lantern around and turned the knob, which brightened and dimmed the flame inside. He did this a few times until a click and a *pop* happened. The light when out.

The glass had fractured.

And so had Abi's mind. Eddie could not find specifics in the panic of Abakoum's thoughts, and he could see no images. Abi thought in his native language. But pain and loss fired through his neurons like they were fully automatic.

"What happened?" Eddie asked.

"Oh no! Abi breakses Mr. Eddie lamp. Abi so sorry! Abi fixes. Abi fix. Very soon. Very much apologies," he said, rushing to the tent's exit.

"N-no. It's okay. Lexi has a handyman at the brothel. He can fix it. But it's not that, Abakoum. Not that. There's something. What happened to *you*?"

Pain.

Ama.

That was one of the few words Eddie could pluck from Abi's thoughts. "Is you mom sick?"

"No, no, Mr. Eddie. Amas is fine. I go now. Much apologies for breaking lamp. I takeses to fix to Madam Regina's. Is okay?"

But Eddie didn't have time to respond. Abakoum rushed out of the tent. Lantern with him.

And the noise, distant as it was, became louder.

CHAPTER 28

That fuckin' prick. That piece of shit. That fuckin' piece of shit. That fuckin' mezza fanook piece of fuckin' shit.

Bobby was livid. He'd figured that he'd had an ace in the hole. He had figured that the surveillance tape on Stacy Thornberg would be enough to put Eddie under Bobby's thumb for a good long while, or at least long enough for him to figure out how to get rid of Eddie before taking Lexi for himself. Most of all, he had thought that Bobby Sr. would be proud to see his son take some initiative. But when Bobby Jr. told his father about his plan (he'd told him everything about Stacy, and the plan to get the money back) his old man had dressed him down. In front of everybody.

I can't handle it myself? We'll see about that, Pops. I'm gonna' handle it just fine. Right here, right now, I'm gonna fuckin' handle this business.

Bobby's hands were white-knuckling the steering wheel of the Deville. He was lucky it was Sunday and that there were no drivers on the road on which he could take out his aggression.

"Motherfuckin' faggot. You listen to me. You LISTEN to me when I tell you to do somethin'!" He yelled, slamming his palm onto the horn of his Deville. Yelling at no one. Honking at no one. Well, no one who was present, anyhow.

It wasn't that Eddie didn't go one hundred percent across the board in his picks. No, Eddie had picked no winners, no long-odd winners, no money-making bets at all.

"Fuckin' with me. Show you to fuck with me," Bobby spat as he mumbled. Little droplets sprayed the inside of his windshield.

"Why the FUCK don't they have wipers on the fuckin' inside. God-dammit!"

The worst part of it was Bobby Sr.'s lack of faith in Jr., his inability to see the larger picture. When Bobby told the old man what he'd done, Bobby Sr. told him that it was his fault that Eddie hadn't picked any winners. Bobby Sr. told Jr. that he didn't know people, that he would never succeed in the family business, and that violence doesn't solve everything. That last one was rich. Bobby Jr. remembered being a kid and walking into Bala Pizza with his dad and watching Bobby Sr. smash the glass display where the pies were slowly roasting and toasting under an orange-red hot light. After Bobby Sr. had busted up the rest of the storefront, he casually went to work on the owner of the store.

But nowadays the old man wanted to play the big shot, he wanted to cull a Presidents' Council of racketeer-diplomats out of the piles of human refuse he did business with to meet once a year at The Pony. Just like they were the International High Commission on Bookmaking, Drug-Dealing, and Whore-Mongering. Bobby Sr. had told his son something like—there's enough pie for everyone, we're lucky things are how they are. Bobby Sr. had also told his son—the Chinese have something they say when they want to curse someone. They say, "May you live in interesting times."

Whatever the fuck that meant.

Bobby Jr. missed his mother. He thought of her now, even as he was barreled down the highway. She would have understood. Ma always did. She was a nurturer. A bona fide feeder and happy homemaker. Bobby never understood how it was that her and the old man ended up together, and he would probably never find out. It wasn't the sort of thing Bobby Sr. talked about. He thought he remembered Ma telling him the story of how her and Pops met, but that was when he was little, a long time before she died. And when she did pass, playtime was over. While Ma had cooked Bobby whatever food he wanted, Pops had put him on a diet in the week leading up to the funeral, telling Bobby he was too chubby for a boy his age. Whatever the fuck that meant. And while Ma had tucked him in every night, with kisses, Bobby Sr. wasn't even in the house when Jr. went to sleep.

Bobby Sr. was obsessed with impressing the snooty Old Money Set. That's why the old man put on those stupid fundraisers and cocktail parties. He'd even tried to send Jr. to boarding school; and even further than that, suggested that Jr. ought to go to college. Fuckin' pansy.

Bobby pulled the Deville up in front of the driveway and looked for the tiny studio carriage-house above the garage where Lexi lived. Yep, there it was, just like that sloppy-titted cow, Fanny, had said. Bobby took his gun from the glovebox, cocked the slide back to reveal the business-end of the barrel, and then let the slide snap back into place, putting one in the chamber. He tucked the gun into his waistband.

He got out of the car, a cigarette dangling from his lip, and looked to see if there was anybody around. Not that it mattered. Bobby was going to do what he had to do, witnesses or none. That's what his old man didn't understand, that you took what you wanted and then paid the bill later if you felt like it. In Bobby Jr.'s mind, all the years of peace had turned the old man soft. Bobby Jr. welcomed war. He almost wanted it. No, he did want it.

Bobby walked quickly, flicking his cigarette into the bushes nearby as he came within a few strides of the steps leading up to Lexi's apartment. He could see that at the top there was a small window next to the door. He made his way up the stairs slowly, feet light as a feather, and peeked in through the window.

Yep, she was there.

Eddie was supposed to have met Lexi more than three hours before. Abi was headed to see Madam Regina, and Lexi was going to take the car off Abi's hands and get Eddie to take him out to the old lighthouse again. After two hours, Eddie decided to take a walk through town and head to the brothel by foot.

He was happy to go walking anyhow, what with how much they'd been driving lately. Aside from that, Abi had taken his lantern to Madam Regina's the other day because Regina's handyman said he could fix it, and Eddie wanted to get it back.

As dusk descended over Kayjigville, Eddie perused the kaleidoscope of colors settling across the cobblestones of Main Street. His eyes lingered over the shop windows glinting with prismatic reflections and light-echoes of primary colors. There was something strange in the air. It was Sunday, sure, but it seemed as though all the shops had closed early.

After a short sprint, he left the macabre shadow of the street's unnerving communal silence and was huffing it up the hill. By the time he reached the top, his head was clear of alien thoughts. The emptiness of Main Street, the unpeopled terrain—both had vanished from his consciousness.

When he arrived at top cluster of hillocks beside the brothel boulevard, Eddie saw there was no one out on the veranda. He walked up the stairs and inside the purple Victorian. He waved at Madam Regina, who was in the parlor off to the left.

"Eddie, honey. How are you?"

"Good, good. Is Lexi here?"

"No, she's not. But now that I see you, I do recall that boy Bobby saying that you should call him as soon as you got in."

A contorted twist of anxiety momentarily disfigured Eddie's face.

"Did he say what he wanted to talk about?"

"Honey, I don't ask, I just take the messages. I don't make inquiries into their substance."

"Ah. Okay."

"By the way, your lantern's fixed. I set it out on the bar top for you, whenever you want it."

He felt better, having it back. Better physically, mentally, and in some other way he did not know, but it was there. Something new, burgeoning. Or something old uncovered.

"Oh, thanks. I really appreciate it. What do I owe you? I don't have money on me right now, but—"

"Don't worry about it. Abi already took care of it, and he told me not to take even a dime off you." She paused; her lips pursed. "Have... have you seen Abi lately, Eddie? He sure was nice and all, when he came in, but something was off about him. He wouldn't tell me what it was."

"Off? In what kinda way?" Eddie asked. After the way his friend had acted the night the lantern broke, he was not surprised by Regina's observation. He tried. He fished for more information in her mind but came up empty. He felt like a shitty FM radio station experiencing interference.

Madam Regina sighed. "Oh, honey. I don't know how to describe it. Just seemed like... like he acted himself, but he sure wasn't. He didn't look it. And you know how he is. He just said everything was 'okay dokay' and 'not to worries about Abi'. But I... I don't know. Just wondered if you noticed anything."

"Sometimes he misses home. He gets in moods. He'll be okay," Eddie replied.

"Yeah. Yeah. Maybe that is it. Okay, hon. Here ya go," she said, handing him a slip of paper with a number on it. "You go on ahead in the bar and close the doors behind you. You can make your call in there and grab your lantern."

"Yes, ma'am."

Eddie did as he was told and walked into the bar, gently, sliding the doors closed behind him. He picked up the receiver of the old rotary and began the cumbersome back-and-forth rolling of the dial. It only rang once before someone picked up.

"Hello?"

There was some muffled noise in the background, like an animal or some kind of groaning.

"Yeah... uh... hi. Hi, this is Eddie."

"Eddie-boy! I'm glad you called, chief. I was starting to worry that you wouldn't get my message and I'd have to do something to get your attention. Well, never mind. 'Cause here we are."

Eddie didn't say anything.

"Eddiiiiiiieeee... you still there, chief?"

"Yeah... yeah, I'm here."

"Good. Now I want you to listen to me carefully. Can you do that? You listening, Eddie?"

"I'm listening."

"Good. Now, I was very disappointed when you picked my horses, Eddie-boy. I thought you were supposed to be able to know things before they happened, buddy. Well, I laid a bet on every pony you picked, and I lost on every single one. Lost me money—big money. I'd like to believe that was an accident, Eddie-boy, but I think you did it on purpose. I think you have some kind of problem with me. I think it's because you don't like me around your little girlfriend. Well, Eddie-boy, I don't like losing. And I especially don't like losing money. So, here's what we're going to do. You're going to come out and meet me by the river. Don't worry about picking up Lexi, I've already got her. You just bring your own bad self out here, and we'll settle up. You know where the old camp used to be? Where that old wooden deck and diving board is?"

An abandoned camp. Large enough for privacy and far enough out so that no one would see them.

"Yeah, I know it."

"Good, Eddie-boy. That's real good. You meet me out there. And don't take your time, pal. I'm with Lexi and we've been waiting a while for you to call already. You wouldn't want me to get bored and use her to pass the time, would you?"

Bile rose at the back of Eddie's throat. He could barely squeak out his answer.

"No."

"Good. That's good, Eddie-boy. I'll see you soon... friend."

Eddie replaced the receiver on the rotary and stood there for a moment, shaking. He reached over the bar, grabbed a bottle of bourbon and ripped out the funnel-top, guzzling down about a sixth of the bottle. His mind was racing. He thought of his options. He could run back to the Carnival grounds and have Abi give him a ride, but that would take the better part of an hour. And what if Abi wasn't there? What would he do then? He'd have to tell Papa what was going on. Or Marv and Andy, and they'd tell Papa too. He could ask Regina to take him out there, but then things might get messy—or, messier than they already were. No. No, he would have to run. He was at one of the highest points in Kayjigville, so he'd mostly be running downhill. If he was quick enough, he'd make it in less time than it would take to go back, find Abi, and get a ride.

Like a maniac, Eddie picked up his lantern, ripped open the front door and started sprinting with his lantern cradled in his arms like he was a running back.

ABOUT FORTY MINUTES LATER

Clara was driving back from visiting Ferriman at his office. She was still shaky, unnerved. That bastard Marivicos had put some fear into her, and she didn't like it. Not one bit. Clara Guadali wasn't supposed to be afraid of anyone. But affairs of late had become much more serious—dire, even. She had to find some way to even the odds, some way to make Marivicos pay for it— for making her feel fear. It had settled in her bosom—the fear had —and snaked like venom into her blood—the fear—and boarded up in her brain—the fear. She'd been humiliated, soundly (if only temporarily) defeated.

Humbled? Well, not quite yet.

She had to think of something. Something, anything. Had to. Can't let Marivicos win. But her blood pressure was up, still up, way, way up. Boiling, even. Boiling. She wasn't just mad at him, at Marivicos; Clara was mad at herself for not having seen all the angles. What did she think? That Papa was just going to roll over and let himself die, just allow her to snuff him and his Carnival out of existence? No, she'd been too optimistic. Clara could see that now. Pride cometh before the fall, and such.

Clara racked her brain for any way to one-up this beast of man, to meet his level of malfeasance. She'd come up empty.

Marivicos had taken something very precious from Clara Guadali. Something priceless, irreplaceable. He'd taken her sense of self and turned it upside down, inside out, and splashed it all over that boat, just as he had done to Clara's strongman.

She was beyond offended. She may not be the pillar of absolute mental fortitude she assumed herself to be, but Clara was still cold. Colder now than ever. She was still calculating. And there was more subtraction she must do. She was still vengeful.

An eye for an eye is what they say, isn't it? He'd stolen the thing most precious to her. Killed it. Decimated it. And she didn't know exactly how she could strip an eye like that from his world.

She paced. Wrung her hands. Screamed. What, oh what did Papa value most in this wretched world?

Greed. Money. His image. What gave him those things?

The alien tug of a smile pulling at her lips surprised her as she thought of Marivicos's son, Eddie.

How would Papa feel if she destroyed that which was most precious to him?

Eddie was drenched in sweat. It was a warm summer day. He'd kept running when he hit the campgrounds, but as soon as he saw the deck with its lolling wood tongue bent over the river, he slowed down to get his bearings. Eddie saw Bobby's car off in the distance—the Deville gleaming in the twilight.

It would be dark soon enough. In his heart, he felt. It would be dark soon enough. But it was still light enough for him to see the pistol hanging casually at the outside of Bobby's thigh.

"Eddie-boy, what's with the lantern?"

Eddie was still clutching the lantern like it was a football and this rendezvous was the end zone. He'd forgotten about it. It was as though it were an extension of himself. Just a part of him. He looked down at it.

"I... I had it fixed."

Bobby started laughing. Something either clicked or broke, because Bobby started laughing like a fool, hard enough that tears trailed from his eyes. He laughed like this for nearly two minutes. Every time Eddie thought he was going to stop, something tickled Bobby again. Eddie knew what that something was; *I had it fixed* was repeating in Bobby's mind every time he was close to the end of his fit.

"God *damn*, Eddie-boy! You know, you make this real enjoyable. I'm not even playin'. It's just... people like me don't get in beefs with people like you too often. I just gotta' say I've enjoyed it. You're like the human version of Mad Libs."

"Where's Lexi?"

But of course, Eddie knew where she was the instant he asked Bobby. She was tied up in the trunk, and Bobby had clubbed her real good. Bobby answered, using the back of his pistol-grip hand to wipe the tears out of his eyes.

"You know, Eddie-boy, don't ya?" Bobby's face sloped toward the ground into a sour grimace. "Don't ya? You know where she is. You know. You know."

Bobby went on, murmuring to himself more than to Eddie. "How is that, Eddie-boy? How can you know these things?" Bobby raised his gun at Eddie, his finger on the trigger.

Eddie didn't speak. He was trying to look into Bobby's head, catch a glimpse, but his extra-sensory faculties were failing him. When he was under pressure and wanted to read someone, it seemed to be that way; like when he tried to read Lexi.

Lexi. She's in the trunk.

"I don't know."

Bobby released his white-knuckle grip on the pistol and lowered it. "Do you know where my Mom is? Do you know?"

"I... I don't."

"I want to see her. I want to see my mom. I want to. Or talk to her. I know you won't do the bets, but I want to see my mom. Or I'll talk to her. I can just talk to her."

It was that time of dusk where you could just barely see a person in the sunless outdoors, but if you had a little light with you, you could see better. If that light was too bright, it would blind you to your surroundings. Eddie dimmed the lantern and set it on the ground so he could better see Bobby.

A crack in the foundation. A little sliver of light cut through the dark. And then, a flood. Eddie could see everything in Bobby's mind. He wasn't a gangster—he was barely a criminal. Bobby was just a spoiled, petulant rich kid, just someone with bad luck, bad moral luck, no guidance, whatever else you want to call it—a combination of fateful misfortune and trained misbehavior. And his mother had been dead for years.

"Can I talk to her? Please?" Bobby's eyes were damp. He clumsily aimed the gun back at Eddie.

Eddie gently raised his hands level with his shoulders, palms facing the gun-toting thug. "Bobby... I... I can try. I've just never tried to talk to... people who have passed on."

"But, do you think maybe you can?"

Eddie nodded. He had promised himself that he wouldn't be doing any more favors for Bobby Rizzo Jr., but he had to go along with this if he wanted to survive long enough to make sure Lexi would be okay. Eddie reasoned that this was more a favor for himself and Lexi than it was for Bobby.

For all he knew, he could be a medium. Maybe. Maybe given time and effort. The first time he'd heard someone else's thoughts, it didn't come through loud and relentless like it did now; it came like a murmur, like whispering through a thin wall. Maybe he could.

"I think it's possible. I can try, Bobby. But maybe we just... maybe right now it's better to let Lexi out. Is she okay?"

Bobby's lip quivered. With a pained face, he lowered the gun and put his hands on his knees. Bobby took some shallow breaths before rapidly rising back up and pointing the gun at Eddie again. Now everything in Bobby's mind was coming at Eddie like a flood.

...*bleeding*...

...*she'll be okay*...

...*can get to the hospital*...

Rage filled Eddie. He would never forgive Bobby for what he'd done to Lexi. The thoughts he'd had about her.

But at that moment, Eddie had an advantage. A slight, tiny, nearly nonexistent strand of compassion. More than that, he still maintained a modicum of self-preservation. Most importantly, he needed to help Lexi. Bobby had hurt her. He'd hurt her bad.

Eddie picked up his lantern, for a brief moment, and looked at the man opposite him. Really looked at him for the second time in so few seconds, and he saw something else.

Bobby was cracking.

Eddie jumped on the chance to talk him down. "Bobby."

"Yeah?"

"I know you didn't want to hurt her, Bobby. And you're right. We can get her to the hospital. We can all go together. I won't say anything, and I can talk to Lexi. I know you didn't want to hurt her. But you have to let her out, Bobby. Please put the gun down. Okay?"

Bobby still had the gun on Eddie, but his outstretched arm was visibly shaking. Tears rolled down his cheeks. "Do you really think...?"

"I can try, Bobby. I promise I will try as hard as I can. If I can help you talk to your mom, I swear to you, Bobby, I *swear*, that I will get through to her. Please put the gun down Bobby."

"Are you mad at me?" Bobby's face looked like a small animal's. Contrition wouldn't be giving its due—it was the most pathetic face a living thing could make.

"No. No, I'm not mad, Bobby. I'm not. But it's important that we get Lexi out, okay? We should get her to a hospital. Okay?"

Bobby de-cocked the hammer on his pistol and lowered it to his side.

...make mistakes...

...the back road, that's faster...

...not a bad guy...

"Okay, Bobby. I'm gonna try it. Okay?"

Bobby nodded. He inhaled a globule of snot as the tears returned. "Okay, Eddie. Thanks, man." A few seconds passed before Bobby spoke again. "Can ya hear her, Eddie? She sounds—"

"Like an angel," Eddie said. Trying. Trying to play along. He could do this. He had to do this. He was a performer. Eddie extended his arms to his sides about halfway, and curled his fingers gently, looking his best to appear as if he could channel spirits.

Bobby's eyes widened. He smiled. "Really? Yeah. That's her. Angelic. Always had that angelic voice."

Eddie nodded. He didn't know shit about Bobby's mother, but Bobby knew about her, and Eddie was grateful for his second sight then. "With the accent, it's even more beautiful. She's speaking English. She says..." he paused and rolled his eyes toward the sky, hoping that his pupils were not visible. "She says: 'You're a good man, Junior. Not like your father. He liked the ladies too much, hurt Mama too much with that. Mama never taught you that, did she?'" Eddie rolled his eyes back to Bobby, who had one of his hands over his heart.

"Yeah. That's Mama. She always said that shit. Mama, you were right!" he yelled the last part as the tears returned. "You were right. I got a choice. Do you still love me even after what I did to the girl? I won't do nothin' like that again. Mama. I promise."

Eddie suppressed the urge to shrug. "She says she loves her baby more than anything. She'll forgive you if you let the girl out of the trunk."

Bobby's internal thoughts trampled Eddie's mind. There were so many emotions, and the intensity of them was almost too much for Eddie to handle. The gist of it all was that Bobby didn't want to be who he was. He felt like he *had* to be who he was. Eddie understood that. Eddie understood that real good.

"Okay, Mama. I will. I'll do that. I'll let that lady out the trunk. She don't deserve what I did. I'm real sorry." Bobby looked at Eddie while he spoke, but his eyes changed when he addressed Eddie. "I'm real, real sorry, Eddie. I shouldn't've treated Lexi like that. I'm sorry. Can you forgive me, Eddie?"

Eddie clutched the lantern tighter in his grip. Pain. Eddie was used to pain. This was different. It was a shared pain. He would never forget what that man had done to Lexi. But... "Yeah, Bobby. I forgive you."

Bobby nodded and reached into his pocket. The jingle of the keys was music to Eddie's ears.

Then Eddie heard a voice coming from behind him. A surge of raging thoughts, and it was growing louder, a quick violence of spiked volume intruding from the anterior. He heard another sound, a muffled screech, crunching rocks and branches, something rotating in place and tearing, an engine. He saw Bobby's eyes go wide, saw Bobby raise his pistol and aim.

"You motherfucker!" Bobby screamed. His hand was steady now. So steady, as he pointed the gun at Eddie, then at the car, then back at Eddie.

Eddie saw a yellow glare reflect off the chrome of Bobby's gaudy gun. Eddie whipped around just in time to see a car coming at him with a deranged looking woman behind the wheel. He jumped out of the way just in time. He heard the loud pop of a gunshot.

Eddie heard Bobby's panic—not words, but echoes from blood and neurotransmitters bundling and snapping apart—but Bobby didn't have time to yell out beyond his own thoughts. Eddie saw him fly up onto the hood of the car, slamming into the windshield and making a bowed crater of microscopic cracks across it. The car kept going, going, and Eddie could hear the woman's toxicity leaking venom, a hot and painful noise that started a burning behind his eyes; so potent was her hatred. For *him*. She was trying to kill *him*. Instead, Bobby went over the car like a catapult and slammed hard on the compacted dirt. As he slammed to the ground, a spurt of blood shot up like a fountain from his mouth.

The car kept going forward. Eddie tried to move toward it, not thinking, not knowing what he might do. The car was barreling toward Bobby's Deville. Eddie tried to do something—to move the car, to make it burn—but he was manacled by the severity of the circumstance, impotent, unable to—

The car slammed into the Deville hard. The airbags went off inside the deranged woman's car, the horn stuck and continued blaring. Eddie ran toward the Deville, sprinting to the trunk. For only a moment he slowed, peeking into the driver's side to see the woman's limp form draped over the steering wheel. Blood was coming from her nose and her mouth.

He got to the trunk and tried to open it. At first, he started looking for the switch, or button, or whatever there was. Already revved up to a panic, Eddie moved maniacally, fumbling his fingertips, despairing of what could become of Lexi if he was too late. All of that for nothing.

Everything smelled toxic: gasoline, burnt rubber, coolant, oil, and every other compound that the land yacht had hidden beneath its metal shell and skeleton. Eddie yanked the trunk upward, attempting to break the lock. He could hear a groaning and a confused cry—from Bobby. Jagged thoughts. *He's still alive.* Just then, the gasoline smell became more potent.

Eddie looked up and saw a small fire coming out of the Deville.

Shit. Shit, shit, shit.

He sprinted to the woman's car and tried to open the driver's side door but jumped back when he felt that it was already too hot.

Shit, shit, shit, shit, shit.

He put the lantern down and slammed his elbow into the side window, but it only made a crack and bloodied his arm. He tried again, much harder and with purpose, with directed intent toward the glass target. Eddie's arm went straight through, smashing through the middle of the window, but scraping and cutting open the top half of his forearm and the bottom half of his upper arm. He reached inside, put his arms under the armpits of the driver and pulled her out, heaving and pressing back with his legs. The fire was growing. Any second, the Deville would explode and take the attacker's car with it in the inferno to come. Eddie pulled the woman by her legs, dragging her as quickly as possible to the edge of the river and set her beside the water. He sprinted back once again to the trunk of the Deville and started pounding on it.

"Lexi! Lexi, can you hear me? Lexi? If you can hear me, I need you to look around for a switch or something to open the trunk from inside. *Lexi!*"

But it was no use. Surely, she was still unconscious. He dug his fingers into the grip above the license plate and pulled as hard as he could. Eddie strained and strained, his neck heating and tight, his fingers feeling like the bones were about to pierce the skin. But nothing happened. He stepped back for a moment and tried to concentrate. He searched his mind for that strange voice—the voice that came to him, sometimes in meter, but always louder when his powers would grow.

Come on, come on, come on.

Eddie's eyes started to water. He felt weak, drained, stripped down to nothing, barren of soul and weak in body. It was all too much. Everything was too much, and this was just one more heaping helping of shit dumped all over him.

Come on, come on, come on.

He pleaded. With himself? With God? With…? Something happened. He felt a sharp pain slicing through him. He felt his stomach clench, his brain frying inside of his head. Once more he gripped the trunk and yanked with animalistic ferocity, yelling into the heavens as he did so.

The trunk cracked open. Lexi was inside. There was a huge gash on her head, and she had two black eyes. She was curled up in the fetal position, wearing only her underwear and lingerie, which was spotted with crimson stains. Her hair was matted with drying red-brown clumps. She was bound at her ankles and wrists with duct tape, an industrial-silver color placed in an adhesive rectangle over her mouth, too. Eddie picked Lexi up underneath her thighs and where her neck met her upper back. The fire was growing higher. He ran with Lexi cradled in his arms, bolting to the river and laying her down near—but not right next to—the other woman.

Eddie got to his feet to go back for Bobby when he felt something hard and cold hit the back of his skull. It hit him so hard that a punchy blast of black and of white dotted stars flashed in his sight. He fell forward onto his face, slamming mouth-first into the ground and lost two teeth in the impact.

As he rolled over, his back now flat against the ground, he saw Bobby standing over him, bloodied and shredded up, holding his pistol. Bobby's other arm was compound-fractured so badly that two sharp halves of his radius and ulna were protruding from his broken skin. Bobby spoke in a frightening, measured cadence.

"You tryin' to play me, Eddie-boy? Bringin' that bitch along with you? You tryin' to play me?"

Eddie was about to say something when the shock of being pistol-whipped stopped him cold. Bobby hit him—once, twice, three times. It seemed to go on and on until Eddie couldn't move, until the pain of each new blow to his face numbed him, a blanket of shock wrapping his body. There was red in his vision.

"You fuckin' piece of shit asshole motherfucker. You didn't talk to Mama at all, you lyin' sack of fuckin' shit. You was just tryin' to stall, huh? Stall until your bitch comes ridin' in to save the day, Eddie-boy. Well *FUCK YOU!*"

Eddie coughed blood and spit out another tooth. "No. No, Bobby. You don't understand. That's not what hap—"

Bobby threw his pistol aside and grabbed Eddie by his belt. Bobby dragged him, pulling as hard as he could, breathing as hard as he could, sweat and blood soaking Bobby's skin. Eddie clawed at the ground, looking for something to anchor himself to, his vision blurry and dim. He desperately groped in the dark, clinging to the earth. Finally, his fingers found something. Metal. Light. The lantern.

Bobby dragged Eddie into the river. Eddie's body was buoyant now. Bobby held Eddie's face down into the water.

At first, Eddie's body shook, writhing in protest. He tried to throw a punch, tried to buck his head backward, tried, tried, tried. He managed to swing the lantern backwards with enough force to connect. A loud crunch came from the effort—it was the harmonizing of broken glass and a broken nose. Dark blood swirled in the darker water. The maneuver didn't stall Bobby long enough for Eddie to surface.

Bobby curled his hand into a fist and hammered the back of Eddie's head until he stopped resisting. After a short while, there was no more protest. Bobby let go and let the current take Eddie's body away.

Clara waited, watching out of the corner of her eye as the good-looking kid dragged Eddie Marivicos out to the water and drowned him. It took her a moment, but she recognized that this kid was the gangster Bobby Rizzo's son. It had taken Clara great effort, but she was able to bolt upward despite her awful pain. Even willing herself forward with everything she had, her body still moved slowly due to her injuries. But soon enough, she'd grabbed the pistol that the Rizzo Jr. kid had dropped.

She stood at the edge of the river and waited for him to finish drowning Marivicos's son. She had wanted to do the deed herself but watching him die would have to do for now. Once Eddie's body was carried away by the current, Rizzo Jr. turned around, only to find that Clara was standing right in front of him on dry land, pointing his own gun at his face. She pulled the trigger. A bullet ripped through his forehead and exploded out the back of his skull in a pink mist. He still stood for a moment, before falling backward into the water. The current carried away a second corpse.

Bobby Rizzo Jr. would no longer trouble Lexi. Or anybody else.

INTERLUDE

The bottom. The very bottom of the lightless river where the black water wavered. But wasn't he...?

Yes, he was dead.

Eddie distinctly recalled being bashed and submerged into the currents, held down until he was unconscious, and then drowned. And while that happened, he was still a transmitter. Loud as ever. Louder, even. The sound of others, the burden of thought, wages of deceit, the genetic cryptology long hidden and locked away from the world. He saw/heard such arcane secrets from the multiple selves whose strands of consciousness wove themselves outside their minds and into Eddie's. He heard them. Even in the darkness, those riddling strands wrapped about him, those sounds. There were no secrets from him; no cipher obscure enough; nothing so obscure that it couldn't weave itself through him. To know all... what a loathsome inevitability.

He could neither breathe, nor would he die (in the traditional sense). Instead, he kept sinking. Deeper, and deeper, and deeper still. Something lent to the disembodied observation-state that Eddie found himself dispassionately occupying. He was watching a movie, listening to a song, seeing workaday folks hustle and bustle. All things like that, just like that. Just watching, not doing. Just sinking, deeper and deeper, the strands neither dragging him down nor pulling him up. Just existing. Being. Watching. All there ever was, all there ever would be. In the river. At the bottom. That was all. All there ever was, all there ever would be.

Then, a light. A bright light. The brightest light ever? Blue but white; white but blue. Blue or white, thick, packed-in bodies of blue and white and white and blue. Thick glow around the edges and in the crevices. Brighter. *Brighter*. A glowing glacier. A radiating opalescence of cerulean sympathy. *Come, Eddie, come down.*

The blue jewel that was ice and stone and diamonds and everything else—it hummed. A deep, deep pulse. Eddie floated down, drawing closer. The pulse quickened, sending a pleasant vibration through the water and through Eddie's body. And that felt very nice; it quieted the other sounds, unwove the strands of secrets that so burdened him. It was good. Peaceful.

Small beads of bright white orbs crackled electrically in the water, and, along with a sound like microwave popcorn swirled around him. Eddie wanted to reach out and touch the orbs, but he was dead. Or not dead, but not alive. He wanted to touch the orbs but couldn't. That was okay.

His precarious clutch upon reality receded into a delicate and letting grasp. The shapes began to blend as the riverbed fluctuated, its color becoming something else, its lightless bottom a grand illumination. The beaded orbs hastened and surrounded Eddie in orbits upon orbits—minuscule and complex highways where light raced upon luminous lanes. The blue of the river turned obsidian, then navy-purple, then navy-black. All at once, in a snap.

A tunnel formed around him. The sides were liquid, ridges with peeking miniature waves and a glistening blue-green glow. But the vacuum Eddie occupied was a non-solid state, too, and he found himself incorporeal; a consciousness only, a body no more. The tunnel whipped around him in a thousand different cyclones, and he was aware of an immense, paralyzing pain, but he could not feel it. He could only know it existed. A completely black portal appeared, opened, and he was pushed through, or rather his soul was pushed through, as he was no longer made of flesh and bone. Now Eddie was out in the furthest reaches of the vast, imponderable infinity of stellar being, beyond the firmament and galactic filaments, beyond the speckled star systems and solar devastations.

He tried to move his hand and a great sweep of blue stars cut across an imponderable nothing-space. He blinked and his eyes were red suns, every flutter of the eyelids causing explosions that, should they have been even within a world's distance of anything else, would have caused an apocalyptic-infernal destruction. He moved his legs, and they were continent-sized points of starlight, billions of them, combined into unbelievably bright strands of cosmic sinew. He was a great titan, a supermassive body of light, his limbs made of planets and stars, his consciousness reaching across dimensions, his entire corpus composed of lights so bright and beautiful and rare that the very sight of him would have struck any regular man dead. Maybe that's why he was so far out. Wherever he was, perhaps at the edge of the known universe, or maybe the edge of the *un*known universe?

"Eddie." A voice. Not a voice, though. Sounds he'd never heard, carrying information to his soul, imprinting, communication that reached from without to within. Harmonies spoken in some celestial tongue. A thousand symphonies of light and sound wired his soul and the seat of thought to some other *thing*. Some sympathetic other. Maybe a thing like him? It called to him? No. *For* him. He could hear, feel, smell, taste it. He could detect it in so many senses, a number of them were nameless.

"Yes?" he answered.

"Oh. Oh! It's *you!*" the voice answered. "It's you! I can't believe it. I'm so happy you're here." It was compassion and love and a familial longing finally ended. He felt all of it and it so overwhelmed Eddie, because Eddie had rarely felt such things. He had to travel outside the known world to feel worldly feelings.

"Who are you?" he asked. *Even though he already knew. He needed the words.*

"I'm your mother."

"But, we aren't people."

"Not right now. Not at this moment. But we *can* be. Well, you *are*. Most of the time. It must all be terribly confusing for you."

"Yeah. It is."

"Well, you can ask me whatever you want. We have all the Time."

"You mean all the time in the world?" he asked. The answer to this, too, he already knew. He already knew all there was to know. But he still didn't have the words. Every question he asked, he asked it so that he would have the words. Something to keep that he could understand if he were human again.

"No, Eddie. We have *all the Time*. We can be in time, or out of time. We can be in many different worlds, each of our eyes, the eyes outside ourselves, they watch the time float by in a thou-sand-million different worlds, each hand of ours reaches and turns the dial to slow or speed the tick-tick-tock of the time-hand. Or we can sit here and be us, just now, speaking, letting time slow or time stop."

"I don't understand anything you're saying."

"Here, let's try this."

A flash. A millisecond of unfelt change. Transformation. Eddie was standing in the barren sweep of space, and a woman stood maybe five yards away from him in the starry blackness. There was no clear up or down, left or right, but as the woman's bare feet elongated and strode, her strides met translucent ripples in the air. Rippling puddles, almost. They were standing before one another. As people, almost. And she was beautiful.

"Is this better?" she asked.

Eddie looked around. A star blazed, ripping across the fount of genesis, though he didn't understand that. "Are we in outer space?"

The woman laughed good-naturedly. It was a healthy laugh; friendly. Eddie liked it. "Yes, and no. That's one of the harder questions."

Eddie took a deep breath, but nothing came in. But neither did he feel as though he required air. Not that there was any oxygen to be had. "Can we breathe out here?"

"Ah, that's a tough one, too."

"I thought you said I could ask whatever I wanted."

She smiled. "Well, I had hoped you would want to start with questions about me as your mother."

"That's fair, I guess. How can I know you're my mother?" He knew. He needed the words.

"I know everything you've ever done."

"Well, maybe that just means that you're like me. You got second sight."

"How many other persons, young man, have you met who *have* second sight?"

Eddie thought on that. "Good point." But he wasn't satisfied quite yet. "But, you seem very…"

"Nice?" she asked.

"Yeah. And…"

"Your father isn't?"

Eddie nodded.

"Well, he was a very different man when I met him. *Very* different. And maybe it is partly my fault for the way he turned out."

"How do you mean?"

"It's a very long story," she answered.

"I thought you said we have as much time as we needed. Or that there *is* no time here."

She smiled. "Clever boy. Very clever boy. Fair enough. Story time, then."

"It is very rare for one of our kind to leave the spaces-in-between. You see, Eddie, my son, we aren't really ever out beyond the stars, or down below the water—not just there, only. We are in both places, in many places. The human mind, it seems, brooks no reaching hand beyond its bounded borders. And so, I am left to tell you of very great things using very paltry meanings. But that's what it is and where we are, I suppose.

"Where was I? Oh, yes. The spaces-in-between.

"You see, Eddie, once in a great-long-while a child is born on Earth and born with a link to the spaces-in-between. Those who possess the latent ability to *see* the interstices of existence that are unseeable to your people; unseeable to humans, I mean to say. The sight itself is a transfiguration, such an elevation that its subject either becomes insane, or in most instances, must be chosen from amongst the insane, because only the insane can tolerate the far-reaching, reality-smashing implications of what they see once transfigured.

"Tracing back up and in reverse on the family line, we come to a branch of the family tree that is weathered, worn, and so far as mental competence goes, broken and torn. Schizophrenics, sterilized victims of eugenics.

"Here is your great-great-great-great-grandfather. The bedraggled Transylvanian forester in rags. Yes, you see him? Good, good, good. Now watch closely. He is raising his axe. He has done this, if not a hundred-thousand times, at least dozens of thousands of times. Now, you'll notice that your great-great-great-great-grandfather, on the downward chop, hesitates.

"The axe-head shimmers very briefly. It wavers, its steel disappearing and reappearing in the air for the briefest of moments. Now, you'll notice the frenzied circuits of his neurotransmitters, freezing and fired in different places. We'll zoom in here. See the bits of electric light disappearing and reappearing? That is your great-great-great-great-grandfather's mind disappearing and reappearing out here and back in Transylvania. That is your great-great-great-great-grandfather being born in our world—born as a speck here in the desert reaches of the cosmos—while remaining animated and alive in the Forests Roma. Soon, in Time, he will become completely insane. That is the first time your great-great-great-great-grandfather managed to contact our kind.

"Now, let us pull back a little further in Time. This place, on your earth, is called Spain, or called Andalusia. You may have heard of it. This particular municipality—or, in the Time in which we are seeing it, vicinage—is home to two brothers. One is the Monzram. The other is the Ilzram. You'll see that in both of their homes, there are reams of manuscripts, shelves bulging out precariously from the rock-walls of their secreted hovel-homes. The Ilzram, younger and more ill-tempered (and unwise) of the two, has been gathering gleanings of darkness from the great multitude of the insane who have peered into our world. The Monzram is engaging in a similar venture, but with greater caution, humility, and circumspection.

"The Ilzram knows he is not a conduit and will never see as we titans in the stars and outside Time see—he will never intimately know the spaces-in-between. So, he enlists a vast array of charlatans, weeding them out, combing through until he can find the small few who will carry out his mission. The Ilzram hopes, against all hope, one of his enlisted charlatans, to whom he has vouchsafed the secrets of his accumulated knowledge, will carry his tome of darkness to one who can see the spaces-in-between.

"A short time later, a disciple of the Ilzram finds one of the descendants of your great-great-great-great-grandfather and makes him an offer. The Disciple offers the Descendent guidance in exchange for a promise. The Descendent must promise the Disciple that if ever one of the Descendant's line should be able to reach the spaces-in-between, said descendent of the Descendent will be trained to use the cumulative knowledge of the Ilzram.

"Your father was the most recent of this generation of trainees, the beneficiary of both the heritable abilities of the Descendent and the trained scriptural knowledge of the Disciple. When your father, or, "Papa" as you call him, was bequeathed the family book, *The Book of Deeds of the Marvelous Marivicoses*, he tried to make contact anyone or anything from our side.

"Eddie, there are dark forces, beings, entities, residing in the spaces-in-between that wish harm on our species. They will attempt to influence those who are touched by this realm. Your father may be under the persuasion of one such being. This is an unfortunate byproduct of the Ilzram passing down vestigial fragments of arcane knowledge in an imperfect physical manifestation, such as that book. The aforementioned entities can infiltrate and corrupt an individual, and that individual will pass down this corruption through generations by the scripture. Be wary of your father's intentions.

"I am, my dear sweet Eddie, unusual amongst the star-limbed gargantuans who heedlessly rip titan strides through the heavens and every unknown kind of world. You see, I like to step through the door, come down to visit every once in a while. There is no experience quite so visceral as being a human. And it was on one of these particular occasions that I met your father. Back then, I believe he was calling himself Peter or something-other—and we... copulated.

"And that, Eddie, is where babies (like you) come from."

Eddie nodded. "Wow. That's... wow."

"I know," Eddie's mother said, "it is really a crazy story."

"Why didn't you stay with him?"

"Ah," she answered, "the inevitable query of the abandoned child. I couldn't stay, Eddie. And part of the reason your father is the way he is... is that he was offered an opportunity to leave. To leave Earth that is, but he didn't. Beyond all that, the most important thing that I am going to tell you is this: *you can't stay either.*"

"What do you mean?" Eddie was stunned.

"I mean... your body. The one you were born into, is dead. This moment right now is when you say goodbye to the world before and join us; join your mother and your kind, I mean."

"But what about my friends? And Lexi?"

"You'll make new friends. And Lexi is... Lexi will be fine, Eddie," she answered sharply.

"And if I don't stay here?"

His mother frowned. "Hmm... I see. This is the problem with *people*. Obstinacy. You all can't help but look a gift horse in the mouth."

"I'm just asking."

"And I'm just answering, son. Why do you think Papa is the way he is? Why do you think he rots... on the outside... on the inside? Why? Because once we open the door, and once you see beyond your previous perceptual limitations, the world of man starts to eat at you. Eventually, it will imprison you."

The two of them fluctuated between a likeness of humanity and a thousand-fold luminescent states of indescribable existence. They dipped in and out of Time and did so without Eddie noticing. Eddie didn't know how long he had been here, but he was certain enough that they hadn't been speaking in any human language; and, he knew that whatever limits Time imposed, he had learned to manipulate his powers out in this grand sweep of infinite space and incomprehensible measures. He flickered back into personhood—he held his (once again broken) lantern that he had carried with him into the water.

"Oh," his mother said, "I see... you brought something with you. Well, that complicates things."

She reached out with her ephemeral hand. It shimmered, glowed, and flowed with the space. It was almost as though her movements influenced Time. He could see and feel it, but Eddie didn't have the words. She tapped the lantern with a gentle *tip-tap*, a strange and simple rhythm, but even that was incomprehensibly beautiful. The sound was perfectly timed with the effect her touch had on the lantern. The cracked and chipped parts of it receded until the piece was whole again. The flame grew and pulsed, until the light of it encompassed Eddie, and through that light, he could view his world—all worlds—as motes of dust. Warmth spread through him. He was so overwhelmed, so enveloped in the light, he felt the tears that were not build behind his eyes, which were everything.

"How does it complicate things? What do you mean?" he asked. He understood her actions as a means of comfort, but perhaps also as a warning.

She breathed deeply—something that almost made Eddie laugh, knowing that neither of them *needed* to breathe.

"I should have considered that thing you brought along. But I didn't. Which leaves us—really *you*—with a limited number of options. The first option is you stay here with the lantern, but risk spontaneous destruction at some point because you've brought something from the other world with you. That is speculative, though. We've never tested out the long-term retention of an inanimate human object out here."

"Ah."

"The next option is for you to briefly return to the river to deposit the lantern, and then return here to be with us. That is *by far* the preferable option."

"I see. And…?"

"And what?"

"And what if I *just* go back?"

Eddie's mother frowned. She looked desperate. She spoke to him pleadingly, "Eddie…"

"Just tell me."

She sighed. "*If* you go back, and *if* you stay back there… you will become something like your father. But in all likeliness, you will become much worse."

Eddie looked gravely to the titanic star cluster that was his mother, and listened.

"You will be tethered to the object you brought with you and you will be tethered to the place from which you transported yourself here. You will become a part of the lantern and part of the river. I don't know what will happen to the lantern, or what will happen because of it, but I know what will happen to you because you went back through that river.

"Slowly, everything that is human about you will die away. The rotting is not always the same for everyone. You've seen it in your father. Your skin might rot. Your eyes might be burnt from your skull. Your memories will leave you as the power you've learned here replaces your human anatomy. You could become a light spectacle, a human firework. In the end, the people that you stayed behind and suffered for will be unrecognizable to you. You will lose your memory, as memory is a specific faculty of humanity; at least memory as *you* know it is.

"Closely before or after you've gone insane, you will probably hurt or kill someone close to you, or someone innocent. Worst of all, you will have to watch all this passively, a prisoner in your own body... at times. You won't know when you've destroyed someone or when you *are* someone, until the moment you realize what has happened. Then you'll live for nothing but your next moment of clarity, which will flood you with feelings of loss and regret."

"Oh."

"Papa was given the same choice. But he's stayed on earth by the half-titan power that rots inside him, worsened by his obsession with his bloody black book."

Eddie was silent.

"And I can see you're going to make the same choice. You'll do the same thing your father did. You'll go back there to rot."

"How do you know?"

"Excuse me?"

"How do you know I'll rot?"

"It's just a thing that's known."

"But I'm different from my father. And he never brought something outside the world." Eddie gripped the lantern. Held it close. The action felt human. Not something an evil, rotting, cosmic titan could do. He hoped he was different. He hoped he was nothing like his father, and that hope drove his choice. He looked at his mother. "I *am* different from Papa," he insisted.

"Yes."

Eddie thought for a minute. "I'm going back."

"Well, that's okay. One way or another, we will be together."

"We will?"

"Yes. Eventually. All of us—we meet again."

"How do you know?"

"It happens every couple of million person-years."

"You've seen it happen?"

"Oh, yes. A few times now."

"Can I ask a few more things?"

"You can ask me whatever you want," she answered.

"What are... what are we? I mean, what are you? Am I like you?"

"Some of us are watchers; giants who sweep away worlds in the name of an angry god. Some of us are like the leviathan lore; great behemoths, beasts beyond size, the size of stars. Some Talmudists said we are *gedolim*—the same word used both to describe the leviathan and the stars in the sky."

"I'm one of those?"

"Something in between. A hybrid, perhaps. It is the reason I want so desperately for you to stay. Given enough time, I could make sure that you would have all of our... all of my... faculties."

"But I don't want that. It's too much. Maybe it would make me insane," he said before pausing to think once more. "I have to go back. For Lexi. I *have* to. To make sure she is okay. And then maybe I can come back to you."

"It won't work that way. The longer you remain in Kayjigville after your transfiguration, the stronger the changes will be, until you are not human at all. The transformation will be very rapid when you return. You must be careful. Eventually, your actions will reverberate, even out here. Your ability to communicate with humans will change drastically, at the same time as your channel to communicate with *us* opens wider and wider. Your actions in your temporal world, depending on their extremity, will ripple up into our higher dimension. And if you cross another… hybrid like you, the consequences could be more severe. The portal back to us may close. You'll be locked in your point of embarkation—in that river. Maybe forever."

ACT III

I'm down twenty to the devil

Hell, I hope he'll take a check

I'll kiss his ass 'til I get level,

then I'll break his neck

— ROGER ALLEN WADE

CHAPTER 29

The lottery hubbub died down. Oddly, that ticket is still unclaimed. The window of time is closing for the winner to collect their prize, and it's quite the aberration that no one has done so. There's some rumor that the state board that oversees the lotto is going to do something about the lost/unclaimed number, but that seems unlikely. Probably they'll just dump the money back into the pool and have another Powerball sort of thing in the near future.

The Carnival took a big hit. That Guadali lady started the *Commodora* line with Old Money Ferriman's backing, and it's taken off like gangbusters. I asked Stacy if she wanted to go, but she hasn't really wanted to leave the house since that night at The Pony. Speaking of which, Bobby Rizzo Jr. went missing down by the river. Probably carried out to the ocean by now. I don't really keep up with organized crime or the various entanglements the feuding families get caught up in. All I know is that the river carries corpses out to the sea fast enough that unsolved murders stay unsolved.

I once treated a cop who said that he and the other gumshoes didn't really consider those murders unsolved anyhow, since everyone *knew* that criminals killed other criminals. They didn't devote a whole lot of manpower to those types of killings; nobody would ever talk, and they thought of it as one less mobster-wannabe working the streets. *And if the devil is in the details, let that red-tailed bastard stay there along with the skeletons of those fuckin' hoodlums. Street-cleanin' is what we called it in my time. Nothin' from nothin' leaves nothin'.*

I had to admit, he had a point there.

Who knows? Like I said, I don't know shit about Rizzo's business, but I know enough to know that when people go missing, it's not because there's a secret flu pandemic.

Lexi, of all people, has come by pretty often, though. She quit working at Madam Regina's and started at a poker table at The Pony. Maybe she quit because of the baby bump. Being pregnant in a brothel is an unseemly set of circumstances, and not an economically favorable state of affairs for any of the parties involved. Anyway, I think she just wants someone to talk to who also knew Eddie.

She's never said the child is Eddie's, and I suppose she really has no way of knowing since she was working at the brothel at the time. But it's the things a person doesn't hear—or the things they think they hear—that matter just as much as what's spoken out loud. From far away, I could see her rubbing her belly and smiling, talking to herself. I could see her running her hands along the convertible she and Abi used to drive Eddie around in, like there was a remnant of the boy left in the drop top.

Lexi comes by most days before going to her shift at The Pony. They don't talk, but Stacy makes cupcakes for her. She hasn't told us how far along she is, but I'd say she's about twelve to fifteen weeks along (although I admit it's been years since I was in gynecology during rotations). Lexi had to buy her uniform herself, and even though being a cardsharp at The Pony offers more prestige and access than whoring, the hourly rate is a mite lower. So, Stacy, Abi, and I pitched in to get her a series of larger black vests and white French-cuffed ladies' shirts. Lexi protested, but Abi pushed back on her enough that she relented. That's what people who've suffered loss do. They relent.

That's another thing. Abakoum has been a bit off lately. For a few weeks, he hardly spoke, or joked with his typical but derogatory good-natured humor. He would force a few chuckles here and there, but for the most part, he was a mite glum. An apparition of Abakoum. But he enlivened a bit when in the orbit of Regina. I don't know what's happened to him. I would assume some sort of trauma—perhaps triggered by the sudden disappearance of his good friend. But Abakoum is not my patient and he's never asked to be, so I'll stop there with my musings about his mental state. Anyway, he's a bit improved now. Still not the same, but Lexi and Madam Regina seem to get him to perk up a bit, and he does the same for Lexi.

Lately, Lexi has taken to showing up in the early morning, long after her shift is over. Stacy hovers in the kitchen, sleepless and unawake, floating around, a silk-robed specter shuffling through her maze of domesticity. She sees Lexi sitting on the Adirondack chair out on the deck and brings her a cup of tea, and when Lexi finally falls asleep in the chair, Stacy brings out a comforter and throws it over her, and I move the patio umbrella over Lexi so the sun won't wake her in the small hours of the dawn.

They never speak to one another.

Still, I think that we're doing what we can to make it easier for Lexi. And I think it's probably what Eddie would have wanted. Wherever he is.

CHAPTER 30

Papa sat, his mind soaked in anger, hate, and venom. Made crazed and wild by poorer chance, he wallowed in his hatred. A sickly skin now covered the thin, emaciated man as he sat, alone, weighed down by the anchor of memory.

The world was—especially for Papa Marivicos—a very dark place. Especially tainted by the loss of his son. Not because he loved his son. He loved the money. His cash cow had tipped.

Papa's memories were populated with the tracings of his ancestors. He possessed, it seemed, *all* of the memories of his ancestors. It was those memories that Papa Marivicos now searched to obtain some sort of inspiration in this desperate eleventh hour.

Guadali's machinations had sent him halfway to hell. The call of the Uumen bogged Papa down. He obsessed over the control he could exert over the marionettes he manipulated and enslaved through its magic. He was caught in a vicious cycle; the more he obsessed over the book, the less he knew of what was going on with the Carnival or the outside world. For example, Papa hadn't cared to know what the Carnival's principal act was since the disappearance of his son. He didn't even know if the Carnival was in the red or in the black. Ironically, his obsession left him hiding away, exerting even less control over the outside world; allowing Clara to take that slice of the Kayjigville pie Papa had been so protective of.

He'd hoped to wreak some revengeful ill fortune upon the small-minded rubes who'd crossed him. But his uses of the Uumen were still unpredictable, and his body grew weaker, and his blood ran drier, and his bones felt brittler. The Marivicos conjure became weaker. With his impotencies came new obsessions, ways of modifying and calibrating the control he could exert through the book. Papa hardly slept. He hardly ate. He drank mightily.

Three knocks on the door.

Papa ignored it. Then, a stronger knock, followed by a sliver of light cutting white and unbearably bright through an opening door. He nearly hissed as he whipped around, but calmed when he saw Marv and Andy at the entrance of his trailer.

Marv was the one who spoke. "Sir, do you have a moment?"

Papa turned to them, one spindly and sick-looking limb draped over the back of his chair. "Anythin' for my boys."

Marv handed an opened envelope to Papa. "This was brought by private courier just a little while ago. It's about Eddie and Bobby Rizzo Jr."

"That mess again… finally the boy's gone and all I hear 'bout is someone else's worthless rat-faced shit-bag of a cum-stain. Will the world ever stop punishin' me and any other seeder with a dick?"

"It—it seems serious, sir."

Papa grunted and snatched the envelope from Marv's hand. "You opened this?"

Andy, who rarely spoke, answered. "Yes, sir, we did."

"And…?"

This time, it was Marv who replied. "Well, it seems that Rizzo Sr. thinks you have something to do with the disappearance of his son. That's not in the letter, but Andy and I did some quick legwork. We found that there had been some sort of extortion scheme that Junior planned to carry out against Eddie. There were other people involved, it seems. Miss Guadali, for instance. Or, that's what we've heard, rumors being what they are."

Papa scanned the letter. "I see. And so Rizzo wants to parlay, I take it."

"He's as much a peacemaker as a kingmaker, it seems, sir. I doubt there's anything he has in mind other than clearly verbalizing a standing agreement so there's no… collateral damage, I guess," Marv replied.

"Yes, yes, yes. Collateral damage. Can't have any of that. Well, did the *courier* happen to mention when this little parlay is s'posed to happen?"

"He did. One week from receipt of this missive. Midnight."

"Good. Good. Then we still got plenty of time."

"For what?" Marv asked, looking as though he didn't want to know the answer.

The ends of Papa's lips curled up, stretching the too-thin and varicose-veiny skin of his face. "To get a little more even."

Clara Guadali was tooling along in her brand-new Benz, on her way to another meeting with Ferriman. She was just about all healed up—the broken nose, the scratches, the minor breaks. At first, after the row with Bobby Jr. and Eddie, Clara was scared that people would whisper and murmur when they saw her bruised face and body. But Clara played it off, as she always did with everything, and made up a bewildering and mildly entertaining story about a car crash involving a mattress delivery tractor-trailer and a varsity bus full of adoring football players. She had told the tall tale so often that it was interwoven with themes of irony, penitence, destiny, and of course, forgiveness.

So, on that front, all was good.

Clara had been quite nervous about Eddie's disappearance. When Lexi awoke from her pistol-grip induced unconsciousness, she saw Clara there and she... smiled. Well, why wouldn't she? After all, Lexi hadn't seen what had happened. Sure, it was *possible* the girl knew about Clara—in the abstract, maybe—but from the look of her then it seemed as though Lexi couldn't give two shits about Clara or what her angle was. That's not to say that Lexi wasn't very, very polite to Clara Guadali (she *was*); it's more so a commentary on the girl's carefree and near-wholly apolitical nature. Besides, there was no one to testify as to what happened that day other than Lexi. And it was Lexi who told the police that Bobby Jr. was a psycho and must have brought the three of them out to the river because he'd finally cracked from the pressure of being under his father's thumb. So, Clara wasn't even thought of as a person of interest, because there was no crime as far as the police were concerned, only self-defense and Clara being a good Samaritan who just so happened to be passing through the scene.

So, on that front, all was good, too.

Then, there was business. Clara had been terrified when Marivicos has made his threats and defiled her boat—but she pressed on. Sure, the experience had left her shaken, but she would not deterred from her... *aspirations.* From her business. And business was booming.

The *Commodora's* grand opening bash had been a hell of a shindig. Anyone who was anyone was there. The attendees weren't just from Kayjigville, but from all over the state. It had been a *very* classy affair. It was exactly the kind of classy, controlled chaos that got notice in newspapers but not over the police scanners. And Clara had greatly underestimated the appetite that people had for gambling out on the water. More than that, Ferriman—who, Clara had to admit, was *freakishly* smart—was both happy and helpful in their venture.

There was something about him, that man, something in

Ferriman that she was attracted to but couldn't *admit*. It wasn't quite his Anglo-Saxon detachment. No, not that. Although, it wouldn't be wrong to say that Ferriman kept his black-dog days to himself. But he would, once in a while, show glistening corners in his wrinkle-wreathed eyes, would laugh much louder, would occasionally even add a mild musical lilt to his voice, so that one couldn't say he was *so* buttoned-up when it came to feeling. He was considerate, too, which was rare enough for the average person, and even rarer among that breed of plutocrat-financiers who occupied the uppermost-uppermost of the world's super-elite. But Clara simply thought of Ferriman as a nice guy.

So, on that front, all was much more than good, too.

Clara pulled up to the gleaming arc-topped glass building and into the reserved parking spot she'd sprung extra for this week. The parking spot represented, to her, a sort of resurrection, the revivification of her fortunes. It was a symbolic victory—this modest painted rectangle framing her vehicle—but a victory, nonetheless. *Soon,* she thought, *I can divorce that cheating milque-toast faggot of a husband and see if Ferriman is game.* She could imagine being happy with him, doing business together, and occasionally going on decadent jaunts around the globe. Clara was very close to being *happy*.

A man dressed in gaudy sharkskin waited on the walkway of the parking lot. The man sported a gratuitous amount of gold and diamond hand jewelry. He was waiting for her, she knew. *Oh, well. No reason to fight the inevitable.*

He didn't even wait for her to get out of the car. "You Clara Guadali?"

"Yes."

She discreetly straightened her skirt as she stood then closed the car door behind her.

"Rizzo's got a message for ya."

Clara was stricken. She paled as her blood drained far, far down, and her body flashed into a frightening shade of paper-white. *This is it.* In less than a second, this hulking gindaloon would proffer a pistol, and she would accept its gun-powdered yield into her bosom, and forever sleep.

Instead, when the man reached his hand into his jacket, he pulled out a folded piece of paper which he waggled in front of her face, but she didn't take it. She was in a state of shock.

"Lady, I ain't got all day." Finally, she took the paper. As the man walked away and toward an old Continental with suicide doors, he called back to her.

"One week from today. Midnight. See you at The Pony, Clara."

The sharkskin goon got in his Lincoln and drove away. Clara stood, holding the paper, still partially paralyzed, trying to process precisely how thin the line between life and death really was, and how one might cross that line on any old morning.

One week.

CHAPTER 31

"Are you okay, Miss Lexi?"

Abi was driving her back home from a doctor's appointment. A sonogram. She didn't speak, only nodded to him. Then Abi pressed her again.

"You want I should take you to Doctor *Khayeen* instead of homes?"

Lexi thought about that a moment and nodded once again.

They drove along the winding backroads, lush parkways, and curve-biting turns lined with looming giant trees. It was a pleasant area—one backed by the expanse of forest that grew large and away from the river and the town. Lexi looked out into the dense foliage of green, to the forest's coppery sheen, like a clockwork of vegetation sprouting here and there and all around. She imagined, as she often did when they were on these back-roads, that Eddie had somehow regained consciousness and made his way out of the river. But in her mind—her awful, spoiling *rational* mind—she knew that the river was a wild one, and it had laid claim to her man.

Was he my man? Had he been my man?

They'd slept together that one time—and now she would be

just another single mother who used to be a prostitute. A *whore*—and depending on how things went with the college fund, maybe she would have to be a whore again. She was angry at Eddie. Angry at him for trying to be a knight in shining armor. She would have handled it. What would Bobby have done anyway? Bobby Jr. was just another petulant spoiled little brat, and once he'd realized he'd gone too far, he would have just brought Lexi back to the brothel and *begged* her not to say anything to his father.

But Eddie was too big for his britches. Another case of suicidal bravado; some inborn need to prove up honor. She was being unfair, she knew. Lexi *knew* this. Losing him, though, seemed harder when examined by the illumination of the past. They say that, of course, about the clarity of hindsight. It doesn't make missing the things you lost any easier. Especially when you're carrying that lost thing's child.

It was Abi who broke the silence again. "We and the Madam are make goings to *Commodora* tonight. You want to should come with us?"

"No. I look like a moose. I don't want to be out in public."

"Haha, Miss Lexi, you are not even closely to have baby months! Not fat. No, no, no, no."

"Thanks, Abi. You're sweet." It was nice to hear Abi laugh again.

It was sometime in the late afternoon when Abakoum dropped Lexi off. I wasn't very surprised. Stacy hadn't said anything to me about it—frankly, my wife had rarely spoken since the clusterfuck at The Pony. But she'd made up a guest room for Lexi and left the door open so I could see the fresh linens laid over the queen and the bleach-clean towels folded neat and laid atop the bed. I took the hint.

An open invitation would be forthcoming, but first I went through the motions of what had become a regular routine with the young lady. I brought out coffee for the both of us and a pitcher of iced tea. I don't normally have caffeine in the afternoon, my late-growing physiology being as sensitive as it is, my own sleep already troubled by my wife's sleep patterns.

Lexi smiled, sullen and sweet, a new kind of sorrowful grin that I'd seldom seen before but had grown accustomed to in the stretch of time since Eddie's vanishing. She quickly drank the coffee and ponderously gazed over the iced tea. Tentative. Wanting. There was some*thing* behind her eyes.

She spoke in a contrite whisper. "You don't have any white wine, do you?"

"Sure do. Would you like a half-glass? Or just a glassful. Whatever you want, Lex."

She thought on that a moment. "Do you think it's okay? I mean, for the baby?"

"My medical opinion? I should say no, but you aren't that far along, and it's a little bit, not a lot. Next week, probably a bad idea to drink. It's probably fine this week. I'm not a gynecologist, though."

"No, but you went to school to be a doctor, right?"

"I specialize in general medicine, and also dabble in psychology, but becoming an OBGYN wasn't in the stars for me."

I went inside and looked in the refrigerator for an already-opened bottle. I uncorked it and poured two healthy helpings of fermented sour grapes for the consumption of two commiserating sour grapes.

As I set Lexi's glass beside her and started squatting into a creaky crouch toward my Adirondack, she spoke.

"I know it's his. The baby. It's Eddie's."

The smart move would have been to just nod—maybe to say *yep*. But that's not what I did. "How do you know?"

"I just do. It feels… different. I think it's a boy."

"Different?"

"You know. Like Eddie."

Ah, there it is. I'd been wondering when we'd get around to this, to this supernaturalism, this rural superstition carried over by the Carnival. Did Eddie's body really transfigure? Hard to say. I *saw* it, that much I know. I saw those things happen. But what were they? What were the lights and the fire, the fury and the noise that came from that troubled boy? Looking back now, the trained-and-educated portion of my mind—says that I'd tricked myself. Of course. How could it be otherwise? Since time immemorial. It's been that way. People deceive themselves. We want to believe. That's what the doctoral cognition said. But the other part of me thought, *felt*, differently...

"I don't know how to explain it, but I know it. I know this baby is his, and it's going to be like him. I'm happy about that. But I'm scared, too. I'm all alone, Doc."

Lexi started to cry. She looked at me, seeming to want more, some further expression of my concern. I thought of reaching my hand over and setting it on hers, but I was worried that we were still not quite on those terms.

"You're not. You're not alone. Stacy is happy to have you here, and *I'm* happy to have you here."

She continued crying. I wasn't sure whether what I said sank in, so I took a deep breath and rephrased, but I still felt I was fumbling.

"Stacy made up a bed for you. We want you here. I mean, if *you* even *want* to be here, and it's *okay!* Shit, sorry—didn't mean to startle... I mean, it's okay if you want to stay with us. It's *good* if you want to stay with us. Shit... am I making any sense?"

Lexi leaned over and placed her hand on mine.

"Are you *sure*? You wouldn't think it lookin' at me, but I can snore loud enough to wake the dead. And... sometimes I fart."

I was so shocked by the sudden resurgence of old ball-busting Lex that I couldn't speak for a moment. But then I started laughing. Loud. And then louder. And then Lexi was laughing too. We were laughing together, happy, shining in the sun even if it was only a few spare moments before the lingering shadows came creeping back. We finally wound down, the guffaws deflating into little after-shocking giggles and titters.

"Well, that's good, Lexi. Staying here, I mean. As a medical professional, I'm surprisingly ambivalent on the matter of farts. It's all just airy shit sprayed in the air, anyhow."

Lexi smiled. "Isn't everything?"

CHAPTER 32

ONE WEEK LATER

Rizzo Senior was waiting.

He sat in one of the ample salons of the mansion, reading a book about horse-breeding. Rizzo was tired. His son's disappearance had made his exhaustion much worse, but he'd been getting tired for a long time. Rizzo had never really wanted to get into this... trade? *Profession*? Racket? But there he was, a washed-up old fuck, still playing gangster, still putting out fires, still quelling and stoking intrigues and violence.

For Robert Rizzo was like his father before him, Lino, and Lino's father before him. Paesanos. He'd carried on the bad blood and animosity. Paesanos had brought the old Camorra vendettas from Naples to be realized, fresh and bloody, in the tenements and the slums of the New World. *Il lupo perde il pelo ma non il vizio* (loosely translates to "a leopard cannot change its spots"). It was as true as it ever was, for people and for families—all sorts of families. *Old habits die hard.*

With a note of concern (and self-interest) in his voice, one of Rizzo's boulder-shoulder brutes broke the old man's reverie.

"Boss, you doin' okay?"

"I'm fine, Terry."

"Can I get you anything? A drink? The paper, maybe?"

"No, no. I'm fine. I'm reading." Rizzo held up the equine reference book to prove his point.

"Well, let me know if you want something. We're all just waiting. Guys'r at the door, room's all set up."

"No, I'm fine, T. I'll let you know if I need anything."

Terry nodded and left. Rizzo liked Terry—a hard worker, a smart guy, a friendly outsider who'd been hired on merit. Rizzo was happy when he had the opportunity to make meritocratic promotions. This world of his, this criminal constellation, was studded with nepotism. There was no shortage of idiot-hires that Rizzo had reluctantly made in the past. Not Terry, though.

Terry is a good man.

Rizzo slunk back in the high-armed leather chesterfield and brought the book closer to his nose. He read on, drifting into a drowse. Eventually, as he scanned the bottom paragraph for what must have been the third or fourth time, he fell into a light snooze. Which was okay. Because Terry was watching the door.

Clara had driven toward The Pony well before midnight. Since about a quarter to eleven, she'd been sitting in the Benz, pulled onto the shoulder along the parkway. From where she was parked, Clara had a prime vantage point for overlooking the old-town part of Main Street. The soft glow of the globed streetlamps and the boxy gas-lamps beamed—tiny eyes glinting and squinting in the crystal-clear eve of the night's end. She thought of how it would be nice to have a house up here, somewhere in the hills, somewhere beyond the flotsam and jetsam of the town's wrathful wretches and squalid skell-folk. A dream within arm's length, it seemed.

An unknown. That's what she was facing down. It was an equation she would be happy to live her whole life without.

Childhood was full of unknowns. The promise of fidelity had been one of those unknowns, and where had *that* gotten her? Not knowing was not being in control. Not being in control was admitting to fear, or humanity, or at minimum, to base human worthlessness. She didn't like it—Clara *did not like it*. No, she didn't like the unknown. Not one little bit.

Quarter to midnight.

She pulled off from the shoulder and up the sloping driveway lined with lush and long green sodding. When the car crested the final gradient before letting out onto the flat drive top, some strange relief flooded Clara's bloodstream, making her heart and veins cooler and calmer.

Maybe she would get out of this meeting without having to do or change anything; probably not. Either way, that's all that it was —a meeting. Just another out of many thousands just like she'd been to in the past. Only words. She was a talker, after all. A persuader. This was her bread and butter. This is what she *did*.

As she drove up to the periphery of the mansion, she spotted the men in suits waiting for her. Not black suits, not *those* men in suits, but more like goons squeezed into ill-fitting pinstripes and peak-lapel three-pieces. There was a Suburban and two land yachts, but otherwise, Clara was surprised at how few vehicles were parked out front. *Maybe they carpooled?*

She thought that maybe one of the goons would direct her where to park, but all of them stood, indifferent to her arrival, smoking cigarettes and jawboning. So, she parked far off to the side, a little bit in the dark, next to a big old cypress.

Clara made sure she had what she needed, consolidated everything in her purse, and stepped out of the car, closing the door behind her.

"Missss Guadali…"

A rotted voice, reeking of cancerous lungs and the smell of

burnt-up paper, croaked from behind her. Clara jumped. She nearly pissed herself. She whipped around to look into the black shadows beyond the pine and saw an inhuman silhouette lined around the edges with a faint crimson glow. The glow faded as soon as she thought she'd really seen it, but the light from the far-off driveway lamps still put some reflective light into two dancing yellow orbs a head above her own. *Eyes.*

Papa Marivicos stepped out of the shadows. "How're you doin' tonight... *sweetheart*?"

He grinned, and it was absolutely awful. She'd never seen a grimace like that, and she'd be happy to never see one like it again. Papa's mouth was mutating, his teeth warbling between longer and shorter, sharper and duller, yellowing and reddening points. It looked like his gums were bleeding. And Clara swore to herself she could see some rotten matter lingering, post-mastication (or maybe even post-mortem). His skin was sallow and loose and grey.

"Mr. Marivicos. I wish I could say that it's a pleasure to see you again, but—"

Papa approached her in sweeping stilt-length strides. He leaned down and whispered in her ear, close enough to touch his tongue to her. "Oh, don't worry. The feeling's mutual."

Clara shuddered and staggered a few steps back. Her foot caught in a peeking root raised up from the dirt, and she tripped backward, falling onto her ass.

Papa laughed and stepped over her, seeming to have grown in height. His ankle brushed against her breast and left some mud on her blouse. "Watch your step. It can be damn near *treacherous* in these parts."

Papa kept on walking, laughing like a maniac as he went. *Fucking asshole.*

She stood up and tried to get a look at herself in the reflection of the car window. Her backside was covered in muck. She thought to clean herself up a little bit but looked down at her watch and saw that it was only two minutes to midnight. So, she hurriedly shuffled toward the entrance, trying to pick off dirt and mud as she went.

Fucking asshole.

"Hey, boss."

Nothing.

"Hey, *boss.*"

Still nothing.

"HEY, BOSS!"

Finally, Rizzo stirred. He felt like his head had been deflated, or like someone had drugged him.

"It's time?"

Terry nodded.

Rizzo walked through the long hallway that led from the salon into an antechamber. There were about a dozen suited goons, none of whom looked like pushovers, lightweights, or amateurs. Rizzo continued on through the antechamber into the meeting room that used to be a library. Papa was sitting at the head of the table, and Clara Guadali was sitting a little more than halfway down on the side of the table, demonstrating a clear aversion to Papa.

Immediately, Rizzo noticed that Guadali was a little worse for wear. "Miss Guadali. Do you need a minute to collect yourself before we get started?"

She thought about it for a moment then nodded. Normally she'd answer firmly in the affirmative and in a firm voice. But Marivicos had spooked her something awful, and she didn't feel in her right mind.

"Terry, why don't you show Miss Guadali to the powder room?"

Terry nodded and showed Clara the way. Rizzo sat down, kitty-corner to Papa Marivicos.

"Thank you for coming, Mr. Marivicos."

"It's the least I could do. I mean… we're all professionals… right?" Papa looked like he was having trouble breathing. He looked like his lungs might pop out of his mouth from over-exertion.

"Yes. Yes, we are. That's why I was glad you were able to come."

"But… of course." Papa smiled wide and sickly.

"Mr. Marivicos, are you feeling alright?"

"You know, funny you should ask. I *have* been feeling a little… different lately. Different… a little different, yes."

"Well. Okay, then. Listen, Mr. Marivicos, I asked you here because I'm not so clear on a couple things. My son… you know who my son is… *was*, right?"

"Well, why do you say it like that? Is the boy gone *missing*, now?"

Rizzo pointed in the direction that Clara had walked off in. "That's why I asked you to come here. I know that you and *her* have been embroiled in some nonsense about your business. Now, I don't care about any of that shit. But I got a notion that *that woman* tussled with my boy and did something."

"Oh, my." Papa smiled wider than ever, his grin seeming to reach up to his eyebrows. Rizzo caught a peek at the man's ragged, raw, filthy predator's mouth—*Christ look at those fuckin' chompers*—and felt the bile rise at the back of his throat.

"Yeah…" Rizzo muttered, his mind disappearing elsewhere for a moment, disappearing, perhaps, into the wretched possibilities presented by Marivicos's maw.

"Now, Mr. Marivicos, I'm not aiming to start a war with anyone, but I do want some answers. And one way or another, I plan on getting them tonight."

"Is that so?" Papa's smile disappeared.

Rizzo looked at the old man and could have sworn he was growing taller as he sat in his chair. But Rizzo stood down pat, his eyes meeting Marivicos's, his gaze unwavering. He'd stared down plenty of hard cases in his time, and Papa was just one more of the many *botz* fools he'd measured dicks with. *Still, it's exhausting...*

"Yes, Mr. Marivicos. I'm getting answers. You're a smart guy. I assume you're a smart guy. Natural enough, assuming you are. Not a guarantee, though. No, not in business... In business, and I know this as good as anybody, there are plenty of fuckin' blockheads. You see, I *know*. What you do, though, is more like... Well, what is it you say you do? Entertainment? Gambling and entertainment? Gambling and freakshows and entertainment... sumthin' like that?"

Papa's smile was now completely evaporated. Instead, his lip curled, his face twisted, his limbs elongated. To Rizzo, Papa looked like he was leaking radioactive blood around his edges; a two-dimensional pop-up doused in a crimson glow. He grew, and he bled.

"Something like that. I have to ask you something, Rizzo."

"*Mr*. Rizzo."

"Uh-huh. Right. I have to ask you something, Rizzo."

Rizzo sighed as he closed his eyes, holding his temples close in the pressure of his thumb and finger points. "Go ahead."

"You probably think of yourself as a powerful fella. Am'I'right?"

Rizzo waited before answering. "I *know* I am."

"Right, right. And I guess that you think that power is one of the greatest levers that can be operated as leverage 'round this town. Am'I'right?"

A longer pause this time. Some of the men peeked around the corner from the antechamber, eavesdropping or watching Rizzo's back.

"Yes. I've got power in this town."

Then Papa let him have it. The full monty. The full Marivicos monty.

"I wonder, though. I wonder. Have you ever seen real power? True power? Power like God and the devil have. Have you ever looked a reptile in the eye and called yourself a better snake than him? Y'ever shook hands with a man made all up of knives, known the whole time you would boil him down and eat his bones? I'd venture you don't know none of that. Because power is a strange thing. Damn strange thing. Lots'a folk say that, *strange thing,* but I know how strange it is. You been chasin' power all the way to the finish line, right up past the checker-line, headstone in sight. Legacy, some men call it. Power and legacy. Legacy and power. But it ain't nothin'. It ain't shit, Rizzo. Power, you see, is strange in its transformations. You don't contain power, you don't chase after it, you don't *seek* it, Rizzo. Power *takes* you, makes you a channel of *its* desires and wants."

"It slaps you in the face!" Papa bellowed, sending an involuntary jolt through Rizzo and bringing the goons just a few steps closer. Baring his teeth, with a sneering grin, he continued.

"Right in the fuckin' face n'tells you what-it-is-you-gon'-do. You look power in its burning, cold dead eyes, and you swear to it you'll eat the fire and pay the price. You'll pay in blood and family, with your soul and your son's spirit, if need be. *That's* what power is, Rizzo. And I bet you ain't got none of it. You're just another geezer greaseball grown too big for his britches. In that way, you remind me of my worthless son, may the devil erase his name after the taking. What you need, Rizzo, is a demonstration."

Papa Marivicos took on the appearance of a gaunt, hollowed out, gargantuan corpse, just past the point where someone might say it was *possible* that a human being could look like that. Something like a skeleton, if it were left in boiling water to disintegrate over a century, slathered up in someone else's dead skin, and covered in red light, baring teeth like an apex predator.

It was difficult for Rizzo to know how to respond to that. He felt fear, *real* fear, in a way he hadn't remembered he could. A fear of youth and inexhaustible indiscretion. An unholy fear that taunts as shadows taunt wary children in their smaller years.

"I want you... I—I want you… to tell me what happened to my son."

Papa laughed. High-pitched and hysterical, a shrill tone that sounded almost like a mourner wailing. It was a phlegmy laugh, too. A sick one. The laugh stopped suddenly, making a ratcheting sound. A croaking death rattle. But the grin had returned. The grin remained. And oh how terrible it was. "Why, don't you know?"

A long silence. Then Rizzo shook his head.

"I ain't had nothin' to do with it, Rizzo. But if you want ta'know what happened to 'im, I'll tell ya. The same thing that happens to everybody. The same thing gonna happen t'you."

Rizzo looked over toward the antechamber for his men, but some invisible hand slammed closed and bound shut the pocket doors around the room. Immediately, there was the sound of hammer-pounding ham-fists bouncing against the other side of the wall in the antechamber room. Papa was standing all the way at the other end of the old library, cloaked in the corner shadows, though his eyes and teeth were still visible.

Rizzo reached for his pistol but was frozen. His heart pounded, his eyes swelled inside of his head, quickly and painfully, till it felt like they would pop out of his skull. He started choking.

His men battered the antechamber doors. It was the sound of hulking shoulders being barreled into them. But they held out, old and sturdy and made in another time; made when lumberjacks were fathers and neighbors that you knew, not just an abstract idea in some faraway forest. A few splinters, a few cracks, but the doors held.

Rizzo eyed the doors, but soon his vision was clotted red and it felt like his organs were being pushed up into his neck. He managed to pull his pistol up level, firing off shots wildly, but Rizzo couldn't see Papa.

Papa seemed to flit in and out of the shadows, even in and out of existence. One of the stray shots went through the door and hit someone on the other side. Even through the high-pitched ringing going off between his ears, Rizzo heard a violent *thud* — the sound of a very big man falling. More yelling. Loud, panicked, yelling. Rizzo's ears started bleeding, and he heard a loud *pop* before he never heard anything ever again. He screamed and was terrified to discover he couldn't hear his own voice, just a moaning vibration in his head. His eyes pushed and pushed and pushed from the inside-out against the regulation of his eye-socket bones.

Rizzo screamed, in the tormented and confused terror of a whelp. "God help me!"

Help, however, was not forthcoming. He knew it was imminent, the end, and before that, more pain, but that didn't stop Rizzo's screaming. Then, another *pop*. His eyes had burst inside his head. Rizzo fell from the height of the tabletop, slamming his face into the edge and breaking his nose on the helpless drop to his knees. Blood and viscera ran from his eyes, his nose was broken, making breathing almost impossible. Rizzo was still on his knees, his forehead leaning against the edge of the table. He was too afraid to pull back for lack of anchorage, too scared to test the new truth of his deaf-and-blind disequilibrium.

He could hear nothing. He could see nothing. But then, a voice.

"D'ya see what I been tellin' ya', Rizzo? D'ya see it? Strange, it is. Prolly never thought in yer' life, never in yer' life… prolly never thought you'd see it. Only now that yer' blind. Blinded, Rizzo. Ain't never touched ya', but still them eyeballs went POP! D'ya see what I been sayin' now? Strange. Power is… strange."

Rizzo couldn't hear it, but Papa was laughing hysterically; he could only hear the transmission of sinister thought raping his consciousness in what were surely his last moments.

"You are blind but now you see. You are deaf but hearing me. And all yer' power, Rizzo. Do you see the illusion? Do you understand it, at least? At last? At last, at least, at last, at peace. The lie. THE LIE, YOU FUCK! The deception—a curtain, a curtain drawn over… well come on! Do you see it now? Your power. Your power that never was. I took it from you, Mr. Rizzo. I TOOK IT GOOD!"

Just at that moment, the doors from the antechamber splintered and busted wide open. One of the goons flipped on a light switch. None of them saw Papa Marivicos. What they did see was awful. Rizzo knelt on the ground with his blood-covered face looking like it had exploded against the edge of the table. The boss had asphyxiated on and in his own gristle.

It looked like he'd pissed and shit his pants, too.

A VERY SHORT WHILE LATER

Clara had locked herself in the bathroom. Just a few minutes earlier she'd finished tidying up and cleaning off the dirt she'd fallen in. She'd been just about ready to come out when she heard some terrible noises.

Squelching. Rupturing. Aspirating. Retching. Shattering.

She reached for the door, with her hands shaking, to make sure the tumbler key in the old lock had turned the bolt shut, and just when she heard the click—*so loud; it seems so loud*—a heavy *thump* cracked the other side of the bathroom door.

"Fuck! Oh Jesus. Oh Jesus Christ…"

A shrieking sound—no, a howl—and it sounded bottomed out. The howl of some bass-driven bellowing beast, some drooling devil with evil in its eyes and blood on its breath. Then, quiet. Complete silence. Stillness. Clara could make out the contours of that auditory vacuum—an emptiness larger than sound. She warily turned the tumbler key back to unlock the door, wincing when it made a *click;* it was the loudest sound any lock anywhere had ever made, she thought. She pulled the key out carefully, stifling a cry when the key clacked against the sides of the lock. *So loud.*

Clara squatted and pressed her face against the lock to look through the keyhole to make out what was happening on the other side. The silence was gnawing. Quiet.

"Hello, little rabbit."

A croaking, wet thrush-like voice spoke. A hemorrhaged eye looked back at her. Clara jumped back, extending her legs all the way and launching herself against the closed toilet. She then painfully slid down and hit her head on the commode. She heard laughing on the other side.

"Run, little rabbit, run…"

Slowly, the laughter trailed away. She heard a single set of heavy footsteps, heard the footsteps recede in their sound and distance. Tears streamed down her face. Her hand reached to the back of her head. She felt a gash. She had hit her head hard. She was bleeding.

Clara waited.

Every minute felt like an hour. *Don't move. Don't move.* She waited… waited. And waited. Petrified. Frozen still.

Don't move.

She wasn't even aware of her sobbing. They were stifled-to-silent heaves, wet and staggered. Clara would hiccup every few breaths and raspberry out a sputtering exhale. Every few moments she heard far away voices and hammering. *Who was hammering?* But she still couldn't move. That monster was out there. That *thing.* It couldn't have been Marivicos. She'd seen him before. He didn't look like *that.* But there was nothing and no one else it could have been.

More hammering. A clatter of wood against wood. Clara couldn't move. Then, she heard the sound of hammering behind her. She spun around and saw that the outside of the awning window above the toilet was being blacked out. *Is that wood?* After that, Clara smelled kerosene. Even in shock, the pieces started coming together.

Oh, my God. He's sealing us in.

Clara sprang to her feet and hopped on the toilet bowl, trying to open the awning window, but it wouldn't budge. She strained desperately, not thinking clearly. Why bother with the one window? Surely, Papa would've left if...

She hurriedly hopped back down, unlocked the door, and ran out. It was dark. Most of the lights had been shattered so she couldn't see. There was more hammering. The kerosene smell grew stronger. Her survival instinct kicked in and she started running toward the front door, though it would surely be boarded up by now.

It was.

More hammering. More kerosene. The smell stung. It stung her nose, at the back of her throat, stank like slaughterhouse hell. She scurried around in the dark, choking on effluvia. She slipped on something and fell, her forearms scraping against the broken glass from the bulbs, ripping through flesh, her clothing and skin drenched in something warm and metallic. *Blood.*

There was a flash through the seams of the boards that had been nailed up around all the windows of the mansion. Marivicos's men had trapped them inside. *Them? No. Me.* A flicker of firelight illuminated through the seams between the nailed-up planks that trapped her within. In little bursts of bright yellow and orange, with little prancing shapes dancing in the shadows beyond the light, Clara could see. Not much, but better than before. And along with the light, there was a roar. It grew, louder, louder, louder. She couldn't comprehend time. It had left her, through panic, through fear, through finality.

One last... try.

Clara ran from point to point, trying new knobs and straining her fingernails against the bottoms of windows. But her nails were reduced to stubs, and there was no place where she would gain any purchase. And all the while, the gathering fire lit the floorboards and seared wallpaper and curtains that she couldn't see before.

Plumes of smoke extruded through air gaps in the old windows and past door thresholds. Clara was soaked in blood; she was soaked in sweat and ash, in tears and snot and mucus. It was hot, growing hotter. After what seemed like forever and a minute, she understood. Understood that it was over. That no matter what... it was over. The smoke billowed and she heard the bowing, creaking floorboards and the entropy of foundations. The heat was too much to stand, and she cried in a spiral of apocalyptic terror. Unholy terror.

This is it.

Clara stumbled around, tiny hiccup-echoes of sobs reverberating from her, traces of sadness now without meaning. She wandered for a while and found her way to the salon. And it was there that Clara finally found her perch, the final place from which she would play witness to her own execution-by-fire. She sat in a leather chesterfield and waited to die.

Clara became calm. There was some part of her that felt relief. Not that she wanted to die. No, that would be foolish with everything that had gone *right* in this last season of her life. But the inescapable grip of God's wrath had reached her, and she saw the logic of it, saw the truth, and found it all very fitting. Strangely comforting, even.

And as the fire closed in around her, Clara thought back to college, to her roommate Sarah Holly Keener, who often recited passages from a strange liturgy of judgment that used to horrify her so. The words came to Clara as her lungs swelled with black smoke and her skin felt like it was being torched:

How many will pass and how many will be created?
Who will live and who will die?

Who in their time, and who not in their time?
Who by fire and who by water?
Who by sword and who by beast?
Who by hunger and who by thirst?
Who by earthquake and who by drowning?
Who by strangling and who by stoning?
Who will rest and who will wander?
Who will be safe and who will be torn?

There was more. But that was all she could remember. And it would all be over soon. So, she rested within her incomplete memory. She was consumed by the fire.

CHAPTER 33

Someone thrashed about in a netherworld between this life and another. Words and concepts fluttered in and out of the entity.

This. I. Is. Am. Part. Is. Are. Thus.

Then a faint glow, imperceptible at first.

Here. Therein. Time. Place. Thus.

Then, tectonics. No, no... continuums. No. Both. Occulting. Occluded. Arc—a secret, a cipher. Written in the dredges. Through the running patterns of black water, with the history of bodies the river kept in its breast. Embedded in rivulets running to its very heart. Secrets written in the land and the river. And then, one more secret, whispering to himself, discovering existence. An entity. Whispering in harmonics and electro-magnetic cadences.

Time. She. Said. She said. She said Time. Thus.

An opening. Pure electricity, blue and wild, wandering, snapping, waving in and out of the *measures*. Yes, tectonics. The secret revealed in the land, and through the land, and under the river. That's where the entity lived. A new thing, from an old thing. Discovering those secrets written in the land and the river. Birthing his own existence.

I. Thus. Are. Thus. Is. I am. Thus. Time. Thus. Here and therein, without and within, in this place. A Time, somewhere in space. I am. Thus. I am.

Then, he remembered. He was Eddie.

Papa Marivicos was sitting in a newly constructed addition to the Carnival grounds. It was a bunker of sorts. Ramshackle, surely, but a bunker, nonetheless. It was all that could be constructed on short notice and within the specifications he'd demanded. Marv and Andy told Papa that the bunker wouldn't exactly be as iron-clad as the *Wolfsschanze*, but it would serve well enough. Well enough to keep secrets. Papa had had to purge some folks because he wasn't careful enough about keeping secrets. That had been foolish.

It was better down here, anyhow. Better that Marv and Andy couldn't see him afflicted with some satanic gigantism, some wraith disorder of brain, breast, and spirit. *Falling apart, he was. That's what they'd like t'say. We'll see, though. We'll see who'll fall 'part.*

The Book was open in front of Papa, of course, but it was hardly even a book anymore. Miasmal smoke came from one picture of a dead man with pipes shoved down his esophagus—that page disappeared into black sparks in the air, one such ember lodging itself in Papa's tear duct (he barely batted his eyes). The picture also showed a gossamer skeleton wing flapping frenziedly in an attempted escape, like a dumb dead bird squashed and trampled, brainlessly trying to flee from a boot. Also pictured was a web-work of diaphanous beams soaked in putrid haze, reeking of a graveyard. *The Book* had gone bad. It had taken too much of Marivicos. It *was* too much of Marivicos. And he needed it —*needed* it desperately.

Well, down in the bunker, he could have it. All to himself. And the only price to pay was his soul. And maybe, his very precarious existence within the grand structure of the cosmos.

His mind was rotting. Papa had turned to the bad long enough ago, but now he had compound interest built up, too. He sang a nursery rhyme refrain that his gypsy granny had sung to him decades ago.

Oac oac diri diri dam
Oac oac oac oac diri diri dam

It was only after a half-hour's repetition of one-half of the song's refrain that Papa realized he hadn't been singing at all, but that the song had just gone around and round in his head—a skip and a trip on the turntable, as it were.

Oac oac diri diri dam
Oac oac oac oac diri diri dam

Memories came to him as the smoke and light danced in the pages of his book's (and mind's) ruination. Memories gleaned, pruned, tweezed from the delicate ancient fibers of a *very specific* branch of the collective unconscious. The Marivicos Memories. How many had there been? How many in debt to the Ilzram? How many children, mothers, sons, daughters in debt to a man they'd never known, mounted with a yoke to a plow broken to pieces and partly buried, dragging them down into the dirt? How many? *Never enough.*

These memories belonged to others. That was clear enough. But they were also *his*. Papa remembered, once upon a time, being a man named Muhamed Mehmedbašić; he remembered being Muhamed and convincing some wayward Serbians to light a powder keg, ignite an oil drum (figuratively speaking). He remembered being Muhamed and hearing *him*, hearing the star-titan of black veins and ill-gotten-gains whispering *make them do it*; and then, he remembered being Muhamed and escaping, fleeing somewhere safe while the rubes took the rap for assassinating nobility and starting the Great War. That had been *him*. And that thing in the stars had told him to do it. *But I'm not that old, am I?* And Papa had never been named Muhamed. Nonetheless, *The Book* told him it was true. So it must have been.

Papa Marivicos turned to one of his favorite pages and *The Book* warbled and moaned a sensual, painful musical tone while it pulsated in unnatural illumination with every touch of Papa's fingers. *Stacy Thornberg. My loyal soldier. New marching orders today, young lady.* The memory of Mehmedbašić came upon him again. What was *The Book* trying to tell him? Words floated through his mind, each accompanied by a flurry of images, of fire and exsanguination. *Ignition, catalyst, implode, explode, death, terror.* There it was. Terror. *Terror.* And it all became very clear for Papa Marivicos. He knew what he had to do.

The *Commodora* was docked at the wharf that Ferriman had suggested adding to the riverscape. It was nine in the evening, and the captain was waiting impatiently but quietly by the ramp. All the passengers had loaded onboard, but they couldn't open the gaming tables until the ship was in motion. That rule, Ferriman thought, was inconceivably dumb. But, then again, most things local politicians did, to Ferriman, were inconceivably dumb.

"Mr. Ferriman, sir. She's achin' to get out'n the river, if y'don't mind my sayin'. Ought we get ourselves goin'?"

Ferriman looked down at his watch, which was just a nervous tic; he seemed to have borne an ingrained time-perfect biological awareness of minutes and seconds ever since childhood. He grumbled, more to himself than to the captain, "She said she'd be here at seven. I can't imagine…" Ferriman turned to the captain.

"Does Miss Guadali usually arrive late like this?"

"Not once, not ever, sir. Clara's been here early 'nough ever'day we've took the *Commodora* out. Real hands-on, Clara is. Bookkeeping and such. Bustin' balls and checkin' off boxes is the lady's business, I reckon. Not been late once."

"I see. Well, you better take her out on the river. I won't hold you up any longer, and I apologize for getting between you and the performance of your duties."

"Ah, it's yer ship, sir."

"But you are the captain, and I'm a man who recognizes both talent in one's profession and rank in one's field."

The captain smiled at that.

"Well, I will see you soon enough, Captain. Good night."

"'Night, sir."

The captain trudged up the ramp and two outfitted deckhands started to pull up the ramp behind him.

"Wait! *Wait!*"

It was a woman's voice calling from the end of the wharf. Ferriman turned around, a sudden hope blossoming in his chest, but it wasn't Clara. A dark-skinned pretty woman came running to the end of the wharf. She breezed right past Ferriman, not even looking at him, and proceeded briskly up the ramp and onto the ship. She breathlessly offered a "thank you" to the deckhands and the captain before scurrying inside before any of the crew could say anything. The captain looked back at Ferriman with raised eyebrows and Ferriman shrugged back at the captain, in turn.

The captain waited to see if there were any more surprise late arrivals. There were not, but a few moments after the lovely lady had boarded his beautiful boat—that he so aptly named— Ferriman noted a curious looking couple staggering toward him. The man appeared seasick, and the two argued as the man frantically tugged on the woman's arm, but she refused to move. The man grabbed the woman, kissed her firmly, then ran off the boat.

Ferriman shrugged and made a wind-up motion with his hand.

Finally, the deckhands raised the ramp.

CHAPTER 34

Where the hell is my wife? Damned if I know. She's been every-where and anywhere in the depths of her own mind, I'm sure. But she's come nowhere near being present here in this house with me.

It's late now, probably somewhere around nine p.m., but I'm too damn lazy to lift myself up and peek at the oversized clock on the wall by the refrigerator. I don't want to make too much noise anyhow, since Lexi is asleep on the couch. If I even move an inch while I'm in my recliner, it'll creak like nobody's business. (I guess Stacy was right about that; she's told me about eight billion times to grease up the chair with some WD-40.)

You'd probably expect a husband to be worried about his no-spring-chicken of a wife being out and about late in the night, especially when that no-spring-chicken left the house *zero* times without me (if at all) in the last few decades.

Unusual times we're living in.

Anyhow, this wouldn't be the night to start stirring any shit. Abi and Lexi's friend from her last "job", Regina, are going out on the *Commodora* for the first time, and Lexi was so happy for them that she finally got herself some sleep. It's hard for her to sleep, that girl. She isn't far along enough to be really uncomfortable yet. That will come in about three or four months' time, when her belly's so swollen she'll lie awake at night staring at the ceiling. Still, she doesn't sleep too well. Could you blame her, with everything that's going on lately? With all this high weirdness and mafioso intrigue and whatnot?

Yep, it's like I said already. Unusual times we're living in.

In a short time, Eddie had calculated the parameters of his newfound existence. He had discovered many things, assorted features, but memory was not one of them. Not yet, at least. More than anything, he was an infant.

This was not because of some retrograde turn of his faculties, but because his reemergence into the river catalyzed a wild change in him.

To wit, he was no longer flesh.

If anything, he was an electrical field sparking within a container that looked very much like a body. He had the *shape* of a human, but he burnt as white flame, glowed a starry hue of lavender, and seemed to be composed of millions of strands of crackling blue lightning. His limbs were boundless, extending as far as the visible manifestation of the electrical field would go, which was very far, indeed.

Silver. Surfer. Thus.

Eddie heard the words, remembered that imagery from his paltry former three-dimensional world, but still didn't understand.

Eddie couldn't remember the pain of before, of the ordinary human life he had been born in.

I. Water. Light. Two. Thus.

Bits. Micro-bits of information. But he wasn't there yet. Not at comprehension, no. He was, analogically speaking, a differential analyzer. The theory that could explain him to himself wasn't available.

Three. Thus.

And there was the matter of the missing pain. Eddie felt no pain. None whatsoever. The excruciating experience of yielding—of breaking down while being bombarded by all the thoughts of any person in his orbit—was gone. Eddie could still *see* everything, *hear* everything, *know* everything that every person thought. But it was now effortless. He was, as his mother had warned him, somewhat half of a god. Perhaps a more cerebral version of that Scandinavian fellow with the hammer.

Painless. Until he wasn't.

Suddenly, he felt something. Something sharp. It didn't cripple him, didn't bring him down as it would before. Instead, it was more an awareness that pain existed somewhere in the world.

Eddie was naturally curious, being the infant that he was. The pain seemed to be moving, slowly, fluidly, gracefully, across a body. *Water. Thus.* Yes, the pain was gliding across water. There was some awful feeling, something in the way of horrid anticipation, that drew his attention.

Water. I. Thus. River. Exist.

Thus.

On the *Commodora*, Stacy found she couldn't control her actions. She didn't understand why. She was a prisoner in her own body; impulse and other assorted influences had guided her actions and behaviors before. Those were strange enough, but this was stranger.

She passed through the observation deck and the bar and strode into the lounge by the bridge. The voice in her head was back, controlling her. She clutched her purse, straining to win the battle waging within her, trying to deny access to herself. All to no avail. For only a moment, Stacy was able to arrest her marionette locomotion. She recognized someone in the lounge; a man dressed in loud summer linens. He was olive-skinned with a neatly trimmed beard, and he stood next to a busty middle-aged woman who wore a loud purple dress.

It was Abi.

Abakoum recognized Stacy and waved to her. He was excited, but his expression also clearly conveyed that he was confused to see her alone on the ship at night, or even outside her home.

The voice came back, directed her, commanded her. She walked past Abi as if she'd never seen him before.

Stacy entered a stairwell that led down to the *Commodora's* restaurant. The maître d' tried to stop her to ask if she wanted a table, but Stacy walked right past him and through the kitchen. No one in the kitchen stopped her. Her presence there was strange enough, sure, but it was a new boat and Clara had warned the crew to expect surprise inspections. For all they knew, this spaced-out lady was one of those inspectors. She exited the kitchen and continued toward the stern, ambling through the main deck as though she'd been there a thousand times before. The boat shook as it accelerated from its docked position.

The voice spoke to her. *Now. You're there. Now.*

Stacy opened her purse and looked down. She watched her hand reach into her purse but couldn't stop or control herself. She pulled out a brick-sized block with an electronic timer wired to it. She watched her finger press a button on the IED, but she couldn't stop or control that, either.

Once the timer started ticking, Stacy placed the IED back in her purse and gently sat down. She leaned back against the wall.

Eddie could feel the pain sharpening, growing into a behemoth. It was a pain that floated soft and easy down the river, even with the barbs of agony emanating from it. He could feel it growing and knew that something was coming soon: a violence, a sadness, a cancerous... something. Above all, it was pain, transmuted into particulate that floated through the ether that only he and a few other monsters like him could access. Yes, it was pain. Human pain.

———

Papa closed *The Book of Deeds of the Marvelous Marivicoses*. He had done all he could. And anyhow, it was time to head down to the river. He had one more loose end to tie up.

———

Still seated, with her back against the ship's bulkhead, Stacy clutched her purse close to her chest. She was sobbing, wracked with preemptive grief, mourning her imminent exit from the world. If she had only tried again, tried at her free will, she might have had time to stop the timer on the explosive.

A crewman came wandering down the main deck vestibule and saw Stacy crying. If he'd had a moment longer, he would have asked if someone had hurt her. Instead, before he could say anything, Stacy tried to choke out her words.

"I'm sorr—"

She wasn't able to complete her sentence.

———

I heard a loud *boom* in the distance, but it was close enough to shake me awake. I was just about to doze off in the recliner when I heard it. I looked over to the couch. Lexi was still there. I thought of getting up to check what had made that great and violent *boom*. But then I saw that Lexi was, mercifully, still asleep. So I stayed in my recliner. *It can probably wait till morning.* The same went for determining the whereabouts of my beloved wife. All of this would wrap itself up on its own. Like a bow. I'd wake up refreshed, Lexi would perhaps be a little less sad after having had some good sleep, and Stacy might even be in the kitchen cooking breakfast for our little ad hoc family when the morning came.

With those surprisingly optimistic thoughts, I drifted off to sleep.

I should have known better.

CHAPTER 35

I was dreaming.

In my dream I saw a wave—a mammoth crescent crashing down from five-hundred feet high. It was dark blue through and through, from its translucent rippling sheath all the way to its murky center. The kind of water that comes down from an apocalypse ocean. The wave reached to the sky, seeming to tear the clouds down into its rolling momentum. The sky was red.

Just before the wave hammered me into oblivion I woke up.

A dream. Just a dream.

But then I heard the same sound, a similar sound.

Outside in the waking world. *What is the waking world anymore?* A torrential rain poured from the sky. At the top of our winding stairwell is a skylight, made of old glass, that hangs a distance above the balusters. A glazier had crafted it long ago. As long as my lifetime, at least. The rain crashing down against that glass aperture was the loudest rainfall I'd ever heard. *Torrential.* A word that gets a lot of mileage in the weatherman's teleprompter, but this rainfall demanded another term. It was a sound and a fury, a force like the apocalyptic ocean-swell of my dreams. It was without a doubt the hardest it had ever rained in Kayjigville.

Just as I roused myself from the recliner, Lexi woke up. She looked bleary. Then startled.

"What is *that noise?*" Her face was riddled with surprise. And maybe fear.

"It's the rain."

"Couldn't be. That's... that's the loudest sound I've—that's not rain, is it?"

I walked over to the stairwell and looked up at the skylight. Lexi asked me again, for reassurance.

"What?" I was having trouble hearing her.

"Is it rain?"

"Of course it is. What else would it be?"

Her hands rested on her slightly swollen belly. Her eyes drifted off to the side windows, as if lured to the rain. She saw something that I didn't, I think. Lexi's eyes were drawn out sideways by some invisible force while my eyes were attracted toward the cacophony above. Both of us were right; both impulses came from some inexplicable necessity.

"It's something," Lexi whispered.

"What?"

"There's *something.*"

"I know."

A bolt of lightning hit so fast and loud; the thunder shook the skylight in its casement. We both jumped. I yelled like a maniac. Lexi yelped. Then, a rapid-fire barrage of lightning bolts hit. Again and again and again—a sound like six and nine guns or depth charges. A cannonade of supernatural electricity in the flooded sky. Lexi started screaming.

"What the fuck is that Doc?"

I don't know why, but I needed to understand what was happening, and that meant looking outside. Lexi saw where I was headed, my hand stretched toward the doorknob as my legs carried me forward. She screamed at me to stop. Well, she didn't scream anything comprehensible, anything that would qualify as the English language (or any other). But I recognized her scream. It was a protest. She wanted this edifice, *this home*, to remain whole—four walls, closed windows, shut off from the world. She wanted me to do nothing that would compromise this refuge.

I opened the front door and stepped out onto the veranda. The streets were flooded, sewers bubbling grey-water backup in small deltas of saltwater refuse, rushing like cyclones. The smell was everything you wished it wasn't, and not like anything you could imagine. A thick froth collected on the top of the several inches of foul effluvia washing over the road, bubbling brown and white and rolling with the kinetic energy of an avalanche. And all around, rain dropped like little bombs, rain in finger-sized pellets of hail slamming into the deluge.

It was biblical.

And loud.

LOUD.

As I surveyed the scene, a transformer blew in a skyrocket of sparks. A bolt of lightning felled a utility pole, ripping the inter-connected cords of power lines and wood poles down, too. It started a domino effect. In an instant, half a dozen streetlamps and power lines went crashing into the flooded streets. More sparks flew, and in a synchronous firing sequence, another trans-former blew. The electricity was gone; the house fell into dark-ness. All of this happened in the span of about four seconds. It looked like the world was coming to an end.

For all I knew, it was.

I thought I saw something beyond the harsh waters that billowed furiously through the river-run streets. I thought I was seeing hovering yellow jewels floating ethereal and dismembered in the raging storm. *I thought I saw eyes.* Not a man's eyes. But maybe it was the flood. Maybe I'd forgotten, like most had forgot-ten, what wrath and Acts of G-d could wreak.

But then the lightning. But then the storm. But then the flood. I was afraid. Certainly, I had seen yellow devil's eyes floating in the monsoon air, forge-fire eyes hissing and sizzling like heated steel dipped into the quench. My eyes couldn't be trusted, owned by my fearful soul as they were, my soul clutched in the fear of my heart.

Still standing at the door of my home, I felt the animal fear, the fear at the base of the neck, the fear of the boundless evil from beyond the eternal precipice of night, the fear of murder and loss. It had come upon me so powerfully that only after settling myself to the sound of the harsh waters and the angry electric sky, could I recognize how fearful I truly was.

Yellow eyes.

A dim red glow that grew in brightness and rage cut a closer and clearer path toward my door.

"Hello? Who's out there?"

No answer.

I turned to look at Lexi. She was standing at the door's threshold, her hands gripping the frame, her eyes pleading with me to come back inside. But it didn't matter. I could have explained that to her, if I'd wanted to, but the air was thick as the sea, and the sky was ignited with slings of immortal light, so it didn't matter at all what I might say to her. Because she already knew. What lips couldn't speak and words couldn't say was written with clear finality in the squall and the flood. We were tiny things in the face of these inhuman events.

I turned around and saw the pair of yellow lights of the shadowy figure as it drew nearer to us.

Teeth, too. Sharp animal's teeth.

Lexi screamed something at me. Something about coming inside. She ran, but I couldn't. I felt fear, of course. But, looking at the figure before me, I also felt a strange wonder. Why else would I plant myself so firmly in the path of this horror?

It looked like Papa Marivicos.

But it couldn't have been him. This monster, red and yellow, sour with stink and blood, was the height of two men. And the monster looked like it was falling apart. It growled at me, and Lexi.

"*Giiiirrrl… Get… HER.*"

I nodded. Not out of agreement. Because my body was disconnected from my brain and it was doing what it would, not what I willed it to.

There was a round of chemicals—powerful, hormonal bites of liquid information bursting through my brain—that gave me five hundred conflicting commands. One part of me said *run.* Another said *strike.* The chorus of other commands clanged noisily in my head, urging a thousandfold variations somewhere between fight and flight.

But I didn't flee. I just stood there nodding my head.

The beast that looked somewhat like Marivicos strode past me, a groaning, creaking moan coming from his joints. I still stood there nodding, and my wavering sight caught hold of Marivicos between the bounce of my head.

I saw his teeth—sharp needlepoints.

And his fingers—the overlong, knotted branches of a desiccated tree.

And his body—warped and lumbering.

As he passed by, Papa flashed a loathsome grin, his lips pulling back to bare teeth and splotched, bleeding gums the color of a cut of raw tuna. Papa tipped the brim of his hat as he continued onward, his tree-stump torso contorting weirdly above his elongated legs.

"*Eeeevening, Doc.*"

Maybe seconds elapsed. Maybe minutes. I wouldn't know, with that animal fear as bloody and fast in my brain as it ever was.

I heard a shriek, a woman's piercing scream. That was what broke the freeze. I turned and ran inside toward the noise.

There was Marivicos, carrying an unconscious Lexi, under his arm. She hung from that spindly mass as though she were a child's ragdoll.

Papa Marivicos looked down at me, and he laughed. Not a jolly laugh. A sick laugh. A muscle-reflex laugh that picked up after the distortions of the body. A laugh inside a frown. Then he snarled and spat through his curling lips.

Don't wuuurrrrryy, Doc. I'll make ssssure sssssshhheee doesn't tuuurrrrn into a… puuuuuumpkiiiin.

Papa swatted me hard in the face, knocking me to the ground. There I lay, somewhere between consciousness and unconsciousness, thinking of my grand-mammy's mumbles of scripture:

And, behold, I, even I, do bring a flood of waters upon the earth, to destroy all flesh, wherein is the breath of life, from under heaven. Everything that is in the earth shall die.

And the serpent cast out of his mouth water as a flood after the woman.

CHAPTER 36

Eddie was lacerated.

Lacerated, yes. But without memory.

Yes. Memory. Thus.

Flashes of images came to him, to what was left of him. Cycles of thoughts previously known but now *incomprehensible,* but for the remnants of experience that lingered. It was as much as Eddie's mother had prophesied, far out in the stelliform isles in the void, beyond the reach of all but the starry titans themselves.

In losing his tether, Eddie was unique from the other titans of the stars. Embedded within him, as a cell or as a growing seed, was planted an ineffable *thing*… a *thing* whose dimensions reached even past the supremacy of his mother's knowledge, a *thing* beyond all other things, gifted to him—to *Eddie*—from an unknowable source.

He was a vessel. A vessel for something that *grew* rather than withered. Because Eddie, in all his humility, and in all his bashful, unthinking piety, had become empty. Empty and left only to wonder.

So it was sadness that awakened him. It was the truly felt suffering of others that brought Eddie to his senses, senses now supremely heightened beyond the physical laws of the earth. He heard the wretched sorrow of the sufferers aboard the *Commodora*. And he heard with special clarity the remorse and paralyzing impotence of Stacy as she sacrificed herself unwillingly unto the altar of blood that Papa had erected before the black gates.

Eddie heard all of them drowning at the bottom of the river. He heard them trapped under steel beams, the air compressed out of the victims' lungs, blood and air leaking from their bodies and into the river's bottom. He felt their veins and their hearts, their lungs and their bowels. Eddie could feel the torch of embers and shrapnel flown into flesh, even minutes past the expiration of the victims. Painless to him, but felt nonetheless. Eddie floated above the *Commodora's* watery grave, his toes dragging across the river's surface and leaving rippling lines as he levitated forward. He moved toward the sunken ship, seeing it clearer than any man could.

He arrived at the crash site. There were bodies strewn along the nearby shore, and floaters bobbing up and down with the river flow, dead in the water, some belly-up and showing their obliterated faces, others mercifully down-facing and drifting away with the current. The prow of the ship was tilted at an odd angle, sinking under its capsize and pushed down by the flood rains. The river spilled out over the shores, and as the ship sank, the sinking prow looked like a hand depressing itself into an overfull sink, splashing water outside of the basin.

Sirens rang out, distant and muffled by the cacophonous meeting of rainwater with the river and with the roaring of fuel-fire burning up the remains of the *Commodora*. Some of the people who swam for shore were screaming.

Eddie felt a piercing knife invading him, a long hot poisonous needle driving itself to the center of his mind.

I see you boy. Come to me, Eddie. Come home.

Papa was close. Very close. The sound of Papa's discarnate cadence thrust deep, burrowing into Eddie. Eddie flailed and fell into the water. Like a hot iron dropped into a washtub, his electric, radiating body sizzled as it dispersed a shower of spokes and angry bursts of light, and then rubber-banded back in a furious elastic motion. Papa wasn't just using his voice; he was poisoning Eddie with it.

C'mon, Eddie. C'mon home. I needja, boy. Can't do it alone. You gon' help either way, Eddie. So, jus' c'mon now and help your Papa.

Eddie felt his hands. He felt his hands. He couldn't see them, but he could feel them. And in those hands—the lantern.

It was then that the memories came rushing back. All the years under Papa's thumb: the weakness, the capitulation, the wholesale razing of romance and marriage, the denial of education, the treatment of Eddie and his children as though they'd been only chattel… enslavement in all but name. And as these memories came back to him, Eddie felt a new kind of pain—pain out past the edge of human perception, pain of a newer, stronger, fiery kind. Pain like the heat of the sun, agony like drowning.

That's when Eddie saw him waiting at the edge of the river, saw Papa watching the *Commodora*'s prow sink into the waterway grown fat from the rain.

Down by the river, Papa demanded that Eddie send him—Papa—through the portal so he could destroy the starry titans from beyond the sky.

"We've got to finish it, Eddie. This is what we've been waitin' for, boy! This is what he wanted us to do, for all these years. I know now! *Him.* Our bloody father. The master of our evil, lustful hearts. We've got the black dog on our backs, boy. I know it… *you* know it. Let's end it. We can kill her together. We can kill *all of them!*"

"Her?"

"Your mother. She has to be stopped."

"I don't understand."

Papa laughed while crying manically. He tore his shredding fingernails at the corners of his eyes, pulling out a tear duct on one side and letting loose a voluminous spatter of blood that the flood-rains barely kept from dyeing his whole face crimson red.

"I knew you wouldn't, boy. But I did it for you. I did all of it for you. So you could finish what I started, Eddie. So *we* could finish it, together. Even the bad things, I had to do them. *I had to,* Eddie."

Something was missing. Something was wrong. "Where's Lexi?" Eddie asked.

"You know, your little slut-whore is pregnant. Did you know that? *Did ya?* If you want that little whore-baby of yours to live, if you don't want me to cut that kid right out of her nasty dollar-store cunt, then you'd better *DO WHAT I SAY!*"

It was then that Papa's thoughts entered the extra-sensory loom from which Eddie spun his familiarity with the past. The young man *peered* into his father's head, and what he glimpsed inside that theater of torment was too terrible.

Too, too terrible. The massacre at the Carnival. Perpetrated, orchestrated, and demonstrated by his father. Beatrice's body twisted, contorted, but not in the usual way, not in a way she'd contorted herself. Papa had done it—lynched her and dismembered her, eviscerated her. He'd killed her and so many others Eddie had considered to be friends.

But there was more. There was more and the absolute horribleness of the thought in Papa's mind was so unthinkable, Eddie could not believe what he heard. That trail of words, strung together, shattered him.

"No. No, you didn't... please... you didn't..."

"I had to, Eddie. Don't you understand?" Papa yelled, his voice cutting through the noise of the storm.

"If they were alive, you would go find them. Eventually. I knew I could stop you sending them letters. I knew I could stash 'em in an orphanage somewhere. But you'd find 'em someday. Especially now 'cause you got the second sight. I had to lay them in their beds, Eddie. For the Forever Sleep, son. *I had to*. I couldn't have you running off."

"They were children… children… my…"

Eddie gripped the lantern. He had the words. He only had to grasp the unwieldy strands of them and weave them together.

"They were *my children!*"

"That they was, boy. That they was. It's better that way. Better. They won't grow up to be broken-hearted. And they won't see what it is we have to do. Come on now, boy. I *need* you. We can do it together. We can kill all of them! For *him*, Eddie! For the Ilzram. For the Marivicos clan. So *he* can come and take us! They don't understand boy. They don't understand us! None of 'em do. But we're *powerful*. Powerful, boy! Don't you understand? And *he* gave us the power. He gave us the knowledge, you worthless cunt-mule!"

Papa's voice trailed off, but not because he was losing confidence in his message. For a moment, he realized Eddie was no longer the human speck of a marionette he once controlled. For a split second, he wondered if he needed to change his approach.

"Sorry… sorry-sorry-sorry-sorry… NO! And no I *ain't*! I ain't sorry. Power is strange, son. You have to do the strange… you have to do the bad things… you got to do it! For *him*."

"I can't see… I can't see where they are. Where did you put them, Papa?"

"I don't know."

"*WHERE?* LISTEN TO ME, PAPA!"

"I… don't… know. Not like I did it personally, ya know? You see, Eddie? There's no way to avoid it now. There're no distractions. I couldn't even tell you if I wanted to! For all I know, the bones of your children are at the bottom of the fucking river!"

Something deep happened to Eddie in that moment. The measures and energies, the entropy and electricity—*every* bit of Eddie that was more than human—suddenly slipped away. It was unexplainable. It was a feat so staggering in its impossibility, so unimaginable to those starry-limbed titans who would never even *consider* transmuting themselves to such a base species, it wouldn't have been understandable to others like him. Not even his mother would have been able to explain. Eddie had stripped himself down to nothing but his base humanity. It may possibly have been the first time ever that one of his kind had done it. Eddie was so defeated, so bereaved, so torn and soul-sick, *so heart-broken,* that he was willing himself to powerlessness.

Papa screamed even louder.

"What are you *doing*? You fucking fool! We need your power! Strange! *Strange*! STRANGE, I SAID! How can we kill her now? How? *How?* None of 'em, we can't, now. We gotta do it, Eddie. We gotta' do it for *him*."

Papa raved, his mutant limbs thrashing about, his boots stomping the mud as spittle flew from his wretched, bloody mouth.

Papa didn't see Eddie move. He was raving like a madman. Madmen are preoccupied with their constructs, their false realities, so the puny gestures of an inconsequential man like Eddie would never garner the attention of a demon so mad as Marivicos.

As a response, Eddie picked up his lantern and he raised it. He lifted it slowly enough that it moved a millimeter at a time, crawling in an arc.

Fear. Eddie was terrified, but fear was the only human feeling with the power to motivate him in that moment. To make him *move.* A lifetime of fear. Of being terrified of Papa. Of waiting for Papa to find out. Fear that he'd let his father go too far. Remorse that he should have *done something sooner.* That same fear reshaped until it was something he could wield against Papa. He would no longer shrink away, hide away, escape. Fear, indeed, could be useful. Maybe even more useful than the strange power Papa knew.

A fire started from the ground, forming a circle around Eddie

—small waves of flames flickered at his feet, they rose and fell in time with the waves of the river. He paused for a moment. The dumb numbness was gone. He *felt*. The scene he'd created looked like hell, but Eddie didn't feel like hell. *This* didn't feel like hell. It felt like *harmony*.

The ring of fire rose as Eddie lifted the lantern. His knuckles turned white, then his hand. His arm was luminescent. He could see his own veins and he noted how they pulsed. Steady, steady, steady. Yes. This was *harmony*. This was *human*.

He raised the structure that housed the original blaze, and the fire at his feet surged until he was surrounded by flames that reached far above his head. He brought his arm forward and the circle of flames writhed into a mass, forming a wall before him. Between himself and Papa, who had begun sputtering, choking. The fire inched away from Eddie and, finally understanding the mechanics of the lantern and the flame, Eddie raised the lantern higher, and the fire surrounded the inhuman form that had never been a father to him. Papa's bones crunched inside his body. When he raised the lantern nearly level with his shoulder, Papa fell to his knees, blood pouring out of his mouth.

He was dying, but Papa continued his diatribe. With all his remaining strength, he pointed a bony finger at Eddie. "He'll come for you, son. He'll come for you. And then you'll be in his debt. You'll be a slave."

"Who? Who will come?"

Papa was coughing up blood. "You'll be his slave just like all the chained are. Just like all the trapped half-stars who are nothing what they think. You'll be his *slave*. Just because we didn't finish the job doesn't mean he still won't."

"Who? *Who?*"

"Chernobog."

But even before Papa answered, Eddie had decided that he didn't care. His father hated him. His father killed his children. He raised his lantern to the height of his shoulder and closed his eyes.

The lantern illuminated brighter. And then, a blue-white fire enveloped Papa. He burst into flame. Papa screamed and shrieked, as his wretched form slowly turned to char and ash. Every horrid fiber of his rot was now host to volcanic ember. The blue-white fire ended Papa Marivicos, burning him alive.

Eddie didn't stay to watch. He simply walked toward the river, the lantern lighting his way. And when he arrived at the water, he walked in. In that moment, he was ready to give himself to the whirlpool of that black river—join all the nameless no ones who had met their nevermores somewhere in its depths. No. In that moment, there was nothing left for him in this world.

"Please stay," a voice commanded him. Softly. Eddie turned, and there, at the shore of the river, was a bruised and bloodied Lexi. His heart nearly stopped. His heart. He felt it there, beating in his chest. The heart beating near him. Two heartbeats.

He turned around.

Got out. He got out of the river.

"I thought... I thought... he'd hurt you. I couldn't see you, in there. I couldn't see you. Maybe you were..." he tried to articulate, but words couldn't serve him, and they couldn't save him from the pain, and they couldn't save him from the loss. They couldn't explain to her why he'd needed to get to the river.

Lexi shook her head. Ashes fell and latched onto her hair like snowflakes. They caught in her lashes. Smoke swirled around them so thick it was almost impossible to make out the red and blue flashes of EMS, police, FBI—whoever was coming.

"Papa took me from Doc's place. I couldn't move through most of it, but I could hear him... snarling. He said horrible things. I can't remember them all, but he wanted you to see it. He wanted to rip me apart right in front of you. He sat me down on some concrete, said 'stay put you miserable bitch,' and for a while, that's all I could do. I couldn't move. Until... I think he was focused on you. He left me in some..." she paused. She shook. Her voice shook. Her eyes were unfocused. "I don't know. It was like a tomb near the river. That's what it felt life, anyway."

"How did you get here?"

Lexi looked up at Eddie. Shook her head. "I knew I'd find you here. I don't know anything else."

"Oh."

"Are you leaving?"

Eddie stood at the precipice of death. A death he wanted. A death he deserved. But there was Lexi, cradling her belly, and even though he couldn't hear her mind, he understood what she worried about. He was torn between dimensions. it seemed Earth would not release him from its grasp. He stepped closer to Lexi and closer to the black sludge at the shore of the river.

"I... I..." he trailed off as he bent down and touched the sludge. Dragged two lines through it with his index and middle finger. Two. Two children lost to its depths. Or the depths of something like it.

"Eddie?"

He stood and turned to look at her. She was bloody and muddy. Her bare legs covered in deep scratches. And she shook so wildly he could hear her teeth chatter. "We need to get you to Doc's," he said, reaching his free hand out to her. Lexi moved slowly.

"I might not be able to stay. It's... it's hard to explain," he said.

"I know."

"There's a chance that I might have to leave. Might have to go."

Lexi stared at the lantern. It swayed in Eddie's grip. She sighed. "Yeah. I don't... I don't wanna talk about that."

Eddie pulled her up slowly and guided her away from the river.

CHAPTER 37

I was sitting on my porch near the spot where that demon Marivicos had swatted me. I alternated between applying pressure to the spot where his talons grazed my face and peering at the blood on my palm. They felt like deep cuts—would likely wear some scars on my face. Sometimes scars have good stories behind them —unfortunately for me, the story behind this one would be hard to relay at a party or in a bar. There I was, standing face to face with a giant mutant of a man, when he paralyzed my senses and swatted me to the ground. Yeah, might as well say a tiger in Indonesia got me.

I was still sitting in my shell-shocked state when I saw two familiar figures approaching from the street.

Eddie and Lexi.

Eddie had one hand clasped around Lexi's, and the other gripping what appeared to be an old kerosene lantern. The pair looked like they'd been to hell and back. Probably looked just like I looked.

I stood to greet them. Where the hell had Eddie been all this time? How did Lexi escape that horrible beast?

I invited the melancholy couple inside. Time to snap out of it and get the gang bandaged up—time to play my part as the doctor. I tried to detach, to zone out, pretend it was all a story. I'm an old pro at that.

I drew my eyebrows so close together, so tight, I developed a headache, mostly swallowing tears so that my G-d damn eyes wouldn't blur. I did not detach emotionally—just visually—but still with an ability to zoom in on wounds, to gauze and iodine smatterings where needed.

Once I ensured no one had any life-threatening injuries, we went to the living room to sit for somewhat of a debrief. I spoke first.

"Well, here we are at two in the morning, likely just bore witness the most horrific things we will ever see in our lives."

Silence. Eddie was holding something in. He wanted to speak.

"Yeah Doc, I *would* like to speak. I'm sorry." Eddie replied.

G-d, I'll never get used to that.

Eddie continued, "It's about Stacy..." He looked down. I didn't have to be a mind reader to know his next words.

My heart sank. I folded my arms and leaned forward. "What do you mean?" I knew what he meant. *Fucking hell.*

"That boat, the *Commodora*, it's... gone. Stacy was on it." Eddie looked away from me before he continued. "Papa made her do it, Doc. She sank the boat. Papa was controlling her mind."

I put my hands over my temples, slid them over my eyes, then back down into my lap. Maybe she made it to shore? Maybe she swam so—

"Doc, she didn't make it. I saw her. I'm so sorry."

We sat in silence.

I didn't know how to respond. *She was mine.*

I excused myself as I sat up and walked to the bedroom. I sat on the side of the bed. My thoughts drifted to the good times I had with my wife. There was before we got married. After we got married. And more recently at the Carnival and The Pony. Was she under his control during her last bout of happiness? Was it an illusion, part of his trickery, part of his mind-fuckery meddling? Maybe this was, too. Maybe he was still fucking with her or me, and she'd come back. She had done so many impulsive things. Maybe she'd get right into bed with me at the end of the night and I'd happily have sex with her. Or maybe I'd happily not have sex with her. All I really wanted to do was lay next to my wife again. Eddie wouldn't fuck with me and she just has to be...

Dead.

Now, I've never had someone shoot a cannonball at my body, blow a hole in my middle and just leave me to deal with it, but I imagined it was quite like how I felt then. I was both frozen and falling into a void.

It was an hour before I repaired enough of myself to move.

Lexi and Eddie were passed out in the living room. I was just about to doze off after a sleepless night.

A knock on the door shook me back into a state of alertness.

I walked into the living room—Eddie and Lexi were back in the waking world as well. I looked at Eddie—the look on his face was... hopeful? Relieved? Frustrating how hard it is to read that kid.

"Who's out there, Eddie?" I asked. I could tell Lexi's curiosity was also piqued.

Eddie got up, approached the door, and opened it without hesitation.

I caught a glimpse of Abi's face. It turned from exhaustion into shock.

"Mr. Eddie? What do... how is... wow..."

Eddie smiled and put his hand out. Abakoum took it, and they awkwardly shook hands before Abi pulled Eddie into a full embrace.

"I thinks the worst for Mr. Eddie. Mr. Eddie went gone for such long! How are Mr. Eddie here?"

They released each other. Eddie had a goofy grin on his face.

"I'm okay, Abi. I had to leave for a while. I might have to leave again... it's hard to explain. But I'm here now."

I started some tea for myself and coffee for the gang. What a gang. A washed-up widower shrink, a pregnant ex-prostitute, a death-defying mind-reader, and a Bouklafian immigrant carny.

I handed out caffeinated brews to the crew and took a seat. I planted myself firmly in this scene, in this situation and nowhere else. That hole wasn't going to regenerate; but I eliminated most of that feeling, leaving a residual dull ache in my chest.

Lexi sat next to Eddie. She crossed her legs and leaned back on the sofa. "Abi, I was worried about you. Regina told me you two were planning a date night on the *Commodora*. I was startin' to think the worst."

Abi sat forward in the old recliner, steepled his hands, and looked down. "Miss Lexi, we... Madam Regina and Abakoum did go date night on boat. We making the good times, but then I see doctor-wife. You wife, Mr. Chain." Abakoum looked back up from the floor to meet my gaze. He didn't know what I knew. I let him continue anyway.

"I sees Stacy, and Abakoum try to say hello and make with the friendly. Stacy no look at me, like we never meet. Abakoum think, whys no Mr. Chain here? Whys Stacy have scared face? Why Stacy act like she no know me? I worry. I tell Regina we go get Mr. Chain because wife is no right in the head."

Abi paused for a moment. He wore that same weary face I caught him with when he first arrived, that face he was prepared to present to me. The your-wife-is-probably-dead face.

"Madam Regina was in the drinks, and happy to see she friends. Regina stays on boat. Abakoum tell Regina he has the bad feelings, that no gut feeling." Abi's voice started as a whisper but grew to a grief-filled boom. "Regina no trusts my guts and no come with Abi. She stay on boat, and shes no call me, and I no see hers at the sex houses."

It was obvious Abi needed a minute to collect himself. I worried about the poor guy thinking it was his fault Regina didn't get off that cursed ship. Of course he was going to think that. He was going to beat himself up for that.

"I no drive two minuteses, when I hear the kabloom. I stop to gets out car, and look back where *Commodora* was. Abakoum saw the black smokes. I want to go back, but then the rains start. The rains so hard, it hurt being outsides. The rains-rocks so hard, it shatters car front window. The waters from river becomes roads, and Abi trapped. I has to run, or water take me away."

Abi maintained a thousand-yard stare.

I offered to let him stay here with us. Four people that had witnessed horrors and had suffered. Four souls with a shared experience that would affect us forever most likely.

Might as well put a sign in the yard: Dr. Chain's Sanitarium for the Traumatized and Supernaturally Afflicted.

ONE WEEK LATER...

Abakoum stayed with us for three days before deciding to return to Bouklafi. He missed his daughters. He wanted to put these wretched few months behind him—forever. We all said our good-byes. He's been told to not be a stranger, and he promises to come back and visit us someday soon. Well, I think his exact words were, "Abakoum will come back to US of A, and will be wealthy prince. I make it rain with monies on Mr. Chain, Mr. Eddie, and Miss Lexi!"

The past week has been... peculiar to say the least. I insisted Eddie and Lexi stay at my place for now—as long as they wanted. I liked having them around. I think the feeling's mutual.

Things were starting to settle down in Kayjigville. The *Commodora* disaster claimed about one-hundred and fifty lives, and the number ticked up with every passing day as they continued to find more bodies during the cleanup. There's also the matter of the flood; that black river rose up and took homes and people with it. The responders are still trying to figure out how many lives were lost.

There's flyers all over Main Street; flyers stapled to telephone poles, street lamps, plastered to windows put there by folks that haven't heard from their loved ones. I've been avoiding my walks down Main; it's a depressing affair knowing that my wife was involved in such a horrible incident that brought so much pain to this community. From what Eddie and Abi told me, Stacy was not herself at the end, didn't have control—was being controlled. Still, I don't feel right walking around right now. People no longer burn others at the stake, do they? I'm probably paranoid, feeling like public enemy number nine or some shit. I'm sure there are a few before me.

I keep waiting for that knock on the door—for the FBI or CIA (or whoever the fuck investigates supernatural terrorist attacks) to drop by and pay the husband of Stacy Thornberg a visit. Well... that knock hasn't come yet. Perhaps they can't even identify Stacy. Maybe the currents carried her away. I didn't entertain that she'd burned alive. I started to, but I don't have to craft some morbid event. I'd rather not know than think that.

Eddie and Lexi have everything they need right now. Eddie had been keeping this old black lantern near himself almost obsessively when they first arrived, but he took to just leaving it sit in his and Lexi's bedroom a few days ago.

Eddie, Lexi, and I were playing a board game when a knock-knock came from the front door. I looked up at Eddie.

"Doc... I actually don't know. I can't hear anyone now. It's... nice."

I nodded with a grin. "No worries, Eddie." I got up to answer the door. Who was next in the unpredictable procession to ole Dr. Chain's house?

I looked through the peephole. Were kids seriously still doing that stupid ding-dong-ditch prank? Already annoyed, I swung the door open so I could yell at the little shits that were likely running off to the next house.

What I saw next had me a bit... thunderstruck. There stood Marv and Andy, Papa Marivicos's right-hand... men. The minions, the tiny henchmen from hell or accounting or whatever. Same thing.

Marv spoke first. "Dr. Chain, we need a moment of your time. We come in peace."

I almost held up my hand in the "live long and prosper" signal but decided I could, maybe not be a smartass, as feral as I felt, I'd have to push that urge down too.

"Eddie, Marv and Andy are here. Are you okay with that?" I called out without taking my eyes off the dwarves.

Eddie approached from behind and put a hand on my shoulder. "It's alright Doc, let 'em in."

Andy didn't do much talking. Marv talked about regret, about wanting to believe that Papa was a good man. There was a slow turn, he said, to madness. He spoke of how Papa ordered the boys —Marv and Andy, that is—to get rid of the kids. Papa Marivicos had ordered a hit on two children. Can't say I was surprised. I was outraged.

"It was a bridge too far," Andy spoke with his eyes down and a poignant attention to the response of Eddie, a social intention that was unusual from either of the brothers, but especially from Andy. No matter; it was the only thing he said before Marv continued.

"We found Gabriel and Camille," Marv said, "and hid them in another home, registered under different names. Papa thought we'd killed them. Their bones… he wanted to see their bones. He saw bones, but not theirs." Marv didn't elaborate on what substituted for the skeletons of Eddie's children who'd survived.

Lexi and I looked to Eddie. He was in a state of shock;

emotionless, expressionless. Marv and Andy seemed to be waiting for Eddie's reaction.

I piped in to give Eddie time to process this new information. "I have a question. My wife. How did he—how did Papa get her to…?"

"We don't know," Marv answered. But he shook with the lie, eyes looking away as facile and half-meant as the answer.

Andy spoke. "The book. That's the truth. The book is what he used. She was likely susceptible to his influence due to her... condition. We don't know how, or more past that. He used the book."

"What book?" Lexi asked.

"It's what he used for years. There was something he used in that book."

Marv and Andy got up from their seats. "We didn't mean for things to get so bad." Marv looked genuinely remorseful.

"There's more," Andy said. "Papa left us in his will... we received his inheritance. Or what was left of it anyway. It's not a lot, but one thing I know for sure—it's not right. We're not his blood."

Marv nodded in agreement. "We believe the money should go to Eddie. And his family."

"Everything you're owed, Eddie... it's in this envelope. Instructions for the inheritance. The location of your kids. And, a surprise."

I nodded (in Eddie's stead, the boy was frozen in time) and Marv let himself out the front. Andy stood there for a second, staring at Eddie. After several moments, he set the envelope on the table where the three of us were sitting, and followed Marv out.

Lexi opened the envelope, glancing between it and the statue of Eddie. "It's all here Eddie... everything they said. Oh my God…"

"What's in there Lex?" I asked.

"The lotto ticket. The one that Eddie predicted. Oh my God."

We spent a few moments looking at the information regarding the kids and the inheritance, and the ticket.

I thought I heard a noise come from Eddie finally, and looked back at him. He was in tears.

"Th... they... they're... alive?"

CHAPTER 38

SEVERAL YEARS LATER

"And the princess was just too pure and beautiful for this world, so she had to go on to the next one, a better one."

Lexi finished reading her bedtime story to the children. Gabriel, the eldest, was getting a bit old for fairytales, and he was also a boy, but Camille and Junior still liked the story. It was the same story Lexi told them when they asked what happened to their biological mother. And because the story was really about his mother, Gabriel listened every time, and he hung on to every word, and every time he asked the same question.

"And her family gets to go there, too?"

"That's right, sweetie. We will all get to be with her again."

"But why can't we go now? If there's a better world out there?"

Dr. Chain, Eddie, Cami, Gabriel, and Junior all looked to Lexi for the answer. This was a new question. One Eddie knew was coming, but he was surprised it happened that evening.

But Lexi only smiled. Her answer came easily. "Because you're good. And this world needs you and your sister and your brother in it so that it can become better. The princess wanted a better place for everyone, and she knew that you were just the people to make it happen."

Eddie slapped his knees and stood up. "Okay, okay. No more stories. It's bedtime. Everyone off to your rooms. Come on."

"I got 'em, say goodnight to Peepaw," Lexi said. She scooped up Eddie Junior, who was already asleep, and cradled him while she ushered the other two off the veranda once they said goodnight to Doc.

"Gotta say, she does a great job," Doc said.

Eddie looked down at his wedding band and smiled. "She does."

"She treats 'em all the same. Like they're her own."

"So do you," Eddie said.

Dr. Chain grinned and turned his head. He was getting on in his years and found himself acting like a pre-menstrual woman when it came to matters of family.

The two sat in silence and listened to the rain hit the roof of the veranda. It was a humid summer night, but a nice breeze came in.

Silence. Something Eddie had so coveted for so long. After committing patricide, oddly enough, the voices were gone. He'd even been away from Lexi long enough at times that he expected they'd kick in again, but they were just... gone. No more. He didn't know why, but he was grateful enough to not ask questions. He also had no one to ask questions to. The only person he could ask would be his mother, and he didn't know if he could see her again. His most central unsolved mystery was why he hadn't turned into his father—or rotted, as his mother had said. Eddie still had all his parts and faculties. He only felt better, more human, kinder, and more compassionate.

It hadn't happened. That was all that mattered. He did wake up, some nights, from nightmares where his skin fell off, or he grew fangs or claws, or developed elephantitis of the arms, or legs, or those grey-matter voices whispered to him. Sometimes he thought he could hear them—the voices of his paternal ancestors, but he knew they weren't real. Still, he felt as though he stood upon a surface that loosely separated him from the heinous horror of his genetics, and the strain of that possibility (inevitability?) weighed upon him. It haunted him.

"Doc, I—"

"What are you two talking about?" Lexi returned just as Eddie started speaking. Lexi looked at him. "Oh! I'm so sorry. Go on. I didn't mean to interrupt."

Eddie shook his head. "You're not, Lex. It's okay."

Doctor Chain observed the two young people who now occupied his home. "You. We were talking about you," he said. Lexi raised an eyebrow.

"Yeah. You know, there's this old saying—I'm sure you've heard it—an adage, if you will. It goes a little something like this: you can't turn a hoe into a housewife. But Eddie, you've sure done it!"

The trio laughed, though Lexi feigned offense. "You old bastard!" she said, grabbing a throw pillow from the patio couch and playfully slapping him with it. "But you're right. And this hoe's off to bed. Long day and all. You coming?" she said, looking at Eddie.

"Yeah, just gotta brush my teeth. I'll be up."

"I'm glad you're still hygienic. Some men stop wiping their asses," Lexi stated.

Doc laughed. "What? This is the first I've heard of this. What sort of animal would stop wiping their ass? And at what point in their life have they given up to that extent?"

"Well, women are supposed to stop having sex when they're married. I've seen some married men who definitely don't wipe their asses. That's all. Once you've had ten bladder infections in a year because some stinky loser paid you to—uh…" Lexi looked at Eddie.

"I don't mind. I never did mind what you did for a living. I mean, I'm glad you stopped. That's... that's gross. The assholes, I mean. Not your work. And yeah, I guess knowing my wife had to deal with... shitty assholes isn't... uh, fun."

"Both literal and figurative," Doctor Chain said, raising his glass in what could have been a toast to shitty assholes, to sex work, to Lexi and Eddie, or to all of the above. "I'm gonna hit the sack myself. 'Night, kids. See ya in the morn."

"Good night, Doc."

"None of that *Walton's* shit tonight, though I think I've made my rounds." Chain handed his glass of whisky to Eddie.

"It's backwash."

"Yeah, well..." Doc shrugged and went inside. Eddie sat the glass on the table. He didn't need to drink so much anymore. Not with the quiet. Not with his wife, who had always been a mystery to him. She still was in so many ways. But he loved her. He loved her and his children so much. More than he ever imagined he was capable of, and while it was an anomaly in his life, Eddie embraced the love. Because he knew what it was like to endure the antithesis of love.

Lexi, as though she was the mind reader of the group, gave him a hug. It almost hurt. For such a thin woman, she had quite the grip. But Eddie didn't mind. She'd only started doing that after the night Papa died.

The house was so quiet. Something Eddie treasured. He could hear murmurs occasionally, but for the most part the voices were gone. Most often, all he experienced was the typical hypnagogic hallucination. But that night was different. Four years of silence and now, it was back. There was a constant thrum of indecipherable, guttural garbage. He'd been hearing it for about twenty minutes. That's what he'd wanted to tell Doc about.

He wanted to brush it off. But he couldn't.

"Okay, Eddie. Goodnight. You just wanna stay out and enjoy the rain through that quiet, don't you?" Lexi asked, breaking through the noise, pushing it to the backdrop of his thoughts, just as she always had.

"Yeah. Just, uh, just for ten minutes. I'll be up soon."

"Sure. I'll see you in ten minutes, or in the morning depending on how fast I'm out," Lexi said, kissing him before she turned to leave.

The assault inside his head grew. He resisted the urge to grab the whisky backwash and drink it.

"Hey," Eddie said, grabbing her arm.

"Hey you," she replied, grinning. But Eddie wasn't in a jocular mood.

"Where's Junior?" he asked.

"In his room, remember?"

"Was he asleep?"

Lexi looked confused. "Yeah. Should… should I go check on him, or…?

"No. It's fine. I just… I'm tired. I forgot."

"Okay. See you soon."

"Soon. Yes," Eddie replied.

But he was more alert than he'd been in years. The low hum of voices resonated through his mind, and they grew louder, almost like a chant. Anxiety gripped his heart and lungs. Something shifted. Something had changed. A corner of darkness formed in his mind. A voice had nestled there, with its sickly sweet callings and unspeakable intent. He knew where it came from—the room Doc had intended to be a nursery for his and Stacy's children.

Eddie rushed inside. As he approached the nursery, the voices crescendoed into a swell so monumental he could no longer hear exterior noise. He opened the door.

Junior stood in the middle of his bedroom; his was head pointed downward at an unnatural angle. And the noise inside Eddie's head only grew worse. He plugged his ears out of habit to keep the unearthly sounds from his battered mind, but it did nothing. It did nothing because Eddie Junior wasn't *speaking* a stream of incomprehensible diabolical words in a language no one on Earth could understand. His mouth was open. His jaw appeared unhinged, even, but his lips were still. Unformed syllables remained unuttered into the Earth. Junior was *thinking* those words. And Eddie could hear them.

Eddie's heart stopped then plummeted. He looked to where his son's eyes were. There, on the ground, was a book. *The Book.* And it swirled and writhed with life. A grey morass of odd and odious things. A black sun, a dead sky. That iniquitous book— there it was. A red marionette puppet dangled over it, the strings attached to Junior's hands, which controlled the puppet so deftly. Too deftly.

Eddie had to fight the voices to even move. But he did.

He dove over the mammoth sanguinary book, ripping the puppet from Junior's hands. The voices quieted, and when he stared up at his son, Junior looked down at him, and Eddie could only see the whites of his son's eyes. Eddie picked the book up, even though it hurt. It hurt badly to even touch the thing.

His son was unresponsive for a moment. Eddie didn't know what to do. He was prepared to get Doc, and he nearly did, when Junior's hazel irises came back into view. The boy blinked.

"Hi Daddy," he said in a monotone. The low bass of the malignant tome still thrummed through Eddie's head, but the flood was gone. The pain was gone.

He gripped Junior's shoulders. "Where did you get that book?" he asked as gently as he could.

Junior stared straight ahead, empty eyes. "It's always been here, Daddy."

Eddie wanted to scream. He wanted to cry, but he held back his tears, and he kept his tone even. "No. No, no, no. It's gone."

"It cannot be gone," Junior said.

"What? Who told you that? Where did you get it?"

Junior pointed out the window. "He told me."

"He *who*?" The hair on the back of Eddie's neck stood up. All the hair on his body did, as though the room was ripe with static electricity.

Junior's tone did not change. "You know who. Power is strange, Eddie," Junior uttered.

"No, no, no. No, no, no. Come with Daddy." Eddie grabbed his son's hand. He tucked the horrid book into a blanket and haphazardly tucked that under his shirt.

"Where are we going, Daddy?"

"Shh…"

Where is it? Where is it?

Eddie took Junior into the hall near the master bedroom. He tried to be quiet as he ransacked the closet. He'd put it there, and he'd carved out a particular part of his mind to house the memory of its location. He gripped its familiar rusted texture in the dark with one hand while his other was still firmly wrapped around Junior's.

After hectic seconds that felt like enough time for whole worlds to be born and die, his hand brushed the handle. He ripped the lantern from the closet.

A match. I need a match.

The book was quieter, but it adopted the rhythm of Eddie's heartbeat, and the tough but viscous hide of the cover tap-tap-tapped against his abdomen—it clung to him, like a parasite finding its host. Eddie shivered, but regained his composure, vowing not to fall apart in front of his son.

His son, who had inherited that demented, twisted strand of DNA.

No!

The arc of Eddie's ancestry would have an end point. It would not curve so much that it became a circle. But he didn't know how to stop such an apocalyptic force. Flashes of choice flickered in and out of his mind as the tap-tap of that grotesque manuscript against his body and the low hum of its call ripped through his awareness. Nothing was optimal. Nothing was certain.

"Hey, bud. Let's go outside for a minute. Whaddaya think?" Eddie asked Junior. But Junior was still. Too still. He did not speak. The tome's bloody binding twisted and turned, and Eddie's stomach lurched. He dry heaved as he led his son down the stairs and into the kitchen. That's where the matches were.

The utility drawer. Eddie never let go of Junior's hand. He placed the lantern atop the counter while he dug in the dark for the long blue-tipped matches. The moment he released the lantern he could feel the indecipherable text of the book. Words flooding his head, his veins, his gut. They marched through him to their own archaic beat and entangled themselves with his.

When he scooped the lantern up, the pacing of those words slowed, but their tapping and the invasion remained. He could feel them. He had the words now, and they'd trespassed, slithering under his skin.

Once they were outside, Eddie took Junior all the way to the edge of the expanse of yard where there was a firepit.

The noise. The voices waxed and waned. They weren't a single language, but a combination of all languages that had ever existed —that composite of dialect that had once come from him (or Melmoth) so many years ago.

He gripped the lantern. Every time he clutched it the book relented its internal infernal march throughout his being. He felt it in there. In his veins, his very blood, where the words had been destined to travel from the day he was born.

Eddie fumbled, but ultimately lit a match. He turned the bronze knob of the lantern.

Come on. Come on. Come on. Come on.

The fire crackled into existence, and the words wound back out from Eddie, shrinking away from him. Some remained. But the regression was temporary. It returned. It would always return, just like Papa had always found out.

He brought the lantern up to Eddie Junior, whose innocent

eyes bore confusion for a moment but quickly reverted to a lifeless gaze.

No.

"Stay here."

Junior said nothing. Eddie gripped the book, ripping it from his body. He ignored the pain that came with excising a malignant tumor from healthy tissue. He tossed it into the firepit, and the pain fled. Eddie turned the knob all the way up, so that the fire heated the glass to a near-melting point. Blinding light filled the backyard as Eddie directed the flame using the lantern just as he had when he'd burned Papa. But this time was different. This destruction wasn't for Eddie.

The binding of the book came apart, and the hisses and whispers roared into his mind causing him to stumble, to falter, but he stayed on his feet even when he felt the fire lick and spread through his spine as it melted the spine of the book. The pages and words were the most painful. The fire reached them, and Eddie's veins burned, burned, burned, but still he would stand and watch the book die. Even if he had to die with it.

The process didn't take long, and when all that was left of the book was ash and bits of the binding, Eddie set fire to those as well. He burned the firepit. The flame of the lantern was strong— otherworldly. It did fine work, incinerating every last despicable utterance written upon those pages.

The book was gone. But its words would never leave the world. They were within him, and he couldn't bear the thought of carrying them throughout the rest of his life. Especially now that he knew Junior had been exposed and was susceptible to them.

He recalled the day that Lexi had first gifted him the lantern.

And at the very second he determined his next actions, a darkness churned throughout his mind, a darkness he'd evaded for years, but now it was collecting its due.

Eddie scrambled over to his son. He lowered the flame on the lantern and placed it in Junior's hand.

"Daddy?" the voice was innocent. It was Junior's voice. Eddie's vision was going black at the edges.

"Why are we outside?"

"You don't remember?" Eddie asked. The timeless language still existed. Eddie felt the words. And the pain. Back. Worse than before. Worsening. Fast. Too Fast. The moment he mentally forfeited that lantern, it happened.

The rot. Accelerated. He'd put it off for so long...

His vision was fading. It was as though a thick film of grey muck coated his sclera, and it only got thicker. He wiped at the corner of his eye and pulled a long, thick string of black sludge from it.

"Uh-uh," Junior said. "Did I sleepwalk? Did you find me out here?"

Eddie groaned, fighting the text, fighting the rot. Fighting, fighting, fighting.

"You don't remember the book you were reading?" Eddie questioned. His voice was rusted and rough. He fought to maintain his regular cadence. For Junior.

"No, Daddy. I was asleep."

Eddie's throat was impossibly sore. "Listen to me, Junior," he said, placing his hand over his son's, which held the lantern. "You see this?"

"Yeah." Junior laughed. A joyful, child's laugh. Eddie's heart strained and fluttered all at once.

"Good... Good. I want you to have this. I'm givin' it to ya," Eddie forced the words out.

"Why?"

"Because it's very important to me, okay? Do you understand that it's very, *very* important to me? That it means a lot to me? And I'm giving it to you now?"

Junior nodded. "Thanks, Daddy."

"Promise me you'll keep it. Forever," he said, his voice

descending briefly into that strange choir he'd spoken as Melmoth.

Junior's smile fell. "Are you okay?" he asked his father.

Eddie's heart shattered then. "Mmm-hmmm. Yep. Promise me you'll keep it and get on back to bed now, you understand me, you *SON OF A WHORE?*" Eddie regretted the words. But he could not stop them.

Junior nodded but kept his distance. The two walked inside, Junior holding the lantern. It was a struggle to make it to the nursery, but they made it. Eddie watched as his son crawled under his comforter and placed the lantern on his nightstand.

These things weren't of Eddie's world anymore. Still, he pushed himself to remain within it.

"Goodnight son. You get yourself some rest. Yesss. Yesss. Some nice, fine rest'll do ya some good."

Eddie had to get out of that room. The desire to harm, to maim, to destroy—he had to go.

He had to get to the river.

He closed the door. The heartbeats of everyone in the house became prevalent to him. He probed the resting minds of his sleeping family. There was weakness in this house, oh yessir. Weakness.

NO! Eddie thought. His body moved without his permission. His legs, as pins and needles punctured them, took him toward his bedroom. Toward Lexi. But he stopped when he reached Doc's door.

He held his hand up. The experience was like being a prisoner in his body. Eddie was still there, somewhere, but he struggled to maintain control. His nails had sharpened, serrated on the sides, and came to sharp points at the end.

There's a weakness inside this here door. The voice floated through his mind. He ran his nails down the door of Doctor Chain's bedroom.

I took my glasses off and placed them neatly on top of my hard-cover copy of *One Hundred Years of Solitude*.

I had been reading for about a half-hour, and was my lids were heavy enough. Night reading, another behavior I could check off the stereotypical-grandpa list.

I reached over to the bedside lamp, clicked it off, laid back down, and began my drift into dreamland.

I heard the creaking of my bedroom door. I cracked open an eye just in time to see the door drift into the rubber stop. I'm at the point where I can't see shit without my glasses (check that off the grandpa list as well), but what my still-functioning-in-the-dark senses could make out shot a surge of adrenaline through my chest.

A pair of yellow eyes. Heavy breathing.

My shaky hands fumbled their way back to the lamp on the nightstand. I flicked it back on and in the process brushed my glasses onto the floor.

It was Eddie. A blurry Eddie, anyway.

"Christ, Eddie. You nearly gave this old man a heart attack."

No response.

"Eddie… you okay?" I asked as I leaned over the bed to search for my glasses.

Still no response. I kept feeling around for the spectacles and glanced back in Eddie's direction. He wasn't standing in the doorway anymore. What the hell was he doing?

The tedious probing of my carpet ended as my hand grazed the prize. I placed the glasses on my face and sat back up in bed.

The room way scarcely lit. There was Eddie, sitting in the recliner in the room's corner. He was bent forward, his face buried in his arms. He sounded ill. He wheezed as his back rose and slumped in rhythm with his breathing. His behavior was more than a little worrisome; it was alarming as fuck. Discomfort crept up my spine and blossomed into goosebumps on the back of my neck.

"Eddie, what's wrong son? Do you... want to talk?"

Finally, Eddie acknowledged me.

His face shot up from his arms. His eyes appeared sunken, and they were a terrible yellow. A yellow that brought me back to a certain rainy night from years before. Eddie's face showcased that old pain, a burden, a torment that only he could know. The inside feelings most of us shove deep and far away from our awareness, and Eddie's shit was severely amplified—and very, very freaky.

"It's Junior... Doc, he's got the darkness in him..." Eddie struggled to get the words out.

"What do you mean? Is he hurt?"

"Doc... he had that... fucking book. Papa's book. I heard him... tryin'a..." Eddie looked out the window, staring at nothing. Staring into the night. I noticed a small amount of blood dripping from the bottom of his chin. "It sounded like... he was speakin' in tongues, Doc."

My first instinct was to offer reassurance, but Eddie always knows when he's being bullshitted. So what can be said? Everything's gonna be hunky-dory, don't worry?

"Doc... I gave Junior the lamp. I have to leave... for good."

I'm not the type to wear emotions on my sleeve, but my stomach sank. I was heartbroken. "How did this happen? Where did the book come from?" My voice shook a bit.

The speed at which Eddie snapped his gaze back to me gave me a start. *I don't fuckin' know, you busybody, what the fuck does it matter?* Eddie snarled. That yellow glow intensified, and I caught a glimpse of his teeth. Sharp, pointed teeth.

I recoiled. Eddie threw his head down, curling up into his torso, hands over the top of his head. He screamed—a muffled yell of a broken (*breaking?*) man—Eddie's voice was in there somewhere, all but drowned out by the other roaring vocalizations that accompanied his own.

He gradually brought his head back up. That awful yellow had dimmed, but even in the poorly lit room I could see the skin on his face was riddled with vascular spiderwebs of heliotrope.

"Doc... please... help Lexi make sure that—"

Eddie's head cocked to the side, his eyes clenched shut, his temples bulged. He dipped his head down between his legs again. More heavy breathing and wheezing.

Eddie was losing this visceral struggle. That much was clear. I wanted so desperately to help—and not just in the *I swear to fulfill, to the best of my ability and judgment, this covenant* way—I considered Eddie family.

"Eddie, son, take slow deep breaths. What do I need to help Lexi with? Please tell me."

Eddie stopped breathing so heavily. I was relieved, hoping that he had relaxed a bit and was in less pain. He was still staring at the floor.

"*You cannot save him.... The children of the Ilzram will always belong to... me...*"

That was not Eddie's voice. It was more of a growl. Was I in over my head? You betchya. I didn't know what else to say. I needed to speak to Eddie, and that sure as hell wasn't Eddie. I tried again. "I don't understand. How can I help Lexi?"

The wheezes started again, and he slumped and fell from the chair to the floor.

I hopped off the bed and knelt next to the poor boy. I gently shook him by the shoulders. "Eddie, Eddie!"

His eyes fluttered then opened wide, and he gasped. He took in air with a wet ratcheting noise. I took his hand and held tight.

"Doc... please... Junior has to keep the lantern. It'll... it'll keep him... from being like Papa," he spoke before another wretched gasp of air. He squeezed his eyes shut before opening them wide again, this time with a look of determination. "Or me."

I squeezed his hand tight. My voice was shaky. "Eddie, I promise I will do everything I can. You're doin' the right thing."

I helped Eddie get back on his feet. I embraced him. "You've suffered enough, son." After holding onto each other for about five seconds, a noise emanated from Eddie's throat—something that sounded like the muffled screams and cries of hundreds of people. I don't really know how to describe it, but G-d damn, did it make my skin crawl. He squeezed me a bit too tight—I'm not going to lie, I feared Eddie in that moment.

"Eddie! Eddie, fight it," I spat out.

As he was latched onto me, I felt claws digging into my back, pushing and breaking through my skin.

Eddie pushed me away—I staggered backward into the wall. The yellow glow had returned to his eyes. He appeared to tower over me. Tiny rivers of dark fluid were streaming from those sunken eye sockets, flowing past his nose, dripping off his chin. A small clump of Eddie's sweat-drenched hair was stuck to my hand—the young man was literally falling apart before my eyes.

"Doc... I don't want to hurt anyone... I have to go now."

Eddie left my room; the dragging of his footsteps receded. The front door opened and shut.

I stepped out of my bedroom and approached the door he had exited. I peered out of the peephole—he was gone.

I turned around and Lexi was there, stifling sobs.

That was the last time we saw Eddie Marivicos.

BLACKOUT

EddieMelmothEddieMelmoth

Bones crippled, bent, broke. Gums peeled back, he spat loose fibrous tissue from his lips. The tissue shriveled and melted into decayed lumps of fat—fat that hissed and sizzled as it graced the shore of the river.

Eddie—or what was left of him—crawled, gasping for air that wasn't there—his lungs hardened and turned to stalactites in his chest. Black esophageal sputum oozed as he gasped and wheezed. He tried to hold in the violent whooping coughs; he felt the organs in his chest rearrange themselves with every barking hack.

Nothing human left. Just a writhing pile of putrid rot, wriggling its way to the depths of the river as a voice called to him.

You won't make it... another marvelous Marivicos for my collection...

The rotting ravaged the tendons, sinew, and fibers of his joints. He couldn't feel his legs—just strands of necrotic weight. Eddie crawled over a rock, snagging himself where the pelvis connected to the femur. As he dragged himself farther, the leg's elasticity gave way—the flesh severed and split.

The trail of viscera behind the creature indicated that there was once a human there.

Mind. No mind. No mind. Just black, black, black. Stench and sorrow. The nerves in the brain rewrote memories, rewrote the world from the birth of time.

Rest with us... rest with your ancestors... rest with your father... YOU WILL NOT REACH IT.

Thus.

Eddie.

The claw-like nails that stretched from his cuticles grasped sand, mud, ground. He pulled himself over the terrain, pieces of which became imbedded in his chest and stomach. He could see the black water rippling and waving. Home.

YOU CANNOT ESCAPE THIS. You and your ancestors have a price to pay... you will pay... your son will pay...

"NO!" he screamed. The word was the last Eddie would ever speak. He cried out, roared in anguish as his mind was overtaken by millennia of interstellar grey-black matter.

The being that spoke to him called him home. But not to the river. To some other place. If his form changed before he reached the river, he did not know what would happen.

River. Get. To. River.

Inches now. Only inches.

But, oh, they were miles. Skin became a hard, leathery hide. His cry had broken the delicate meaty pieces holding his mouth together. His lower jaw was left in the wet sand, another obstacle to crawl over. The yellow glow from his sunken eyes locked in on the water.

As his claws touched the cold, black river, he was overcome

with paradoxical sensations. A crypt. A tomb. Home. Haven. The river repelled him.

It. No longer a man.

Reaching into the damp sand, the thick sludge, there was a desperate need to die right there, but a desire somewhere, somewhere cerebral, urged him—*it*—onward. That black water burned him. What it would do to the rest of him, it did not know.

His mind was slippery. One moment it was aware. The next it was not. Fighting to decide between two unknown deaths.

Less than inches now. Foul smoke arose and coated the river like a fog. He was a white-hot rod of iron dipped in water, and it evaporated at his touch. His vision became hazy in the fog. No more yellow glow, just hollow sockets.

One final push. Deep enough now for the circular current to carry him to the center and drag him down.

If he had eyes, he would have seen the swirls of that grey-black matter. Little lights like constellations in the sky. He sensed the pulling and tugging of his rotted form into a spiral.

What is a hurricane within the water? In the calm, quiet eye now. Black, black, black.

The curtain fell.

FINALE

She couldn't remember much. The smell of smoke and blood,
perhaps. The fear, the desperation; and then, finally, the accep-
tance. She was disoriented by her surroundings. A large black
liquid abyss, flat and stretching out in infinite directions. She
could smell char and burnt flesh, polymers and cloth fibers singed
and mixed in with it.

Am I dead? She looked down at her hands, and they were
mangled things burnt down to the bone. She looked down at the
black surface and extended her foot, cautiously pressing it against
the slick obsidian. The sight of her own foot revolted her. It was
boiled and disfigured into meaty cords of firewood, but she kept a
close eye to see what her next step would do on this unknown
plane.

Before she could fully set her foot down, however, she found herself rocketed forward—hundreds of feet, thousands of feet, hundreds of thousands of feet. The propulsion took milliseconds or millennia. She couldn't tell which. And when she stopped, she was still looking down at her foot, burnt and mangled as it was, setting a step into the black liquid plane. When her foot came down, only the faintest ripple slid outward into the black—barely a trace of her having moved. There was no light, but everything was perfectly clear; she still stared at her foot.

Then she looked up.

A monster, but worse than that. He sat upon a royal throne made of bright white gold, which was too radiant to look directly at. A vile beast—anthropomorphic and demonic—halfway between a bleached demon and Edvard Munch's *Skrik*. Something like a Gallen-Kallela painting of an ancient Finnish god or wretch or sacrifice—*Kullervo*—or maybe a grotesque take off of Blake's *Nebuchadnezzar*. A bald-headed king with writhing flesh and insects moving in and out of slits in his skin; no crown. A monster, at least thirty feet tall while seated on the throne. It was nude, and she saw its mutilated genitals hanging freely between its open legs. Its eyes were turned upside down and they were bleeding. The monster was rail-thin, but every bit of sinew looked like some hyper-compacted musculature, so dense it seemed as though the muscle of a creature five times its mass was packed into its body. Its greying white skin *exhaled*, and small trickles of blood flowed from different points all around its anatomy.

The monster wore a velvety blood-red regal mantle that shimmered with a long train. The train carpeted the throne beneath, and spotted fur pushing out so it could be seen around the creature's haunches and massive shoulders. The beast had no nose, no ears, no hair. No nails; but lengthy fingers sheathed in gold rings that came to points, like velociraptor claws. A yellow saliva oozed out of its mouth, falling down onto its naked chest. The whole front of the beast was naked except for the outer thirds of its right and left sides which were covered by the royal mantle.

The longer she looked at this, this—this thing, it grew taller and more fearsome, or it *seemed* to.

"It is very, *very* good to see you."

The woman couldn't respond. She was frozen.

"I'm sure you have some questions. It was quite a row you went through on your last day."

The voice was a man's baritone. It came as a great shock to her that its voice was pleasant; soothing, even.

"I see you've crisped a little. Took up in a fire, yes? Died in a fire, I saw. Awful way to go. Just *awful*, darling. I'm so sorry that happened to you."

She still didn't have it in her to respond. *Shock*, she thought, but couldn't form more than that single word in her mind.

"Well, since you seem to be caught up in your own thoughts, I'll speak for the both of us."

It stood from the throne, rising high as it did. Mercifully, the drape of the royal mantle fell naturally enough to only allow a sliver-sight of skin running down the middle. "I'm a fanatic. No— your word…a *fan*. Yes, I've spectated your evils. Very good, nice, good. Almost—"

It drew in a rasping ratcheting wet and phlegmy breath, then spoke in a sorrowful, almost tearful—but feigned way, "I was just *heartbroken* when things didn't go as you'd planned. Really, my dear. *Heartbroken*." It paused to look at her, as if anticipating some response. She was no longer in shock, but she had nothing to say.

"It really is so shameful when others ruin one's carefully calcu-lated machinations. Oh, I love that word, don't you? *Machinations*. But, that's alright. Because what do we do when we fall off the horsey?"

She suddenly looked up. Her father used to say that. *What do we do when we fall off the horsey?* That's what he said.

"We get back on it and give it a nice whip," she finally answered.

It smiled at her, showing teeth like a deep sea dragonfish; teeth that enlarged as his mouth opened into a vomitous grin. Some pus-like slime and clotted blood mixture slid slowly down from its gums to the tips of its needle-point teeth. "That's right. *We get back on it and give it a nice whip.* So, my dear, would you like to hold the whip?"

She nodded.

"Good," It laughed, the diseased blood spittle running from its mouth.

"W-whooo… whhh… h-h-ho?" she attempted speech, but had difficulty adjusting to her flame-ruined anatomy.

"Who am I?" The creature finished her thought for her.

She nodded.

"My dear… I am Chernobog."

THANK YOU FOR READING *BLACK RIVER LANTERN!*

As an author, I know that there are many choices when it comes to modern literature; I am grateful to my readers. When writing this book, I made an effort to weave together elements of family drama, paranormal/supernatural horror, comedy, and tragedy.

I hope you enjoyed the story! If you feel so inclined, take a few minutes to leave a review on Amazon or GoodReads. It's with the help of readers like you that authors like me can continue to thrive as we endeavor to bring our stories to life.

Again, I thank you for reading *Black River Lantern* and for any review that you might be willing to take the time to share.

Want to stay up-to-date with the latest books and news from Alex Grass?

Sign up to receive my mailing list and, as a subscriber, you'll receive a free special sign-up bonus. In addition, you'll be able to stay informed on future releases, take part in book cover reveals, read updates from Alex Grass, and more.

Visit the blackriverlantern.com website to sign-up today and to get your free download!

ABOUT THE AUTHOR

Born in Harrisburg, PA, Alexander Grass lived in Philadelphia, Israel, and a few other places before settling in Brooklyn with his wife and three kids. As a teenager, Alex was in a thrash-metal band called Shock Syndrome. He later worked in construction, landscaping, driving in a car auction, and worked in parts and shipping for a Honda dealership. After obtaining his GED, he went to Penn State online before attending Cardozo Law School on scholarship. While at Cardozo, Alex was a Floersheimer Student Fellow in Constitutional Law, and a law clerk for the Institute for Justice and for the New York County Defenders. After a stint in rehab, he dropped out of law school to become a person who is good at writing word-sentences.

Made in the USA
Middletown, DE
12 September 2021

48151868R00210